I0831869

Stone Heart

A BOOK OF UNDERREALM

Garrett Robinson

STONE HEART

Garrett Robinson

The author greatly appreciates you taking the time to read this work. Please leave a review wherever you bought the book or on Goodreads.com.

Interior Design: Legacy Books, Inc.
Publisher: Legacy Books, Inc.
Editors: Karen Conlin, Cassie Dean
Cover Artist: Sutthiwat Dechakamphu

1. Fantasy - Epic 2. Fantasy - Dark 3. Fantasy - New Adult

First Edition

Published by Legacy Books

To my family
It's been a long, hard year.
I survived it thanks to you.

To my parents
The only thing I wish you'd done differently
is sticking around to see this

And to everyone who's waited patiently
for this new foray into Underrealm.

You're why I get back up and carry on.

I hope this is worth the wait.

GET MORE

Legacy Books is home to the very best that fantasy has to offer.

Join our email alerts list, and we'll send word whenever we release a new book. You'll receive exclusive updates and see behind the scenes as we create them.

And we'll send you a free ebook copy of Nightblade, the #1 Amazon Bestseller, as our way of saying "Thanks."

Interested? Visit this link:

Underrealm.net/Free

THE BOOKS OF UNDERREALM

THE NIGHTBLADE EPIC
NIGHTBLADE
MYSTIC
DARKFIRE
SHADEBORN
WEREMAGE
YERRIN

THE ACADEMY JOURNALS
THE ALCHEMIST'S TOUCH
THE MINDMAGE'S WRATH
THE FIREMAGE'S VENGEANCE

THE TALES OF THE WANDERER
BLOOD LUST
STONE HEART
HELL SKIN

THE BOOKS OF UNDERREALM

CHRONOLOGICAL ORDER

NIGHTBLADE
MYSTIC
DARKFIRE
SHADEBORN
BLOOD LUST
THE ALCHEMIST'S TOUCH
WEREMAGE
THE MINDMAGE'S WRATH
STONE HEART
THE FIREMAGE'S VENGEANCE
HELL SKIN
YERRIN

Stone Heart

A Book of Underrealm

Garrett Robinson

ONE

A warm sun rose, its crisp rays bathing Sun's face, and with it came an unpleasant truth.

It is the day after I left my family.

It was hard to believe that only a scant few hours ago, she had fought a vampire. It was even harder to believe that she had won. Since then, she had had a few hours' sleep before Albern had woken her to take the second watch. But despite having slept and woken already, she could not shake the thought that this had to be a dream. She was sure that soon she would wake again, the way she sometimes did in dreams, rising through layers of illusion before finally emerging into the waking world. Any moment now, she would find herself in the luxurious tent her parents' servants had built for her, and hear Mother commanding her to get ready for another day's ride with the caravan.

Yet here she remained, sitting against a tree just inside the edge of an unknown forest in western Dorsea. The dew beneath her felt real enough, as did the rough bark of the tree against which her head rested. A chill wind blew across her face, the last of the night's cold wisping away with the coming of the day. It was almost *too* vivid to be real.

Had she made a mistake? Never had she entertained the thought of running away from her kin, except as the most passing flight of fancy. When the opportunity had presented itself, it had *felt* like the right thing to do, but now she was filled with doubt.

Albern stirred in his bedroll.

Sun looked over at him, watching his stubbled chin as it waggled, the old man murmuring as sleep began to creep away from him. Albern of the family Telfer, a figure of legend in his own right, and longtime companion of the mightiest warrior Underrealm had ever seen—if you believed the stories. And Sun found she *did* believe them, no matter how outlandish Albern's claims seemed. Not only that, she wanted to hear the tale go on.

In the end, that might be all that matters, she told

herself. *You may have your doubts, but ask yourself: do you regret your decision?*

She could not bring herself to say that she did.

Albern's eyes opened. He lifted his head slightly, looking around as if disoriented. When he spotted Sun sitting by the edge of their campsite, he seemed to focus at last, and he gave her a little smile.

"Good morn," he said, his voice a frog's croak. He cleared his throat and tried again. "Good morn. No sign of danger while I slept?"

"There were many," said Sun. "A pack of wolves arrived not an hour ago. I told them how old and bony you were, and they slunk away in search of better game."

"No respect for your elders," said Albern, grinning as he sat up nimbly despite his missing arm. "Then again, I had none myself at your age. We shall have a bite to eat and then head off to Lan Shui."

"And what are we doing there?" said Sun.

"I mean to visit a woman there."

Sun arched an eyebrow. "A woman?"

Albern laughed. "Not a lover, if that is what you are implying. Though I would not have you think I am incapable of such things, despite my age. I can still—"

"Sky above, stop talking," said Sun. She went to his pack to fetch some meat and bread, then thought better of it and found some twigs to stoke their fire. It had dwindled down to coals. The forest turf sank pleasantly beneath each footstep, soaking in the morning moisture.

"Noble children," scoffed Albern, pulling his blanket closer around his shoulders.

With a short while's work, the fire sprang to life again, and Sun laid sturdier branches across it to help it grow. She went for the food, then, handing some of it over to Albern. The old man tore at the meat with teeth that looked surprisingly healthy, if somewhat stained with age.

"I have a question," said Sun.

"You may or may not get an answer," said Albern.

"I thought so, but I have to try. Is this . . . is this what you do now?"

Albern frowned at her, then glanced around as if expecting to see someone else there. "Now, just what do you mean by 'this?'"

"Not *this.* I mean last night. Hunting vampires. Is that your . . . your trade?"

That made him smile. "No. I am not a monster hunter, except when I need to be. And when I am, it is not only vampires I seek. I have fought all sorts of creatures. After all, you do know *something* of how I lost my arm, do you not?"

Sun's jaw clenched. She had begged him for that story already, but the man was maddeningly reticent. "Something, but not as much as I would like."

Albern chuckled. "You shall have to suffer under

what I am sure is the crushing weight of your disappointment, at least for a while longer."

It was impossible to be *too* angry at the old man when his attitude was so genial and friendly, but that did not stop Sun from trying—nor from trying to hear the story she had wanted him to tell in the first place. "Now that I have agreed to go with you, will you not, *please,* tell me—"

"I will not," said Albern. "Our arrangement remains the same. I will keep telling you stories, as long as you want to hear them—but I will choose them. Can you accept that?"

"I suppose so," grumbled Sun. "I thought that would be your answer, in any case. But I have my own condition. You are a storyteller, and if you say you must tell your stories in a certain order, I will believe you. But we are also traveling companions, and in that, I do not call you master. I do not want to follow along at your heels, chasing you like the wolfhound from your tales. If we are to ride together, I want to be treated as your equal. A partner, not a lackey."

Albern looked mildly surprised. But then his gentle smile grew into a wide grin, and he clapped his hand on his knee. "Why, I could not agree more—and I apologize for making you feel that you were ever anything less. We *are* traveling companions, and neither lord of the other. I vow I will not forget it. What more can I do?"

"Tell me of this woman in Lan Shui, for one thing," said Sun.

"Ah, gladly," said Albern. "She is a medica, and I am seeking her services."

Sun's heart seemed to pause for a moment. "I—are you ill?" A sudden fear clutched at her heart, that the man she had just befriended might be in peril, about to be ripped away from her just as she had begun to value his company. And another, smaller part of her—a part she was somewhat ashamed of—wondered if she was about to be cast out alone upon the road, just as she was wondering if she had made the right choice in the first place.

"Oh, sky no," said Albern, and his easy smile dispelled her terror in an instant. "Do not worry yourself in the slightest. It is simply that old bodies need a little more care than ones your age. My friend in Lan Shui makes sure I stay healthy."

"Ah, I think I see," said Sun. "Because you are ander?"

"Well, yes and no," said Albern. "That plays a part—but age catches up with all of us, and it causes quite a bit more problems than a wending ever has."

Sun let a little sigh of relief escape her. "Well, I am glad to hear it. At the risk of imitating Mag, I have to say: if you were to die before telling me the tale I wish to hear, I would have to kill you."

Albern laughed loud and long at that, and the

sound rang hearty and cheerful among the dark trunks that surrounded them. A bird chirped indignantly as it leaped into the air from a branch above him.

"I shall endeavor not to earn your wrath," he said. "In any case, after I have seen the medica, I have other business. There is something near Lan Shui that needs looking into."

"Another vampire?" said Sun, trying not to quail visibly.

"I should certainly hope not," said Albern. "It seems to be a more mundane sort of evil. Banditry, mayhap, but we shall see. These are the errands I mean to take care of in Lan Shui. After I have seen to them—with your help, if you are willing to give it—we shall plan where to go next. Together. Is that acceptable?"

"Of course it is," said Sun. "You could have simply told me so in the first place."

She had meant no insult by it, and she thought she spoke the words lightly. Yet Albern's smile faltered. When he spoke, it was in a subdued, almost mournful tone.

"I am sorry, child," he said. "You are right, of course. It is only that as I tell you these tales, I cannot help but think of the times I traveled with Mag. And when I rode by her side . . . well, the two of us were so close, you see. We almost knew each other's minds. Many things passed between us, plans and decisions, that never needed to be spoken aloud."

He fixed Sun with a gaze that was suddenly clouded. She shifted where she sat. Her meat was in her lap, untouched and now forgotten.

"I hope this causes you no discomfort," said Albern, his voice scarcely above a murmur. "But you remind me of her in many ways. I suppose I fell into old habits. But that was a different time, and I must always remind myself to see the world around me—as it is, not as I remember it. I should know better by now. Can you forgive me?"

"Of course," said Sun, answering a bit too quickly.

"Thank you." The old man's smile grew. "But I must also ask a boon. I reserve the right to surprise you with *some* things. Any good tale must have a few twists and turns, after all, lest we grow bored of it. But I promise that the next part of this story should be very interesting to you—especially considering what you have told me about your family."

Sun could not help herself—she smiled like a girl whose parents had just promised her a treat. "I cannot wait."

"Then let us get ourselves upon the road, and I will talk as we ride."

"You mean as *you* ride."

Albern chuckled. "Your point is well taken. We must see about getting you a horse of your own."

"I would greatly appreciate that."

They packed up their camp—a quick process, for they had not unpacked all that much, simply a few bedrolls and some small dishes for eating. As they had laid it all out the night before, Sun had thought she would have to do much of the work, but in fact Albern was much quicker at it than she. The same was true now; his bedroll was on the saddle long before hers was, and by the time she was ready to gather up their simple dishes, he had already bagged them all and slung the sack, too, atop the horse. As she had last night, Sun chided herself for her assumption. It was plain that Albern had been traveling all across Underrealm for many years since he had lost his arm. He had adjusted himself to taking care of the small business of life long ago, and was likely a much better campaigner than she was.

Albern climbed into the saddle and smiled down at her. Their breath poured out in a heavy mist in the still-chilled morning air, mingling far above their heads as it stretched up in search of the light clouds floating overhead.

"Are you ready?" he asked.

"Of course," said Sun.

He nodded and nudged the horse into a walk. Sun strode by his side, one hand hanging idly from his left stirrup, as the old man continued his tale.

TWO

Autumn clung to the land, slow to relinquish it to winter. The days were cloudy, casting that gentle semblance of sunlight that illuminates the shadows nearly as much as everything else. It rained often, and sometimes it snowed lightly, but we hid beneath our oiled cloaks and rode on regardless. The trees all around us were a thousand shades of red and orange and gold, casting their leaves into the wind to gently brush against us as we carried on.

Our journey had taken us some weeks. After proceeding to the city of Bertram from Lan Shui, we had eschewed the King's road and struck out west, carrying on all the way to the coast before turning north. There the road is often within sight of the ocean, that endless expanse that stretches forever, a blue blanket strewn with a thousand diamonds. In northwestern Dorsea, just before we turned east for Opara, Dryleaf had fallen ill, and we had halted for a few days to let him recuperate. As we drew at last to the borders of what had once been my homeland, I held on to a hope that our hunt might be at its end.

You will remember, of course, that in Lan Shui we had learned that Kaita was heading for Opara. You will also remember that we thought that message came from Pantu, the young boy who had once been a servant of the Shades, but that it had actually been Kaita in disguise. But of course we did not know that as we approached the city. We thought we would go unseen, and that our quarry had no idea we were even after her.

During our travels, I had engaged in a small project of my own. I told you of Jordel, the Mystic with whom I had journeyed through the Greatrocks, and who had perished before that journey's end. I had promised the boy, Gem, that I would write a song for him, a song of celebration for a life more eventful than most. I had not had the time to begin it in Northwood, and the road to Lan Shui had provided little opportunity, for we were in a dangerous land. But on the long road to Opara, I spent many nights on watch and many days idle in my saddle with little else to do. And so I had begun my ballad. It was grueling work, for I had never tried my hand at songwriting in those days. It is not as easy as some think—not if you want to do it properly. Sometimes I could summon no words at all. Other times, a part of the song would stick in my mind, repeating itself over and over again, demanding to be improved, until I was rocking back and forth in my saddle, muttering and humming to myself under my breath.

"Are you going mad over there?" said Mag, drawing me out of my thoughts. "We can seek a healer in the next town."

I looked at her somewhat ashamedly. Mag sat straight in her saddle, prouder than any Mystic knight, her green cloak fluttering in a light wind. Though the journey had been long, and though we had faced darkness along it—not only the vampires we slew in Lan Shui, but highwaymen and brigands in the wilderness—she looked better than ever, hale and healthy and with a focus honed like a razor's edge. Indeed, if I was honest with myself, she looked far more natural, far more *whole,* somehow, than she had back in Northwood. Mag had been happiest there, in those days she had spent with Sten. But there are the things that make us happy, and then there are the things that come to us naturally, and it is an exceptionally fortunate few who can find both things in the same place or circumstance. I think Mag belonged on the road, on a campaign, such as it was, whether or not it was what she desired.

"Forgive me," I told her. "I had not realized how loud my voice had grown."

"Really?" she said, arching an eyebrow. "I have been unable to pay attention to anything else for some time."

On Mag's other side, Dryleaf chuckled, his sightless eyes drifting aimlessly. I had been most worried for the old man when he had fallen ill, but now he seemed even stronger than when we had met him in Lan Shui. He, too, seemed to be a man who belonged on the road—and in his case, it did seem to be his great love, as well. I knew he had been a wandering peddler for many years, long before he met us.

"Oh, do be gentle with Albern, dear girl," he told Mag. "Any art requires time and patience, and songs most of all. They come to us in dreams, in our mind's wanderings, a piece at a time. Then we must sit there with the parts of them, shoving them about like a child with a tinker's puzzle, often going days or weeks without seeing the way they fit together. And then, all of a sudden, the pieces form into a whole, and then the world is forever blessed with a new and beautiful thing. Nothing can fly through the ages like a song."

"Thank you kindly," I said, nodding before I remembered he could not see it. "Your support is greatly appreciated, though I can defend myself against this one." I pointed past Mag at the old man and gave her an admonishing frown. "Do you see? That is how one true friend supports another. With encouragement, not heckling."

"If I were heckling you, I would have found some rocks to throw," said Mag. "Carry on with your mutterings, then. There are many beekeepers in this part of the kingdom. Mayhap one of them will sell me some wax to plug my ears."

I reached over and tried to shove her. Mag snatched my arm and nearly pulled me from the saddle, before catching my shoulder on her knee and launching me back upright. I snatched wildly at the saddle horn to steady myself. Foolhoof, my gelding, snorted loudly and danced beneath me, as though he had sensed an opportunity to try to escape.

"You hush," I told him, slapping his shoulder—but gently. "You will not rid yourself of me that easily." I glared at Mag. "Even with her help."

Mag laughed aloud, dragging a smile out of me. "If I wanted you out of the saddle—"

"—it would already be done," I finished. "You should be more careful with me, you know. You may be able to best me in a fight, but I am learning to write songs. I could immortalize you in verse as an utter buffoon. That sort of victory lasts forever, Mag; you can only trounce me as long as we are both alive."

A curious expression came across her, one so tragic and . . . and *weary,* that I felt at once that I should apologize, though I did not know what I had done wrong. She smiled at me, but I thought I saw her eyes glisten as she did it.

"You are welcome to your eternal victory," she said, and the spell broke. Her voice was so cheery, her smile suddenly so genuine, that I felt I must have imagined what I had seen. "I prefer to defeat the person right in front of me, rather than the idea of them many years later."

I laughed, for it seemed clear that that was the response she needed. Mag and Dryleaf joined in the merriment, while Oku barked and ran two quick circles around our horses.

We fell silent as we rode on. Yet I thought long upon what I had seen, and the way Mag sounded. My words must have reminded her of Sten, I thought. So much had happened since the battle of Northwood, that sometimes I forgot it was barely two months before that Mag and Sten were still living happily in that town, foreseeing no darkness in their future.

"You know, Albern," said Dryleaf after a time, "I could offer my services in your attempt. I have written a fair few songs in my time, and received praise from kings and princes for them."

"I know it, friend," I told him. "I would have guessed it from the moment I first heard you sing. But this is too close to my heart to share with anyone. At least for now."

Dryleaf pursed his lips and gave a deep nod, pushing his long beard into his chest. "A song of mourning, is it? Very well. You will know when you have healed enough that my advice will be more help than hindrance."

I glanced again at Mag, but from the corner of my eye so that she would not notice. Mayhap I need not have worried. Her gaze was distant as she let it rest on the horizon, and I doubted she had heard a word Dryleaf or I had spoken.

The old man had said I would know when my heart had healed. But some wounds, I wagered, never healed at all.

THREE

THE NEXT DAY, WE REACHED THE CITY OF OPARA, which stands at the foot of the mountain Tahumaunga.

I do not know how far you have traveled, but I doubt it is as far as me, and I can tell you this: there are few sights as glorious, as awe-inspiring, and as frightening as that fiery peak. Tahumaunga looms over the land all around, its crest often wreathed in smoke, which drifts away south and east. There are taller mountains in the nine kingdoms, but none stand so tall in isolation, dominating the horizon and commanding one's attention.

There are tales from the time before time that say it spouted its flames often, sending great rivers of molten rock cascading down its slopes and flooding the wilderness all around. But those flames had long since subsided when Roth's armies conquered the nine kingdoms. Now it belched forth its fires mayhap once in a lifetime, and they were gentle and slow when compared to the mountain's ancient fury.

Opara had been built at the foot of the mountain long ago. The King's road did not pass through it, but it was still sizable, for it was an important waypost on the kingdom's southern border. The Tongarn river poured from underground caverns within the mountain, and the city had been built around the place where the waters reached the lowlands. The south gate stood open as we approached, but the guards there raised a hand to stop us, and one stepped forwards to take Mag's reins, for she was at our head. He looked at each of us in turn with a studious gaze. He and his companions wore the black and red armor, trimmed in white, that marked them as servants of the Calentin king. A curious feeling, somewhere between longing and discomfort, came over me as I beheld them.

"Good day, friends," said the man, a short and stout fellow. I do not know how many Calentin citizens you have met, but we often decorate ourselves with moko—a sort of tattoo scarred deep into the skin of the face. Moko covered this guard's chin, which jiggled when he spoke. "Whence have you come?" One of his fellow guards edged closer and knelt a pace away, extending a hand towards Oku.

"Southern Dorsea, and before that, Selvan," said Mag. "We hail from the town of Northwood."

"A long way to travel," said the guard. "I am Ari, of the family Parata. What is your business in the kingdom?" Oku had drawn tentatively closer, and finally he allowed the other guard to scratch him behind the ears.

"I am Kanohari," I said, speaking before Mag as a way of reminding her not to give her true name. We had discussed this before. Mag and I would use false names, in case word of us somehow reached the weremage and warned her of our approach. Dryleaf would need no such precautions, we thought, since he meant nothing to the Shades. "I am returning home, and these are my friends, accompanying me on the journey."

As I spoke, I dismounted and threw back my hood. The guards' faces lit with recognition, and Ari gave me a warm smile. My father was a Heddan, but my mother was of old Calentin blood, and the features of my homeland were plain upon my face, even if my skin was a bit pale.

"Welcome home, countryman," said Ari. He pressed his fist to his forehead. "How long away?"

"Too long," I said, giving him a smile that I did not feel. "Many years."

He chuckled and clapped a hand on my shoulder.

"Well, you will lose that Selvan accent before long." He shifted his attention back to Mag, giving her a nod. "You are true friends to accompany your fellow on such a long journey." Behind him, Oku had gone belly-up to allow the other guard to scratch him. One hind leg kicked wildly at the air.

"Oh, do not worry," said Mag, smiling at me. "It has all been a long ploy. I mean to get him drunk and then steal all his coin."

"She is joking," I said quickly, scowling at her.

Ari chuckled, but then his countenance grew stern. "You are welcome to Opara, but I am afraid we must inspect your belongings. Orders from the Rangatira, and none but his servants are exempt."

"Of course," I said easily. Yet in my mind, a warning bell began to toll. Inspecting travelers at the border? That was something I might have expected in the eastern regions, the mountain passes where I grew up. But the southern border had never been a place of great watchfulness. It had never needed to be, for Dorsea knew better than to bring their aggression here, and they turned it instead upon Selvan, or Feldemar or sometimes Hedgemond.

Fortunately, we carried nothing suspicious upon us. We were indeed simple travelers, even if our ultimate goal was not quite so simple. After perusing our rations and travel gear and Mag's considerable stock of coin, the guards waved us on through the gate. Oku leaped up with a yelp and, after giving the guard's face a quick lick, he came pelting after us. Ari raised a hand to wave farewell, and then they were out of sight.

Riding into those streets was a strange sensation for me. The scent of cooking food wafted on the air towards me, bringing the aroma of dishes I had not smelled in years, but recognized at once. Most people around us had moko, and more than once I caught myself staring at it, tracing its twisting designs with my eyes.

I was something of a rarity, you see. Most people of Calentin do not travel very far from home, and so I had not seen them often since I left. Yet the smells, the sights, and the few snatches of song I could hear in the streets and alleys, all of it came together to pitch my mind straight back to my youth, as though I had never been gone.

"Those guards were very friendly, even if they did search our belongings," remarked Dryleaf. "That is one thing I have always liked about Calentin. Not only is it a beautiful kingdom—or I considered it so, back when I could see—but the people are simply wonderful. They seem so happy here, tucked in their own corner of Underrealm and untroubled by the affairs of the wider world."

"Calentin has its own troubles, and they are plenty." The words came harsher than I intended. Dryleaf cocked his head in surprise, and Mag gave me a stern glance. "Do not look at me like that," I told her. "I speak only the truth. No kingdom is an idyll."

"We know it, but that is no reason to be such a grouch," said Mag. "We are leagues and leagues away from your family. No one here will recognize you."

I gave her a small and sheepish smile. She had seen to the heart of my poor mood right away. "I know that. But this is the closest I have come to my family's domain since I left them."

"Ah," said Dryleaf, nodding sagely. "Bad blood, is it? Well, this is your home kingdom, and you would know more about it than I do. At least we do not have to go to your family's lands. That is one hopeful thing."

I hid a grimace and turned my attention back to the streets. But Oku seemed to sense something of my dark mood, for he whined and stepped closer, nudging my foot with his head. "Thank you, boy," I told him, and looked up at Mag. "Do you see? Even the hound knows how to be a good friend."

Mag snorted and leaned over from her saddle towards mine, wrapping me in a one-armed hug that almost lifted me into the air. "Here. Is this affection enough for you?"

"Release me before I faint," I wheezed.

She let go and pounded me on the back, which only hurt worse. "That is more than enough support for now. I shall give you another dose tomorrow."

"Please do not. I quite enjoy having ribs."

Dryleaf laughed aloud, and I felt my dark mood dissipate somewhat. Mag sometimes made me feel inadequate, but that was through no fault of her own. It was only that she was impressive in so many ways. Yet she was always a true friend, never letting me wallow in my own misery, and doing anything she could to pull me out of it. In that moment, I appreciated it a great deal.

"Let us return to the matter at hand," said Mag. "We are here for the weremage. We need a place to start looking."

"A difficult proposition," I said. "She could be anyone. We could encounter her at any time. In truth, she could have been one of those guards at the gate, and we would never have known."

We had discussed this, of course, on the long road north. Dryleaf had raised the idea of telling the Mystics about the weremage—hunting down rogue wizards was their duty, after all. But Mag and I refused. The Mystics would never allow us to join them in hunting the weremage down. They never partnered with others for such a task, except in very rare cases where they had no other choice—or if they were an exceptional person, like Jordel, who had been far more trusting than most. Indeed, if we had told the Mystics of our aims, not only would they have barred us from the hunt and brought the weight of the King's law against us if we persisted, but it is unlikely they would even have told us if they were successful. We had to do this on our own. The weremage had slain Mag's husband, slain my friend. She would die by our hands. On that we were agreed.

Mag nodded at my words. "Our one advantage is that the weremage does not know we are coming for her. The only way she could have found out is if the satyrs sent word. No other servants of their Lord found out about our hunt and lived to tell the tale. And certainly none of them know Pantu told us we could find her here."

"Yet we cannot hope to simply run into her on the street," I said.

"You should seek out these Shades, I think," said Dryleaf. "We know she meant to join some of them here. A weremage can be nearly impossible to hunt, but unless all the Shades are also wizards, they will be easier to pin down. Find them, and you will find her."

"I think that is our best hope," said Mag. "It will still require a good deal of work, but that can wait for the morning. It is already late, and we still need to find a bed for the night. Albern, do you know where we should seek lodgings?"

"No," I said, shaking my head. "I visited Opara but rarely, and that was decades ago. We shall simply have to choose an inn by the look of it."

"I think you two will be better at that than I," said Dryleaf, chuckling. "Though I think I will be a better judge of the food and the beds."

It took us some time to find a place that looked suitable, and by the time we found it, darkness had begun to creep into the sky overhead. The sign hanging over the door named it the Ugly Squirrel—a joke, it seemed, for the building was beautiful, with a grid of dark beams framing tight wooden slats that had been painted a deep crimson. But then we met the place's owner, and his face more than made up for the building's beauty. His forehead swooped down low over his eyes, which pointed in different directions, and his jaw was misshapen so that he looked to be constantly grimacing. His name was Nuhea, if I remember correctly, and he was a delight. He chuckled as we introduced ourselves.

"The name is for me, not the inn," he said, lisping slightly. "For even ugly squirrels make their nests in beautiful trees."

He took our orders for food and lodgings, summoning hands to care for our horses and carry our few belongings to our rooms. But I noticed him giving me little glances from the corner of his eye—or at least, I thought he did, for it was hard, sometimes, to tell where he was looking. I was somewhat unnerved, even though I knew there was precious little chance of the man recognizing me. In hindsight, I now think that Nuhea must have seen something of my mother in my features. He must have thought I looked familiar, though he could not place why.

In any case, we paid him for his trouble and retired to our rooms, where food was soon delivered to us. We ate quickly and readied ourselves for sleep—though Mag and I still traded watches through the night, just in case. Weary as we were, we had no wish to be surprised, on the off chance that we had been spotted entering the city.

It was our weariness, however, that kept us from noticing the woman who entered the inn just behind us. Her skin was pale and her hair was fair, though she hid both under a grey cloak. She watched as we dealt with Nuhea, she took note of the rooms to which he brought us, and then she slipped out into the night.

FOUR

KAITA HAD BEEN WAITING FOR US IN THE STRONGHOLD of Maunwa not far away.

She had been there for some days. When we had ridden from Lan Shui, she had trailed us for a little while, stalking us in raven form, until she was sure we were heading for Opara as she had intended. Then she had cut straight across the countryside towards Calentin, bypassing the roads and traveling a long, harsh route through the wilderness. It had been taxing, but she was eager to reach the city far ahead of us.

But when she reached the Shades there, she found

a nasty surprise. The old captain in the area had been given a new assignment. The new captain was a woman named Riri, and the hatred between the two women was thinly veiled, even in service of their Lord. For some days Kaita had been trying to get Riri to prepare for our arrival, but every council had devolved into an argument before long, and so they had barely gotten anything done.

Now Kaita sat in Riri's council chamber again, bored nearly senseless, listening as two officers delivered reports of troop movements, of information and intelligence gathered about the constables, the Mystics, the Rangatira and his rangers. None of it mattered to Kaita. She had only one aim: to continue to lead Mag and me north, to the lands I had once called home. Just as Rogan had commanded her.

And then the door opened, and the woman with pale skin and fair hair entered the council room, casting back her hood.

Kaita looked up, every nerve in her body suddenly alight. The look on the woman's face told her that her long wait was over.

"They are here," said the woman. She nodded to Kaita. "The travelers matching the description you gave."

"At last," hissed Kaita.

Riri gave her a cool look for a moment before turning to the messenger. "Where are they?"

"The Ugly Squirrel. One room for all three of them. I have a contact there, we could strike—"

"We do not aim to kill them," Kaita snapped. "Our job now is—"

"You are not in command here," said Riri. Kaita scowled. She did not need the reminder; Riri had not let her forget it for so much as a moment since her arrival. Riri looked to the messenger once more. "Thank you. That will be all. The rest of you may go as well."

The messenger nodded and left, and the two Shade officers at the table took their leave. Kaita waited in frustrated silence as they shuffled out of the room—too slowly, she thought, and she wondered if Riri had secretly given them an order to annoy her as much as possible.

When the room was finally empty, Riri studied her for a moment. Kaita said nothing. Riri liked to wait for Kaita to speak, and then interrupt her. It was just the sort of petty, vindictive trick she had always cherished—and she had used it often enough against Kaita in the last few days. And so Kaita remained quiet, refusing to give her the pleasure.

"Well?" said Riri at last. "What do you think they mean to do next?"

"They will look for me," said Kaita. "We will have to watch them."

"It is dangerous for my people to visit Opara too often," said Riri. "The High King knows about us now.

The nobility is on alert. We are only here to watch for Calentin troop movements. Our secrecy is more important now than ever."

"You do not have to tell me that," said Kaita. "I know Rogan means for us to remain in the shadows, for now. I was there in the room when he said it—and, too, when he commanded us to begin *striking* from those shadows."

Riri's hands clenched on the arms of her chair. Kaita wanted to smile, but she was smart enough to conceal it. Riri had never understood why Rogan kept Kaita so close. She had never understood that Rogan knew just how useful Kaita was, in a way no one ever had before.

Even those who had claimed to, when Kaita had been young.

"In any case," said Riri, "sending my own people into town to watch these stragglers will endanger our more important work. You brought this problem to Opara. You can watch the strangers."

"I can," said Kaita, fighting not to say it through gritted teeth. "But I cannot stay in raven form all day. And even if I could, night will come, and I have to sleep sometime. You cannot simply bury your head beneath your blankets and hope this blows by. If Mag speaks with the King's law, they will come hunting for you."

"They would not find us," said Riri calmly. "None of their agents have come this far outside the city in a long while. The only danger would be if one of our soldiers were caught—which is why I will not continue to send them to Opara on your errands."

Her foolishness grated on Kaita's nerves. The constables might not have made a habit of visiting the stronghold of Maunwa, but it was far from concealed. It was an entirely foolish place to make one's secret hideout—but then again, it played very well into Riri's idea of her own importance. Why should she lurk in caves or some backwater buildings, when she could set herself up in this place of strong stone and imagine herself a grand lord? Never mind that she had only a dozen soldiers at her command.

But Kaita had pointed this out already, and Riri had ignored her. She must adopt a diplomatic tone now, if she wanted Riri to see wisdom.

"Do not underestimate the redbacks," said Kaita. "You do not want them to be on the alert. That is what is important now. The sooner you help me lead Mag and her party north, the safer your mission will be. Abandon this place, and leave evidence that points a trail north. Albern and Mag will discover it. It is only a matter of time. Speed the process, and you can have them out of your life all the sooner."

Riri frowned. It was a good point, though she clearly would not admit that. She scratched one nail against the wood of the table. For just a moment, Kaita thought she might agree.

"No."

Kaita balked. "No? That is all you have to say?"

"It is all I need to say," said Riri. "I am the captain here. I take my orders from Rogan, not you. And the last thing Rogan told me was to keep entirely out of sight, remaining unknown to anyone. And he said that if we were discovered, that we were to eliminate any witnesses. You have been a fool, and have led our enemies right to our doorstep. But I believe you when you say that Rogan wishes for them to be killed. I will do so, fulfilling my duty to him while also cleaning up your mess."

"Are you . . ." Kaita stopped, aghast. "Are you mad? You will not do anything of the sort. If you try, you will die. Mag will slaughter you and anyone foolish enough to follow your orders. I must lead her to Tokana. No human can defeat her, but our allies in the north can."

"Oh, Kaita," said Riri, giving a scornful smile. "Simply because you have proven too incompetent to deal with her, does not mean that I am."

Kaita shot to her feet. "Incompetent?" she roared, as her eyes began to glow. "Never forget who you are speaking to."

She lunged, sprouting a pace taller. Her clothing sank into her flesh even as her hands turned into a lion's massive paws. The air hissed as her razor claws came slashing forwards.

Riri ducked the grasping talons. A knife appeared

in her hand, too fast for Kaita to see where she pulled it from. Twisting, she avoided another swipe.

Her dagger flashed. Kaita felt a stabbing pain in each thigh. A thick, guttural scream erupted from her enlarged throat.

Unable to keep her feet, she crashed to the floor on her front. Riri was atop her in an instant. She snatched Kaita's arms and wrenched them behind her back, squeezing until Kaita screamed again.

And then Riri seized her temples. Her fingers dug into the flesh there, pushing, crushing. Kaita's whole body went rigid. She tried to cry out, but all that came was a choked gasp.

She felt the magic slipping away from inside her. Her body slowly resumed its natural form. Her tight blue and grey clothes sprouted out of her skin again. In a few heartbeats, she was herself, and still pinned under Riri. Tears sprang into her eyes at the agony in her legs.

"I will release you so that you can heal those wounds," said Riri. "But only if you will promise not to be so foolish again. Swear to me."

"Only Rogan and our father receive vows from me," said Kaita, gritting her teeth and trying to pull an arm free.

Riri twisted harder. Kaita had to bite her own tongue to hide another scream. "Then I can hold you here as long as I need to."

"All right," said Kaita, hating the whimper in her own voice.

"Say it."

"I swear."

Riri let her go and rose, backing away quickly. But Kaita could not even think of breaking her word. She could only think of the pain in her legs. She focused upon it, and her eyes glowed once more. Slowly, painfully, the flesh turned fluid and melded together. The skin rejoined last, sealing the wound. Kaita gave a sigh of relief and let her magic slip away once more.

She got to her feet. Her arms still pained her; no weremagic could heal a twisting like that. Leaning heavily against the table in the center of the room, she glared at Riri, who now stood by her chair.

"Darkness take you and your Mystics' tricks," snarled Kaita.

Riri smiled. "You have remained the same girl you were in our youth, but I have not. I have grown stronger. And if I have learned the secrets of the mage hunters, now I use them in service of the Lord—a service you have been unable to render. Go now. If Rogan wishes for you to continue your work in Tokana, then you had better scurry off. I shall finish what you could not."

"When Rogan hears of this—"

"Oh? And will *you* tell him?" Riri gave a derisive bark of laughter. "The once great Kaita, scurrying to the heels of her master when she is defeated. I think you will not. I think you will try to forget that this ever happened, out of shame."

Kaita fumed, her breath coming hot and fast, a haze settling over her vision. Almost she reached for her magic again. Almost she transformed and attacked. Never mind defeating Riri—she wanted to kill her.

She smiled instead.

"Very well. You wish to fight the Uncut Lady? You are welcome to her. I wish you every chance of success."

Riri arched an eyebrow. "What are you playing at?"

Kaita did not answer. She turned and stalked out of the room, throwing the door open so that it slammed against the wall outside. Two guards stood beyond, both of them looking nervously over Kaita's shoulder. They must have had strict orders not to enter unless Riri called for aid, but it was clear they had wanted to. They stared, dumbfounded, as Kaita swept past them.

The low stone hallway ran a short distance before reaching a double door. Kaita flung these open to reveal a large main chamber, the centerpiece of the fortress. It was no grand place—not as finely decorated as the Shades' fortress at The Watcher, and not as venerable as their former stronghold in the Greatrocks. It had been built long ago by kings whose names were long forgotten—forgotten because they never rose to the greatness of Roth's generals in later days. Only recently had the Shades reclaimed this place for their own use.

Many of Riri's soldiers sat in the hall now, eating

their evening meal. At the loud crash of the doors, most of them looked up, and the rest followed suit as the hall slowly fell silent.

"Hear me," called Kaita, her voice ringing in the still air. "Hear me, my siblings. Your father loves you, as he loves me and all his children. And if his love has a flaw, it is that it leads him to trust those who are not worthy."

Footsteps came down the hall behind her. Riri was coming.

"Father would want you to survive," Kaita went on, more quickly now. "And I say this: if you wish to live, abandon Riri. She is a fool, and she will throw all of your lives away. But if you remain, and if any of you live, your father's mercy will remain—in me. Go north. Find me in Tokana. I will welcome you with an open heart, ready to return you to our father's embrace."

Riri skidded to a stop behind her. Kaita turned and smiled, pleased to see the look of shock and fury on Riri's face.

"What under the sky are you doing?" growled Riri. "This is worse than insubordination. It is treason!"

"Bold words from one who refused Rogan's orders," said Kaita. "Strike me down, if you think you can. But you had best pray word of it never reaches Rogan or our father."

Riri's hands tensed. For a moment, Kaita thought

she would actually try it. But finally Riri thrust a finger towards the chamber door leading out.

"Go. Never let me see your face again, lest I plant a dagger within it."

"No, you never will see me again," said Kaita. "You will die shortly after I leave, after I continue my service to our father. You think you have grown strong since our youth, and that I have remained the same. But I *did* change. I have grown wise, while you have remained foolish. Farewell, *Ririti.* For the last time."

Kaita turned and swept from the stronghold.

FIVE

"Why did Riri hate her so?" said Sun.

"They knew each other when they were girls, as you will have guessed," said Albern. "Their feud began then, and it worsened the older they grew. That is not always how it goes, of course. Many times we make enemies in our youth, only to reunite with them later and laugh at old, petty grievances. But that usually requires our paths to draw apart for a time, only to reunite when years of wisdom allow us to see our early days with a more honest eye. Kaita and Riri never had that chance. They were never apart for long, and their conflict worsened each time they clashed."

"They were not sisters, were they?" said Sun. "I have no siblings, but I have known others who do. They fight more than it seems possible two people *can* fight."

Albern chuckled at that. "I have seen the same. But no, they were not."

They journeyed now through green lowlands, across fields that stretched for leagues to the west and east. In the west they met suddenly a great spur rising up out of the land—Sun recognized it from the story Albern had already told her of Lan Shui. To the east, the land climbed into the foothills of the Greatrock Mountains, which stood imposing above them, reaching for the sun, which was still climbing into the sky. The cool air had warmed now, and Sun had cast off her cloak and opened the ties of her outer skins as she walked, trying to keep from overheating. A raven soared above them. Sun glanced at it and was unpleasantly reminded of Kaita, and the way she had stalked Mag and Albern from the air for so long. She shuddered and returned her attention to the road.

"It is all so different," murmured Albern. When Sun looked up at him curiously, he waved his arm at their surroundings. "The landscape, I mean."

"When was the last time you were here?"

"Longer than a while, less than an age," he said,

chuckling. "Some time after the Necromancer's War, but not long after. Leaving for such a length of time makes all the changes seem far more stark. When you remain in a place, or when you see something every day of your life, you can miss the subtler changes as they happen."

Sun peered up at him, for his face was still somewhat shadowed by his hood. He had not thrown it back, despite the sun. "You mean as someone grows older?"

"Certainly, but it is true for more than just people." Albern rolled his shoulders. Sun was beginning to recognize that as a sign that he was about to tell another, smaller story, as part of the whole. "I am of the family Telfer, as you know, and my kin dwell in the northeastern mountains of Calentin, in a land called Tokana. That is near the northern end of the Greatrocks, whereas we are now close to their southern tip.

"Our main stronghold is nestled in the mountains, on a ridge overlooking a small dale. That dale was my favorite place when I was a child. The way the land seemed to spill down into it, tumbling from the heights to level out and grow smooth far below our home. The city surrounding our keep was built into the folds of the land. In the morning, the clouds would surround us like a blanket, and as the day wore on, the sun would cast that blanket away from us, welcoming us to its warmth. The stars . . . I have never seen so many, never seen them so clearly. It was like the sky viewed from the ocean on a clear night, but more so.

"Of course, I know now that I was viewing things through the eyes of childhood, and circumstances are rarely as good *or* as bad as we think they are when we are young. But still, it was a beautiful place. I would often go walking and riding, for I was always a lover of the wilderness. When I was very young, my middle sister, Ditra, would accompany me, along with a few attendants. When I was older, I ventured alone.

"In the center of the dale was a tall kauri tree. Every time, I would stop and spend a little while observing it. I told myself stories about it. I imagined climbing it one day, though I never did. The idea of it was something beautiful, and I feared that if I ever went to it in fact, if I put my hands on it, I would find that it was real, and inevitably disappointing.

"The tree never changed. It was always there, always watching over the valley. Kauris are evergreen, so it did not even lose its leaves in the winter. I imagine it was growing, but that was impossible to notice from so far away. And because of the tree, I thought that the land, too, was unchanging. To my mind, the city of Kahaunga was much the same every time I went out on one of my adventures, and the wilderness beyond was always a joy to ride through. I have told you that Mag's happiest days were in Northwood with Sten. Mine were in those mountains, before I grew older and realized something was wrong in my life.

"That changed when, one day, someone cut down the kauri tree."

Sun frowned at him. "What? Who?"

"Some logger, I imagine," said Albern. "I never found out. But the next time I went riding, something felt wrong. It was like going on a journey and realizing after a week of travel that you have forgotten your cloak, though you would have sworn it was on your shoulders. Or, I suppose"—he raised the stump of his right arm—"it is like suddenly missing a limb. It took me some time to realize that the tree had been cut down, and it shook me. It shook me far more than it ought to have. But then, once I had recovered from *that* shock, I began to look around, and I realized that things were even worse. The dale no longer looked as it once had. The town had spread. It was a city now. A pall of smoke hung in the air, the smoke of many cooking fires and smiths' forges. I realized suddenly that the once-brilliant stars above me had grown dim and red. It had happened over time, so that I hardly noticed. And now that I studied it more closely, I realized that *many* trees had been felled in the dale, not just the tall kauri. Now there were more rooftops than trees in the valley. The tall kauri was only the latest victim; I had missed all the others because it had held all of my focus.

"I ran to my mother, the Rangatira, and demanded to know what had happened to the kauri. She dismissed my concerns with a snort, saying that it had had to come down for the good of the people in the dale. I myself thought that the dale had been better before everyone had torn it down to the turf. Mayhap the kauri had only been a pretty thing for me to look at, as my mother tried to tell me, but I did not think so at the time.

"That was in my fourteenth year. Until then, I had been mostly happy with my life. But seeing the great changes that continued to spread around me . . . it made me realize that I, too, had changed. I was never quite as satisfied again. I left before seeing my twentieth year."

"You did?" said Sun, jerked suddenly out of the spell of the story. "Why, I have only seen nineteen years. You left at the same age as I did!"

Albern smiled down at her. "Correct. Do you not think that is odd? Do you understand a little better why, when I first heard about a daughter of the family Valgun sneaking away from her family, I thought I might understand why?"

Sun grew somber. "Mayhap. But your family does not sound quite so bad as mine."

She expected him to refute her, but he only pursed his lips. "Mayhap. I suppose we shall both have to see. For now, let us return to Opara, where Mag and Dryleaf and I had taken our lodgings."

We woke in the morning after a restful night, more restful than any we had had since we set out from Lan Shui. In truth we slept overlong, waking a good few hours past dawn. The smell of food drifting up from the kitchen filled my nostrils as I stretched upon the bed, which I had taken after Mag had replaced me on watch. She sat with her back against the room's door, dozing, but her eyes snapped open as she heard me groan.

"Good morn," she said. "I think I shall fetch us some breakfast."

"Make sure to bring some to Oku as well," I said. "He is likely angry with us, for spending the night inside and apart from him, after so much time of being able to share our tents."

"Your tent, mayhap," said Mag, sniffing. "I never allowed him into mine."

"That is patently untrue," I said. "But in any case, I would much appreciate it if you got us some food."

She nodded and went to do it. I had Dryleaf up by the time she returned, and we ate in silence, enjoying our sliced sweet potato and sour bread.

"Sky," I breathed, once I had finished eating. "That was good."

"A taste of home for you, I imagine," said Dryleaf.

"Time for business, then," said Mag, before I could answer Dryleaf and tell him that I barely remembered the dish, for I had spent longer outside of Calentin than within it. "We must determine how to hunt down the Shades, and hopefully Kaita."

"I am afraid I do not know where to start," I said.

"This place is almost as strange to me as if I had never been here before."

Mag grinned. "There is someone we can call on."

I frowned at her. "Who?"

"Victon."

My eyes shot wide. "Victon? Victon is *here?*"

"He is," said Mag. "We sent each other letters on occasion. After he retired from the life of a sellsword, he moved here to Opara and began a winery."

Dryleaf's brows shot for the ceiling, and he licked his lips. "Did he? It has been some time since I have been able to enjoy a good, rare vintage."

"Victon," I said, shaking my head. "I can scarcely believe it."

"I hope he will be happy to see us," said Mag, "and that he will be able to aid us."

Laughing, I said, "Happy? I have never known Victon to be anything but a happy man. Let us ask the innkeeper if he knows where the vineyard is, and then let us report to our old captain."

SIX

You may remember my mentioning Victon earlier. When I joined the Upangan Blades, he was my first sergeant. We fought together for a good long while, and unlike many of my other superiors, he and Mag and I were always fast friends, partially because of something that had happened when I had only been with the company for a few months.

He and I were scouting through the jungle towards an enemy camp when a bear plunged out of the underbrush and attacked us. I was a few paces ahead of

Victon, but my focus was on the tracks we were following, and so Victon noticed the bear first. He leaped forwards to shove me out of the way of its charge. It struck him instead, sending him careening into a tree. He sagged to the ground, groaning.

I gave a shout and drew an arrow from my quiver. The bear turned on me at once. It came roaring towards me with a fury that told me it must have cubs nearby. Nothing else could have provoked it into such unreasoning rage.

As it charged, I managed to loose a single arrow. But panic sent my shot wide, and the arrow only entangled in the fur of the bear's shoulder. It struck out, and I barely threw myself out of the way in time. Its paw snapped my bow in two. I ducked behind a tree as it swiped again. Its claws ripped through the tree, nearly toppling it.

Even as I prepared to run for my life, Victon came charging with a cry. He went for a stab, but the bear rounded and struck him a heavy backhanded blow. He crashed to the ground. The bear reared, ready to fall upon him and crush him with its massive bulk.

I had been about to flee, but seeing Victon helpless gave me just enough courage to rejoin the fight. I drew my short sword and charged. I stabbed the beast in the side, but fear had weakened my sword arm. A few fingers' worth of steel pierced the bear's flank, but that was all.

Still, it turned and thundered in rage at me, forgetting Victon. I barely managed to duck another swing. The creature's speed and ferocity were incredible.

I had only one thought: I had to draw it away from Victon. There was no use in both of us dying out here in this sky-forsaken wilderness. I ran off into the jungle, hoping to lose it. But the bear was never more than a few paces behind me. My breath grew short. I could practically smell the thing, and I thought I was doomed.

But then came Mag.

She had been assigned to the same squadron as me, and she and a few of our fellows had remained behind to wait for Victon and me to return. She heard the sound of the bear's attack from far away through the jungle and came running as fast as she could.

Even as I was searching for some place I could climb, or some hole I could hide where the bear would not be able to follow, I heard the tone of its roaring change behind me. I turned and found Mag had engaged with the beast. This was long before she had acquired her spear in Dulmun, so she had a simple broadsword. But she had not even bothered to draw it before flinging herself at the beast.

It growled and swiped at her, but Mag evaded the blow with such ease that she looked lazy doing it. Then her boot flew up and struck the bear hard in its chin. I heard a *crunch,* and its head snapped back. It gave a confused grunt.

Before it could raise another paw to strike, Mag

leaped forwards and jabbed at its eyes with fingers she had pressed together like daggers. I heard a wet *thunk* as she pierced one of the bear's eyes, and it gave a terrified scream of pain and fury.

It struck, but again Mag avoided the blow. When she came back up, her sword was in her hand. It sank into the soft flesh underneath the bear's foreleg, piercing deep into its rib cage. Its cry came out wet and wheezing.

The bear turned and fled. It limped on three legs to favor the fourth that Mag had maimed. She turned to me, the battle-trance like a mask over her expression. It shook me then, as it always did.

"Are you all right?"

"Victon," I gasped. "It is heading for Victon."

She seized my arm and pulled me up, and together we pelted after the beast.

Its trail through the jungle was plain to see—and then, half a span before we reached the place I had left Victon, it turned right and vanished into the underbrush. I stopped at the spot, and Mag ran a few more paces before she stopped and looked back at me.

"What is it?" she said.

"It turned. Headed off that way." I pointed where the trail had gone.

She saw the trail after I pointed it out and nodded. "I am going after it. We have to make sure it does not wander into our enemy's camp and alert them. See to Victon."

Without waiting for my answer, she bolted off between the trees. I carried on towards the clearing where we had been attacked. There I found Victon. He had crawled to a nearby tree and sat with his back against it, panting and grimacing, holding his side. Blood seeped out from between his fingers.

"Victon!" I cried. "Are you all right?"

I ran to him, and he smiled up at me, his white teeth shining against his dark skin. "Fine," he said, chuckling. "Its claws got me, but not very badly."

He lifted his hand, and I could see it was true. There was a gash, but nothing life-threatening unless it became infected.

"It needs cleaning," I said, reaching for a flask of ale at my side. "I wish I had something stronger, but this will sting badly enough to do the job."

"How comforting. Wait." Victon seized the flask and took a deep pull, wincing at its poor taste. He handed it back to me. "All right."

I poured it on the wound. Victon growled out his pain and then laid his hand back on the wound when I was done, putting pressure on it with the edge of his cloak.

"There now," I said. "The healers back at camp can tend to it further."

"Mag?" he said.

"Went after the bear. She did not want it to wander towards our enemies, lest they discover other soldiers are here in the jungle."

"Smart of her," said Victon.

"Yes, it annoys me," I said lightly. "No one should be that good a fighter *and* have a mind for strategy."

Victon chuckled. And just then, Mag returned to the clearing. The battle-trance was gone from her, and there was a deep frown on her face.

"You finished it?" I asked her.

"No," she said. "It vanished."

"You lost the trail? It was not exactly trying to be stealthy, after the trouncing you gave it."

"For which I thank you, by the way," said Victon.

"Yes," I said. "It is not everyone who can defeat a full-grown bear with only her hands."

Victon stared at me incredulously. "Her hands?"

"At first," I said, smiling. "I think she wanted a challenge before she deigned to draw her sword."

"Oh, be silent, both of you," said Mag. "And I did not lose the trail. The bear vanished."

I rolled my eyes and grinned at Victon. "That bolsters my confidence, at least. She may be better with a sword than anyone I have ever seen, but she is as useless in this jungle as you are, sir."

Victon burst out laughing, though it looked like it hurt him. "You two have saved my life, and that is not something easily forgotten. Thank you. Now help me up."

We stooped to lift him, and I walked him off through the jungle with his arm around my shoulder.

Mag took his other arm, bloody sword still bare in her hand.

"You are too kind, by the way, sir," I said. "I did not save your life. That honor was Mag's."

Victon grinned again. "You drew it off, and you tried to fight it, at least. We cannot all be the Uncut Lady."

Mag grimaced. I had only recently coined that name for her. Victon and I laughed again. Our true friendship began in that moment, and it would last for the rest of our lives.

And it is rather important to me that you know this story, for reasons that shall become plain.

Our innkeeper did indeed know where the vineyards could be found, and he seemed somewhat jealous when we said we and Victon were old friends. It seemed that Victon was rather well known in the area, and his wine much sought after.

With Dryleaf in tow, we rode for the place with light hearts, for we were eager to see our friend again after so long. We cast our hoods up and moved quickly, doing our best to pass unnoticed, just in case the weremage was in the city and happened upon us by chance. We still thought we had the element of surprise. Of course, you know that all our precautions were in vain, but we did not.

We spotted Victon's place almost from the moment we passed through the city's eastern gate. He had a very large estate, hectares of vines stretching across the feet of Tahumaunga, which loomed high above. There was a west wind that day, and so the air was clear, the mountain's lazy smoke blowing away from us. Once we were a good distance out of town, Mag threw back her hood.

"If the weremage is watching us from the sky, that is because she already knows we are here," she proclaimed. "And it is far too wonderful a day to stay sweating under that hood any longer."

I smiled at her. We let the horses proceed at their own slow pace, with Foolhoof occasionally trying to wander off the road towards a particularly delicious-looking patch of grass. Oku padded happily beside us.

A light wooden fence surrounded Victon's land. It would have been proof against nothing more determined than wandering deer, and the gate at the front stood open. We walked up between the rows of vines, seeing no one nearby. Only when we drew closer to the house at the end of the path did we finally see six figures, bent and plucking the last of the year's grapes. So deep were they in concentration that we drew very close indeed before one of them noticed us. Her plump face, brown skin further darkened by the sun, crinkled as she squinted at us.

"Visitors," she said, loud enough for us to hear.

Two of the figures, the ones closest to the path,

raised their heads. One of them was a young man, the other a woman, and from their jet-black skin and features, I knew them for Victon's kin. When they saw us, they stepped away from their vines and came walking up. The rest of the workers gave us only a cursory glance before returning to their jobs.

"Good day," said the woman as she approached. "I regret to inform you that we have no stock available for sale. Last year's wine is not yet ready, and it is all reserved, in any case."

"That is ill news," said Mag. "Or it would be, if we were here looking for wine. We have come to see Victon. He is an old friend, even if he is now of such stature that others must greet us when we visit. Am I to guess that you are his children?"

They looked uncertainly at each other. "We . . . are," said the boy. "How do you know our father?"

"From the days of our youth," I said. "Or hers and mine, at least, for Victon is older than either of us. We were sellswords together, in the days when he fought for the Upangan Blades."

A flash of recognition shot across both their faces. They looked up at the two of us with renewed interest, and the girl's eyes shone. She pointed to Mag.

"You . . . are you the Uncut Lady?" she asked.

Mag scowled. I strangled a bark of laughter before it could break free. "I am Mag, if that is what you mean."

"Sky above," said the boy. He came to me, extending a hand. "Well met, friends. And what is your name?"

I am afraid I looked quite thunderstruck. It was Mag's turn to hide her laughter. "You mean Victon never told you about me?"

They both looked embarrassed, and the boy slowly drew back his hand. "He . . . he might have?" he said, making it sound like a question. "Only not well enough that we would know you by sight."

"I am Albern," I said. They both blinked. "Albern of the family Telfer?" I said, struggling mightily to hide a note of desperation.

At last the girl's face lit, and she smiled. "Oh, of course! The Uncut Lady's follower!" She turned to her brother. "You remember. He was the one who ran away from the bear."

"What?" I rather shrieked.

The boy, who appeared not to have heard me, burst out into laughter at the girl's words. "Oh, *him!* Sky save me, Father always makes me laugh when he tells those sorts of stories." He extended his hand again. "Well met, Albern. I am Nuru of the family Victon, and this is my sister, Zuri."

"Well met," said Mag, recognizing that I was quite incapable of speech for the moment, though I did take Nuru's hand and shake it. "You know the two of us already, and our elderly companion is called Dryleaf."

"And are you an old friend as well?" said Zuri. "I do not recall Father mentioning you in his stories."

"I am sorry to say I am not," said Dryleaf, who was still wiping away tears of laughter at my reaction. "Though from everything I have heard, as well as your excellent manners, I think I will enjoy meeting your father to a rare extent."

"Come with us," said Nuru, gently taking the bridle of Mag's horse, Mist. "Father will be overjoyed to see you."

"It will be our pleasure," I managed to growl. Zuri approached Foolhoof, and the dark-taken gelding actually nuzzled into her outstretched hand. "Oh, have you decided to forsake me, too?" I asked him.

Zuri looked up at me, aghast. "What?"

"The horse," I said, dismounting and letting her take the reins. "Never mind me. Thank you."

SEVEN

THE HOUSE WAS LARGE, BUT NOT OPULENTLY SO. THE walls were light brown stone, but the roofs were curved red tile, which I had not often seen outside of Dorsea. It made for a wonderfully attractive combination, especially with the great wooden doors through which Victon's children led us inside the house.

Victon was napping, and so we met his wife, Nuri, first. She was positively radiant, with a round waist and eyes that danced, her skin even darker than her children's. She was delighted when her children introduced us, and she went to fetch Victon as soon as we had finished our greetings. When he emerged, still blinking bleary eyes from sleep and leaning heavily on his crutch, his face beamed with a smile that burst into laughter as he saw us.

"Sky save me if I expected this today!" he said, coming forwards and seizing us in a hug. "What are the two of you doing here? I thought you were both living in Selvan."

That cast a shadow over our mood, and he saw it. His own smile faded a little as he watched ours die.

"We were," said Mag. "Much has changed."

He looked us both over, taking note of Dryleaf. I suspected he was looking for Sten. They had never met, but of course Mag would have mentioned him in her letters.

"I can see that," said Victon at last. His smile returned now—still happy, but somewhat more weary. "Well, come in. We are about to eat. I shall fill you with food and flood you with wine, and we shall talk of what we must, and what we can, and what we wish."

Rarely have I enjoyed a meal so much. The courses were a mixture of Calentin food and dishes from Victon's homeland of Feldemar. First we ate sour flatbread and sweet potatoes, but dipped in a delicious sauce made from beef grease and filled with spices. Then the beef itself came, smoked with manuka wood and cooked with whitefish, soft and tender and soaking in still more sauce. With it came plates of greenshell oysters, dipped in pepper and garlic.

I remember every bite of that meal to this day. I can see Oku, who waited patiently at the side of the room until I offered him a morsel of food. He trotted forwards to eat it gently from my fingers. Mag fed him as well, but only when she thought I was not looking, which of course I was. Victon called Oku to him at one point, and the hound came obediently.

"A finer wolfhound I have never seen," said Victon, holding Oku's face between his weathered hands. "Who has ever seen such a well-mannered boy? Not I, no, not I." Oku nuzzled his hands and licked his face, and Victon laughed and ordered the kitchen to give him whatever bones they might have. Oku lay happily in the corner for the rest of the meal.

I remember, too, the wine, which was not only plentiful, but among the best I have ever tasted. It was just sweet enough for you to drink it in great swallows, and more than heady enough to send us into peals of laughter at even the slightest joke. It was dark and smoky, with the faintest hints of charcoal that mingled perfectly with the well-smoked meats we ate. I had a few glasses, and I am positive Mag had more than a bottle. Wine and ale had never had much effect on her.

The food I remember. The conversation, however, comes to me now in bits and snatches. We told Victon of Northwood, and what had happened to Sten. Then we told him of our journey through the Greatrocks, of the satyrs we found there, and of all that happened in Lan Shui. When we told them of the vampires, Victon's face paled, and his wife reached over to clutch her son's arm.

We finished our stories around the same time that the whole table finished their meal, and we all leaned back in our chairs, groaning pleasantly at the tight feeling in our guts. I looked to Victon.

"I cannot remember the last time I enjoyed myself so thoroughly, old friend. Barely half the day has passed, and yet I wish I could lie down."

"But you can," laughed Victon. "I have a room for just such a purpose. Walk with me a moment, and I will show you my land, and then we can rest."

He walked us out of the back of the house and pointed at the different plots, telling us the different sort of grapes he had, which I am sure are important to a vintner, but which I cannot remember at all. In the middle of the fields were built a series of houses, each seeming just as grand as Victon's own. When we asked him who lived there, he smiled.

"Why, those who work the fields with us, of course."

"They must be grateful to you, for building them such fine homes," said Mag.

Victon cocked his head at her with a wry look. "Grateful to me? They built those homes on their own. I only helped a little."

Mag seemed somewhat at a loss. "Forgive my mistake. I thought the field hands were your servants."

Victon laughed at that, slapping one hand against

his hip and the other against his crutch. "Servants? Giving and taking orders? Sky above, Mag, have we not had enough of that in our lives? We make the wine together. We sell the wine together. We live together. Some even bed together when they think their parents are not looking—is that not right, Nuru?" He took his son's arm and gave it a little shake.

"Father, please," said Nuru, blood rushing into his cheeks.

"The only trouble we have tending our fields," Victon went on, "is when he and one of the Turei boys suddenly go missing. But we always find them before too long, and their cheeks are a little rosier when we do."

"Father!" cried Nuru, aghast.

Victon laughed harder and led us all back into the house. He brought us to a room full of couches, each of which was laid with many tasseled pillows, and we lay down as we continued to talk. I learned that Nuru was an ander man, like me. He had come to realize he was ander much younger than I had—I was a bit of a special case, for it usually happens in childhood. The two of us spent a good deal of time speaking privately of our wendings, and all the other little details that only another ander person can understand.

Sometimes Dryleaf would be reminded of one of his stories, and then he would tell it. He was better at it than any of us. We listened attentively whether he spoke or sang, and he made Victon's family weep with the beauty of the songs he gave them, so ancient that I had never heard them before, and rendered in the high speech that had once been common in the courts of the nine kingdoms. We talked until dinner, and then we talked all throughout that meal—even better than lunch had been, and with still more wine—and then we talked for a good long while afterwards.

But sometime in the evening, when the sun had long since set and the moons were making their intrepid way across the sky, we came to business. Victon's children had long since gone to bed—Nuru somewhat sooner than Zuri, for I had spotted another boy lurking outside the room, beckoning to him. It was only the five of us now, and Oku in the corner, of course. Mag sat up on her couch. Victon and Nuri rose as well, sensing the mood in the room shift.

"Victon," said Mag. "This day has been the best of long memory. I have not Dryleaf's gift with words, nor even Albern's, and so I cannot tell you what a balm it has been to all of us after the long road that brought us here. But we did not come here only for a visit, however long overdue that might have been."

He sighed, leaning forwards to scratch at the stump of his leg. "Well, of course not. That would have been a long journey to make to see my ugly old face." Nuri reached over and slapped his arm lightly, and he grinned. "Tell me, my friends. What do you need?"

"We told you of the weremage," I said. "We are

hunting her here in Opara. We know she still works with these Shades, and we think she came here to join more of them."

Victon frowned and scratched at his stubble. "I have heard nothing of any rogue weremage. Nor have I heard of these Shades. I did not even know about Northwood; there was some rumor of an attack on Selvan, but I took that for Dorsea's usual malcontence. What could bring them here? Opara may stand on the border, but it is hardly a hub of trade."

"The Shades have long been devising a plan both hidden and evil," said Dryleaf. "We should not presume it will be easy to guess at."

Victon reached over to take Nuri's hand. "I suppose I was a fool to think I was done with war forever."

"You still can be," said Mag. She left her chair to kneel before him, putting her hands on his leg. "We will take care of this matter. You left your fighting days behind you."

"So did you," said Victon. Then he chuckled and pounded on his stump with one hand. "But I suppose there is more than one reason I should not return to the field."

Nuri's brows lifted. "Not to mention the fact that your wife might kill you if you tried."

"Another fair point, and one I had not considered," said Victon. "Yet I may still be of some use. I may not know where to start looking for your renegade wizard—but I know the person who *will* know where to look. It happens that I am acquainted with Conrus of the family Matara."

I squinted, thinking, before I recalled the name. "The Rangatira? It . . . might not be wise for us to speak with him."

"Oh?" said Victon, looking vaguely alarmed. "Are you in some trouble with the King's law?"

"No," I said. "But I do not wish my return to Calentin to be widely known, especially among the nobility." I had known Conrus when I was very young. That was a long time ago, and I had had my wending since, but still I did not like the thought of presenting myself to him.

"Yet we could hardly ask for better assistance than we would get from a border lord," said Mag. "Worry not, Albern. I will do most of the talking."

"And I will visit him with you," said Victon. "He has been expecting a bottle of my special reserve for about a week now. I meant to entice him to visit, but it seems fate has given me a better use for an unpaid favor."

"Fate," I laughed, like a fool. "If you say so, old friend."

"But come," said Nuri. "It is far too late for you to make your way back to the city tonight. You must stay here with us, and the lot of you can go in the morning."

We made all the right sounds of protestation, but

she did not have to work very hard to persuade us. Nuri set us up in some of the finest rooms in their very fine house, and we slept even better than we had at the inn the night before.

EIGHT

Nuri woke Mag, Dryleaf, and me just after sunrise. We broke our fast with her and Victon. I had a slight headache after all the wine, and Dryleaf looked to be feeling even more delicate, but none of the others seemed any worse for wear.

Our meals were done, and we were picking through the remains of the tastiest remaining morsels when Victon clapped his hands. "We shall make for the Rangatira first thing," he proclaimed. "I readied one of my finest bottles last night before I went to sleep."

"Will you be accompanying us?" Dryleaf asked Nuri, who was sitting beside him.

She arched an eyebrow. "Do you wish for me to?"

He lifted her hand to kiss it. "How could I wish for anything but more of your astonishingly beautiful company?"

That made Nuri giggle, even as she shook her head. "I could ask no greater compliment, for the blind see the only sort of beauty I have ever cared about. But no, I have many duties here, and I will be little help to you."

When we were ready, we left the house. In the front courtyard we found that the horses had already been brought from the stable, as well as a horse for Victon. Nuru and Zuri were there, and they grinned at us as we emerged into the strengthening daylight.

"A good morn to you all," said Nuru. "Did you sleep well?"

"Wonderfully," said Dryleaf. "And I thank you for your courtesy."

"Mag," said Victon, "will you do me the honor of helping me to the saddle? I learned how to do it myself after the leg, but it is still easier with help. And I could ask for no greater honor than being squired by the Uncut Lady."

"Squired, is it?" said Mag with a wry smile. "Of course I will."

She took his belt and helped heave him up, while

I went to aid Dryleaf. Once the two of them were mounted, Mag went to her mare, and I went to Nuru, who was holding Foolhoof's reins. The gelding eyed me suspiciously.

"Did he give you any trouble?" I asked Nuru.

"Not a bit," said Nuru. "He was most well behaved."

"Oh, you will obey *others,* will you?" I said, glaring at Foolhoof even as I rubbed his nose.

He snorted on me, and a bit of phlegm splattered on my hand.

"Do you see?" I asked Nuru, shaking it away. "This is what I must suffer through."

Nuru laughed. Then he held forth a hand. I took his wrist and shook. "It was an honor to meet you, as well as a pleasure," he said. "I am always pleased to meet another ander person, and more so when they are a companion of the fabled Uncut Lady. And a stalwart warrior in their own right," he added quickly, as I gave him a sour look.

"Well spoken, at least at the end," I told him. "Mag has stayed in touch with your father over the years, but I have not. I will do so from now on. And once I have a place where he can send me letters, I would be most pleased to hear from you as well."

The boy's face split in a brilliant grin. "I promise I shall write until you are sick of me."

I laughed and climbed atop my horse. With Victon leading the way, we rode away from his home towards the city. The streets were nearly empty, for it was not yet time to go to market, and all the farmers were already out in the fields. Victon took us to our destination with the unswerving air of one who had made this journey many times before.

In the center of Opara stood the Rangatira's keep. It was surrounded by a strong stone wall, the back side of which pressed close to the river. Guards patrolled the top of the wall, but they had the sluggish look of soldiers who almost wished for trouble, simply so they would have something to do.

The guards opened the gate once Victon explained why he had come. I looked down at Oku.

"Kip, boy," I said.

Oku looked up at me and whined.

"I am sorry. But we will return soon."

He trotted off to the side of the gate and lay there, watching as we vanished through it. Attendants took our horses, and Victon led us to the great doors of the keep, which also stood open. A page there raised her chin and looked upon us expectantly.

"I have come to see the Rangatira, bearing a gift I promised him," said Victon, raising the bottle of wine. "And I speak on behalf of my friends here, who have come to beg a boon."

The page looked us over. "Very well. We will take your weapons."

"Of course," I said, unbuckling my sword. I left my bow, for it was unstrung, hanging on my saddle. Mag looked somewhat disgruntled, but she handed over her spear and shield. The page handed the weapons to a doorman before leading us into the keep's great hall.

There were tapestries on the walls inside, as well as many fine weapons with gold inlay—pieces for ceremony and show, but they looked fit for battle if need be. Lord Matara clearly had not forgotten his primary purpose as an agent of war. The furniture was solid and sturdy even when it was beautiful, and the doors looked well-kept and easy to bar against intrusion. Through the hall we were led and into a small chamber off to the right. There were many cushioned chairs inside, and the page beckoned us in.

"I will deliver your request to Lord Matara," she said. "He is in council at the moment. You will be summoned when he is ready."

Mag looked exasperated, but I spoke quickly before she could express it. "Of course," I said. "Thank you for your assistance."

She gave a thin-lipped nod and vanished, closing the door behind her. I helped Dryleaf over to one of the chairs and eased him down into it.

"Oh, this is a fine seat," he said with a sigh. "Though not as fine as your couches, Victon."

"I despise all this waiting." Mag wore a scowl, and she did not sit, but stood in the center of the room with her arms folded. "You nobles seem to have perfected the art of making people wait on your beck and call."

"I have not been a noble for some time," I said.

She was about to respond when the door to the chamber opened again. It had only been a few moments, and so we all turned to it in surprise. There stood the page again, looking almost as startled as we were.

"The Rangatira is ready to receive you," she said, as though she herself could not quite believe it.

I barely kept myself from asking, *Already?* But Victon gave us a knowing grin. We helped Dryleaf stand again, and followed the page back out into the main hall and up a short flight of stone steps to a large door at the end of the room.

Beyond lay the Rangatira's audience chamber. It was the bottom floor of the keep's central tower, and so it was circular, with a wall towards the back that obscured the staircase leading up. In front of that wall stood a small dais—nowhere near so grand as the king's, as I knew from personal experience, but imposing enough. And upon that dais was a chair, where sat the Rangatira. He was a little older than I was, with a thick and braided beard that reached the middle of his chest. Some grey flecked that beard, as well as his temples, just like mine. He had extensive moko on his cheeks and chin. Upon his brow was wisdom, and in his eyes burned the fire of courage. His arms were thick with both muscle and fat, and he was clothed in practical clothes that were fine enough for his office, but not ostentatious. I felt myself instinctively straightening my posture, standing like a soldier in formation. This was a leader, and no mistake.

"You address Conrus of the family Matara, Rangatira of Opara and of southeastern Calentin," said the page.

I bowed with a fist to my forehead, and after seeing me, Mag did the same. After I straightened, I went to Dryleaf and carefully guided his hand to his forehead. But before I helped him bow, Lord Matara raised a hand.

"That is not necessary," he said. His eyes shifted to the page. "That will be all, thank you."

The page bowed, fist to her forehead, and left. The chamber settled to silence as Lord Matara studied us. At last he beckoned to Victon.

"Greetings, old friend," he said. "I see you have finally brought that which you owe me."

Victon beamed his most charming smile and approached with the wine. "And it is my pleasure to do so."

The Rangatira smiled in return and came down from the dais to accept the bottle. He turned it over in his hands once before placing it on a table near his chair, and then he came over to us, studying us with keen eyes.

"You are the ones who have come to ask a boon?" he said.

"We are, my lord," said Mag, bowing again.

He turned to her, clearly assuming that she was our

leader—which suited me just fine. "My duties keep me rather busy, and so I must be brief," he said. "How may I help you?"

"We were hoping, lord, that we could inquire as to whether there has been any unusual activity in Opara of late?"

Lord Matara frowned. "You shall have to be more specific. Odd goings-on are all I seem to deal with. That is the lot of a Rangatira."

Mag gave me a quick glance. How to inquire without tipping our hand?

"Rangatira," I said. "Has anyone, by chance, reported any sightings of a rogue weremage? A Calentin woman of about my years?"

The effect on him was immediate. His dark face grew darker still, and he glanced quickly back and forth between the two of us. "A weremage? I cannot say that I have heard of one, no. But that is a matter for Mystics. Are the two of you redcloaks in disguise?"

"We are not," said Mag quickly. "But we have a special interest. Have there been any crimes recently, mayhap, something outside of petty theft or a street brawl, where the perpetrator has not yet been caught?"

"Nothing that has come to me," said Lord Matara. "Though I could make some inquiries. But what do the two of you want with a rogue weremage? You would do better to turn this matter over to the Mystics and let them track her down, if you can give them a report as to the crimes she has committed."

I sighed and reached for my right sleeve, drawing it up to the elbow. There, on the inside of my forearm, was my family's mark. I showed it to Lord Matara.

You will already be familiar with noble marks. The family Telfer's is made of three arrows pointing down, and behind them lies a bow. It is somewhat reminiscent of the Mystics' symbol. There mine sat, etched into the skin with black ink.

"We have come from the family Telfer," I told Lord Matara. "We have pursued this weremage a long way, and Lord Telfer's grudge against her is quite personal. For that reason, we would rather not involve the Mystics. The redcloaks would not allow us to pursue our hunt, but would take it upon themselves. We would prefer to handle things quietly."

I could see Victon's surprise. Of course, he knew I was a Telfer. But he also knew that I had not been home in many years, and this story was rather different from what we had told him. But he was wise enough to play along.

The Rangatira, for his part, suddenly looked rather stony. Instead of answering, he turned and walked back to his dais, climbed the stairs, and sat down upon his chair. The message was clear: this was no longer a personal matter, a favor bestowed by him upon his friend, Victon. This had just become official business.

"Why did you not tell me this before?" he said sternly.

"As he said, we wished to handle this matter quietly," said Mag.

He kept his gaze fixed upon my face. "I do not know that I know you," he said, "though you have the Telfer look."

"I do not know that I know you either, Lord," I replied, "though you look like a Matara."

The words were mayhap brazen, but they drew a small smile from him. "What is your name?"

"Kanohari."

His gaze slid past me. "And she?"

"This is Chao," I said, pointing to Mag. "She is an old friend of the family, and a loyal companion in a fight."

"And the other?"

I frowned, though I tried to hide it. When it came to matters of Rangatira and rangers, I did not know why he should be so interested in my companions. "He is Dryleaf. An advisor, and one with much expertise in the matter that drew us from home."

"The matter of wizards, you mean," said Lord Matara.

"I do," I said. "Forgive me, Rangatira, but why do you ask? By which, I only mean that so many questions tell me something is amiss here in Opara."

Lord Matara considered me, for a moment, deep in thought.

"When was the last time you were in Telfer lands?"

Quickly I added the time up in my head—not the true answer, of course, but the time it would have taken us to get here from Tokana if I first rode into Feldemar and then traveled in haste.

"What is the date, my lord?"

"The eighteenth of Yanis."

"Then it was over a month ago," I said.

Lord Matara nodded. "That is as I thought. There have been recent developments that I have only recently been made aware of. The High King has sent word to the nobility across the land, asking us to be especially alert for strangers passing through our domains. But if you are supposed to know why, it would be proper for you to hear it from your own lord, not from me."

That put a tremor in my heart. And despite myself, I could not keep from asking the obvious. "And yet, my lord, if you are supposed to be suspicious, why did you allow us to enter your council chamber?"

"Because you came with Victon," he said. "And I have verified that this *is* Victon. I have my own wizards, and though you did not notice them, they probed your party for magic as you entered, to ensure he was no weremage in disguise."

"A wise measure," said Mag.

Lord Matara glanced up at her, looking annoyed for a moment.

"Forgive her, my lord," I said, glaring over my shoulder at Mag. "She has been a family friend for so long that she has grown somewhat lax in decorum, and she is such a skilled warrior that my lord tends to overlook it."

To my immense relief, he smiled at that. "I suppose there are some in Opara whom I treat the same—Victon among them, though that is for his wine, and not his skill in battle. Though I have heard that that was prodigious in earlier days."

"Nearly an age ago now, Rangatira," said Victon, giving another bow.

Lord Matara smiled before turning back to Mag. "If you are so skilled a warrior, I would enjoy sparring with you sometime, if you remain in Opara long."

Before Mag could say something else idiotic, I replied, "I am afraid that is not our plan. We wish to find and eliminate this rogue weremage, and then to return home as quickly as we may."

He nodded. "Fairly said. Very well. If you have been hunting this weremage for almost a month, there is little chance she has anything to do with the matter the High King warned us about. That is reassuring, but it also means I cannot spare my personal attention for the matter. I will send for my lead ranger to assist you."

He lifted a hand in a clear gesture of dismissal, though a kindly one. I bowed, fist to my head once more, and ushered Victon, Mag, and Dryleaf from the room.

NINE

"Sky above, Mag, would you *please* try to keep at least a modicum of respect?" I said, once the page had escorted us back to the waiting chamber and the door was closed.

"I was plenty respectful," she said. "And I took his measure before I spoke. That was a man who respects bravery and a good laugh."

"She is right," said Victon with a chuckle.

"He seemed an honorable man," said Dryleaf. "I could hear a strength in him."

"Strength, and wit, and many secrets," I said. "I

knew him, when I was young, before I had even seen fourteen summers."

"Before your wending, then," said Mag. "No wonder he thought you looked familiar."

"The years have altered my appearance at least as much as the wending," I said. "Not all of us have retained our youth so well as you."

She gave me a brittle smile. Dryleaf sighed as he settled back in his chair cushions. "It is good for you that you were not recognized," he said. "It seems you do not have as much to fear in your homeland as you thought."

But I was not entirely convinced. Certainly, here in Opara, it was far less likely that anyone would recognize me than it would have been in Tokana. But all it would take was one member of my family—even distant kin—and then I knew word would make its way back home. To my mother.

I feared to think what might happen then.

Victon spoke up. "This is where I should let you go your own way, I think," he said. "I know little of these matters."

"Of course," said Mag, clasping his hand and pulling him into an embrace. "Thank you for everything, Victon. We will try to see you again, if we can. Will you be all right, getting back to the farm on your own?"

"I told you I can mount my horse," he chuckled. "Besides, the Rangatira's servants are always willing to help me."

"Then thank you again," I said. "May the sky smile upon you, and the moons light your way through the dark."

"I enjoyed our time together more than any I have had in a good long while," said Dryleaf, reaching out to allow Victon to take his wrist. "May the time before our next meeting be short, and may the reunion be joyous."

"With your presence, of course it will be," said Victon. "I would give much to have you tell more tales and sing more songs for my family."

"Nothing would please me more," said Dryleaf. "Once this business is taken care of."

"Of course," said Victon. Then he took Dryleaf's shoulder and gently placed his forehead to the old man's. "Until next time."

He left. We settled ourselves into chairs to await the arrival of the lead ranger.

"I was interested in that secretive business the Rangatira mentioned, about the news from the High King," Dryleaf said, once the chamber had settled to silence again.

"It must be the Shades," said Mag.

"That was my guess," said Dryleaf. "Yet Conrus thinks our weremage has nothing to do with them. I wonder just what Enalyn told the nobility."

I could not help getting somewhat rankled. "The least you two could do is refer to Lord Matara and the High King by their proper titles."

Mag waved an airy hand. "We leave such niceties to you nobles," she said. "You just told me I have a poor grasp of decorum."

Before I could argue further, a thought struck me like an arrow between the eyes. I grinned, prompting a confused frown from Mag.

"Mag," I said, struggling through a throat that had suddenly gone tight. "If the High King warned the nine kings of the Shades, that means she received the message."

She looked every bit as thunderstruck as I felt, her hands clenching to fists. From his place in the cushioned chair, Dryleaf turned his head back and forth, arching an eyebrow.

"Eh? What message?" he said. "You did not tell me you were on speaking terms with the High King."

"Not us," I said. "Friends of ours, ones who barely escaped the destruction of Northwood. They were trying to deliver news of the Shades to the High King's Seat, but they were pursued. We had feared for their safety."

"I see," said Dryleaf, nodding gravely. "Then I am happy for you both that they survived."

"Mag, we know where they are," I said. "We can find them. We can go to the Seat and find—"

"Of course we can," said Mag, giving me a small smile—but a stern one. "Once the weremage is dead, we are free to go wherever we wish. We will visit the Seat then. I swear it."

I felt crestfallen. In my joy over realizing that Loren had survived and fulfilled her mission, I had almost forgotten about the weremage, about anything but my sudden desire to mount Foolhoof and ride for the Great Bay as fast as his legs could carry me. But of course, we had come this far, and there was still the weremage.

"Naturally," I said. "After we have finished here."

"And speaking of which," Mag continued, "if the nobility knows of the Shades, it could become a problem for us. If the Rangatira seeks information about them, but he is trying to keep their existence a secret, then his servants might withhold information from us. It is understandable, of course, but contrary to our aims. But I know how to solve the problem."

Before I could ask what she meant, the chamber door opened. In stepped a person whose golden badge marked them as the lead ranger. They were twixt, short and thinly built, with sharp eyes and hair cut only a finger away from the scalp. Their clothes were much finer than mine, but had clearly seen just as many miles and just as much wear. The tunic's sleeves ended just past the elbow, and I saw scars and calluses on the fingers that told me at once this was an archer, and a well-practiced one.

"Greetings," they said. "I am Tuhin of the family Matara. I serve the Rangatira."

"His lead ranger," I said, stepping forth and offering my hand. "Greetings, friend. I am Kanohari of the family Telfer."

They took me by the wrist and shook, sizing me up for a moment. They had to look up into my face, for they were a head shorter. "Well met indeed. It is a long while since I met a ranger from Tokana."

I smiled weakly. "And a long while since I met one from Opara."

"I have met the Lord Telfer, you know. She came to visit some years ago. An honorable woman, though a hard one."

This caught me so thoroughly by surprise that I was unable to respond for a long moment. I was terrified of my mother discovering my return, but I had managed to put thoughts of her aside—until Tuhin spoke of her so brazenly. A response seemed far out of reach, but I summoned it.

"She certainly is a hard woman," I said at last, forcing a weak smile.

Tuhin chuckled. "Doubly so to her rangers, I imagine. Still, it seems to get results. When she came, she only brought Maia, her lead ranger, but he was a fine man. Rarely have I met a ranger with such skill."

I began to get a sick feeling. I knew no one named Maia. It had been many years since I had spoken with my family, of course, but I had thought that my middle sister, Ditra, would have been the lead ranger. Had something happened?

But of course, when we were younger, Ditra had been more like me—nearly as "soft," as my mother would have put it. I could well imagine that Mother might have decided not to elevate Ditra to the position.

Especially not after what had happened to Romil, my other, eldest sister.

"Maia is a fine man indeed," I said, feeling as though I had pulled the words from the depths of a bog.

"If they set you to this task, you must be a capable warrior," said Tuhin. "And if by any means I can help, I shall. Out of respect for them both."

Though I felt sick, I nodded and waved to the others. "This is Chao, and my elderly friend is Dryleaf."

"A pleasure," said Dryleaf, holding out his hand for them to take it. "The Rangatira's lead ranger! We stand in mighty company. Why, I would guess you have wandered nearly as far as I have."

"I can only hope, Grandfather," said Tuhin warmly. "Well met. Now, I hear we have a weremage to hunt. A dangerous prospect at the best of times. You should tell me all that you can."

They beckoned us over to the chairs, which we moved to surround a table near the back of the room. Mag and I carefully explained what had drawn us here, though I took the lead in the storytelling, changing the details to match the tale that we had come from Tokana. They listened as I described a road east into Feldemar, which then cut south through that kingdom into Dorsea, and then circled back around to head north into Opara.

Tuhin frowned. "Why would she come back towards Calentin if she fled it in the first place?"

"Because she has friends here, or so we have gathered," I said.

Tuhin nodded slowly, pursing their lips. "Hm. If she is lurking near here, there are only a few places she could be—especially if she has company."

"We hoped you would be able to point us to some of them," I said.

They leaned back in their chair, looking pensively at the table and tapping their chin. After a while they rose and went to a cupboard at the other end of the room. From it they pulled a wide scroll, which they unfurled on the table to reveal a map of Opara and the surrounding area. On the eastern end of it was half of Tahumaunga, the fire mountain, with many notes scratched around the area of its foothills. Some had been rubbed away, leaving only a smudged stain behind. Tuhin leaned over it.

"If the weremage is up to no good, and is trying to avoid the law, there are many places she could be hiding," said Tuhin. "Of course, being a weremage, she could be anywhere, even in plain sight."

Mag nodded. "We think it will be easier to find her

by way of the friends we mentioned earlier. Someone in one of the previous towns we passed through heard her talking about coming to Opara to join them."

"And what sort of friends are they?" said Tuhin.

Mag shrugged innocently. "She is a criminal on the run from the law. I imagine they are other criminals." Then she fixed Tuhin with a piercing look. "Though of course, the Rangatira seemed rather suspicious of the whole matter. Tell me: are the two of you worried about the Shades?"

She might as well have pulled the ceiling down on us with mindmagic, so great was the effect upon Tuhin. Dryleaf's brows shot for the sky, and his grip tightened on his walking stick. I tried mightily to keep an expression of calm, but I must admit I wondered for a moment if Mag had quite lost her mind.

"How do you—" began Tuhin.

"When we were following the weremage through Dorsea, the rumor of these 'Shades' was thick across the land," said Mag. "We heard they have already attacked a town in Selvan—some place called North Forest, or some such." She gave a look of surprise so genuine that I almost believed it. "But you look shocked. Are they meant to be a secret?"

Tuhin frowned. "They are. Blast. My lord will not be pleased to find out that rumors of the Shades have spread to the commonfolk—though I am happy to hear that it seems to have started in Dorsea, and not here in Calentin."

Mag cocked her head, her eyes widening slightly in perfectly innocent curiosity. "Who are they?"

Tuhin shook their head slowly. "The Rangatira has told me that you should hear that news from your own lord. But if your weremage has something to do with the Shades, then—"

"Oh, we are certain she does not," said Mag, shaking her head emphatically. "There was not even a rumor of them in Tokana. We only heard about them in Dorsea, and never related to our search for her. And we heard less and less about them the farther we came north."

I understood at last. As long as Tuhin thought we knew nothing about the Shades, they would not speak of the matter with us—but they would harbor a secret suspicion about our weremage, and might even withhold information. But by assuring Tuhin that yes, we did know of the Shades, but that we were certain our weremage was in no way related to them, Mag hoped to put Tuhin's mind to rest on the matter. It made sense, though it still seemed a wild risk, and I wished we had had time to discuss it first.

Tuhin was silent a long time. Their brow furrowed, and they looked between Mag and I. "What did this weremage do, exactly? Why did Lord Telfer command you to hunt her in the first place?"

"She killed someone," I said quietly. "Someone dear to us, and dear to Lord Telfer. It was a spiteful, personal fight that spun out of control." Mag's expression turned grim.

Tuhin sighed. "I am sorry to hear it," they said. "Very well. If the weremage has friends hiding her from the law, and they are not lurking here in the city, that should narrow it down. She is likely somewhere in the foothills of the mountain."

"We came from there just this morning," said Mag.

Tuhin nodded. "So I heard. There are many folds in the land in that area. Opara is an always-changing place. People move here, and people move away. Abandoned homesteads are common near the edge of the wilderness. So, too, are neglected strongholds even farther away. Some are built by bandits and thieves and left empty when we drive them away, but then there are abandoned fortresses, relics of ancient kings, some stretching back to the time before time. They often have an evil air, and criminals usually avoid them, but not always." They thrust their finger at the map. "We should begin with the stronghold of Maunwa. The last time it was occupied was three years ago. After we drove bandits out of the place then, the Rangatira kept a watch on it. But that watch was relaxed a year ago, and now it is visited but rarely."

An evil stronghold in the mountains. I did not much like the sound of that. But Mag had focused on something else Tuhin had said.

"You said 'we' should search the stronghold? Kanohari and I had planned to go on our own."

Tuhin grinned up at her. "Did you? Well, I am the

Rangatira's servant, and it is my duty. He assigned me to help you."

I gave them an easy smile. "We are grateful, of course."

"It seems your plans are set," said Dryleaf, who had settled back in his chair. "Though I am afraid I will not be much help in such a venture."

Tuhin nodded and knocked their knuckles once on the table. "It is settled, then. The day has worn on too long for us to go now. I will arrange for you to be quartered here in the keep tonight, and we will set out first thing in the morning."

"You are too kind," said Mag. "But we have lodgings in the city."

"I would rather not have to seek you out," said Tuhin lightly. "And besides, you are servants of a Rangatira. It is only right that we should house you while you visit our domain, as well as spare your coin." But they had a careful look in their eye, and I wondered if they wanted to ensure we did not try to investigate the fortress on our own.

"Then I suppose the matter is settled," I said, just as amiably. "We thank you for your help."

"Of course," said Tuhin. "Let us get you to your rooms. Our servants will rouse you before dawn, and then we shall all see what may be done about your weremage."

We set about retrieving our things from the Ugly

Squirrel, and Oku was allowed within the keep walls to bed with the other hounds they kept. But as we set about readying ourselves for another night's rest, I found myself wondering whether Tuhin's presence by our side would be a help, or if they might inadvertently keep us from the end of our long hunt.

TEN

It takes a special sort of person to be a ranger like Tuhin. One must be a fighter as well as a tracker, and able to survive alone in the wilderness for weeks on end. I never wanted to be one. Not because I lacked the skill—I was better in the wilderness than most, and a good archer, as well as a passable swordsman. But I did not want to fight for my mother, to be another soldier serving at her command. As a consequence, my mother thought I was rather useless, and that was the only quality she could not forgive in a person. She doted—as much as she ever doted—upon my eldest sister, Romil. And she tolerated my middle sister, Ditra, because Ditra at least tried to play the part our mother demanded.

When I was young, it was hard for me to tell how much of Ditra's demeanor was an act, and how much was genuine. She could adopt a hard-bitten, stern manner when she wished to please our mother. When she was following orders, she would grow stone-hearted, cold, even ruthless.

But I knew another side of her. She was kind to me, and to others, when not under my mother's eye. She was assigned several retainers close to her own age as she grew older, and she grew to love many of them—or at least to bed most of them. I was not supposed to find out, but I did, though Ditra swore me to secrecy.

It happened when I was fifteen, and Ditra would have been . . . oh, she would have been about nineteen? I had woken after a nightmare. I had such dreams often in my youth, though never after my wending, which tells you something. In any case, when I woke up frightened in the night, I would creep down the hall to Ditra's room. Never to my mother's, certainly never to Romil's.

And so there I found myself, creeping along the hallway in the thin moonslight pouring through the windows—when suddenly, the door to Ditra's room opened.

Out came her retainer, cloaked in shadow and little else. I could scarcely see her in the darkness. But she saw me, and she fled at once as if in terror. I stood staring after her, and only after a moment did I realize that Ditra now stood in the doorway. She was clothed in a thin robe, one hand on the door's edge, red upon her cheeks and a scowl upon her face.

"Do not say a word," she whispered in the dark. "Not one. If Mother finds out, she will put me in the stocks."

"Mother would never do that!" I protested. But Ditra gave me a long look, and I wilted under it. "I mean . . . well, obviously, I would never say anything in the first place."

"Good girl," she said, because none of us knew any better in those days, least of all me. "A bad dream?"

I nodded, though I had almost forgotten why I was there. The nightmare was fading. "A small one. Do not trouble yourself over it."

"Oh, come in," she said, opening the door wider. "But sky above, please pay attention in the future, will you? And if you should come by in the future, and my door is closed, knock before you open it."

"I will," I promised her.

"Very well," she said. "Tell me what you dreamed."

I entered her room, which smelled sweet, and told her all about the dream, which I do not remember now. And at last I fell asleep in her arms, and felt just a little safer than I had before.

That is what a ranger should be. It is why I always thought Ditra would be an excellent ranger, if she had *not* had to serve my mother. But it is why I never thought I would be a good one. Because Ditra could always make me feel safe, but that was not a gift I felt I could give to anyone else.

A ranger's first duty is always to keep their people safe. Or at least to try, even when faced with threats against which they are powerless.

On the same night that Mag and I conferred with Tuhin, there was trouble in my homeland of Tokana.

In a small village north of my family's stronghold in Kahaunga, a woman named Whetu and her husband Paora had just put their children to bed for the night. They were sharing a cup of wine before they, too, went to sleep. They rested in wicker chairs in front of their home, watching the stars make their slow turn through the sky.

Whetu had been a ranger long ago. She was the one who heard the sounds first. A heavy stomping, along with a deep, guttural snuffling.

She shot to her feet. "Paora," she whispered.

Paora rose, though more slowly. "What is it?"

"Something is coming. I think—"

A loud, heavy crash shattered the stillness of the night. Towards the northern end of the village, someone screamed.

Whetu turned. "The girls."

They ran inside the house to the back room. Their

daughters were sitting up in bed, listening in terror as more screams rang out in the darkness. Together Whetu and Paora scooped them up, running for the front door.

CRASH

The wall to their left shattered inwards. A piece of wood whizzed through the air to jam straight into Whetu's thigh. She managed to bite down on her scream, turning it into a grunt instead, but her daughter fell from her arms onto the floor.

"Whetu!" cried Paora.

"I am fine," wheezed Whetu. "Get the—"

Her eldest daughter screamed, pointing at the new hole in the wall. A massive face was looking through it. The skin looked stony, with small formations of crystals looking as though they had erupted through the skin, and moss clinging to the cracks. Two tusks were visible in the bottom jaw, and two in the top. Huge ears, like miniature sails, swept back from either side of the head, twisting every which way. Small, beady eyes glinted with the light of a nearby fire.

The troll opened its mouth and roared.

"Run!" screamed Whetu, forcing herself to her feet. She seized her daughter's hand and pulled her along, half-dragging her out the door and into the night, forcing herself to keep up with her husband despite the pain in her leg.

Together the family fled south, beyond the bounds of the village and up a rise. Most of the other villagers had gathered there. Whetu and Paora stopped in their midst, clinging to their daughters as they turned to look back at their home.

Trolls were ripping the village apart. There were at least a dozen that Whetu could see. Wooden timbers cracked in their grip as they ripped roofs and walls off of houses, as though they were peeling away the skin of great beasts to reveal and eat the insides. There were only a few stone buildings, but even those could not stand before the monsters—the trolls simply smashed their fists into the stone, and after a few blows, it crumbled before them. A fire had caught in one of the buildings, and tongues of orange licked up into the night. The trolls gave that building a wide berth.

"Why did they attack us?" said one of the villagers.

Whetu's expression was grim. The village had been her home ever since she had retired from the Rangatira's service. Ten years she had lived here, and they had been the happiest years of her life. Watching the trolls rip it apart was like watching them tear her life into pieces and scatter them to the winds.

"Who knows?" she said. "It does not matter now. We must make for Kahaunga."

"She is right!" cried Paora, turning to the others. "We will be safe there. The Rangatira can protect us."

Whetu held her tongue as she pushed through the crowd, leading them off south in the darkness. She wanted to say that Paora's hope was misplaced. They needed to reach the city because they needed food and shelter. But if the trolls attacked Kahaunga, Lord Telfer would not be able to keep them safe. No one would.

Whetu wanted to say it, but she did not. She was no longer a ranger, but she had been. And a ranger was supposed to make her people feel safe. No matter what.

ELEVEN

We were guests of honor in the Rangatira's keep, and our quarters were more than comfortable. Mag distributed our possessions between the bedrooms we had been given. Dryleaf smiled broadly as I walked him about the place, letting him run his fingers along the bookshelves and push them into the deep, plush cushions of the furniture.

"We have gone from comfort to comfort the last few days," he said. "Why could not the road from Bertram have been this gentle on my old bones?"

I laughed. "If only it had, friend. Let yourself relax. You will remain here while we set forth tomorrow."

"Naturally," said Dryleaf. He gave a sigh. "I never thought I would rest inside noble quarters again. It has been some years since I resigned myself to dying in Lan Shui."

"It was our pleasure to change your fate," said Mag.

Dryleaf chuckled. "Oh, I do not know if anything can do that. It depends upon whether you believe in fate or not, I suppose. But I certainly never suspected that I was destined to embark upon another adventure so late in life. The Birchwood was all I ever wanted, for a good long while."

At that moment, a knock came at the door. Supper had been brought for us, though the sun was still well above the horizon. We would go to bed early that night, so that we were well rested when they came to wake us up before dawn. Servants set the dishes out for us, and we began to tuck in. The fare was nowhere near so fine as the meals at Victon's had been, but it was still better than anything we had had upon the road.

"What was it about the Birchwood you so loved?" I asked Dryleaf as we ate. "Why there, and not any of the other wondrous places you must have visited in Underrealm?"

"A fair question," said Dryleaf. "The Birchwood is a place of small wonder, but great peace—which is a wonder in itself, if a less obvious kind. There was something about the trees. Not the sight of them, mind you—that matters little to me, especially now. But there was a feeling to them, a peace beneath their boughs. Four branches of magic there are, wizards will tell you. Yet I have often found myself wondering whether there are other, older magics in the world. It seemed there was always a spell of tranquility upon the Birchwood—something that relaxed your muscles, that made you wish to dip your feet in the cold, clear water of its rivers. I was happy there."

His expression darkened. "Though others were less fortunate. The other reason I wished to return was to look after some friends."

Mag's face twitched. I noticed it, though I did not understand it.

"Old friends?" said Mag.

"Not old the way I am," said Dryleaf. "They were only children, and I had known them for most of their lives. I was mostly concerned with the girl, though there was also a boy who loved her. It has been . . . well, it has been many long years since I was last able to visit them, and when last I was forced to leave them . . . well. The girl, Loren—"

Mag and I had both frozen, her with a bite of food halfway to her mouth. A dawning realization had been creeping upon me as Dryleaf spoke, and when he spoke Loren's name to confirm it, I nearly choked.

"—she had parents with evil hearts," Dryleaf went on, not noticing our sudden silence. "I always worried for her, and as time went on, I would return to visit her more and more frequently. The boy, Chet, was moonstruck for Loren from a young age, and I worried it might get him into trouble with her parents. Particularly her father. I did not know exactly how to help them, but I thought, if I could be there when she came of age, I could somehow . . . some way . . ."

He fell silent. Still I could not move, could not speak. But now Mag was looking at me from across the table.

"Albern," she said quietly.

I stared at her.

Dryleaf frowned. "What is it? Is everything all right?"

Mag turned to him. "Dryleaf . . . this girl from the Birchwood . . ." She fell silent, seemingly unsure what to say.

He pursed his lips. "Yes?"

"We told you of our friends who rode from Northwood," I said. "The ones who delivered word of the Shades to the High King."

Dryleaf went very still. His sightless eyes brimmed with tears.

"It was Loren," said Mag. "And Chet was with her."

His jaw quivered as the tears spilled down his cheeks. When he spoke, his voice had dropped to a whisper.

"Loren is alive?"

We told him everything. Everything we knew, that is, which was not, in fact, everything there was to know. Loren had told me only bits and pieces of what had happened on the long road between her departure from the Birchwood and our meeting in Strapa. But I told Dryleaf everything that had happened after that, and he asked me many questions, so that no detail was missed. He went very pale when we told him of the attack on Northwood, and gave a great sigh of relief when we told him how Loren had escaped the fighting. That was the end of what we had seen, and as my tale subsided, Dryleaf asked me another question.

"Her parents," he said. "Do you know what became of them?"

"We do not," said Mag. "She was not very willing to speak about her home, or her past."

Dryleaf sighed. "No, I suppose she would not have been. Something evil lurked in their souls, and they took it out on their only daughter. Theirs was always a house of secrets—secrets, and pain. I feared that if she remained in that home, she would not survive it."

"You should be happy, then," said Mag. "She escaped, and if I know anything about her, she will never again fall under their sway."

"No," said Dryleaf. "That seems clear. And my heart sings to know that Chet is with her now. He has loved her a long time, and though I suspect Loren never felt quite the same way—or at least not to the same degree—it will be good for her to have a reminder that not everything in her past came from suffering."

"And she has the children as well," I said. "She may not have known them as long as Chet, but they are a great source of comfort to her. She thinks she protects them, and I suppose she does. But they are better for her than she realizes."

"Good, good," said Dryleaf. "It sounds as though she went through many hardships on her road—and she may still face hardship even now. But as long as she has Chet, I am confident she will be well cared for."

"How did you first meet Loren, anyway?" said Mag. "Why did you keep returning to the Birchwood to see her?"

Dryleaf tilted his head. "You have met her yourself. You know how remarkable she is. She was always that way, and I knew she could do great things, if she could only escape her horrible home. It was always something that just seemed to happen to me: finding the lonely and the lost, and trying to make their lives somewhat easier, if it was in my power to do so. Loren was not the only one, though she was a particularly urgent case. I knew an orphan girl in Cabrus, who has run away now, and is lost in the nine kingdoms. A merchant boy in Idris, who finally broke his family's shackles and lives on his own now. A child of nobility in Hedgemond, who needed more love than her mother felt she could spare. She is a Mystic now, and a fine officer of that order."

My expression darkened, and I picked at a loose thread on my sleeve. I was not from Hedgemond, of course, but Dryleaf's words would have been most apt for my own mother.

"But these others had already managed to escape, sometimes with my help, sometimes on their own. Loren was the last. She never knew me as Dryleaf, by the by. In the Birchwood, they call me Bracken. But after Loren, I had thought I would be done. My bones were already getting too old for travel, and the Birchwood seemed a good place to live out the end of one's life. I had only just resigned myself to do so in Lan Shui instead, when you arrived."

"But Dryleaf," said Mag. "Or, wait. Should we call you Bracken?"

He waved a hand. "No, no. One name is as good as another after all these years, and I will not say the name my parents gave me, for there is a reason I left it behind so long ago."

"Very well," said Mag. "My question is: what now? You know Loren was making for the Seat, and you are free from Lan Shui. Do you wish to run off and find her?"

"We could make arrangements," I said.

Dryleaf settled deeper into his chair and sighed. "I will not lie to you: I greatly wish to go. But no. For now, at least, it is enough for me to know that she escaped her parents. I am content to remain with you for a while yet." His lips curled in a smile. "You may need my help, after all. And besides, it seems likely that you shall cross paths with Loren again, and mayhap sooner than later."

"That is my wish," I said.

"Then until that day," said Dryleaf, "I will happily ride by your side, if you will continue to have me. But wait!" Suddenly his face lit up, and he gave a broad grin. "We must write her at once."

I blinked. "Write her?"

"Why not?" he said. "We know where she is."

I looked to Mag. Writing to Loren had not even crossed our mind on all the long road since Northwood—but then, we had no idea that she had succeeded in her mission. And with that came a chilling thought. "Mag," I said quietly. "She thinks we are dead. She must."

"Sky above," breathed Mag.

"And I doubt she thinks I am still breathing," said Dryleaf. "Had I thought her parents would let her read a letter, I would have written one long ago. As far as she knows, I simply disappeared."

That settled it. We asked one of the stronghold's servants for paper, quill, and ink. Together we sat down and drafted a letter, which Mag rendered in a firm hand. When we were done, I folded the parchment up and handed it to Dryleaf.

"I will see to the arrangements tomorrow, while the two of you are off on your adventure," he said. "Someone should be willing to walk me to the constables' station to send it off."

"Thank you," I said. "I only wish I could see her face when she reads it."

"As do I," chuckled Dryleaf, "though that chance passed long ago."

"At least she will know we are alive," I said. "And if we should meet her upon the road, and you wish to go with her then, no one will begrudge you that—least of all me."

Mag gave me a careful look as I said it. I thought she must be wondering if I, too, would ride off with Loren, were I given the chance.

But now it was time for bed. We had spoken a good long while into the night, and we had to rise early for tomorrow's hunt. I helped Dryleaf to his bed and retired to my own room, undressing by moonslight.

Sky above, let our hunt end tomorrow, I thought to myself. *Let it be over, so that we can find the children again, and see that they are safe.*

But of course, you know enough about the Necromancer's War to know my hopes were in vain. And even today, part of me wishes I had not waited.

TWELVE

One of Lord Matara's servants awoke us before dawn. Mag and I left Dryleaf asleep as we roused and dressed ourselves and then made our way out of the stronghold. The moment we set foot in the courtyard outside the keep, Oku came dashing up to us, yipping in excitement. I knelt and scratched him behind the ears.

"Did you sleep well, boy?" I said. "I hope so. We have a long journey ahead of us."

Oku licked my fingers and trotted over to Mag,

sniffing at her leg. I looked studiously away so that she could pat his head and think I had not noticed.

Tuhin soon joined us, leading a horse by the reins. Two stablehands followed, bringing Foolhoof for me and Mist for Mag. We mounted and rode through the streets of the city. Tuhin was silent as we went, and I thought they might still be ridding themself of the last vestiges of sleep. Yet they seemed alert and watchful, peering down each street as we went, though there was no one around. They even looked up into the sky. It struck me that they were likely looking for any sign that the weremage was stalking us.

Once we had left the city through the eastern gate and were a good distance away from the wall, I finally spoke. "Did you see any sign of pursuit?"

"No," said Tuhin. "But I am always cautious when going on an expedition, especially when pursuing a wizard. They are not to be underestimated, especially weremages."

"I have fallen out of such habits on our long road," I said, "but I will try to resume them. I have grown nearly as lazy as Mag." I looked over at her. "Remind me never to grow so inattentive again."

"But what if I am too lazy to do so?" said Mag.

Tuhin smirked. "You can rest easily, Albern," they said. "I saw no one paying us any undue attention."

"That is a relief," said Mag. "Wake me if you see any signs of danger. I will be dozing in my saddle, as it seems is my wont."

"Oh, be silent," I grumbled, "or we will make you ride at the head of the party."

"But I do not want to," said Mag, giving an exaggerated frown. She reached to her belt and pulled out a copper sliver. "We should flip for it and let fate decide. Tuhin, have you ever heard of latrine duty?"

"Do not answer that," I said quickly, even as Tuhin opened their mouth to answer.

Tuhin shook their head, still smiling, and took the lead. They made their way down the same eastern road we had taken to reach Victon's estate, but they soon turned north, on a smaller road that curved east after a time, wrapping around the foot of the mountain.

Dawn broke at last, and we increased our pace now that we did not have to worry about striking a rock or sudden pit in the dark. Though we traveled east, the sun did not immediately fly into our eyes, for we had entered a series of low but steep hills that thrust up around the road on both sides. The road grew faint, but it still had very clear edges. I could tell that it had once been well-tended, and mayhap paved with stone.

And then I noticed the tracks.

"Tuhin," I called out.

"I see them," they said, pulling their horse to a halt. Mag and I stopped as well.

"Would anyone else have a good reason to use this road?"

"Not much of one," said Tuhin. "There is no good hunting this way, and there are no dwellings at all."

Mag frowned at me. "What in the dark are the two of you talking about?"

"Signs of others," I said, pointing at the road.

She shook her head. "I see nothing."

"What did I tell you?" I said, giving Tuhin an exaggerated shrug. "Lazy."

While Tuhin hid a laugh, Mag nudged her horse closer and punched me hard in the arm. I gave her an easy smile.

There were not all that many—around a dozen distinct trails that I could make out. They could easily have been made by the same person going back and forth several times. I saw no hoofprints, though if someone wished to approach Opara on horseback, they would likely have looped around and approached by the north road.

"We carry on," said Tuhin. "But we should abandon the road. I wonder if we should leave the horses."

"Though it is tempting," I said, frowning down at Foolhoof's flattened ears, "I would rather draw closer first. How far away is this stronghold?"

"Another two hours if we press the horses, mayhap three or four on foot," said Tuhin.

"Then let us ride for another hour, off the road, before we leave our mounts."

"A fair plan," said Tuhin, and they turned their horse at once, walking off the road and into the hills.

We wound our way through the dips between the hills, slower now without the bridges that crossed shallow cracks in the land, or the rises that had been leveled to accommodate it. Tuhin led us skillfully, though it was clear they had not been here for some time. After a time, the land dipped into a gentle gorge, through which ran a narrow stream with gentle banks. The land began a steep climb after we crested the other side. Soon we came upon a broken land, with steep cliffs that threatened to drop us a span or more to the ground below. All around us were piles of black rock, pitted and pockmarked, signs of the mountain's ancient fury.

"This is where I think we should leave the horses," said Tuhin. "They will be no faster than we will be on foot, especially on the fireglass."

Mag arched an eyebrow. "Fireglass?"

I pointed to the black rock. "Leavings of the mountain. Lava after it cools off."

"Ah," said Mag, arching an eyebrow. "The mountain is not going to drop its leavings on us, is it? I am not fond of dangers against which I have little power."

"Not every danger can be staved off with a spear," I told her, slipping down from the saddle. "Worry not, wanderer. We will not let the mountain's rage consume you."

Tuhin chuckled and waved a dismissive hand towards Tahumaunga. "It is only a grumpy old man these days. You are lucky we do not wander at its feet during the days of its youth, when the tales say it was as wrathful as a dragon."

We found a small cluster of trees well away from the fireglass, with brilliant green turf springing up on the ground all around. Oku danced about as we dismounted and brought the horses together. With a hatchet from my saddle, I quickly cut a few sturdy posts from the branches of the trees, and we gave the horses a loose tether that would allow them to wander. They began to nibble at the grass almost immediately, except Mist, who nuzzled Mag's shoulder first.

"There there, girl," said Mag. "We will return before you know it."

"A fine mare," said Tuhin, patting Mist's flank as she began to graze with the others.

"Far better than that one," said Mag, pointing at Foolhoof.

"Do you expect me to argue?" I said, arching my brows. "He is never more than a bad mood away from being turned into sausage."

"That is simply cruel," said Tuhin. Foolhoof raised his head to nudge them gently with his neck, the dark-taken traitor. "Do you see? He is a gentle soul."

They ignored my sudden grumbles and led us off again. Soon we were breathing somewhat heavily. The land kept climbing, and we had to take many sudden turns and detours to avoid pits and cliffs that seemed to appear out of nowhere. Mag, curse her, did not seem winded at all, despite her shirt of metal scales. But then, that was to be expected. I kept Oku close by as we went, and he was more than capable of matching our pace.

I began to notice that Tuhin was looking around uneasily as we went. "What is wrong?" I asked them.

Tuhin's mouth twisted. "The land is quiet."

I felt a tenseness creep down from my neck into my shoulders. "Do you think we are being watched?"

"I am not certain," said Tuhin. "I have been searching for signs, but I have found none yet. We should be wary, just in case."

"I am always wary," said Mag.

"That is a lie," I said.

It became clear, the farther we went, that the cliffs we kept encountering were in fact one long cliff, the edge of a trench that ran for miles. Tuhin's guidance meant we encountered it rarely, and only when they became turned around for a moment. But I realized after a time that it was far too straight to be natural. It was a man-made trench that must have been dug in ancient days. I remembered Victon's words, that it had been put here to divert lava away from Opara and into the surrounding land. I marveled at the thought of it. Magic must have been used in its making, for I could not imagine that even an army could have dug so deep, and for such a great distance.

"Halt," said Tuhin suddenly.

We stopped short behind them. Just ahead of us, the path delved into a slice through a hill, both sides slick with fireglass. Half a span in, the path curved sharply to the right and out of sight.

"Maunwa is on the other side of that passage."

They unslung their bow from their back, and I did the same. Mag had her spear ready, for she had been using it as a walking stick. Now she hefted her shield off her back and onto her arm. Tuhin pressed close to one side of the path, creeping forwards to the sharp turn. I was just behind them, with Mag bringing up the rear.

Tuhin came to the corner at the end of the path and stopped. I pressed forwards a bit, trying to see around. Tuhin saw me edging towards them and beckoned me closer. I leaned over, my shoulder to theirs, and looked around the bend.

Only a few paces from where we stood, the steep-sided path emerged into the open air. And there, mayhap three spans away, sat the fortress of Maunwa. It perched upon the top of a rise, but behind it the land fell off into the sheer cliff of the trench. A thick iron gate sat in its northern wall, visible from our vantage point, and a road ran out of it—the same road, I knew, that we had been following before we left it for the wilderness.

An uneasy feeling came over me. I had approached a stronghold in the mountains in much the same way not that long ago. Then, as now, I had anticipated foes within, and then I had lost someone dear to me.

I shrugged the feeling away. Yes, there might be

Shades here, as there had been when I had led Jordel to his doom. But I had not had Mag by my side, then.

"I see no one on the walls," I murmured to Tuhin.

"Mayhap it is abandoned," they said, frowning. "Yet I am still uneasy. We should check to make sure."

We crept forwards. I whispered hasty instructions to Mag and Oku to stay well behind the two of us. For all her skill at fighting, Mag was no master of stealth.

I followed Tuhin's lead until we were out of the narrow path, and then we split up and cut wide, creeping between rocks and mounds of fireglass. I kept my eyes firmly fixed on the stronghold, wary for any sign of movement inside. But there was nothing. The gate remained open, and it looked as though it might have been that way for years.

Of course, we could not know that the Shades were aware of us. We could not know that Kaita had warned them, and that they were fully aware we had left the city, thanks to an agent of theirs in the Rangatira's keep. Nor could we know that they had sent their best scouts to shadow us, agents so stealthy that even Tuhin did not detect them, except as a vague sense of unease. We did not know they had us surrounded.

Until they struck.

THIRTEEN

I HEARD THE WHISTLE OF AN ARROW A BLINK BEFORE IT struck Mag, too late to do anything about it. Too late for me, at least, but not for her. She whirled on the spot. Her cloak billowed around her with the movement, and the arrow passed harmlessly through it.

"Down!" I cried, flinging myself behind a boulder that jutted out of the ground, its bottom half embedded deep in the earth. Oku yelped and pressed against my legs. But no sooner had I hit the dirt than I spotted a flash above me. Sunlight reflecting on metal. Without thinking, I threw myself down and rolled.

An arrow splintered against the rock. If I had been a moment slower, it would have struck me in the chest.

I came up ready to fire. My shaft sped for where I had seen the archer above me. But they were too wily, and had already hidden themselves. My arrow passed futilely through the air.

"Agh!"

Tuhin cried out as an arrow impaled their right shoulder. I spared them only a glance before looking wildly around.

The archer who had fired at me had been opposite the one who shot at Mag. They were in a half-circle that wrapped around us, and we could find little cover out here, despite the boulders. For a mad moment, I thought of running for the fort, but that would put us in open ground long enough for them to fill us with arrows. I looked around desperately.

There. A small depression, not quite a cave, in the side of the hill nearby. It would block vision from above.

I sprinted for Tuhin and seized them by the back of their shirt. Ignoring their grunt of pain, I dragged them towards cover. Oku came pelting after us, whining.

"Chao!" I cried over my shoulder.

Mag had been peeking out from behind a boulder, looking for a way to approach the archers above. She glanced over, saw what I was doing, and ran to join us.

"Dark below," I grunted, releasing Tuhin once we were in the half-cave.

"Thank you," they gasped, seizing their wound and squeezing to keep it from bleeding.

"Save your gratitude until we survive this, if we do," I told them. "Do you have bandages?"

"Here." They drew them from a sack at their belt.

I snapped off the arrowhead and pulled the shaft out of the wound. Tuhin grunted in pain, but they kept their wits and handed me the bandages. I wrapped them around the shoulder, and Tuhin helped me hold them in place until I was done. When I finished, they sighed in relief and leaned back against the cool earth.

"Again, thank you."

I stepped away from them to take stock of our situation. In the half-cave, the Shades could not see us. But neither could we see them, and we could not step out to shoot at them. I had an arrow nocked, but it felt useless between my fingers. My mind whirled, trying to devise a strategy.

"These friends of your weremage are ready for a fight," said Tuhin with a grim smile.

I snorted. "Fortunately, so are we."

"I should have been more watchful," said Tuhin, wincing against the pain of their wound. "I grew lax after we left Opara."

"You were the only one who thought anything was wrong on the road here," I pointed out. "You and Oku. I should have been less moonstruck by the fireglass and the trench. But this is no time for blame. We must—"

"Stay alive," barked Mag.

Before I could even look at her in surprise, she ran out into the open. Oku gave a sharp bark and ran after her. I reached for them both with a cry.

But though arrows came streaking for us, they missed. Of the two that would have struck Mag, she caught one on her shield. The other passed through her cloak, and I gasped, certain it had pierced her side. But she ripped it from the cloth and flung it on the ground—it had rebounded from her armor. She darted out of sight, Oku hard on her heels.

"What under the sky is she doing?" gasped Tuhin. "There are at least a dozen of them. We need to flee, not fight!"

"That is not how Chao prefers to go about things," I said, shaking my head. "But as tempting as it is to let her take care of them, I cannot allow her to fight alone. There was a tree not far from the stronghold. I am going to sprint for it. It is close enough to the trench that I will have one direction, at least, from which they cannot fire at me. While I give you cover, you must try to go in the same direction as Chao. You can lose yourself in the hills."

"I will go with you," said Tuhin. "I can still run, and I might draw arrows away from you."

"I can do it alone."

"Of course you can," said Tuhin, and they sprinted into the open air.

"Dark take you!" I cried, sprinting after them.

They kept their lead, and the two of us dodged and weaved, taking sudden turns to try and confound the archers. Arrows hissed all around us. One found Tuhin before we reached the tree, but it merely stuck in their cloak.

We fell to the ground on the tree's other side. It was a thick oak with high branches, and for a moment I simply sat there, panting and pressing the back of my head against the rough bark. At last I risked a glance out. I ducked back at once, as five arrows streaked through the air towards me. Three stuck into the tree, the other two embedding themselves in the ground near our feet.

"Only five arrows," I said. "Chao has been busy. We should help her finish the job."

"That shall fall to you, I am afraid," said Tuhin, pointing to their shoulder with a rueful smile. "Unless you think I should throw arrows at them with my good arm."

"As amusing as that would be, I think not."

Quickly notching an arrow, I darted around the other side of the tree and fired at the last place I had seen one of our foes. Their head popped into sight, but a heartbeat too late, and I missed. They fell back behind cover again, and I did the same—but then I froze as I heard a scream from their location.

I risked another glance out. There she was—Mag, standing just in the spot where I had fired my arrow. She had plunged her spear down where I could not see it, but when it came up again, it was red with the blood of the woman I had tried to shoot. I heard a furious barking from Oku, and then Mag vanished.

"Sky bless and dark take her, both at once," I muttered, as I hid once more.

"Chao?" said Tuhin.

"She killed another one. Mayhap more. I think I am going to try to draw their fire again, to give her as much opportunity as I can."

"There are many rocks close by, and I think they are far enough away from the hills. We should each run for one."

I nodded. "One. Two. Three. Four!"

We pelted out from behind the tree. But only two arrows came streaking down this time. *Sky above,* I thought, *did Mag kill that many already?* I struck the ground hard, groaning as my ribs slammed into the rock I had hidden behind, and I heard Tuhin grunt as they did the same several paces away.

From the edge of my vision, I had taken note of where one of the arrows came from. I drew, leaped up, and fired. This time the arrow flew true. A man in a blue cloak appeared just in time to take the shot in the eye. His head jerked back, fletching protruding from the socket, and he toppled out of sight.

"One!" I called out, hiding again. "At least Chao is not having all the fun."

"You two have very odd ideas about your entertainment," said Tuhin, and I gave a shout of laughter.

Footsteps.

They came pounding across the turf, running from the pathway through which we had emerged. From the sound of them, they were making for the stronghold. Mag? No, the steps sounded too light.

I risked a look out. A young woman in a grey cloak was sprinting for the gate. I looked up at the surrounding hills. No shots came flying towards me.

Dropping my bow, I broke from cover and ran after the woman.

She was panicked, her dark skin flushed with exertion and fear. She did not hear me until I was almost upon her. At the last moment I leaped, and only then did she begin to turn to see me. I struck her hard in the side, and she crashed to the ground with me on top of her.

Her hand darted for a knife at her belt. I seized her wrist with one hand and struck her in the face with the other. It dazed her for a moment, and her head lolled to the side. I drew the knife and threw it away before flipping her over to lie on her face, dragging her arm behind her back and holding her immobile. With my free hand, I patted her waist and boot to make sure she was not hiding another weapon.

"I think it is over, Tuhin," I called out. "Help me secure her."

Tuhin emerged into the open, though they still walked hunched over, darting from rock to rock. When no more arrows were forthcoming, they straightened at last and came over.

"Here," they said, drawing a pair of iron manacles from a pouch at their belt. These they clamped around the woman's wrists, securing them behind her back. Together we hauled her to her feet. The woman's eyes were wild, and they darted about frantically, seeking some means of escape. Her shoulder-length hair swung across her face with her movements, though it could not entirely obscure the sizable birthmark that covered her left cheek.

"None of that," I told her. "I am afraid your time here is over. Please do not make more trouble than you already have. I would hate to have to sling you over the back of my horse as we ride back to the city. I have seen a long journey made that way once, and it was most uncomfortable."

"I have done nothing," the woman said. Her voice was low, but thin, and it shook with terror.

"Nothing lasting, though not for lack of trying," I said. "But you shot my friend here, or one of your companions did. Tuhin, what penalty do you think the Rangatira will mete out for such a thing?"

"Oh, imprisonment and hard labor would normally be enough," said Tuhin, raising their brows. "But then, I am a representative of the King's law. The punishment for *that* shall be much more severe."

"Dark below, you are frightening the poor girl," called Mag.

I turned. She had just emerged from the path. Oku padded at her heels, looking up at her and whining. A great deal of blood had spattered across Mag's clothes, and she had her hands on another one of the Shades. This one had her blue hood cast back, and her hair was wild as she struggled and jerked in Mag's grip.

And I knew her.

FOURTEEN

The woman Mag had captured was a noble—or at least, she had been. Her family lived in Opara. They had served the Rangatira when last we had met, far back in my youth. I struggled to remember her name. Riri, that was it. And yet there was no trace of recognition in her eyes.

Shock and a flood of memories caused me to slacken my grip. The woman I was holding noticed it, and she bolted towards the stronghold, her arm tearing out of my hands. But with her hands bound tightly behind her, she could hardly hope to outpace me. I caught up after only a few paces, catching her and wrestling her to the ground once again. It was only when I looked up that I realized we were hardly a pace from the edge of the trench, and spans of empty air stretched before us to the hard ground far below.

"Careful," I told her. "You almost went over. And if you are not cooperative with my friend, she may pitch you over regardless."

"Are you all right there, Kanohari?" said Mag. She drew nearer, her hand firmly clutching Riri's arms behind her back. "I caught one on my own. I thought you would be able to handle another, with help."

"Cease your boasts," I told her. "Are there any more hiding out there?"

"None," said Mag. "I accounted for all of them. There were twelve. Only these two remain. I left this one alive because she is in charge." She hefted Riri's arms up, bringing her slightly off the ground, like a prize on display. Riri snarled and made a fresh break for freedom, but she could not budge with Mag holding her. "I heard her giving orders. The one you are holding escaped while I was killing one of her fellows, and I trusted you would catch her."

"Assuming your faith is genuine, I appreciate it," I told her.

I noticed something odd. Oku had remained close by Mag's side. He kept nuzzling her leg, as though checking to make sure she was all right, and small whines issued from his throat. Mag ignored him.

"Well, now to get them both back to Opara," said Tuhin. They pulled out another pair of manacles and went to bind Riri.

"There is one problem," said Mag, as Tuhin did their work. "I saw no sign of the weremage."

"There is more than one problem," said Tuhin. When we blinked in surprise, they gave us both a stern look. "These are Shades."

I did my best to look shocked. "These two?"

"And their companions," said Tuhin. "They wear blue and grey, which we have been told are the Shades' colors. And something tells me you are not quite as surprised by this news as you are trying to appear."

Mag shrugged. "How could we know? The weremage dwelled long in Tokana. We had no reason to suspect her involvement with them."

"Hm," said Tuhin. "Or mayhap you thought the Rangatira would not let you join the hunt, if he knew you were in fact hunting Shades."

Mag's expression of innocence was perfect. "Would he not?"

"Hm," said Tuhin again. Then they rolled their eyes. "Since we have, in fact, cleared out a hidden stronghold of Shades, I suppose I have done my duty, and I need not press the matter."

"We thank you," I said. "But we are, in fact, after the weremage, and that mystery remains. Unless she is one of these two."

It was only then that I realized Riri had gone very

quiet. She looked no less enraged, but she had stopped trying to pull away from Mag. Her eyes went from Tuhin to Mag, and then to me, calculating, assessing.

"I think that if she was disguised as one of these two, she would have taken a more dangerous form already, trying to kill us," said Mag.

"You cannot be sure," said Tuhin. "And you have forgotten someone else." They gave a small smile.

I frowned at them. "Who is that?"

"Me," said Tuhin. "You lost sight of me for a moment there. It would have been easy for her to replace me, if she was nearby, and watching. If you are going to hunt a weremage, you must always be alert, and never trust anyone—least of all the ones you feel certain about."

An uneasy feeling crept through me. "But if you were her, you would never tell us this."

"Unless it were part of a grander ploy," said Tuhin, raising their brows. "I could be luring you into a false sense of peace. Why, after this, I imagine the two of you would march me straight to the Rangatira, where I might be able to strike him down."

"Except the Rangatira has his own wizards to detect that sort of thing," said Mag.

Tuhin gave an exasperated look. "But the weremage might not know that, and I rather wish you had not mentioned it in front of the prisoners."

Oku pulled his attention away from Mag for a moment and trotted to Tuhin. Tuhin knelt to greet him, and Oku sniffed at their wounded shoulder. He gave it one brief lick and then went back to Mag, whining at her again.

"Oku seems to trust you," I said.

"I could fool him, too, if I were particularly skilled at magic," said Tuhin. "There is only one way to ensure we know who the weremage is."

"Please," interjected the younger Shade woman in my grip. Her eyes had begun to brim with tears. "I only served them for the coin, I do not—"

"Shut your mouth, girl," said Riri harshly.

"This is ridiculous," said Mag, looking annoyed. "The weremage would never tell us everything you have."

"They are masters of deception," said Tuhin.

"They are not the weremage!" said the younger girl, tossing her head at Tuhin. "She left!"

"Hoko!" cried Riri.

"She might have appeared to leave, but remained behind," said Tuhin. "You would never know, girl. There is only one way to tell for certain."

"What is it?" I said. "Though I suppose you will tell us, and then tell us that we cannot trust what you have told us, because you could be the weremage."

"You are getting the idea now," said Tuhin, grinning broadly.

They came towards me and the younger Shade—Hoko, she had been called. She recoiled, but Tuhin ignored it.

"There are two points just behind the temple," they said, pointing to their own head. "Just here, where the skull dips. As I understand it, the magic passes through there, no matter what form the weremage takes. And if you strike them—"

They lunged forwards, striking with their uninjured hand in a chopping motion. Hoko reeled under the impact. But nothing happened—no glow in the eyes, and no shifting of her form. Tuhin strode towards Riri next.

"Do not touch me, kingsworn scum," snarled Riri.

But Mag held her still, and Tuhin struck her just as they had done to Hoko. Riri grunted at the blows, but again, nothing happened.

"That is most interesting," said Mag.

Then she moved almost faster than I could see. First she shoved Riri in my direction, and I caught the woman's arm in surprise. Mag struck Tuhin twice, once in each temple, before I realized what had happened. Tuhin nearly fell over from her strikes, but somehow they kept their feet. Their gaze looked unfocused for a moment.

"Yes," they said weakly. "Just like that."

"Chao!" I said indignantly.

"No, she was quite correct to do so," said Tuhin, raising a hand. "I could have been the weremage, and I could still be, if I have been lying. You should bind my hands for the journey home."

"I will keep you close," said Mag. "You will not

escape us unless I want you to. Assuming you are, in fact, Tuhin, where did you learn this skill?"

"I was never a Mystic, but I have served alongside them many times," said Tuhin. "This is a trick I learned from their mage hunters."

Suddenly a memory came to me. I, too, had traveled with a Mystic—Jordel, who had also been a mage hunter, once. I had seen him do something I would have called impossible, if I had not seen it myself. He pressed his fingers to the temples of Xain, the wizard, and forced him to use his firemagic.

I met Mag's gaze. "I think they are telling the truth. I have seen something like this before."

"You should bind me regardless," said Tuhin.

"I have already said you cannot escape from me if I do not wish you to," said Mag.

A thought struck me. "Tuhin," I said. "You are trying to warn us about yourself. But you have said nothing about Chao. We both lost sight of her. She could be the weremage, for all you know."

Tuhin grinned. "I wondered when you would think of that. Oku trusts her. Animals have a sense for these things, and none more so than wolfhounds. For a weremage to be able to fool Oku, they would have to be so powerful that you would not have survived the long road you took to get here."

I glared at them. "But you just said Oku's trust of *you* was no proof."

Tuhin shrugged. "Not if I am a strong enough weremage."

"This is making my head hurt," said Mag. "We should be getting back to Opara, lest we return after dark."

"Then you must take the three of us to the Mystics," said Tuhin. "They will know the same trick I have already told you, and they will tell you I am who I appear to be."

"The Mystics?" cried Hoko in terror.

All of us turned to look at her—including Riri, who suddenly fixed the girl with a razor-sharp glare.

"Why, yes," I said. "We need to know what happened to the weremage who had been working with you. And no one is better at gathering information than the Mystics."

"I will tell you!" shrieked Hoko.

"Hoko!" said Riri sharply, tensing in my grip.

"The weremage went to the Telfer homelands! Tokana!" cried the girl.

I froze.

"Hoko!" snarled Riri. "Dark damn you, you traitorous sow!"

"Save your breath," said Hoko, who sounded close to sobbing. "I have been under the Mystics' knives before. I will not go there again for anything—not for you, and not for the Lord."

The girl's words rang in my ears. Tokana? My homeland? What would draw the weremage there?

"Why?" I demanded. I shoved Riri away and gripped Hoko by the shoulders. "Why Tokana?"

I had meant to shove Riri towards Mag. I failed.

She spun with my shove and charged at my back, bent almost double. I heard her just in time to step aside and turn to see what was the matter.

Riri caught Hoko in the stomach with her shoulder.

She did not stop. Both women pitched headfirst over the edge of the trench.

"No!" I cried, running to the edge. Mag leaped forwards and seized my arm, drawing me back.

Riri remained silent, but Hoko's scream lasted an obscenely long time before being sharply cut off.

"They are gone," said Mag quietly.

I ripped my arm out of her grip, and she let me. "Dark take me," I said savagely.

"You were distracted," said Mag. "And you have reason to be."

I glared at her, but I could not do so for long. I turned away, even as Tuhin stood on the edge of the cliff, looking down to where they had fallen.

"We . . . we should investigate," they said after a moment, sounding like someone coming out of a dream. "The stronghold, I mean. We should ensure no one else lurks within. And one of you must remain with me as a guard. Or mayhap we should stay together—I could heal this injury and overpower only one of you."

"Sky above, Tuhin, *you are not the weremage,*" I growled.

They gave me a grim look, only faintly amused now. "You do not know that."

"Let us all search Maunwa, then, and be quick about it," I said gruffly. "The sooner we can return to Opara, the better."

"Do not look too worried," said Tuhin. "If the weremage is heading for Tokana, that means you can set your steps for home."

They could hardly have said anything *more* worrying, though of course they could not have known that. I struggled to don a smile. "That is good news, at least."

But it was not. I knew it, somehow. Just as I knew that this had just become very, very personal.

I did not know exactly why the weremage had turned her steps towards Tokana. But I knew, down to my core, that my family was in terrible danger.

In raven form, Kaita watched the whole thing from the air. When we captured Hoko and Riri, she spun lower in the sky so that she could hear. Hoko told us that the weremage was headed for Tokana, and Kaita felt an enormous wave of relief.

That relief turned to grim satisfaction as Riri and Hoko pitched over the cliff.

Dark take her, the fool, thought Kaita.

Her anger at Riri faded quickly. Now she was free to journey to Tokana. She would travel by air. It would be exhausting, but she had the strength. The end of the game drew near.

Kaita could not defeat Mag herself. But even the Uncut Lady would be helpless against the trolls.

And if she were not—if even the trolls proved unequal to the challenge—Kaita had Rogan's word. If the trolls could not finish what she had started, then Father would give her the strength she had long craved.

But that would come later, if it came at all. In the meantime, at long last, she was going home.

FIFTEEN

Albern fell silent and glanced down at Sun. The corners of his mouth curled up, though he seemed to be trying to fight the smile. Sun frowned. What was the old man smirking for? Then she realized she was fidgeting with her fingers as they walked. A flush crept into her cheeks as she stilled her hands.

"You look fit to choke on whatever unasked question plagues you," chuckled Albern. "Spit it out."

Still she hesitated, and when she did speak, it was slowly. "You said you would only give me certain stories. I do not want to ask for a tale you do not wish to tell."

"I will only tell you what I wish, but you can always ask," said Albern. "I do not promise to answer, but I might."

That was good enough for Sun, and her words came out in a rush. "Whenever you speak of Kaita, you say she thought of Calentin—and now Tokana, I suppose—as 'home.' Was it the Shades' home, or *her* home? Did she live there as a child? Did you know her?"

Albern shook his head. "I did not know her, because she was not a noble."

Sun frowned. "What does that matter? I was a noble as well, but I knew plenty of common folk in—"

"Calentin is not Dulmun, and my family was not like yours," said Albern. "The commonfolk in Tokana obeyed us, but when I was a child, we were not particularly well loved. Nor did we mingle often. My mother, in particular, was very strict about it. You recall the story of Ditra and her retainer? She feared Mother would punish her severely if they were found out, and she was correct."

It still made no sense to Sun. "Still, you must have known *some* commoners in your youth, unless you never left your family's stronghold. But you have already told me that was not the case."

He sighed. "You are not entirely wrong. My mother's attitude is, mayhap, an excuse I use to feel better about the way I acted. We all like to think better of our younger selves than we might deserve. The truth is that I rarely tried to befriend anyone outside my family, or even converse with them. I never paid much attention to anyone but other nobility, and even that was scant compared to the attention I gave to the wilderness. You might not believe it, but I think I have spoken more to you, in the short time we have known each other, than I ever spoke to my eldest sister, Romil."

Sun balked at that. "That cannot be true."

"Stories and truth," said Albern with a smile. "But that is how I remember it. Romil saw me as little more than a family asset, and a poor one at that, and I wholeheartedly returned her lack of affection. The only person I was close to was Ditra, and even we drifted further apart as we grew older.

"It was not until I was free from my home, out from under the sway of my mother, that I began to appreciate the people around me. I had been so starved for friendship and affection that I began to bestow them with great vigor. You think I am friendly now, but I doubt you would have so enjoyed my company if you had met me when I was your age. I was too focused on my family, on how they treated me. In short, I thought only of my own difficulties. Once I had put them mostly behind me, it felt like my attention was suddenly free, and I was able to behold a world I had never noticed before. And only then could I spare enough thought for my own desires to decide what I wanted to do with my life. That is when I realized I was ander. I could never see it in Tokana, when I was too focused on my dissatisfaction with my family to see how I was dissatisfied with myself."

Sun shook her head. "I still want to know why you left your home in the first place. You have told me of the tree in the valley, and your mother's lack of care. But neither sounds dire enough to flee your homeland, especially as a noble."

"You did not ask about this before."

Sun threw her hands in the air. "I did not want some dark-taken answer that 'Every part of the story must be told in its proper turn, or the whole thing will collapse.'"

Her imitation of his Calentin accent was passingly fair, and Albern laughed loud and long at it. "I suppose I can explain a bit more of my decision without ruining the whole tale," he said at last, wiping a mirthful tear from his eye as his laughter finally subsided. "I did not leave because of the tree. As I told you, that was only what first made me aware of my discontent. The urge to leave built steadily after that. My mother's unkindness was another part of it. My father was a bannerman first, a parent second, and he died when I was young. All I had was Ditra, and she was only a few years older than me. She was not a good substitute for a parent. And why should she have been? She had no one to learn from—certainly not our mother."

He cut himself off suddenly, and the smile he forced was bitter. "That sounded resentful."

"You *seem* resentful," said Sun. "But not without good reason."

"I should have left this bitterness in the past long ago," said Albern. "I should not still be angry about it, but I am."

It made Sun uncomfortable to hear such familiar sentiment from someone so much older than she was. "I understand," she said. "Truly, I do. My parents act the same way."

"As I suspected," said Albern with a sigh. "It is as though . . . as though people become parents, and suddenly they feel a sense of duty to 'the family.' But they forget, or so it seems, that the family is made of people. A family is not a name. It is not a legacy, not a list of ancestors, not the house you live in. It is the people. Your kin, by blood or by law. If the people are not well, the family is not well."

He paused again—but this time with a wince of pain, and his hand moved to his side, clutching near his ribs. Sun's heart skipped.

"Are you all right?" she said.

"Fine," he said. "It is . . . something. I am not sure. Mayhap it is an old injury, or mayhap just a product of age. It is one of the reasons I wish to see the medica."

"Ah," said Sun. "You seem to be traveling quite far to meet her. Have you known her long?"

"Oh yes," said Albern, his smile returning. "She

is the one who performed my wending when I was your age. She is hardly any older than I am. That was quite a shock, when first we met. There I was, having only seen nineteen summers, having only just realized that I was not my mother's daughter, as I had always thought, but her son. I had just left home, and I was very anxious about the wending, as most are. And in walked a young woman in a medica's robes, who had seen only twenty-two years, and who *looked* even younger than I was.

"Well, I must have seemed nervous, because Dawan laughed out loud. 'You think I am young, do you?' she said. 'Well, you are right. But I am one of the High King Enalyn's personal medicas. Masada, the one who performed Enalyn's own wending, was my mentor, and when he passed into the darkness, I took up Enalyn's service myself. If I am good enough for the High King, I daresay I am good enough for you.'

"Her manner was so forthright, and yet so friendly, that I was immediately put at ease. We got along famously after that. And though she had to travel often, being a medica, we always stayed in touch—better, in fact, than I would stay in touch with Mag in later years. And whenever I was due for a new visit, to ensure my health had remained good since the wending, I would always seek her out if I possibly could."

Sun was staring at him in fascination now. To have the High King's own medica . . . she would not have been more surprised if Albern had revealed that he and Enalyn were closely related by blood. Albern was looking at her carefully, and he continued studying her while she attempted to gather her thoughts.

When Sun spoke, it was not about Dawan. "What happened in Opara next?"

Albern chuckled. "In Opara? Not a great deal. But on the road north, and in Tokana . . . why, yes. Quite a bit happened."

SIXTEEN

As I have mentioned, my family has long dwelled in our stronghold in the city of Kahaunga. And in Kahaunga, while Mag and I were returning from our fight with Riri and the Shades, the Lord Telfer received dire news.

She was in her council chamber, poring over the map of her lands. Her lead ranger, a man named Maia, was by her side. He stood off to the side, leaning against the wall, one hand idly toying with the hilt of the sword on his hip. He knew better than to interrupt his lord when she was deep in thought. She had been a stern woman as long as he had known her, and she did not take kindly to being interrupted.

There was another woman in the room, waiting somewhat less patiently than Maia. Her name was Callen of the family Incab, and she was a representative of the Calentin king. One such representative is stationed in the home of each Rangatira, to provide counsel and to send independent reports to the king. Callen was a reedy woman, and Lord Telfer had never liked her—a sentiment that Maia fully shared. They particularly resented the woman's presence in the room at that moment, but Lord Telfer could think of no proper way to dismiss her.

A knock came at the chamber door.

Lord Telfer growled as she looked up. "What is it?"

The door swung open, and a messenger made her hasty way inside. She pressed a fist to her forehead and bowed.

"Lord Telfer," she said. Her voice was too loud in the modest chamber, full of the frantic energy of one who is both eager to please, and terrified because they bear ill news. "The trolls have attacked another village."

Callen's brows rose in faint surprise. "Sky save us," she said in mild worry, turning to regard the Rangatira.

Lord Telfer ignored her. She straightened, her hands gliding across the smooth parchment of the map before her. "Another? Which one?"

The messenger shook her head. "No name, my

lord. It was little more than a collection of homes. One of the survivors is here."

"Here?" snapped Lord Telfer. "Why would you bring—"

The door swung a bit wider, and another woman entered the room. It was Whetu, the woman who had once been one of Lord Telfer's rangers, but long ago.

"Whetu!" cried Maia, stepping forwards to embrace her. They pressed their foreheads together for a brief moment. "It is good to see you once more."

"If only the circumstances were otherwise," she replied. Stepping past him, she put a fist to her forehead and bowed to Lord Telfer. "My Rangatira."

"Be at peace," said Lord Telfer. It was a soldier's command, and Whetu had not been a soldier for a long while, but Lord Telfer did not much care at the moment. "Report."

Callen looked at her Rangatira in faint surprise. "But this is a villager."

Maia's eyes flashed with anger. "She was a ranger."

"Was," said Callen, tilting her chin up ever so slightly.

Lord Telfer slammed her hand on the desk, and the room fell silent. "Report," she snapped. "The rest of you, keep your flapping lips shut."

"The trolls destroyed our village," said Whetu. "Every building was destroyed. Our crops and any stores of bread were raided. The trolls ate most of them before we managed to escape."

"Was anyone slain?" said Lord Telfer.

Whetu shook her head. "No, Rangatira."

"How many trolls?"

"I did my best to count. I saw at least a dozen, but there might have been more."

A dozen, thought Maia. That was a sizable pack.

"Why did you not get a full count?" said Callen sternly.

Whetu did her best not to glare at the representative. She pointed to a bandage on her leg, red with blood. "I was injured. And my husband and I had our daughters to think of."

Callen snorted dismissively. It was a rich reaction, coming from her. Maia knew full well that the king's representative would have fled at the first sight of a troll, and likely kept running until her heart gave out.

But Maia had a thought, and he grew troubled. "Whetu," he said quietly. "Where was your village?"

"Ten leagues out."

Lord Telfer's eyes shot wide. "Where? In which direction?"

Whetu met her gaze with a grim look. "North, Rangatira." She came forwards and pointed to a spot on the map. "There. It is not marked on the map, but it was there."

Maia gave his lord a swift glance. He could see the sudden tension leap into her muscles, the way her knuckles whitened as they gripped the edge of the table. There was a sense of building energy in the air, as though a firemage had summoned a ball of flame and was threatening to unleash it. He gave his lord a moment to answer, but when she remained silent, he turned to Whetu.

"Thank you," he said, nodding. "That will be all."

Whetu nodded and turned to leave the room. The messenger who had brought her left as well, relief plain in her expression at the chance to escape whatever explosion was about to take place.

"That settlement," growled Lord Telfer. "It was clearly within the bounds of the pact."

Maia restrained a sigh of exasperation. "Rangatira," he said carefully, "the last *two* settlements were within the bounds of the pact." *Not that anyone listened when I mentioned that,* he added only in his own mind.

She shook her head. "Those were questionable. They could have been interpreted to be within the trolls' territory. But they were close enough to the border that it could have been viewed as a mistake. This time it is obvious. The trolls are making a statement."

"A statement?" scoffed Callen. "They are trolls."

Lord Telfer's fist tightened again, but this time on the hilt of her dagger. Maia held his tongue. He was the Rangatira's closest advisor for a reason. His disarming smile, his wry wit, his charm—these helped stave off Lord Telfer's darker moods, and she knew enough about herself to know how valuable that could be. But Maia had no quip for this, nothing to say that would diffuse the sense of danger in the air.

He turned to the king's representative. "Callen, may I speak with my lord alone?"

She frowned. "This is an important matter. My counsel may be—"

"It concerns a private affair," said Maia, giving his best smile. "I promise, I shall tell you as soon as we have finished. We consider your advice invaluable, and will request it as soon as we have finished."

Callen's eyes narrowed. Maia knew she did not entirely believe him. But she gave a conciliatory nod and left the room.

"If she had remained in here one moment longer . . ." Lord Telfer let the words trail off.

"Yes, I rather thought our situation might be further complicated if you were to throttle her," said Maia. He leaned over the map. "You are right, my lord. The trolls are encroaching upon our lands. That has never happened before. I do not see how it can continue without coming to war."

"War," said Lord Telfer, her expression souring. "War, against those creatures."

"Rangatira, how can we . . . what would that mean? We have never gone to war with the trolls. Not since the days of—"

Her eyes flashed as she looked at him.

"—not since ancient days that no one remembers, and few tales speak of," he finished, quickly catching his mistake. "We know how to fight them, though it has not happened in an age. But we have no great stores of oil, and if they continue to advance at their current pace, we will not have time to gather more. If it comes to battle, many will die."

"And if we continue to allow this invasion?" countered Lord Telfer.

"The trolls have not killed anyone. Not yet. And after a dozen villages, I cannot believe that that is an accident. It has to be their intent—not to slaughter our people, but simply to drive them from lands the trolls see as their own."

"Yet the pact is clear."

"And have we ourselves not violated the pact for almost a century?"

Both her hands came crashing down on the table. Maia straightened at once, snapping his hands to his sides.

"These are my people!" she roared. "We never pushed into lands the trolls occupied! We never raised a hand against the beasts! We only took what space we needed to live on, only felled the trees we required for new homes. Go and find the refugees who flood into Kahaunga every day, and tell *them* they have violated the treaty. See if that is sufficient comfort to them after losing their homes."

"I apologize, my lord." Maia stared straight ahead, just over her shoulder. "I spoke without thinking."

"You are my counsellor, yet you offer no council,"

said Lord Telfer. "You invent theories why the trolls are behaving this way, but you provide no solution. What would you do about it?"

"Send me to treat with them," said Maia. His eyebrows rose imperceptibly, as though he was struggling to keep his expression neutral. "Or send Callen if you wish. She is a diplomat, after all."

Despite her anger, that made Lord Telfer snort. "She has other uses here. And I will not throw your life away to the trolls. You are too valuable to me."

She turned away. That meant the matter of his insubordination would be set aside, for now. He *had* spoken out of turn, but he had said many worse things through the years, and received no reprimand. Maia was useful. That meant he could get away with much. Only occasionally did his lord feel the need to remind him that he could not get away with everything.

"We will have to decide what to do about the trolls," said Lord Telfer after another long, uncomfortable silence. "But in the meantime, we will protect our people. Send out our messengers to every mountain settlement—all those beyond the pact's borders. And anyone within a league of our side of the border as well. They must leave their homes and join us here in Kahaunga. Tell the rangers to be vigilant. The trolls are not to be trusted. Muster every soldier that can be gathered, in case this should indeed come to war. And finally . . ." She sighed and played with her ear with two fingers. "I will compose a message to the king. I am not yet willing to ask them for aid, but I must inform them of these events. Have our fastest messenger ready to take my scroll."

"Of course, Lord Telfer," said Maia, nodding. He turned at once and made for the chamber door.

"Maia," said Lord Telfer, just as his hand came down on the doorknob.

"Rangatira?" he said, looking back over his shoulder.

"When you are done—and only when you are done—speak with my daughter. Tell her I cannot confer with her tonight."

Maia hesitated a moment. "My lord . . . if she asks to visit you here in your chamber, instead?"

"Refuse her," snapped Lord Telfer. "This is no situation for one as soft as she. She would be useless, and I must have all my wits about me."

Once again, Maia had to restrain a sigh. "Yes, my lord," he said, and left the chamber.

He knew, of course, that Lord Telfer loved her daughter. He only wished that, for once in her life, she would show it. Even if only to him.

The trolls were still picking through the remains of Whetu's nameless village.

Chok, their leader, stood on a hillock overlooking the village, resting on his haunches with both fists planted on the ground. His back was straight, his shoulders thrown back. His thick tongue, corded and muscular like a man's arms, dug crumbs from his back teeth. As the trolls of his pack searched the buildings for plants and grains and the other foodstuffs they so loved, he gave a rumbling *huff* of pleasure. They had eaten well already, and the feast would last well into the next day.

His gaze turned upon Apok as she stepped out of one of the human homes. Her shoulders crashed into the doorframe as she passed, but it did not slow her in the least. The wood shattered under the impact, shards and splinters of it raining upon the ground. Apok paid no attention, but merely climbed the hillock towards Chok, a large cloth-wrapped bundle under her arm.

She reached him and bowed her head. Chok rose up to his full height, rolling his shoulders, a sign of calm and peace. Apok lifted her bundle and unwrapped it to reveal several brown loaves of bread.

"More food?" she asked, lifting one of them towards him.

Chok grunted and took it. He broke it in half and handed one back to her before shoving the rest of the loaf into his mouth. An involuntary moan shook him as he tasted the sweetness of the baked bread. Trolls had not, in those days, learned to grow their own crops or cook their own food. The mountains they chose to live in were not well suited to farming, and they had never much wanted to bother with it in any case. But they relished the taste of the good crops we humans grew, and when they were baked or cooked into bread and other foodstuffs, with no spices to hide the natural flavor, trolls would go to great lengths to acquire and devour them.

Apok ate of her own half-loaf, only eating once Chok had already consumed his own. She watched her leader from the corner of her eye, and Chok saw it. It made him somewhat uncomfortable. Apok was a loyal follower. She did not question his plans in front of the others, and she never countermanded him. But Chok knew she did not approve of the pack's recent actions, these attacks upon human settlements, pushing ever farther south and west. Yet even now, she only watched him, speaking no word of whatever doubts she may have held.

"This was a good day," rumbled Chok. "We have done well."

And it was true. It had been a good day. An anger had been growing inside him, building since long before their first attack on the humans. He did not like it, but he could not deny it. Now that they had pushed even farther south, past the border of the pact, just far enough to remind the humans of their power, the anger had finally abated.

But it flared up again as he saw Dotag approaching.

Where Apok was a good follower, Dotag always cast doubt on Chok's plans. Where Apok obeyed Chok's orders, Dotag would only do what he was told if he was harangued, or sometimes beaten into it—even if he had suggested the plan in the first place. Every troll in the pack knew that Dotag longed for Chok's place at the head of the pack. But Chok would die before giving it to him.

An involuntary growl rumbled through Chok's body. Apok heard it and turned quickly. When she saw Dotag approaching, her ears spread wide from her head, and she hunched her shoulders. She did not growl, but it seemed as though she wished to.

"This was a good day," said Dotag.

Though he had said the same thing only a moment ago, Chok felt a surge of irritation. He did not want Dotag's agreement. He did not need Dotag's approval.

"Get ready to leave," said Chok. "Be ready to go when the sun rises."

Dotag frowned. "We have not done what we came for."

"Tell me if you think the humans will challenge us again," said Chok, speaking louder now. "They broke the pact, and we have driven them back beyond its borders. They will obey it now, because they know we will return if they do not."

"There are more villages," said Dotag. "There is the city. We can go farther."

Chok snarled and took one leap forwards, landing almost within arm's reach of Dotag. He slammed his fists into the ground. "Stop asking for more like a greedy whelp. Look at the bounds of the pact. We are past them. We came here to keep the humans out of our land. After this, they will not creep into our mountains again. Get ready to go home."

Dotag showed his teeth. "Gatak told us—"

"Do not speak as if Gatak leads us!" roared Chok. "Tell me where she is. Tell me how many times the moons have changed since we saw her. Be wise, and be silent."

Now he did step within reach of Dotag. He could sense Apok just behind him, ready to help if it should come to blows. But he did not need her help to defeat Dotag. Age made him huge and strong. None of the pack could challenge him—not that any but Dotag would dream of trying.

Dotag took a submissive step back, but despite his fear, he glared up at Chok. "Gatak will return. When she does, you will not be so brave. She brings a new master. One stronger even than you."

All the anger within Chok came surging up. He leaped forwards and seized Dotag's neck, throwing him down on his back. Both stony fists rose and came crashing down on Dotag's chest. The smaller troll gave a rumbling shout of pain. Chok wrapped his massive right hand around Dotag's cringing face and brought their eyes within a handbreadth of each other.

"How would *you* know what strength is?" he growled at Dotag.

He shoved Dotag's head into the ground and turned, striding away from the village. Just before he crested a hillock and passed out of sight, he gave a great roar and slammed his fists into the ground, creating two craters large enough for a child to sit in. The trolls in the village looked in that direction for a moment, and then they returned to their scrounging.

Dotag fought his way back to his feet, trying not to wince at the pain in his chest. Apok looked disgustedly at him, and other nearby trolls gave him quick sneers. He glared at them, showing his teeth again.

Chok had to die. Dotag had wanted to kill him and take control of the pack for as long as he could remember, for seasons beyond counting. The pack thought Chok was strong, but he had a weak heart. Chok could not see the coming future. Not the way Dotag could.

He had intended to wait for Gatak's return before he challenged Chok. But as he lumbered into the village, searching for more scraps, he began to plan.

SEVENTEEN

We returned to Opara. Tuhin tried to insist that we bring them to the Mystics for inspection, but we refused. If we took the matter to the Mystics, there would be awkward questions about *why* we thought the Rangatira's lead ranger might be a weremage, and that would be bad for everyone involved. We settled for taking Tuhin back to the Rangatira, and his own wizards confirmed that Tuhin was who they appeared to be.

"Well, at least you know something more than you did," said Tuhin amiably. "And you now have a valuable skill indeed, as you continue to hunt your weremage."

After that, we had to report to the Rangatira. Tuhin told him that we had not found the weremage, but that we had stumbled upon a cluster of Shades in the wilderness. Lord Matara looked quietly suspicious, but he did not question us, and he set about making plans to increase his guard so that the Shades would not be able to claim another stronghold in his lands.

We took advantage of his gratitude to solve another problem. Now we meant to ride into Calentin, across the domains of two different Rangatira on our way to Tokana. Armed travelers needed an official writ to pass through another lord's domain, and that writ had to state the purpose of their journey. We were able to convince Lord Matara that we had not received such a writ when we began our hunt, since we had ridden out of Calentin, not into it. Tuhin spoke on our behalf as well, urging the Rangatira to help. He agreed, giving us a writ in his own hand. It would let us ride unhindered all the way to Tokana.

All our affairs that afternoon took only a few hours, but I chafed at what seemed an unforgivable delay. I could not stop hearing Hoko's words in my mind. The weremage was headed for Tokana. I did not know her aim, but I knew it had to be evil. Despite what I have told you already about bad blood with my family, the thought that they were in danger from the Shades filled me with a sick terror, and I could not pull my thoughts away from it. And we did not know when the weremage had left. At best, the journey home would take us just over two weeks. Who knew what havoc she might wreak in that time?

I was all for riding out that very night, but by the time we were done with Conrus, the sun was close to setting. Mag insisted we spend one more night in Opara before we set out, and once he heard our tale, Dryleaf agreed with her.

"You have been long on the road, my boy," he told me. "The journey here might have been gentler to you than it was to me, but not by much. Sleep in a soft bed while you can, lest you find yourself ill prepared for the end of your road."

Mag and I had heard that wisdom many times in our days as sellswords, but now I chafed at the advice. Still, with both of them set against me, I had to relent. We spent another night in Conrus' keep, sleeping in comfort and with good food in our bellies. But I asked his servants to wake us at least an hour before dawn, and when they did, I roused the others quickly. We were riding north before the sun showed its face.

Thus began our journey north through Calentin. My hope that we could reach Kahaunga in two weeks proved futile. The early days of winter unleashed their full strength upon us. Snow and ice-cold rain plagued our road north. I bought sturdier cloaks—two for Dryleaf—and pressed on as hard as I dared. But still I despaired at our pace.

My sour mood, however, hardly seemed to affect my comrades. Mag and Dryleaf knew the importance of our mission, so they were not exactly jovial. But they did not fall into dark periods of silence, as I did. They complained about the road, but in a jovial way. Once, when we were forced to make camp in between towns because I had pushed us to ride into the early evening, we were huddled around a meager fire beneath some trees. The rain made it impossible to see more than half a span in any direction. Suddenly Mag looked over at Dryleaf and laughed.

"Well, old man," she said lightly. "You are on the road again. I daresay it is not as pleasant as you had dreamed, when you were back in Lan Shui."

Dryleaf chuckled. "You are wrong, dear one. I feel almost young again. But remember, I had been sitting in the same spot for so long. Years of holding still. Of course it feels good to be moving again now—I have only been doing it for a few weeks. Let us speak again in a few months, and I will tell you how I feel then. I only hope I do not hold you up again the way I did in Dorsea."

Despite my foul temper, his guilt made me feel guilty in turn. "We have told you not to trouble yourself over that," I said. "No one can help it when sickness finds them in the wilds."

"Yet it happens to young folk like yourself less often than to the old."

"Less often to me, mayhap," I said. "But never to

Mag at all. She has never been sick a day in her life, that I have seen. Even when dysentery would sweep through our camp, forcing the captains to patrol the tents and ensure every fool washed their hands and boiled their water before drinking it, Mag never suffered from it. They used to say she was Elf-blessed."

Mag shrugged. "And I always said that I simply took better care of myself than you did, and I say it again now."

"I took perfectly good care of myself," I countered. "Certainly better than you. Some folk have all the luck."

She shrugged again. Oku, who had been lying near my feet, raised his head and licked my hand. I scratched his ears.

"Do you see?" I said. "Even Oku agrees with me."

"Oku was not there," Mag pointed out.

"He is wise beyond the measure of a normal wolfhound," I insisted, lowering both hands to fluff his face. "Nothing escapes him."

The hound licked my face, and I laughed as I wiped it off. Then I sighed. "I know I have not been the cheeriest companion since Opara," I said, only just loud enough for them to hear over the rain. "Thank you for putting up with me."

"We understand, my boy," said Dryleaf. "And I hope we have not seemed indifferent to your plight. No one blames you for worrying about your kin."

"Friends have a duty to friends, and soldiers on

campaign to each other," said Mag, speaking so lightly that it almost sounded false. "Do not try too hard to hide your worries behind an insincere smile. The two of us will not let you sink too deep into an evil mood. Have I not already said that you are awful at taking care of yourself?"

I scowled. "It was not I who ran off into the mountains alone after enemy archers, eschewing the hiding place that kept the rest of us safe."

Mag and Dryleaf both chuckled, and the old man shook his head. "You should listen to your friend, my dear. Just wait until age catches up with you. You will not find yourself so impervious to sickness then, nor to injury."

We fell into silence, and Mag stared at the flames for a while longer, deep in thought, while Dryleaf and I ate and went to sleep.

I kept working on Jordel's song as we went north. It would not leave my thoughts, as though Jordel himself were there and anxious for me to write something to commemorate him, before the matter passed from my mind. As if I could forget a man I had loved so well, with whom I had shared a bedroll more than once while we traveled through the Greatrocks—a tryst springing from lack of options as much as anything else, but no less earnest for all of that. Dryleaf heard me singing or writing it in snatches, and though he kept prodding me to share my work with him, I was not yet ready.

"You have spent a great deal of time on it," he said.

"Not that long," I told him. "I started shortly after we left Lan Shui. And I want it to be perfect."

Dryleaf scoffed. "My boy, there is no such thing as perfect, especially when it comes to songs and stories. I think you are letting your own conceit get in the way of your work."

"Conceit?" I said. "I only want to ensure it is a fitting tribute to a friend. A friend who was important to me."

"Your friend," said Dryleaf. "What would he think, if you sang him the song you have? Right now, with no further work upon it?"

I scowled, for I knew the answer. And I gave it, even as I tried to explain it away. "Jordel would praise it. He would tell me it was wonderful, because *he* was wonderful, and always full of praise. But that does not mean he would be right. He would say the same thing if I wrote and sang it with a troll's grace. I have to make it worthy of him."

Dryleaf kept staring sightlessly northwards, but dissatisfaction twisted his lips. "You have told me you are inexperienced when it comes to this sort of thing. I would advise you to trust my judgement. But I know, too, that such advice is hard to hear, especially at the beginning. If you wish to keep it to yourself, I will stop hounding you."

I could hear wisdom in his words, and it made me feel guilty. But still I was not ready. "Thank you. And I promise: when it is ready, you shall hear it."

The old man nodded. I think now, looking back upon it, that he knew his job was done. He had planted a seed of thought in my mind, the idea that my own pride might be standing in the way of my accomplishment. Dryleaf's wisdom had been valued in Lan Shui for a reason. I think he knew that, in time, I would see the truth of his words, and come to him for the help I was not yet ready to admit I needed.

And he was right.

EIGHTEEN

As you might suspect, the Shades had a stronghold in Tokana not far away from my family's dwellings. From there they carried out their plans, organizing their efforts according to the instructions they received from Rogan far away, but dealing with ordinary day-to-day matters on their own.

And then, some time before Kaita rejoined them, they received another visitor—one they did not expect, and far removed from their usual routine. It started with shouts as guards on the wall raised an alarm. Before anyone knew what was happening, the gate burst inwards with an ear-shattering crash.

Chok, leader of the troll pack, thundered into the bailey. Standing in the center of it, he slammed his stony fists into the ground and let out a roar. Everyone in the stronghold heard it, and the Shades on the walls dropped their bows in fear.

A Heddish man named Phelan had been placed in charge of the Shades at the outpost. To his great credit, he emerged from the central stronghold to speak with Chok—though he brought a guard of six Shades to accompany him, all armed.

"Ch-Chok," he stammered, trying and failing to wear a diplomatic smile. "What is it? What is wrong?"

The massive troll stumped up to the man, walking on all fours, his fists leaving broad cracks in the stone. He loomed over Phelan, nearly twice as tall as the man, glaring down at him with eyes that smoldered under heavy brows.

"You are still here," he growled, speaking in the common tongue of Underrealm.

Phelan blinked. "I . . . I do not understand."

"You are still here," repeated Chok, his voice rising in irritation. "You helped us drive humans from our lands. You told us where to strike and when. Now they are gone. But you are still here. These are troll lands."

"But Chok," said Phelan, doing his best to sound placating through a voice that still quaked with terror.

"The Telfers are our enemies, just as they are yours. That means we are allies. We work together."

"We worked together," said Chok. "Because they went past the bounds of the pact. Now they are gone. Only you remain. A human in troll land is the enemy."

The last word came out in a growl that Phelan could feel in his chest, and he very nearly soiled his grey breeches. "But you . . . we thought you would keep pushing into the Telfer homelands. Gatak told us—"

Chok roared in his face, and Phelan lost control of his bladder at last. The troll raised his fists, and Phelan knew he was about to die. But even as the guards behind him raised their blades, Chok slammed his fists into the ground on either side of Phelan, splintering the stone.

"Do not pretend Gatak speaks for us!" roared Chok. "She has been gone for months. She is your creature, not ours."

"She is an emissary," whispered Phelan, unable to put any more strength into his voice. He hoped the troll did not notice the piss now running down his legs. "She struck the deal in the first place."

"Tell me where she is now," snarled Chok.

"She will arrive soon!" cried Phelan desperately, with a small surge of courage now that he was in more familiar territory. "And when she does, if you and your pack have pushed the Telfers out of the mountains, you will receive a great reward. More crops than you can handle. As much bread as you can eat. That promise comes directly from the Lord, who never lies."

Chok seemed about to answer. But then another stone-shattering crash came from the direction of the gate. Chok whirled.

Dotag stood in the entrance to the stronghold. The troll's shoulders were raised in an attempt to seem larger, and his nostrils flared in and out with each breath.

"You come here?" he roared, speaking in the trolls' own language. Most of the Shades in the courtyard looked at each other uncertainly, for the words were unknown to them—but Phelan understood. "You come here and threaten our allies?"

"Allies?" roared Chok. "They are in our mountains. They are no different from the humans we drove from our territory. The only difference is that these ones hold you under thrall."

Dotag snarled and took a leap forwards. "I am no slave to humans."

Chok advanced, more calmly than Dotag, and leered. "You would have us lick their boots in exchange for one loaf of bread. You are nothing."

Dotag struck, fist ripping through the air. But Chok caught the blow. He seized Dotag's arm and threw him. The smaller troll flew through the air, over the heads of the Shades, who scattered out of the way. He crashed into the keep wall, buckling it. A hole the size of a human now gaped in the stone.

"You think to challenge me?" roared Chok.

The Shades fled. But even as he cowered near the edge of the courtyard, Phelan waved frantically at his soldiers stationed atop the wall. He motioned to them, cupping his hands and tilting them over, as if pouring a bowl of liquid onto the ground.

Dotag shook his head, woozy from the impact. This time he was more patient, waiting for Chok to strike first. When the larger troll's fist came flying, Dotag ducked. Chok struck the wall instead, widening the hole he had already made. Dotag struck twice under Chok's arm, and the larger troll grunted as he fell a step back.

"You fight like a coward," he rumbled.

"I fight to win," snarled Dotag.

Chok attacked again. But his blow was a feint, and when Dotag sidestepped it, Chok struck with his other fist. It connected under Dotag's chin, sending him staggering backwards. He struck the outer wall of the courtyard, and only barely managed to throw himself out of the way as Chok's following blow slammed into the stone. Above them both, a Shade lost her footing and pitched over the other side of the wall with a scream.

"You are weak!" cried Chok, coming after Dotag, who tried to scramble away. Chok caught one of his flailing legs and spun, launching him into the keep again. He struck the double wooden doors headfirst, splintering them both.

Phelan looked to the top of the keep. His soldiers were ready. He clenched his fists, beseeching his Lord for good fortune.

His prayers were answered. When Dotag saw Chok coming for him, he scrambled back, deeper into the building.

"Cowering with your human friends," sneered Chok. "Tell me again how strong you are."

Chok reached the front of the keep. He stooped, reaching inside and trying to seize Dotag.

"Now!" roared Phelan.

The Shades atop the keep lifted their huge wooden levers. A massive vat of oil tipped as they strained against it. As it came spilling out, they plunged torches into it, setting it ablaze.

A waterfall of burning oil crashed down upon Chok, dousing his whole body.

The troll screamed in agony and stumbled back. The burning oil coated him, roasting his softer insides, his iron-hard skin no proof against the blazing heat. Blinded by the inferno, he flailed wildly about, seeking something he could hold to steady himself.

Dotag charged out of the keep. He brought both fists around in a wide arc, smashing them into either side of Chok's head. The troll leader stumbled back, dazed. Dotag punched Chok in the gut, and he bent double, groaning. Dotag clenched his fists together and brought them down on the back of Chok's head, crushing it into the stone courtyard.

He did it again. And again. And again, until Chok stopped moving.

Slowly, Dotag backed away from the corpse, his shoulders heaving mightily with every panting breath. He lost his balance for a moment and fell on his rear, propping himself up with one arm. Then he seemed to realize that he was still in a human stronghold, and they were looking at him. He fought back to his feet, shaking his head to clear it, and turned to look at Phelan, who was now cowering near the keep entrance.

"I lead the pack now," said Dotag. "We will do as the Lord has bid. But I want Gatak."

Phelan, hoping that the danger had passed for the moment, emerged into the open. "She shall soon return. We will send her when she does."

"See that you do," snarled Dotag. "And when we drive the other humans out of the mountains, we will expect your reward."

Phelan could do little more than nod. He watched as Dotag went to Chok's body and lifted it in his great, muscular arms. He struggled under the weight, but he carried it out through the gate and off into the mountains.

Dark take me, thought Phelan. *I need a new pair of breeches.*

Once he was out of sight of the Shade fortress, Dotag dropped Chok's body. Then he began the messy process of scraping off the oil and the burned skin that covered most of Chok's form. The other trolls could not know that the humans had helped Dotag with their fire.

After removing most of the evidence of burning, Dotag found a large rock. He slammed it into Chok's corpse over and over again, mashing it to a pulp almost beyond recognition. The wounds, the exposed flesh, and the black blood all worked together to hide the last signs of flame.

Dotag took up Chok's arm and began to drag him along again.

It was nearly sundown by the time Dotag returned to the rest of the trolls, still carrying Chok's body. As soon as they saw him appear over the rise, the trolls moved forwards. At their head was Apok. She saw what Dotag carried in his arms, but she could not quite believe it. Her heart sank as she finally recognized Chok's face, mashed to a pulp but still bearing his telltale ripped ears.

"What have you done?" she cried.

Dotag answered by throwing Chok's body down before the pack. He snarled and puffed out his chest, slamming his fists into the ground. "I have taken leadership from Chok. He was weak, and he was a fool. I am stronger than he. I lead the pack now."

Apok cried out—but a peal of grief, not an angry roar. She fell on her knees by Chok, gingerly touching his chest. Chok lay unmoving, his eyes staring past her, unseeing.

Dotag ignored her, looking over her head at the rest of the pack as they gathered near. Some of them looked at Chok's body in wonderment, some in shock. But none bore the same anger, the same grief, as Apok. They seemed attentive. Ready to hear what he had to say. Ready, mayhap, to obey.

"The humans are our enemies," declared Dotag. "We have driven them from our lands. But how long did they dwell there? They ignored the pact. Now we will teach them to fear us. These mountains are ours, as our ancestors declared in the beginning!"

He thrust a fist in the air. Some of the trolls joined him, unleashing great, bestial roars.

But Apok looked up at him, still cradling Chok's body. "They are within the bounds of the pact already," she said. "And they were never close to us. They never took any land we had already claimed. If you attack them now, you will be marked as a betrayer."

"They betrayed us first," snarled Dotag, pressing his face close to hers. "They cast aside the pact. They cannot claim its protection now."

"Yes!" cried a troll in the pack. "Let us drive them from our mountains!"

"And let us start with these strangers who still lurk in their stone walls!" roared another. "We will cast them down!"

Dotag's attention was diverted from Apok for the moment. "No," he said at once. "The humans who serve the Lord are still our allies. They have not betrayed us. And they have promised us rewards beyond our reckoning if we drive the others out of the mountains. We will not harm them. They serve the Lord, and so do we."

Apok did not speak again. She did not call him a weakling for allying with the humans. But her eyes said much.

Dotag ground his teeth with a sound like shattering rocks. But she had not challenged him, not openly. He could not kill her, not now in front of the others. They would never accept him as their leader if he did.

Apok would live. For now. Until he could find another way to get rid of her.

"We move south," he declared, turning his back upon Apok. "We must be ready. Our allies will tell us when it is time to strike, and where to attack. Until then, we wait. We wait for battle."

And for Gatak, he said, but only in his own mind.

NINETEEN

In the middle of the month of Febris, Mag and Dryleaf and I reached Tokana at last.

I will admit that when we crested that last rise to look upon the city where my family had long dwelled, I feared the worst. We had been almost a month on the road. I was certain the weremage had arrived well ahead of us. Whatever evil the Shades were plotting in my homeland, I knew it would be directed against my family. I half-expected to find our keep razed, and the city burned to the ground, with mayhap an army of Shades still camping on the remains.

Instead, I found that things looked almost exactly the way they had when I left home two decades before. So much so, in fact, that I was struck by a wave of memory so powerful I pulled Foolhoof to a stop. Mag and Dryleaf, too, halted their horses. For a long while I sat there, at that familiar point where the road reached the crest of the plateau, and surveyed the city before me.

The land ran relatively even to the north and south, until after dozens of spans, it finally climbed into new peaks, too sharp and steep for any dwellings. But to the north was a great lake in the mountains, and it spilled into a river that came running south into the dale before us. The wide ridge upon which we stood fell off to form the dale's western slopes, and it was here that Kahaunga had been built. After centuries, the town around it had been spilled into the dale and become a true city. The colors were bleak with winter, except for the kauri trees. I sat there, feeling tiny and inconsequential against the size of the city before me, and the swelling heights of the mountains all around, and I did not notice as tears streaked silently down my cheeks, born of a feeling I could not understand and would not have dared to name.

At last, Mag nudged Mist closer to me and took my arm. "Come, you great fool," she said gently. "I would rather not camp here on the mountainside when there are inns so close by."

I scrubbed hastily at my face with my sleeve. "Of course," I said quickly. "Forgive me."

"There is nothing to forgive, lad," said Dryleaf kindly. "Homecoming is never easy when one has been long away."

I nodded. But his words reminded me, too, that this was my home, and one place above all others where I did not wish to be recognized. If word reached my family that I was in Tokana . . .

Somewhere on our journey I had acquired a scarf, and now I pulled it up and around my face to hide my features, while at the same time I pulled my cowl down low over my eyes. It left me with only a single small slit to observe the land as we approached, but I felt more comfortable at once. There was almost no chance that the guards at the wall would recognize me, but I was unwilling to take even such an infinitesimal risk.

"The Rangatira here is named Thada," I told Dryleaf and Mag. They knew she was my mother already, and I did not wish to say so aloud, even though no one was nearby to hear. "She is the ruling authority, and I imagine her daughter, Ditra, helps her in her duties. Have our writ from Lord Matara ready—it will get us through the gates."

Sure enough, when we reached the wall, the guards asked about our business, paying special attention to Mag's spear, and to my bow and sword. They found Lord Matara's writ to be in order, but they did not let us through immediately, first asking us a few more questions about our business in Tokana. We had prepared a story: we were seeking to deliver a message to a member of Lord Matara's family, who was here on diplomatic business.

The guards looked at each other in surprise at that. I frowned, forgetting my desire for discretion for a moment, and spoke. "My good servants, why so many questions? A writ is normally enough to secure passage across the kingdom."

"Normally, yes," said one of the guards, an elderly man with a thick beard who did not take too kindly to such a challenge from an uppity youngster. "But you have been on the road, and have not heard the news. The High King's Seat was attacked near the end of Yanis, and the High King herself narrowly escaped death in the battle."

The words struck us like a hammer blow. Mag and I shared a glance, and Dryleaf went very still in his saddle.

"Attacked?" said Mag. "By whom?"

"The kingdom of Dulmun," said the guard. "A good distance away from us, you might say, but they have many citizens across the nine kingdoms. If you serve a Rangatira, you should be able to appreciate a little extra caution, given the circumstances."

"Of course," said Mag. "If only the Dulmish king were as loyal as you good people, this would not be such a dark day."

That seemed to pacify them, especially the old one, and they waved us on after only a few more questions. Dryleaf had remained silent all the long while, answering only when one of the guards asked him a question, and then only in brief, clipped words. As we passed from earshot of the guards, he spoke at last, scarcely above a whisper.

"The Seat. Loren."

"I know," I said.

"She may be fine," said Mag. "Loren is a clever girl. She has survived worse."

"Worse than a battle on the Seat?" I said. "They may say it was Dulmun, but I do not think that is the whole truth. The Shades were involved, or I am a fool."

"Both things may be true," said Mag. Before I could respond, she quickly went on. "If Enalyn survived, her forces must have won the battle. And you know Loren is not a fighter. She would not put herself in the middle of a conflict like that."

"Those who do not wield blades can still die upon them," I said.

"And one battle will not be the end of it," said Dryleaf. "Who knows what may have happened since?"

"Not I, and not you," said Mag. "I am as worried about Loren as either of you. But we cannot know what may or may not have happened to her, and even if we set out for the Seat this minute we could not find out for months. Keep your mind on our task here, and once we have completed it, then we can look after her."

I sighed. "Very well. It is true enough that we cannot get answers either quickly or easily. And the weremage will not wait idly if we decide to go find Loren."

Dryleaf shook himself. "You are right, of course. And if she survived, she will receive our letter soon. Mayhap she already has. That is some small comfort, at least."

"It is," I said with a smile. Mag murmured in agreement, though she seemed troubled.

We turned our attention back to the city around us, and I tried to remember what I could, in order to direct us to a good inn for the night. But I felt that with each new corner I turned, I found some way in which the city had changed. I could not be sure if it was only my poor memory, or if things were truly so different as I thought, but I suspected the latter. I thought much of the tall kauri tree that had been felled in my youth, and I knew that that had not been the end of the changing of my world.

Kaita reached the Shades before we reached Tokana, of course, and she received word the day after we arrived.

Phelan, the captain of the stronghold in her stead, delivered the message. He knocked twice on her door, hard. After waiting three heartbeats for a response, he opened it and stepped in. In his hand he held a lantern, and he lit a taper from it, which he used to illuminate two more lanterns on either side of the room.

"Commander Kaita," he said, keeping his eyes studiously away from the bed. "There is news."

Kaita was already sitting up, as was the girl who had joined her in her bed that night. The girl looked somewhat embarrassed at the intrusion, but Kaita ignored her and donned a thin robe. The room was cold for such a threadbare garment, but the chill was as nothing to Kaita.

"Considering I gave you permission to wake me in only one instance," said Kaita, "I think I may venture a guess as to what news you have brought."

"She has reached Tokana."

"With the others?" said Kaita.

He nodded. "The old one known as Dryleaf, and the ranger."

"The Telfer man is not a ranger," spat Kaita.

Phelan did not seem to know quite what to say to that, and eventually he settled for, "They brought the dog as well."

Kaita tried to suppress her irritation. Though our journey to Tokana had taken us longer than we wished, we had arrived just a little too soon for her purposes. Matters with the trolls had progressed more slowly than she would have wished.

"What of the Telfer patrols?" she said.

"We still encounter them occasionally," said Phelan. "Or rather, we see them. We are always careful not to be noticed."

"Are they still out at night?"

The man frowned. "They are. And they have increased their guards since the trolls crossed the border."

Kaita's fingers played with her hair, braiding it absentmindedly as she considered her plans. "Very well. The trolls' efforts must be increased. Gatak shall have to go and visit them, especially now that Dotag has taken leadership. And keep someone—or several someones—watching Mag at all times. But sky above, do not let her notice. I shall join our agents monitoring them, when my other duties permit me."

The man bowed. "As you say, Commander."

"That will be all."

He nodded and left. The room settled to silence, and the girl in Kaita's bed looked uncertainly at her.

"Would you like me to go?"

"If you wish," said Kaita. "Or you may stay. It is your choice." She removed her robe and lay back down on the bed, staring at the ceiling with her hands clasped under her head.

The girl looked annoyed. "In that case, I think I will take my leave."

Kaita barely heard her. The first real notice she took was when the room went suddenly dark, as the girl snuffed the lamps before leaving. But she remained deep in her own thoughts.

Mag and I had arrived in Tokana at last. Kaita had lured me all the way home.

Soon, the long hunt—which had lasted much longer than the paltry past few months—would come to an end.

TWENTY

I WAS, AS YOU HAVE GATHERED, RATHER TERRIFIED OF being discovered by my family. To help you understand why, I should tell you something of my eldest sister, Romil, and of something that happened soon after I had fled from home.

My mother had no tolerance for what she saw as my "foolishness," by which she meant my desire to be happy. She still thought I could be useful to her, and so she sent Romil to bring me home. Romil was very like my mother, which is to say that she was cold and uncaring. Growing up, we hardly ever spoke to each other more than was absolutely required. My mother did not mind. As long as we obeyed her, she cared little for how we felt about each other.

It took Romil some months to find me. I had already had my wending and joined the Upangan Blades before she came stomping into our camp one day. Sentries challenged her, and Romil almost came to blows with them. But I happened to be passing by, and I saw her arguing with them.

The sight of her froze me in place. I had managed to convince myself that my family would simply . . . let me vanish. That my mother, who had never seemed to care about me one way or another, would forget about me, and be satisfied with two daughters who seemed willing to serve her. I should have known it was a fool's hope.

I approached them and put a hand on the sentry's shoulder. "She is with me," I said. He gave me a doubtful look, but he went off on his patrol, leaving Romil and me standing there facing each other.

She studied me, and I studied her in turn. Behind her was a retainer of our house, but I barely noticed. I could only see Romil. She wore our family's colors proudly. A bow was on her back, and an axe hung at her belt. She had done her hair in a single long braid that fell to the small of her back. Her expression was a mixed one—appraisal, and faint amusement, but mostly anger.

"You look different," she said.

"A wending sometimes has that effect."

She grunted. "So it does," she said. "I hope it has made you happy, as well as cleared your head. It is time for you to return. Mother commands it."

"I no longer follow Mother's commands," I told her.

Her fingers tightened on the haft of her axe. "Of course you do," she said. "You are a Telfer. Mother has need of you, and wending or no, you can still be of use."

It was, of course, a rather abominable thing to say, and I cannot with any honesty speak in her defense. The time after a wending is a delicate one. Doubtless you know the ritual one's friends and family are supposed to perform, for the sake of the ander person. The kindest thing I can say for Romil is that I do not think she spoke out of malice. Mother had given her a duty, and that duty was the only thing she cared about. My feelings mattered to her not at all.

Her response sent my blood rising, and I answered somewhat more rashly than I should have. "I am so glad to hear it. That I might still be *useful* to her. But I regret to say that I am not going anywhere, least of all with you."

She stepped forwards and seized my arm. A few paces away, the retainer's hands balled to fists, though she bore no weapon. "Of course you are, you idiot," snarled Romil. "You have had your lark as an honorless sellsword. But the game is over now. You can ride behind me on my horse."

"No!" I cried, recoiling. But her grip on my arm was like an iron band. "Let go of me!"

"What is all this about?"

Never before or since have I been so glad to hear Mag's voice. I looked over my shoulder to see her approaching from the midst of the camp. Near her was the sentry who had first spoken to Romil. He gave me a grim look over Mag's shoulder—he must have sensed trouble brewing, and gone to fetch her.

Mag stepped up close, and Romil had at least enough sense to let go my arm. She stared Mag up and down with a haughty expression I was well familiar with.

"Who are you supposed to be?" she said.

"A friend," said Mag. Then, as if afraid Romil might be confused, she added, "Not *your* friend, of course."

Romil looked past her to me. "You keep charming company, Vera."

My stomach did another ugly turn. Again I spoke without thinking. "My name is Albern now."

Romil's eyes shot wide, her expression incredulous. Then she gave a loud, ugly laugh. "Oh, it is, is it? I suppose I should have expected as much. You always had the strange notion that you were somehow better than the rest of us, though you never did a thing to prove it."

"And that is about all I need to hear from you," said Mag. "Leave. Now."

"I do not even take suggestions from sellsword scum, much less orders," growled Romil. "Walk away, if you know what is good for you."

Mag looked over her shoulder at me. "I do not much like her. Should I—"

"Leave it." I looked past her to Romil. "That goes for you as well. I am staying here. You can tell Mother you tried. And that you failed."

Romil's face grew dark with anger. "I have not failed at anything, you witless girl."

Mag struck faster than I could see. Her fists cracked twice against Romil's face, flinging her senseless to the ground. I stared at her fallen form in horror and grief. The retainer tensed as if readying for a fight, but Mag stopped her with a look.

"You would be unwise to push the matter," she said. "Take your master and ride away with her. Go back to your lord. Tell her whatever you wish, but get this wretch out of my sight before I send her back with more than a headache."

The retainer did as Mag commanded. I could not even watch. My head hung between my knees as I sat on the ground, angry tears pouring their tracks down my cheeks. As Romil rode off, slumped over her horse's neck, Mag came to sit beside me, throwing an arm around my shoulder and holding me until my grief subsided.

Albern looked suddenly down at Sun. "Do you understand why I am telling you this?"

Sun blinked up at him. "You said I should know something of Romil."

"That is not the only reason. You know, by now, that our families are not entirely dissimilar. Mine tried to drag me back home. Yours may do the same. But your life is your own, and your future is a choice no one can make for you. And if they try to convince you otherwise . . . well, you have a friend who can help you now, just as I had one to help me then."

Sun blinked at a sudden smarting in her eyes. "Thank you," she said, quietly, for she did not trust herself to speak any louder. "That means a great deal."

Albern nodded. "So long as you know. Now, let us return to the tale."

TWENTY-ONE

After a good night's rest at a fine inn near the western edge of Kahaunga, our party woke and began our search for the Shades. First we spoke to our innkeeper and some others in the common room, trading stories of travel through the kingdom for information about events in Tokana.

We learned very quickly about the trolls' recent incursions into Telfer lands. When I first heard of it, I thought it was an Elf-tale, someone spreading stories meant to give the listener a thrill. But when we heard the same thing from three different people, the truth became clear. The trolls were encroaching upon Tokana, and no one in the city knew why.

But I had some idea.

I led Mag and Dryleaf back to our room to speak in private. Calentin inns are tolerant of hounds, so Oku came as well. He flopped down on a small blanket in the corner, tongue lolling from his mouth in a smile. But he looked at all of us with keen eyes as we talked.

"This situation with the trolls," I said as soon as the door closed. "We must learn everything we can about it."

Mag frowned. "Why? It seems a local trouble."

"The trolls are an exceptionally peaceful people," I said. "My family has never had conflict with them. For them to now show aggression . . ."

"You think it has something to do with the Shades," said Dryleaf, pursing his lips.

Understanding dawned in Mag's eyes. "As with the vampires."

"It must be," I said. "The Shades are provoking them to carry out these attacks. Either they are drawing the trolls in with some lure, or they are driving them out of the mountains towards us. Though I know not how such a thing could be done. The trolls are formidable in battle, and very difficult to harm. Only a well-fortified stronghold would have any hope of defending against them, and even then not for very long."

"Are you certain?" said Mag. "Human lords squabble with each other over borders all the time, with little or no provocation."

I shook my head. "The trolls are not human. Nor are they beasts like vampires, possessing little wit. They are cleverer than satyrs, though much slower to anger—which is why you must fear their wrath all the more, for once stoked it can be impossible to quell. They are the titled lords of the Greatrocks, from Calentin's northern border to the city of Woad far to the south. The Calentin king and their border guards are permitted to have settlements on the only three passes that provide easy passage through the mountains, and the trolls rule the rest of it. For them to attack our domain goes against the pact."

Mag shrugged. "They forged a pact, and now they have broken it. It may be treacherous, but these are uncertain times."

"This is not some petty squabble between human lords," said Dryleaf. He leaned forwards in his chair, both hands wrapped tight around his staff. He looked suddenly very old. "The trolls first came into the mountains not long after Roth's armies had conquered Underrealm. That is more than twelve hundreds of years ago. They came from the rocky deserts to the north. No one knows why. When they first came, Calentin tried to fight them, seeing them as just another invader. But the trolls were implacable, as well as being nearly impossible to kill—and even more so in those days, when no one had ever dealt with them before.

"In the end, a captain of the Calentin army first had the idea for a treaty with the trolls. Roth's forces had forged the nine kingdoms, but conflict between kings did not end with the foundation of Underrealm. Calentin had long struggled to keep the Greatrocks secure against incursions from Feldemar, and their forces were stretched thin with the effort. The trolls could protect the mountains better than Calentin ever could, and they would mostly occupy lands that mankind could not settle anyway."

Dryleaf paused for a moment, and then he turned his head in my direction. "That captain's name was Albern, of the family Telfer. And for forging that ancient pact with the trolls, he and his descendants were named lords of the northern Greatrocks, where they live to this day."

Mag looked at me in wonder, and I gave her an embarrassed smile. "Yes. That is where I took the name after my wending. I had heard tales of Albern of the family Telfer all my life. It was quite the legacy to live up to." My smile dampened a bit. "Some in my family felt so overshadowed by our history, in fact, that it consumed them, and became more important to them than the present."

Mag nodded slowly. "And this pact," she said at last, "between the Telfers and the trolls. It has lasted ever since?"

"Without once bringing us into conflict," I said. "Sometimes our people have settled in lands that, strictly speaking, are beyond the borders. But the trolls also come into our lands on occasion. As far as anyone can remember, the relationship has been amicable, and any problems have been resolved quickly. The trolls are easy to deal with, and they enjoy most human foodstuffs, which makes them easy to bribe if all else fails."

"Yet now they are agitated, and no overtures towards peace seem to have been effective," said Dryleaf. "Assuming the Rangatira has made such overtures."

"She would have," I said. "But it is clear they were unsuccessful."

"Because of the Shades," finished Mag. Her face was solemn, but a light danced in her eyes. "I understand. If we investigate this matter with the trolls, it should lead us to the weremage. And we can hope that slaying her will end the problem with the trolls as well."

"We can hope," I said grudgingly. "Whatever the Shades have done to direct the trolls' wrath at Kahaunga, I only pray we can turn it in another direction before they have torn my family's home down to its foundations."

"I have faith in your abilities," said Dryleaf with a smile. "The name of Albern may save these mountains again."

"Not if we never get started," said Mag. "Where do we begin?"

"If we are right in our guess, the Shades will be found lurking somewhere in the mountains," I said.

"They could not interact with the trolls from here in the city."

"They say the trolls have been pushing into human territory," said Mag. "What if we find them when next they attack, and follow them back to their home? If they have been dealing with the Shades, we can find them that way."

"No," I said at once, and more sharply than I intended. "You know little of trolls, and so you cannot understand how dangerous such a plan would be."

Mag shrugged. "We have faced danger before. No one thought we could fight a vampire and win."

"This is nothing like that," I said grimly. "You were fast enough to wound the vampires with your spear, and to avoid their blows. But speed will not help you against a troll. You can strike it as much as you like, but your spear will do nothing against their hide. Nor will my arrows, unless I hit one in the eye. And such a small wound will do little beyond angering them enough to crush us beneath their fists. The only thing that can truly harm them is fire, and only the Rangatira's forces have the oil one needs to fight a troll."

She grinned at me, which only served to make me more annoyed. "We will be careful," she assured me. "We will not let the trolls see us. I may know little of them, yet I know they do not have eyesight or a sense of smell as good as our own. They should be easy to track, and without them ever being the wiser."

I huffed through my nose. "We can try. But if you

have any sense at all—a doubtful prospect at the best of times—you will follow my guidance when it comes to these beasts. I would rather not see you meet an undignified if long overdue end, crushed by a troll in mountains far from home."

Mag snatched my shoulder and pulled me into a side-armed hug, bouncing me up and down and ruffling my hair. "There is the cheerful Albern I have so missed. This whole matter will be resolved in no time."

I heaved a great sigh, knowing she was wrong, and knowing, too, that I would never be able to convince her.

TWENTY-TWO

We returned to the common room and asked the innkeeper about the last settlement the trolls had attacked. She told us everything she knew, including where to find it. It was a small town called Ahuroa. Hearing the name sent a chill up my back. I had visited it in my youth, both with and without my mother.

Ahuroa was an overnight journey away from the city. We left Dryleaf at the inn, with a plan for him to continue gathering information in the common room and mayhap elsewhere in the city. Mag and I took Oku, as well as our travel packs, and set out into the countryside. My mother was much on my mind as we made our way through the city streets. I remembered journeys we had made, with me riding beside her just as I rode beside Mag now. I remembered trips to Ahuroa, when she had me wait in our dwellings while she tended to business. And I remembered returning from journeys I had made on my own, and Mother being furious that I had left the city without telling anyone.

Indifference when I did my duty, and wrath at any dereliction. It was a fair encapsulation of what life had been like with her.

The guards at the north gate were less watchful than those we had met the day before—leaving the city, it seemed, was less suspicious than arriving at it. When they asked what business we had in the wilds, I told them I had a cousin who had not come with the other refugees from Ahuroa. The trolls had not killed anyone, so I said he must be lost in the wilds. The guards eyed our weapons, but Lord Matara's writ permitted us to be armed, and they wished us luck as we rode out.

The moment we passed into open country, I felt my whole body ease. It was a relief so sharp that it stunned me. Only the day before, I had ridden these same mountains in the open air. One night in Kahaunga had made me tense as a bowstring, yet I had not realized it until I felt it bleed away. A rueful laugh slipped out of me, and Mag glanced over.

"There is no one else around, so I know I did not miss a joke."

I shook my head. "I was just reminded of riding from the city as a child. I always found my home less comfortable than solitude in the wilderness."

Mag was silent for a little while. "I suppose that was true for me as well," she said at last, her voice low. "I spent many years in the woods on my own, when I was young, and forests are still my favorite place to be by myself. They remind me of the peace I knew before I went out into the wide world—before I met you, if I am being honest. It is why I fell in love with Northwood. The trees were only a stone's throw from my tavern, and I would walk among them often."

I will admit I was shocked. Mag had rarely spoken to me of her youth before we met, and I had never pried. She would tell me if she wanted to, I knew. Hearing her suddenly speak of it now was not unlike when I had heard the satyrs speak of a Lord—the words were not strange on their own, but the source turned them quite shocking. I very badly wanted to ask her to tell me more, but I could hear the nervousness in her voice. She was clearly uncomfortable having said so much. I worried that if I pressed her, she might not speak of it again. And so I said nothing.

We rode on for a while in silence after that. Northwest of Kahaunga, the mountains rise up to sharp peaks, which fall steeply away until they flatten out in the little dale overlooked by the stronghold, with gentler slopes on the eastern side. We rode a narrow path that had been cut into that sharp western face, mostly used by rangers who needed to reach far villages and settlements with speed. It gave us a wonderful view down into the dale—though that was spoiled, for me at least, by the sight of how far the city had spread across the mountains. Many trees had been felled, so that the once tranquil forest had been cleared to beyond the dale's eastern edge, and homes and settlements had begun to edge up the slopes there. Though it was early morning, a thin pall already hung in the air below us, the smoke of hearths and cooking fires trapped by the mountains, giving the lower city a blurred, hazy appearance, like something half-glimpsed in a nightmare. It was a darker, dirtier thing than the thick, grey cloud cover above us.

At last our path turned around the edge of a mountain, and we were in the wilderness proper. There the road struck the top of a wide ridge, and we were able to kick our horses to a trot, making better time. Oku padded along happily with us. On occasion he would go ranging far ahead, though never out of sight, and then sit by the side of the road until we had caught up to him, before making two turns around our horses' hooves and then running forwards again. The road grew somewhat narrow again, and began to wind around the side of peak after peak.

Shortly after we lost sight of the city, we came to

the first stone bridge spanning the gap between two slopes. We stopped at its western end. By the lip of the cliff into which the bridge had been built, there was a small shelf just visible. I tried to ignore it, tried to avoid looking at it entirely. I did not succeed. A dark and hazy memory swam into my mind—a relic of my youth, and a reminder of something I would much rather have forgotten.

Mag, meanwhile, sat staring at the bridge in wonder. It was a half-span long, with its foundations set into the mountains on either end. But it had no supports in the middle, only open air between the bridge and the ground, which was a span below.

"How did they build it?" said Mag. "With no pillars, and no way to have any while they worked?"

"There are tricks," I said. "Not that I know what they are. I am a guide, not a mason. I will admit the bridges never held much interest for me."

"Keen eyes and a dull mind," said Mag. "I am hardly surprised. But an evil mood, as well. Why are you so grumpy?"

"Bad memories," I said. "Let us ride on."

We crossed the bridge. Soon the chasms before the peaks grew less deep and less sheer, and the ground rose to meet the road. We came to another small dale like the one where Kahaunga had been built, and there was the lake that flowed off into the river that ran through the center of the city. But most of the ground here was hard and rocky, ill suited for farming. This vale could support no more than a single small village; I saw it there, on the other end of the lake, its homes perched at the water's edge. A few boats were out on the water.

Our side of the lake was far less gentle. We had to pick our way between boulders and across craggy breaks in the land, sharp fissures that pinched to nothing a few paces down. Oku moved more slowly now, sticking close to us, unsure of his footing on this new terrain.

I found myself growing tense again, distracted, almost irritable. I had to force my attention back to the path ahead of us. It had turned from a solid road to little more than an animal trail, and almost all my focus was required to pick the right path through the rocks and avoid dead ends.

Almost all my focus, but not quite. Suddenly I realized why I was so distracted. My mind was not wandering—it was drawn to something. Tiny noises, which I had passed off as an echo from the stones, but which carried on when we paused for breath.

We were being followed.

I drew an arrow, nocked, and turned in a flash. I paused for a heartbeat before loosing, not wanting to harm some innocent passerby.

There, high above. A woman in grey clothes and a blue cloak, with hard-bitten features.

I fired. If I had not hesitated, I would have struck her in the thigh. As it was, the fletching nearly grazed her rump as she scrambled out of sight.

"Up there!" I cried.

Mag did not question me. Slinging her shield onto her arm, she sprang off of Mist and up the slope towards the woman who had been hunting us.

TWENTY-THREE

I SPARED NO THOUGHT FOR THE HORSES. I RAN AFTER Mag.

"Oku, tiss!" I cried, and Oku came bounding after me.

Mag had outdistanced me, but she was looking for a way to climb up towards her prey. The woman dodged nimbly through the rocky terrain, clearly familiar with it. I only caught sight of her for a blink at a time, never long enough for a clear shot. She was much higher on the slope than we were. Mag ran for a sharp incline that would take her up. But when she tried to climb, the land broke under her feet.

"Too soft!" I cried as I ran past her. "We have to find another way!"

Mag growled and tried again. She planted the butt of her spear in the ground to help her, and it held. She climbed up, but ever so slowly. I lost sight of her a heartbeat later.

We were nearing the southern end of the dale. Not far away was the road we had taken to get here. If I could reach the road before the woman, we would have her trapped. I kept glancing up as I sprinted, catching flashes of her blue cloak between the rocks. It would be a near thing. I pushed myself harder, my legs flying.

I rounded a boulder and saw the road a span away. The woman was still moving between the rocks, but there was a half-span of open ground before the road. I nocked an arrow and drew, waiting for her to emerge into the open. Oku gave a thunderous bark and leaped ahead of me, trying to intercept her.

"Kaw!"

A streak of black feathers swept down upon me. Pain lanced across my face as I felt talons bite into my flesh. I cried out and lost my balance, crashing down upon a rock that struck me in the ribs. Wheezing with the pain, I fought my way back to my knees.

In the air above me, the raven wheeled and screeched again. Oku, hearing my cry, had stopped, and was now looking back. The woman we had been pursuing was mayhap a dozen paces from the road. But I knew the raven that had attacked me was no ordinary beast.

"Oku, attack!" I called out. The hound hesitated. "Haka!" I cried.

He turned and went after the fleeing Shade.

I turned my attention back to the weremage. An arrow was in my hand faster than blinking. I loosed it at the raven even as it wheeled and dived for me again.

The arrow impaled its wing. The raven screamed and crashed into the ground behind a rock a half-span away. I moved forwards slowly, readying another arrow.

Magelight flashed. The weremage's form swelled as she took her human shape, and I caught sight of her behind the rock.

Emotions torrented through me: anger for what she had done to Sten; triumph at the fact that we had found her at last; and fear, for Mag was not there to assist me, and I had no idea where she had gone.

"Mag!" I screamed, my voice echoing off the hard land. "I have her!"

The weremage cried out in pain as she dragged the arrow through the back of her arm. Her eyes flashed again as she sealed the wound. I drew and fired, but she cowered behind the rock, and I missed.

I stopped in my tracks, drawing another arrow. She

could not hide forever. Slowly I backed up, step by step, risking only the briefest glances to see my footing.

Another flash of magelight.

The mountain lion with the white tail sprang into view. It was the form she had used to kill Sten. A fresh surge of anger struck me, throwing off my next shot. The mountain lion snarled and leaped to the side, the arrow missing by almost a pace.

I threw the bow aside and drew my sword from my belt. The weremage stalked closer, hackles up, a low growl rumbling from her throat. Fear now joined anger in my gut, churning it, threatening to make me vomit.

"Do it!" I screamed, forcing the terror away. "Do it, you sow!"

The lion roared. It sank back onto its haunches, ready to pounce.

And then a furious stream of barking made us both pause. Oku had abandoned his pursuit of the Shade to help me. He streaked in from the left, a blur of brown and black fur. Teeth flashed in the dull grey sunlight as he drove the mountain lion back a pace. She swiped at him, and Oku dodged it, barking louder.

Then Mag came dashing into view. She was higher up on the slope down which the other Shade had come. I watched as she took in the scene in a heartbeat.

Her battle-trance came over her, the dead-eyed expression crashing down her face like a portcullis.

She charged from behind, but the weremage heard her coming. She looked back over her shoulder, and I could practically see the fear shoot through her as she saw Mag. With a desperate swipe, she drove Oku back and darted towards the road to Kahaunga.

"After her," called Mag, her voice toneless. I recovered my bow, and we gave chase together.

I managed to get off one more shot before the weremage vanished around the first curve in the road. It streaked just past her white tail. We sprinted after her, the slapping of our boots echoing off the mountains.

"Mountain lions cannot run forever," I gasped as we ran. "Bursts of speed, but little endurance."

"Save your breath for running," said Mag tonelessly.

We had only one advantage. The weremage could not turn into a raven and fly away again. If she tried it, I could shoot her down, and she knew it. And in just a few moments, we would reach the bridge. That was a wide open space, and I would have a clear shot.

The hunt was about to end. The other Shade might have escaped, but that would be something to deal with later.

Then we rounded the path leading to the bridge, and I heard the sound of thundering hooves. Confusion made my steps falter, even as I saw the weremage dashing across the bridge in front of us. Beyond her was a party of rangers in Telfer colors, riding towards us on horseback. They were less than a span from the other end of the bridge.

"Now, Albern!" snapped Mag. "Shoot her!"

I shook off my surprise and fired. The arrow flew true, sinking into the weremage's flank. She roared in pain.

An arrow in her side, and a party of riders ahead. The rangers had drawn up short, some reaching for their bows, others snatching spears from holsters on their saddles. The weremage was finished. She had to be.

And then she turned.

At the other end of the chasm, at the edge of a cliff which the bridge had been built to span, there was a small shelf.

A small shelf I had avoided looking at. The source of a bad memory I wished to forget.

The mountain lion leaped down to the shelf. And then she vanished over the other side of it.

From where we stood—and from where the rangers sat on their horses—it looked like she must have plunged to her death. But I knew she had not. I knew that over that shelf was a slope, steep and rocky, and worn smooth by ages of rainfall and exposure to the open wind.

I knew that. And so had the weremage. She had scouted this area better than I thought she could have. She had only run this way because she knew she had a means of escape.

"Albern," said Mag, her voice still monotonous with her trance.

My attention was dragged reluctantly back to the present situation. Now that the mountain lion had vanished, the party of rangers had turned their focus on us. They were advancing slowly across the bridge, weapons raised. Two had dismounted, and they held their spears ready as they approached.

"Drop your spear!" called one still on horseback—a thicker woman with a shaved head, tattoos all over her lower face. "And you, your bow."

"That mountain lion—" I began.

"Your weapons!" she shouted.

I ground my teeth in frustration—but I dropped my bow. "Do it," I muttered to Mag.

Her battle-trance dropped away, and anger showed plain in her features. "Albern, the weremage—"

"We have no choice," I said. "Unless you wish to slay a whole troop of my family's rangers. I believe you could do it, but I hope you will not."

She growled and dropped her spear into the dirt.

The rangers relaxed a bit and came forwards more quickly. We backed a few paces away from our weapons. Oku looked alert, but he did not growl at them, even as the two on foot scooped up the bow and spear.

"Who are you?" said the woman. Now that she was closer, I could see a badge on her chest—my family's symbol, the bow and three arrows, crafted of silver instead of iron. A captain, directly under command of the lead ranger.

"I am Kanohari," I said. "This is Chao. You must

listen to us. That mountain lion you just saw—it was a weremage. She is on the run from the King's law."

That gave all of them pause. The whole party gave confused glances to their captain, who frowned down at us from atop her horse. "A weremage?" she said.

"Yes, and she is—" I bit my own words off, glowering at the ground. "She is getting away."

It was too late. By now, the weremage would have reached the end of the slope. She had already had plenty of time to resume her human form, heal herself with her magic, and then take a raven's form to fly away.

She was gone. She had escaped. Again.

Suddenly one of the rangers leaned forwards, peering at our faces. "Wait. I remember you."

I looked up at him in surprise. And then I recognized him. He had been one of the guards at the gate when we arrived to Kahaunga the day before. My heart sank.

"Who are they?" said the captain.

"New arrivals to Kahaunga," said the guard. "They came through the west gate yesterday, along with an old man."

"On what business?" said the captain.

"They said they were delivering a message to a cousin of the Lord Matara." The ranger's frown deepened. "Which does not explain why they are out here in the wilderness."

"We have Lord Matara's writ," said Mag.

The captain's brows drew close. "If you serve a Rangatira, you know that visitors are not allowed to hunt in another lord's domain, with or without a writ."

"We were not hunting," growled Mag. "We pursued a weremage. She attacked us. Why else would we *chase* a lion through the wilderness?"

The captain paused again. She gave an uncertain glance to the guard beside her, who had begun to look doubtful.

Mag could contain herself no longer. "She is a *Shade,* you fools!"

"Mag!" I said, but too late.

A shock passed through their party. The captain's face darkened, and all doubt vanished from her expression.

"If you know what that means," she hissed, "then you know better than to be shouting it out loud."

"We have hunted her across two kingdoms," I said, spreading my hands and adopting my most disarming tone. "My friend spoke in haste, but she is not—"

"Enough," snapped the captain. I fell silent. "If you speak the truth, and she is a weremage, then she is well beyond our reach by now. And if you are lying, then you have broken Calentin law. In either case, this matter is out of my hands." She turned to her party. "Bind them. We are taking them to the Rangatira."

A pit formed in my stomach, a bottomless hole that threatened to engulf me. I searched desperately for some excuse, something I could say that would save us.

Nothing came. And so I remained silent, as the two guards on foot approached and took Mag and me by the arms.

TWENTY-FOUR

Albern led Sun around the edge of the hill, and suddenly, there was Lan Shui. He paused the tale, and they both stood looking upon the town.

Sun found herself speechless. She had never seen Lan Shui, and yet Albern had described it in such detail that she felt as if she had been here before. It was nestled by a river that thundered down out of the Greatrocks, the peaks stretching tall and mighty above it. The western spur, which had seemed so large before, was now dwarfed by mountains that were no longer hidden by nearer hills.

"Lan Shui," said Albern. "It has been a long time since last I beheld it. Come. I am hungry, and I long for something to drink."

He nudged his horse forwards, and Sun followed. Though she kept studying the town as they approached, her mind drifted back to the tale Albern had been telling her.

"She got away," said Sun. "Kaita, I mean. You were both such capable fighters, and yet she escaped you."

"As she did in Northwood," said Albern.

"She had help in Northwood," said Sun.

Albern looked down at her, brows raised. "I am afraid I do not see your point, unless you mean to imply that we let her get away."

"Of course not," said Sun quickly. "It is only that . . . it must be the unluckiest thing I have ever heard of."

Albern chuckled. "Luck. I have told you already—"

"That you do not believe in luck," said Sun. "That you trust fate instead. Yes, I have heard you. Many times. But if that is true—if you were not *meant* to kill Kaita then, and you were *meant* to find me in that tavern, and all the rest of it—then why do anything at all? Why make choices? Why . . . why try? If you are *meant* to do one thing or another, if it is all a path laid before you in advance, then what does it matter what choices you make?"

Albern's smile grew a little sad. "It is tragic to see such cynicism in one so young."

"I speak of *your* beliefs, not my own," grumbled Sun.

"And you apply a fatal viewpoint to them," said Albern. "Think of this. One thing is certain for all of us: death lies at the end of our road. That is a certainty. That is a fate no one can escape. So if we know we are fated to die, would you say we should not live? Of course not. Our choices are everything. They make us who we are. And I believe they do shape events. Sometimes, a greater force—fate, I call it, though others have other words—it stops us from making the choice we want to make. But that does not mean our choice is invalid, or that we were wrong for making it. Think of it as a war of forces, a conflict between the things we can choose and the things we cannot. We may not be able to control everything, but we must never stop trying to help when we can, however we can."

It was another one of Albern's sayings that had the sound of deep wisdom, but which made Sun most uncomfortable for reasons she did not entirely understand. It kept her silent until they entered Lan Shui, waved on by a guard at the gatehouse who gave them only a cursory inspection. Within the walls, she let herself get distracted by the sights around her. A strange cast seem to cover the buildings around her, as well as the mountains and green fields beyond. She was reminded of Albern's tale of the place, of the desperate battle he and Mag had fought against the vampires within these walls. Could she, in fact, see scratches on the walls from the vampires' claws? Or did they come from a more mundane source, or did she imagine them entirely?

But, too, she thought of the story he had just been telling her, about his little party riding into Telfer lands. The experiences were very similar, and the sensation she had now was familiar as well, the malaise of riding into a foreign town as a stranger, an interloper in another's domain.

"It is different, being a traveler, is it not?" said Sun. "I have not often had the experience of riding into a town or city, unless I was a distinguished guest of some lord there. It is odd to be just a . . . a person. A person who knows no one, to whom nothing is familiar."

"Yes, it can be strange," said Albern. "But I think your discomfort will fade with time, and with practice. Strangers are usually kind. More often than not, you will find yourself welcomed in the places you visit, as long as you bring no evil with you. The experience Mag and I had when we first arrived here, or when we encountered those Telfer rangers in the mountains, is a rare one. Here in Lan Shui, Yue only distrusted us because the town was in danger. In the mountains, the Telfer guards only suspected us because they were on high alert, for the trolls were threatening their home. The kindness with which we were received at the gates of Opara, and at Kahaunga, is the norm, not the exception. In times of peace, people are given to hospitality, and even charity."

Sun looked nervously around at the town again. "Then what sort of welcome do you expect in these times?"

Albern gave a little frown and did not answer.

He pulled his horse to a stop in front of an inn. Sun read the sign over its door: The Sunspear. But she could not reconcile Albern's stories of the place with the sight before her. This building looked almost brand new. And when Albern saw to his horse's lodgings and led her inside, there was a young woman behind the bar, not the older man from his tale.

"This looks . . . rather different from what you told me," said Sun quietly.

Albern paused in his advance across the room. "Oh, yes, it would. Many buildings in Lan Shui were destroyed in the Necromancer's War. The innkeeper who used to own it—the one we met, and who I told you about—was killed. But the inn was rebuilt, and his daughter owns it now. That is her behind the bar. If you find us a table, I will fetch us a meal and some drinks."

Sun did as he asked, finding a spot in the corner. Albern soon arrived with a savory stew that made her mouth water, as well as a mug of beer for each of them. For a time they said nothing, only tucking into their fare and drinking deep. After a quarter-hour they both leaned back in their chairs at the same time, sighing.

"I asked after Dawan," said Albern. "She is here. I

have sent word that we arrived, and she should come to see us shortly."

"That is good," said Sun. Then she frowned. "I think."

Albern chuckled. "It is. I only hope it does not take too long. I wish to see to our other business outside of town before the end of the day."

Sun's stomach did a little turn. "I suppose I wish to do so as well."

"It is all right if you are a little nervous," said Albern. "But come. I will return to the tale to take your mind off it, if that is all right?"

"Of course," said Sun.

"You mentioned earlier how strange it was that Kaita escaped," said Albern. "But you have little inkling, I think, of just how right you are. To understand, you need to know how I left my home in my youth, when at last I had decided to do so. I should not have escaped. You might call it sheer luck that I managed it. But I think I was *meant* to get away that night, and it is a tale worth telling."

TWENTY-FIVE

I HAD JUST REACHED THE AGE OF NINETEEN. THERE were two storms that night—one outside our stronghold of Kahaunga, and one within. It was my mother, you see—Lord Thada of the family Telfer, Rangatira of Tokana. She was furious about something or other.

No. That is not fair to her. Because of how she treated me, I sometimes speak lightly of the very real problems she faced as a Rangatira. In this case, a group of Feldemarian bandits had ventured into our pass.

My mother had sent a party of rangers to drive them out, and three of our soldiers had fallen. One had been a captain who she had particularly favored. I think she had been meaning to take him as a husband—you will remember that my father was long dead by this point.

In any case, I was in my room, and I was grieving, though for quite a different reason. I had had a hunting hound for much of my youth, a fine beast I had called Kowi. He had died that day. A few days before, while we were out on a trail, he had slipped and fallen when a shelf of land collapsed underneath him. The fall, and the rocks that landed on him after, broke most of his body. I carried him home, and there he lingered for a few days. Our master of hounds had urged me to put him out of his misery, for he had no chance of surviving. I refused, because I loved him, and because I was still very young, and unwise about some things. So when Kowi had finally died, I was abruptly saddled not only with the grief of his loss, but with the guilt that I had made him suffer longer than he had needed to.

It was in this state that my mother found me, alone in my room, my pillow soaked through with tears. I was drunk as well, for I had stolen two bottles of wine from the kitchen and gone through both of them. My sister Ditra was away on a diplomatic trip to the south, and so she had not been there to comfort me. I longed for her company—and so you can imagine my disappointment and dismay when I looked up at the sound of my door opening, and found my mother looking down on me instead.

"Vera," she said, for this was before any of us knew I was ander, "I have need of you."

For a moment I could only blink up at her. "What?" I said at last.

Her mouth pressed into a thin line. She crossed the room and pulled me up off the bed, giving me a shake. "I said I have need of you. You will need to ride out. Get some more useful clothes."

"I . . . what are you talking about?" My voice still shook with sobs, and there was a slur in it as well.

"You are drunk," she said with deep disapproval. "Soldiers from Feldemar have killed three of our people. We are going to retaliate. I am sending you out with the raiding party. It is about time you learned something of real combat."

I snatched my arm away from her, drawing back. "You are riding to Feldemar?"

"No," she said, her gaze steely. "You are."

"You are not even coming with me?" I said. "I have never fought before. I have never killed before!"

Her mouth shriveled into a scowl. "I am well aware of that. But you have had training, just like any of us. It is about time you got your arrows wet. The journey through the pass will sober you."

"No," I said, my voice coming out as little more

than a whisper. I shook my head and spoke louder. "I will not."

I could almost feel the tension rise in her body. "You will."

I tried to push past her. "Leave me alone."

She snatched my arm and shoved me down on the bed. Ignoring my protests, she dragged up my arm and pulled back my sleeve, exposing the family mark. "Do you see this? Do you know what it means? It means you are pledged to the service of this family."

Her grip was too strong, and I could not break free. "I never wanted that mark!"

"It is your duty," she said. At last she let me go, flinging my arm away as though it were something dirty. "You are a child of the family Telfer. It is an honor, and it comes with a responsibility. Yet here you sit, weeping into your sheets about a mangy hound, drinking yourself into a stupor as though you lost someone important."

Before I knew it, I was on my feet, my nose only a few fingers away from hers. "I had him since my eighth year," I said, my voice dropping to a growl. "He was my friend."

"He was a *dog,* you witless girl," said my mother. "And he was mine. Not yours. I am Rangatira. You are not even fit to be one of my rangers—but I will forge you, like a blade, until you are. Get dressed. Do you think I acted this way when your father died?"

"I am sure you did not," I said. "But then, you never really cared about him, did you?"

She slapped me. I suppose it was not as hard as it could have been. Certainly I had taken harder blows in weapons training. But still I went crashing back atop my bed, cradling my cheek with one hand.

"If you were not my daughter, I would put you to death for disobeying me, and I would be within my rights to do so," said my mother calmly. "But being my child will not protect you if you continue in disobedience. Your Rangatira has given you an order. You will obey it, or you will face the King's law."

She turned on her heel and marched from the room, slamming the door shut as she went. Slowly I realized that she was not angry for my words about my father; she was only upset that I continued to disobey her. That was all that mattered. How *useful* I could be to her.

I lay on the bed, fresh tears staining my face and the sheets. I tried to force my sobs to subside, but it happened slowly.

The King's law. Would she truly brand me as a traitor? I thought she might. What would be the penalty for defying one's lord? I knew a soldier could be exiled for that, or executed. But I did not think, even then, that she would order the death of her own child.

That left exile.

And with that thought, my mind was made up. If I was going to be cast out of my home, then I would not wait for her to pronounce that judgement. All the unease that had been building in me for years, all my discontent and dissatisfaction came welling up in me at once.

Ditra was the only person in Kahaunga whom I loved, and she was growing ever more distant as my mother dragged her further into her duty to the family. There was nothing to hold me here. And if I stayed, I would either be miserable for the rest of my life, or accept my fate, as Ditra had, and become one of my mother's warriors, a sword for her to wield, an arrow for her to loose at her enemies.

I would not let that happen.

Quickly I dressed myself—in "useful" clothing, as my mother would have put it, though the plans I was forming would be little use to her. I fetched a pack from my closet and filled it with more clothes, as well as my box of flint and steel. I paused, thinking that mayhap I should run to the kitchens and get some food for my journey. But I had no time. My mother would soon send guards to find me. I would have to hunt on the road. That was fine; I journeyed often through Tokana, and I was able to keep myself well fed as I did so. I slung the pack over my back, took up my bow from where it rested near the door to my room, and left.

No one saw me as I snuck out of the stronghold, but my heart did not ease as I made it into the city. All the guards knew me, and even if I pulled my cowl down over my face, my clothing was too fine for them to think I was simply some passerby. And it was night, besides—no one wandering the streets in the moonslight would pass without suspicion.

Thus I tried to remain alert, watching in all directions for anyone approaching me. But it was hard. My head was still heavy with the wine I had drunk. I know I stumbled, I know I crashed into at least a few buildings as I lurched through the streets. I barely remember any of that. The next clear memory I have is of approaching the city's north gate. I stood there for a moment, trying to think how I could get through.

Then there came shouts, and the gate swung open. A party of rangers on foot came through from the outside—returning from patrol, I guessed. Whatever the case, I seized my opportunity. As soon as the gateway stood empty, I ran towards it. I tripped at the last moment, but I fell to the ground outside just as the gate slammed shut.

My escape had not gone unnoticed. A cry went up, and they labored to open the gate again. I scrambled to my feet and ran. It was not long before I heard them behind me—many voices, shouting in the darkness, hunting for me by moonslight. But that was dim and fey, for rain was falling, and the thick clouds in the sky obscured everything. Despite my drunken state, I was able to keep my distance from my pursuers because I knew the land so well.

My feet carried me north on the same road Mag and I would travel all those years later, searching for the weremage. And they brought me to the bridge. But as I came to the place, the clouds obscured the moons completely, and everything went almost pitch black.

I crashed into someone, and we both fell to the ground.

At first I panicked, thinking one of my pursuers had caught me. But then I realized the person had been in front of me. They had just crossed the bridge from the other direction. They were making for the city.

The clouds parted for a moment, and in the flash of moonslight I saw a face. But it swam in the darkness and my own drunkenness. All I could focus on was the black cloak, trimmed with red. The colors of my family.

I screamed and backed away on hands and knees.

Because, you see, I knew about the shelf by the end of the bridge.

I fell onto the shelf and crawled to the slope on the other side, pitching myself over. It was slick with rainwater, and I flew down it faster than a hawk diving upon its prey. My stomach lurched, and I vomited over the side, my sick splashing upon the valley floor far, far below. But at last I came to the end of the slide.

For a long while I lay there, panting, heaving, feeling ill in both body and spirit. At last I looked back up the slide. The ranger must have seen me. But whoever they were, they had not followed. They had to have recognized me. Yet they had not followed.

I thought that mayhap they had cracked their head when I knocked them over. That they had been knocked senseless, unable to understand what they had seen, unable to call the other guards and point them in my direction.

I thought about them fairly often over the next few months. I hoped they were all right. I thought they must have been; we had not struck each other all that hard. But then how had I escaped? It made no sense.

Do you understand, Sun?

You will.

TWENTY-SIX

THE RANGERS ROUNDED US UP AND WALKED US BACK to Kahaunga, positioning us in their midst. They did, however, show us the courtesy of fetching our horses, when we told them they were a little farther up the road. For our part, we made no trouble for them on the way back to Kahaunga. Oku followed faithfully at our heels, seemingly unconcerned by the new company we kept.

As we went, the captain questioned us, asking where we had taken lodgings and where she might find the old man we had come to Kahaunga with. I barely heard her, and so Mag answered. They went to the place, and one of the rangers went inside to fetch Dryleaf. He emerged with a bemused expression, his hand on the guard's arm.

"Are you there, Kanohari? Chao?" he said.

"Here, Dryleaf," said Mag.

"Ah, good. Your plan of secrecy and stealth has gone swimmingly, I see."

Mag stuck her tongue out and blew at him. Dryleaf smiled.

"Well, I am told the Rangatira requires an audience. We should be honored."

Mag laughed, and even one or two of our guards gave a brief chuckle before biting it off. Dryleaf flashed them all a smile and went to take Mag's arm for guidance. Before we left, Mag looked down at Oku.

"Oku, kip," she said sternly.

The hound cocked his head at her, and a low whine issued from his throat.

"Do as she says, boy," said Dryleaf.

Oku lay down in front of the inn. But he did not take his eyes off us, even as we set off down the street and out of sight.

Our captors led us through the city towards my family's stronghold. I found myself unable to speak, unable to do much more than stew in terror at what lay before us. We were being brought to see my mother. Would she recognize me? Could she? I had not had my wending when I left, and many years had passed since then. But still, she would have to know my face. I was her child.

Then I realized how little that had ever seemed to mean to her, and I felt even worse.

The stronghold gates swung open as we approached, and the rangers led us inside. The captain ordered most of them away, bringing only three with her as she escorted us into the stronghold. Memories struck me like a fell wind as I stepped through the door, leaving my knees weak. Mag saw it, and she put a hand on my shoulder to steady me.

"Easy," she murmured. "We will all be fine. Let me do the talking."

"Gladly," I said, my voice weak. I pulled up my hood and dragged it down low over my face.

The captain stopped us before the huge doors leading into my mother's audience chamber. There she left us with the other rangers while she ducked inside. Our guards removed our bindings. I stood stock still as they did it, staring at my own hands.

"What happened?" said Dryleaf quietly.

"The weremage was following us," said Mag. "We almost ran her down, but our friends here came upon us and mistook our intent."

The rangers gave her a sidelong look, but they remained silent.

"How unfortunate," said Dryleaf with a sigh. "Well, hopefully the Rangatira will understand."

My limbs had begun to shake. My mother, being understanding? It was more than I could imagine.

Another moment's silence stretched. Then Dryleaf cocked his head.

"You said she was following you. The two of you did not track her down?"

"No," said Mag.

"So she knew we were here."

A cold dread came over me. She *had* known we were here. It was too far-fetched to assume that she and the other Shade had simply stumbled upon us in the mountains.

"She . . . must have seen us when we arrived to Kahaunga," said Mag, though her voice was tinged with doubt. "It is not as though she—"

"—led us here," I said. "She led us here."

Dryleaf gave a grim nod. "You *have* been given quite a trail of breadcrumbs."

"What, since Opara?" said Mag. "I find that hard to believe."

"Mayhap even earlier," I said. "Always we have gained one piece of information at a time—never enough to bring her down, but only to lead us to the next step in the road."

"But that was true in Northwood," said Mag. "Are you saying that in the mountains, and in Lan Shui, she . . ."

And then she, too, fell to silence. But where I was now wracked with fear and confusion, I saw a burning rage rise in her eyes. Her fists clenched, knuckles turning white.

"But that begs a question," said Dryleaf. "Why? Why all this? You do not even know her name, Mag. What grudge could she bear you that would be worth all this?"

"Only one answer matters to me," snapped Mag. "The same I have sought since the beginning: her head on the end of my spear."

In front of us, the chamber door creaked open. The ranger captain stepped out.

"Follow me."

I steeled myself, following Mag and Dryleaf into the chamber. I remained behind them, forcing myself to stay as calm as I could. Mag would do the talking. Mother would hardly even glimpse my face. She was never interested in visitors, unless she thought they were of some value to her. She would never notice an attendant in the back.

The door closed behind us. I risked a glance up at the dais from beneath my cowl.

I froze.

The room was just as I remembered it, long and wide with a high ceiling. The walls had a series of short windows near the top, impossible for anyone to climb in, just enough to provide some ventilation for the fires that burned in two hearths. The stone pillars running up both sides of the room were of gleaming white limestone, while grey limestone made up the floor. But that grey was now covered with many rugs, which had not been the case in my youth. I saw the furs of bears and mountain cats, but also of creatures from more distant foreign lands. They were well swept and clean, and they made a soft surface for us to walk upon as we approached my mother's dais.

But the woman in the chair was not my mother.

Oh, she had the same sharp chin, the same piercing eyes, the same wide nose. She even wore her hair in tight braids bound up close to her scalp, as my mother had. But she was much younger than my mother. Only a few years older than me.

I looked into the face of my middle sister, Ditra.

This was such a shock to me that it was a good long while before I noticed anything else about the room. When I did, it was only to see that there were a few guards posted along the walls, and that just behind Ditra's chair was a young man wearing the Telfer family colors, as well as a badge of my family's symbol made of gold. Her lead ranger. I did not recognize him, but I remembered Tuhin's words back in Opara: his name was Maia.

My gaze was pulled back to the center of the dais, back to my sister sitting in my mother's chair, wearing my mother's stern countenance, crowned with the silver circlet my mother had borne as her mark of office. It was like seeing my mother all over again, but younger, the way she had looked when I was but a child.

In the end I realized I had been staring too long, and I ducked my head again. For her part, Ditra had not seemed to recognize me in the slightest. Mag and Dryleaf stood in front of me, and so she paid attention only to them, likely thinking me some sort of retainer or guard, and not an equal member of our little party.

That, too, was very like our mother.

Her lead ranger stepped forwards and raised a hand, causing us to stop a good five paces away from the dais. "You stand before Lord Ditra of the family Telfer, lord of Kahaunga, Rangatira of the domain of Tokana."

My sister tilted her head up slightly. "Well met, travelers," she said. The words were courteous, even if her voice was steely. And suddenly her likeness to my mother was greatly diminished in my mind. Yes, she spoke in a stern tone, but *that* was my sister's voice, a voice I knew better than any but Mag's, a voice I treasured beyond anything else in my life.

I ducked my head still lower, struggling to contain tears. I did not entirely succeed, and I had to pretend to scratch my cheek to wipe them away.

We all bowed low with our fists to our foreheads. "Well met, Rangatira," said Mag. She had given me a brief, confused glance when we entered the hall, but seeing my state, she had not looked at me again. "I am Chao, and this is Dryleaf. We are honored to stand in your presence."

"Kind words, coming from the mouth of one who has been found breaking the law in my domain," said Ditra.

"I have long had great respect for the family Telfer," said Mag, "though it has been long since I was able to visit your noble dwelling. May I ask, where is the former lord, Thada of the family Telfer?"

The chamber fell silent. The lead ranger frowned down at us, but more in confusion than anger, I thought. Ditra had gone rather still in her chair, and while she did not exactly scowl down at Mag, she looked even more solemn than she had a moment ago.

"She passed into the darkness some time ago," she said. "I find it hard to believe you could have met her, for you look as if you would have been very young when she died."

I felt as if the ground had tilted beneath my feet. I gripped the back of Dryleaf's robes, holding him for support, trying not to come unmoored from the very earth. Dryleaf, for his part, tried to keep still, though I am afraid I may have put a great deal of weight on the poor man.

"I am often told that I look younger than I am," said Mag in a quiet voice. "I am sorry for your family's loss. How did she die?"

The lead ranger shifted again, but plainly in annoyance this time. Ditra, too, seemed angered by the question, and her lips drew tight.

"I hope I do not offend," said Mag quickly. "It is

only . . . we had the chance to speak once. And I *was* young, as you said. It was a conversation I have never forgotten."

Ditra seemed to relent slightly at that, though she looked no more pleased. "She was riding in the mountains," she said. "Feldemarians attacked and killed her. It was shortly after the death of my older sister."

I could scarcely withstand the storm of emotions now raging within me. And yet, somehow, I did withstand it. What I was feeling . . . it was happening, but I could not let it affect me. I could not let it show in my face. I could not let it reveal anything about me, or draw Ditra's attention to me.

I had been afraid of being recognized when I thought I would have to face my mother. Now I was terrified. And so I controlled myself, despite the agony it caused me. Emotion would be of no help. It would ruin everything. It would cause me to make a mistake, and that would endanger me and my friends. So I simply . . . did not permit the emotion to affect me. I removed it from myself, to a place where it could hold no sway over my actions.

At that moment, I first began to understand Mag's battle-trance. I could not allow my thoughts to control me, and so I simply . . . left. I put myself in another place, so that I could do what I had to do to survive. A part of myself was destroyed as I did it, like I had ripped myself in two. But it was the only way.

And with that realization, the first seed of a question was planted in my mind. What had happened to Mag, long ago, that had made *her* feel this way for the first time? And how, when it was so agonizing to me, had she continued to use it, over and over again, until it became one of her hallmarks in battle?

But all of this passed through my mind in a flash, the way these moments do, to be considered later. Meanwhile, Mag and Ditra continued their conversation.

"No words can express my sorrow," said Mag. "Though years have passed since your loss, I offer my deepest sympathy."

"I am comforted by your kind words," said Ditra, who did not particularly sound as if she was. "But that is not why you stand before me. What are the three of you doing in my lands?"

"We were sent north," said Mag. "We serve Lord Matara."

Ditra frowned. "And what service are you providing him?"

"He ordered us to hunt down a rogue weremage who had been plaguing his domain," said Mag.

"A rogue weremage," said Ditra flatly. "And he did not give this matter to the Mystics?"

Mag hesitated. Dryleaf cleared his throat, drawing Ditra's attention. "Lord Telfer," he said. "This matter concerns secret words that all the Calentin lords have recently heard from the High King's Seat."

Ditra's face betrayed nothing. But she turned and

motioned towards Maia with two fingers. He waved to the guards stationed along the walls, and they slowly filed out of the room, closing the door behind them. Ditra turned back to us.

"This concerns the Shades," she said.

"As we told your rangers in the mountains," said Mag, "though mayhap we spoke in haste. The weremage we are hunting—she is a Shade, and she is operating with others in the area."

"Why would Lord Matara not have sent word of this to me at once?" said Ditra. "And this does not explain why he would not take the matter to the Mystics. A rogue weremage falls under their jurisdiction, and even more so if she is a Shade."

"As for your first question, the Rangatira did not know the weremage would come here," said Dryleaf. "Nor did we. We pursued her away from Opara and followed her trail through the kingdom, only arriving here yesterday. In hindsight, it would have been wise of us to come to you before we continued our chase. But we have been on a long trail, and we thought we saw its end within reach. As for your second question, the Mystics in Opara were notified. But they only recently discovered a cabal of Shades in the wilderness near their city, and they have been much preoccupied with rooting them out. They approved of the Rangatira's request to let us handle this matter."

It was a brilliant stroke, all the more so because I knew Dryleaf had made it up on the spot. If Ditra tried to investigate the truth of his words, she would find that yes, a cadre of Shades had indeed been found outside of Opara. As for the Mystics, they would be reticent to give any information about matters concerning a rogue weremage, whether or not they had already heard of her.

"You told my rangers something different when you entered the city," said Ditra.

"Because Lord Matara told us that we were not to speak of the Shades to anyone but another Rangatira," said Mag. She nodded to Maia. "And those they trust, of course."

Ditra considered that for a long moment. I noticed Maia eyeing her out of the corner of his eye, though the man tried not to be obvious about it.

"Why has this weremage come here?" said Ditra at last. "What are she and the other Shades planning?"

"We are not certain," said Mag. "But news has reached us of your recent trouble with the trolls. We think the Shades may have something to do with it."

"I think you know little of trolls," said Ditra, arching an eyebrow, "if you think they have allowed themselves to be influenced by humans—Shades or otherwise. Trolls will treat with us, but they will only take advice and counsel from among their own."

"Of course it sounds unlikely," said Dryleaf diplomatically. "We would say the same thing, if we had not heard of something like it before. Word reached Opara of the Shades doing something similar in Dorsea. They hatched a plan around a magic ritual, one that summoned vampires and drove them into a frenzy of hunger. A town near the Greatrocks was almost destroyed, and would have been, if not for the actions of a few brave heroes."

Mag's mouth twitched.

"Vampires?" said Maia incredulously. "No one can command those savage beasts."

"Yet they did," said Dryleaf, bowing his head. "I hope, then, that you can understand why we think they may have something to do with the trolls."

"That is evil news, if it is true," said Ditra. "Yet I have never heard of, and cannot imagine, any such ritual that would command a troll."

"Nor have we," said Mag. "Yet we suspect it all the same. It was one thing we hoped to learn on our expedition. If we are correct, it is a clear pattern—a strategy the Shades may be using in other places, in other kingdoms, even now."

Ditra tapped her chin with one finger. "Stirring up creatures from the wilds to sow chaos and disruption . . . these are the tactics of a foe fighting a war of stealth and subterfuge."

"Guerilla tactics," said Mag with a nod.

"They cannot stand toe-to-toe with the High King, and so they instigate battles between her armies other forces, to supplement their numbers." Ditra slid her hands along the arms of her chair and pushed her shoulders back, stretching. "If this is part of their strategy, it will be very useful information in the coming days. I will send word of this to the king, and advise them to relay it to the High King."

We all bowed deeply. "Thank you, Rangatira," said Dryleaf. "You prove yourself wise beyond your years—or at least, so I guess from the sound of your voice."

Ditra gave a little smile—almost, it seemed, against her will—and said, "Thank you, Grandfather." Then her eyes swept across us again. "So you and the quiet one in the back are rangers?"

Dryleaf and Mag paused for a moment that stretched too long. I realized that they were reluctant to answer, afraid they would miss some intricacy of Calentin politics and make a misstep. Though I badly wished to hold my tongue, I spoke. "No, Lord Telfer. Simple soldiers. We have no marks."

"So he has not fallen asleep back there," said Ditra. I ducked my head lower, hoping it looked like I was embarrassed, and not trying to hide my face. "I can believe the two of you are soldiers, especially since you have Conrus' writ." She turned to Dryleaf. "But I think your fighting days are behind you, if you will forgive my saying so—was it Dryleaf?"

"It was, and it is, Rangatira," said Dryleaf, smiling broadly. "And you are correct. I am one of Conrus' advisors. In my youth I had many dealings with the Mystics, and I learned from them many secrets of dealing with rogue wizards. These two are sellswords working for hire."

I winced, but it was too late. At the word "sellswords," Ditra's small smile vanished, to be replaced with a dour expression.

"Strange that Conrus would trust mercenaries with such an important task," said Ditra. "Stranger still that he would relay to them the information he had received from the High King. Foolish, one might even say."

"We have served him for many long years," I said quickly. "The Rangatira knows he can trust in our discretion. Indeed, we would have joined his rangers long ago. But we were somewhat involved in a disagreement with him and the Rangatira Hauru of Tonga, and Lord Matara was reluctant to bring us into his service, for fear of causing offense."

Ditra's stern look did not relax any, but she did lean back in her chair with a sigh. "Sky save us all from politicking," she said irritably.

"On which point we could not agree more," said Dryleaf. "And I hope you will believe me when I say that I have rarely encountered two more worthy soldiers in all my years of being a councilor. And with that, I believe we have taken up as much of your doubtless precious time as can be spared. Though if you wish it, I would be honored to sing for your dining hall tonight, or any night that you would have me."

She seemed to be more irritated than ever, though she still maintained a thin veneer of decorum. "I do not wish it. My position leaves me no time to sit idly and listen to songs."

Mag, sensing the tension in the room, spoke again. "In that case, Lord Telfer, we would beg your leave. We should set about our business of tracking down this weremage. With your permission, of course."

"Normally, I would not give it," said Ditra. "This matter has moved into Tokana, which means it falls to me to settle it. But my rangers are already stretched thin to ensure none of my people are harmed by the trolls. Therefore I will permit you to continue your hunt. You may speak with my lead ranger, Maia, if you require anything from us." She waved a hand at him, and he gave us a slow nod. "I will also order the soldiers of my house to be on the alert while they patrol. They know the Shades' colors, but any information you have on the weremage would be useful."

"She has Calentin features," said Mag. "When we have seen her in human form, she has worn her long black hair in a braid down her back."

"That narrows it down not a whit," said Ditra. "What of her animal forms?"

"We have seen two, though there may be others," said Mag. "A raven, and a brown mountain lion with a white tail."

Ditra did not respond to that. Her eyes did not widen, her hands did not clench. I doubt that Mag or Dryleaf noticed anything change in her appearance. But I thought sensed *something* in her demeanor. Maia, however, did not give her a second glance, and I told myself I must have imagined it.

"That is something to go on, at least," said Ditra. "I will relay it to my rangers. You are dismissed."

"Thank you, Rangatira," said Dryleaf, bowing low once again. Mag and I did the same, and then I took Dryleaf's arm, guiding him along as I followed Mag out of the room.

TWENTY-SEVEN

I MANAGED TO KEEP MY EXPRESSION IMPASSIVE AS WE made our way out of the stronghold and into the city streets. But I could not keep my grip on the emptiness inside of me forever. Once we were out of sight of my family's home, hot tears slid from me, and my arm began to shake under Dryleaf's hand.

"There now," said Dryleaf gently. "We will be back soon."

Mag looked over her shoulder at his words, and when she saw my face, she came to me at once. "Here," she said softly. "I will take him."

She gently lifted Dryleaf's hand from my arm and placed it on her own. I cast my hood down lower and wept, trying to stay silent at first, but in the end I let myself feel the grief that had been building up in me since I first saw Ditra on my mother's chair. When we reached the inn at last, Oku came bounding up, but he seemed to sense my mood and did not bark at us. Once we reached our room, I sat on the edge of the bed and cast my face into my hands. Mag helped Dryleaf to a chair in the corner, shrugged off her shirt of scale mail, and then came to sit by me, wrapping her arm around my shoulders and pulling my head to her chest. Dryleaf bowed his head, and the two of them sat in silence while I poured my woe into Mag's tunic. She did not speak a word, but only held me tighter, occasionally patting my hair. Oku curled up at my feet, his head resting on my boot.

It did not take all that long, considering. I had mourned the loss of my mother long ago—though because she had not been truly gone, there was always at least some hope that we might reconcile our differences. What I mourned in that moment was the loss of that hope. The knowledge was heavy upon me that it was over now, and things would never be right between us.

And, too, I wept for the sight of my sister. My sweet, loving sister, the only one who had comforted me when the world had not cared, now sitting in our mother's chair, and every bit as hard as she had ever been.

But at last my tears subsided. I scrubbed the last of them away on my sleeve, shaking my head and trying to bring myself back to the moment.

"Thank you," I said quietly. "Thank you both."

"You have nothing to thank us for, dear boy," said Dryleaf. "You have had a hard day."

"We do not have to talk now," said Mag. "If you need time—"

"I do not," I said. "I would rather get to work. It will keep my mind from matters of grief."

"As you say," said Dryleaf carefully.

"Do you think my idea unwise?" I said, trying not to sound irritated.

"I think that open wounds need time to close, or they may become aggravated," he said. "And that goes for others as well. The Rangatira still harbors some grief."

"She seemed very comfortable on that chair," I said bitterly.

"She sounded like a lord secure in her position, it is true," said Dryleaf. He paused before continuing, picking at a thread on the knee of his robe. "Are you certain you do not wish to tell her you have returned?"

"No," I said at once. "She would not react well."

Dryleaf subsided. I could almost taste his unspoken questions, but he had enough sense, bless him, to let them be.

"Then if we are resolved, let us speak of what has happened," said Mag. "We know the weremage is in the wilds to the north."

"And we can guess that she was watching us before that," I said. "That means she will know where to find us. We should find new lodgings, quickly, before she has time to put a new watch upon us."

"Will that help?" said Dryleaf. "If we mean to go out into the wilds again, we will encounter her eventually. Then she can take her bird form again, and follow us back to wherever we are."

Mag frowned. "That is a fair point. But we must have some way to ensure you are safe when we are not here."

"You are worried about me?" said Dryleaf, smiling broadly. "You two are the ones riding out into danger."

"And leaving you unguarded," I said.

He waved his hand. "Why would the weremage care about me? Besides, this room is just beside the inn's common room, and the lock on the door is sturdy. She could not hope to strike me here without causing quite a bit more trouble than she has seemed to seek thus far."

"Very well," I said. "But you must be wary. That ranger in Opara had many wise things to say about trust and weremages. We will establish a password, and you must never unlock the door for either of us until we have spoken it."

"If it will make you feel better," said Dryleaf, inclining his head magnanimously.

"Then we should set back out and continue searching the site of the trolls' attacks," I said. "Not today—

it has grown too late. But tomorrow, and every day, until we have tracked down the weremage."

"And ended her," said Mag.

"So we all hope." I paused, looking down at my hands as they rested in my lap.

Mag smiled. "Very well. Let us continue with our original plan. Back into the mountains tomorrow. The way will be easy without having to worry about Lord Telfer's patrols rounding us up."

"Easy," I said with a bitter smile. "I only hope we do not encounter any trolls in those mountains. If we do, you will learn just how 'easy' they are to deal with."

While we conferred at the inn, Lord Telfer was having her own discussion with Maia. It turned out that I had not, in fact, imagined her reaction when we told her of the weremage's animal forms. For a long while after we left, she sat in her chair, chin resting on her fist, her eyes seeing nothing. Maia stood silently by, knowing it would be foolish to disturb her until she was ready for him. In the end she sighed and stood from her chair.

"Let us retire to my chamber," she said. "We must discuss these matters."

"Of course, Rangatira," said Maia, giving a half-bow. He followed her to the back of the room, to the door leading to a staircase up to her private chamber. There Maia moved towards the chairs surrounding her table, but Ditra walked past them to her window, and

Maia stayed on his feet. Another long silence dominated the room.

"Wine, Rangatira?" said Maia at last.

"Hm," she said.

Deciding to interpret her answer in the affirmative, he poured two cups. She took a sip when he put hers into her hand, but her gaze remained fixed out the window. Maia joined her in looking at the valley. From this vantage point, high in the keep's central tower, they could see almost the whole dale. The day was still cloudy and grey, and the sun was lowering behind them, but it still gave more than enough light to see signs of movement far below. Thousands of people milling together, going about their lives.

But Maia knew, though he could not see it, that there were refugees in the city, servants of his lord who had been forced to flee their homes, and who now choked the streets, the inns, anywhere they could find to sleep. Kahaunga looked much the same as it always did, but there was an unrest in the city now, a fear under the surface, and a tension that threatened to burst, like the snowy clouds in the sky above them.

For her part, Ditra's thoughts were only partially for the city. Mag and I had brought her evil tidings, and she was pondering them. But apart from our news, she was thinking of me. She could not understand why her thoughts should so dwell on a quiet man in a brown cloak standing behind his companions, who were clearly leading our little mission. She had gotten a good enough look at me to know that I was half Calentin and half Heddish, but that was common enough, especially in Tokana.

In the end, her thoughts turned away from me to the weremage. A weremage who took the form of a brown mountain lion with a white tail.

Sky above, thought Ditra. *After all these years.*

At last she nodded, as though in answer to a question. Maia stood straighter. He knew his lord. She had decided something, or she was ready to do so.

"Yes, Rangatira?" he prompted.

"You have been seeing to the patrols and organizing the housing of those who have had to flee from the outer villages," said Ditra. "You must give those duties to another. I require something else of you."

"Of course," said Maia. "What is it?"

"I need you to track down this weremage."

Maia was somewhat surprised, but he hid it well. "As you wish. I shall be working with the newcomers, then?"

"No," snapped Ditra, turning on him with such a furious glare that he swallowed through a suddenly dry throat. "No," she said again, less angrily, taking a deep drink of her wine. "You must do this on your own. Find her, if she can be found in the wilderness. Find out where she is and what she is doing. Take no action against her until you have done this and reported back to me."

"As you command," said Maia. "But Rangatira . . . the newcomers are searching for her as well."

Ditra lifted her chin as she regarded him. "Are you a ranger of the family Telfer, or are you not? I am certain they are capable fighters, if Conrus took them into his service. But they are strangers to this place. They do not know these mountains. You will find Kaita before they do."

Maia frowned. "Kaita?"

Ditra went very, very still.

"The weremage," she said after a moment. "They mentioned her name was Kaita."

For a moment, Maia was unsure how to answer. Of course we had *not* mentioned that her name was Kaita, and Maia knew it. But the look in his lord's eyes told him he would be most unwise to mention it.

"That must have escaped my notice," he said at last.

"See that it escapes any mention as well," said Ditra. "Tell no one what you are doing. And if you discover anything about the weremage or her whereabouts, you are to bring it to me immediately. Do you understand?"

"Of course, Rangatira." Maia gave a low bow. "If I may ask, does this have anything to do with—"

"You may not." Ditra turned from him to look out the window again. "We are done."

Maia bowed once more, though she did not see it, and then he left.

TWENTY-EIGHT

"I have a question," said Sun.

Albern smiled. "I enjoy your questions immensely."

"You hardly ever answer them," said Sun with a frown.

"Sometimes that is what makes them enjoyable."

Sun rolled her eyes and drank more of her beer. They had both finished their meals long ago. "You said you were going to tell me another story about Mag. But this story seems to be about you."

He seemed to consider that for a long moment,

pursing his lips and nodding. "Yes. Yes, I suppose it is. This part of the tale took place in my homeland. A great deal more happened to me—at least in my own mind—than happened to Mag. Are you not enjoying the tale?"

So disarming was his smile that Sun felt he would truly not be offended, no matter her answer. But the truth was that she *was* quite enjoying it. And yet hearing of the manner of his return, the way he had been marched into his own home like a prisoner, had caused her own chest to grow tight, her breath catching in her throat.

"The thought of returning as you did terrifies me," she said. "I almost felt ill when you described it."

He nodded. "It may be the freshness of the parting that makes you feel so. You may feel differently in twenty years. In fact, I hope you do. Because whatever else may be said about my return to Calentin, it was good for me, in the end."

Just as Sun was about to ask him what he meant, a voice spoke nearby. "Are you boring some poor girl to death with tales, young man?"

Sun gave a start and looked up. Standing just beside the table, so close it seemed impossible Sun could not have heard her approach, was a woman. She looked to be somewhat younger than Albern. Her dark skin and long locks of hair spoke of Feldemarian descent, but she wore robes of gold, trimmed with white. Her face was round and soft, and she filled out her robes nicely, her form falling to the floor in wide curves like the bouncing of a child's ball.

"Dawan." Albern stood at once and embraced her, and she patted his back gently. He slid around to another chair on the far side of the table, offering his own to her. "My heart sings to see you again."

"It should not be doing that," said Dawan, her brows rising. "I shall have to take a look at it."

Albern chuckled, and Sun did the same, once she realized it was a joke. She had not stopped studying Dawan's face. "Albern told me you were older than he is," she said. "I can hardly believe it."

Dawan laughed, a deep, rich sound that made Sun feel comforted and warm. "I have lived a life of great comfort and safety, even when travel has taken me away from the Seat. Meanwhile, this fool keeps throwing himself into one dark pit after another. Always climbs back out, however, which is good, especially if he is now picking up traveling companions as young as you are."

"As kind as always," said Albern, giving her a smile. Dawan returned it. Then she clasped her hands before her.

"I have much to do here and elsewhere, and less time to do it in. May we retire to my room?"

"Of course," said Albern.

He drained the last of his mug, and Sun hurried to do the same. They rose and followed Dawan out of the common room into a hallway. She stopped at the second door on the left and opened it. As Albern and Sun filed in, Dawan remained by the door. When they were inside, she paused and looked to Albern.

"Would you prefer for us to be alone?"

"That is up to Sun," said Albern. "I do not mind either way."

"I would like to stay, if that is all right," said Sun. The truth was that she was not even sure what she was staying for, but curiosity had a hold on her now.

"It is," said Dawan. She closed the door and locked it. "You will have to go if I ask you to, however."

"I will," said Sun.

Dawan motioned her to a chair on the other side of the room, and Sun sat. Albern rested on the edge of the bed. Dawan went to him and took his face in her hands, tilting it back and forth and looking at him from all angles.

"Your eyes are still sharp, I see."

"They are, thank the sky," said Albern.

Dawan nodded. Then she placed her hands on either side of Albern's throat. From behind her, Sun saw the soft glow of magelight from the woman's eyes. She gave a little gasp before she could stifle it—as a child of nobility, she had often seen wizards performing magic, but it still sent a thrill through her every time.

From what little Sun knew of spellcasting, she thought that Dawan was using her alchemy—transmutation, wizards called it—to look into Albern's body, inspecting for any signs of injury or illness. They both remained completely still for a moment, Albern's eyes closed as he let Dawan inspect him. After a short while, the glow in Dawan's eyes faded, and she sighed.

"All seems well here. Your shirt, please."

Albern nodded and began to peel his tunic away from his body. It was stained with sweat and with much travel, but Dawan did not flinch as she helped him lift it off and hung it on a hook by the door like a fine garment.

"Where was it?" she asked, peering at his chest.

"Here," said Albern, pointing. It was awkward, for the spot was under his left arm, but he had no right arm to make the motion with.

"All right," said Dawan. She did not use her magic at first, but poked and prodded at his torso like any healer Sun had seen. Albern took her ministrations without comment, his gaze wandering idly about the room. Once he met Sun's eyes and gave her a gentle smile, which Sun returned with some embarrassment.

"You do not have to remain if you do not wish to," he said.

"I am all right," said Sun.

Albern nodded and said no more. When Dawan had finished looking him over, she again placed her hands on his body, her eyes filling with magelight as she touched him first in one place, and then another. It took considerably longer than Sun would have expected. She thought that alchemists could see straight through something in just a heartbeat, but that seemed not to be the case.

Dawan finished at last and stepped back with a sigh. There was a second chair nearby, and she sat down in it, seemingly fatigued for a moment.

"I can see it," she said. "It does not appear to be from your wending, which is a good thing. And I do not think it is an illness, either. It looks to be the remnant of some old injury, likely from a battle."

Albern pursed his lips. "It has never troubled me before."

"You are old," said Dawan flatly, though she softened the words with a smile. "Medicas can do much with the body, but they can do nothing about such injuries, nor about age itself."

"Well, then," said Albern, nodding. "That is the best news I could have expected, and I am glad to hear it."

"It would not be so agitated if you settled down and led a quiet life," said Dawan.

Albern smiled. "Mayhap one day."

"Days run short, my friend," said Dawan quietly. "For both of us."

He shrugged. "Who knows what the future holds?"

"Only one thing is certain," said Dawan. "But come. These thoughts are too gloomy. Let us finish your inspection." She turned to Sun. "You may remain, as before, but I will ask that you avert your eyes."

"Oh, I . . . of course." Sun felt her cheeks flame as she looked away. She was vaguely aware of some activity between Dawan and Albern on the other side of the room, but she busied herself studying the grain of the wood floor beneath her.

"Have you suffered any pains?" said Dawan after a bit.

"As you have said, I live a hard life."

"Aside from the usual, of course," said Dawan, her voice betraying only a hint of annoyance.

"No," said Albern.

"Good," said Dawan. There was more activity just beyond the edge of Sun's vision. "All right, girl. We are done."

Sun looked back. Albern was fully clothed again and smiling at the medica. Dawan had gone to a table beside her bed, where a small bowl of perfumed water stood. She dipped her hands in it, wiping them gently before drying them on a cloth. When she finished, she fixed her gaze on Sun, and there was a keen interest in her eyes.

"Have you ever seen a medica at work on an ander person before?"

"No," said Sun quietly. "I have known ander people, of course, but this is . . . new. I have always been somewhat curious about it."

"Well, you will rarely have a better chance to ask questions," said Dawan, spreading her hands. "What do you wish to know?"

Sun leaned forwards, flattening her hands against each other before her chin. "I have seen medicas heal wounds, but then I have heard that they do not truly *heal* wounds."

"That is true," said Dawan. "In the case of grievous injury, the best we can do is a sort of . . . a sealing. It holds the wound shut so that our charge does not bleed to death. True healing must come from within. Our seal will wear away after a time, and there can be aftereffects."

"Why?" said Sun. "Why can you not truly heal the wound? And why is a wending different? The changes an ander person goes through do not wear away."

Dawan licked her lips slowly, shaking her head as though frustrated. "And there you have asked the greatest question of our art. The answer is that no one knows. A therianthrope can heal their own wounds, but though a transmuter's power is a mirror of that branch, yet we cannot heal others. And no one knows why."

Sun blinked, confused. Albern saw it, and he smiled. "Therianthropy is what wizards call weremagic, and transmutation is alchemy."

"Ah," said Sun. "Thank you."

Dawan smiled and shook her head at them. "In any case, to understand why it is this way, we would have to know why bodies grow the way they do in the first place, and that is a mystery beyond anyone. All I can tell you is that we consult with our charges for a long time, making sure the patient knows exactly the way they wish their body to be, and that they have put that picture in our mind in as much detail as they possibly can. It is easier the younger they are, but then, most who are ander know it from an early age. But only once this picture is clear can we use our magic to realize it. If our job is done well, the body accepts the changes very naturally."

"With no . . . no changing back to the way it was before," said Sun.

"Correct. It is called reversion, in our craft." Dawan paused, considering. "This is not part of our training, but . . . in my own experience, and from what I have seen, it is . . . it is as though the body was always *supposed* to be that way in the first place. We only use our magic to get it back on track, if you will. It is more like righting a ship so it can resume its course, than truly 'changing' anything. Which is why many ander people do not get a wending at all. They enjoy themselves just the way they are. The body was never off course in the first place."

"I still do not see how that is different from an injury," said Sun. "Is a wound not just a body getting 'off course,' as you put it, in what is clearly an attempt to relate to my Dulmish sensibilities?" She smiled.

Dawan gave a loud guffaw before she could help herself, and then turned it into a more dignified titter. She glanced at Albern. "Oh, I like her. As for your question, girl: that might be the case, but it does not mean medicas can accomplish true healing. We cannot, and the results can be very dangerous if we try. Things can be different with a disease, or some injuries a person may be born with. Sometimes our magic can treat such a disease, other times it cannot. But since the side effects can be so severe, it is rarely attempted unless a life is at stake."

The room settled to silence. As Sun pondered what the medica had said, she realized that Albern and Dawan were both looking very intently at her. It was the same look Albern had given her earlier that day, when she had asked him about the time he left home. Suddenly she felt self-conscious, and she rolled her shoulders as if casting off a cloak.

"What is it? Did I say something wrong? I did not mean to . . ." She trailed off, for she did not know what she had not meant to do.

"Nothing like that," said Dawan. She came over and crouched before Sun, looking at her from eye level. Her warm, soft hands wrapped around Sun's own. "I must ask, and there is no wrong answer—even no answer. Do you think you might be ander?"

Suddenly Sun understood their reaction. She smiled at them both. "Ah. I see. I . . . I have thought about it. I do not think so, though I am not entirely sure."

"And you do not have to be," said Dawan quickly.

"Of course not," said Albern. "I am glad to hear you have given thought to it, though. That was more than I had done, when I left Tokana."

"Now I know why you were giving me all those looks this morning," said Sun. "You could have simply asked me."

"That is a conversation that must be had in the right time and place," said Albern. "As I know better than most."

"He is not entirely a fool," said Dawan. But the look she gave Albern was so fond that Sun could not believe any of the chiding in her tone. "And with that, we are done here."

Sun stood from the chair. She had not realized how much time had passed until her leg muscles suddenly screamed in protest. "Sky above, I need to walk."

"I am sure you will, if I know anything about Albern," said Dawan.

Albern stood from the bed, tugging gently on his tunic to adjust it. "Thank you, Dawan, as always."

"You are most welcome, old friend." Dawan went and gave him a quick peck on the cheek. "And do not try any of your tricks this time. I have already given the innkeeper gold—more than enough to cover my time here. You will not be able to sneak a payment to her for my services."

His face twisted in a scowl. "Dark take you. Old age has made you wily."

Dawan laughed. She went to Sun and took her

hand for a moment, squeezing it. "It was an honor to meet you."

"Honor does not begin to describe it," said Sun. Then, seized by an impulse, she stepped forwards and embraced the medica. Dawan seemed shocked for the space of a heartbeat, but before Sun could pull back in embarrassment, she felt the woman's plump arms wrap around her.

"Please," whispered Dawan. "Please, take care of him for me."

Then Sun did draw back, but in surprise. She looked into Dawan's eyes and found them glistening. But her face was turned from Albern, and she had spoken so quietly that Sun knew he had not heard.

"Thank you again," said Sun. She gave Dawan a look, hoping the medica could see the answer in her eyes.

"And you," said Dawan, nodding.

Albern ushered her out. Dawan closed the door behind them. "You see?" said Albern. "What did I tell you? Dawan is one of the nine lands' greatest treasures."

"She is," said Sun fervently. "I wish we could have stayed with her longer. But I will accept, as a poor substitute, a return to your tale."

Albern chuckled. "Very well," he said. "I will tell you a bit more—but as we walk. Remember, I had other business in Lan Shui, and I still mean to take care of it."

"Agreed," said Sun, following him out of the Sunspear.

But as they walked through the streets and out through the north gate, she caught herself looking often back over her shoulder, thinking of all that Dawan had said.

TWENTY-NINE

THE DAY AFTER OUR MEETING WITH DITRA, GATAK finally returned to the other trolls.

She strode into the pack's midst soon after dawn, the sun just cresting the eastern horizon and shining on her back. The smaller trolls roaming around the edges of the pack saw her first. They went stock still, staring in wonder as she approached. Gatak ignored them. Ambling on all fours, she picked her way between the trolls who were still sleeping. The air buzzed with their snores.

Apok stepped into her path.

Gatak was larger than most of the trolls, but Apok dwarfed her. Gatak looked up, betraying no concern. They stared at each other for a long, silent moment.

"You have been gone for many turns of the moons," said Apok at last.

"Yes," said Gatak.

"Where have you been?"

"I have traveled far," said Gatak. "I have seen the end of the mountains. I have seen the eastern sky and the western sea."

"I think you have been lurking with your human friends," said Apok.

"They are friends to all of us," said Gatak. "Their Lord promises many gifts."

"Chok did not think so," said Apok.

Gatak showed her teeth. "And where is he?"

Apok's nostrils flared. But before she could answer, a barking command came from behind her.

"Apok! Enough!"

Dotag strode up, shoving Apok aside when he reached the two of them. For a moment he stood there, looking Gatak up and down, his ears folding back in contentment. Looking around, he found another troll who still slept, his arm curled around a half-eaten loaf of bread. Dotag snatched it away.

"For you," he said, proffering the loaf.

Gatak growled in pleasure as she took it from him and ate it in a single bite. But she tossed her head as she swallowed the last of it.

"Good," she said. "But old."

Dotag's face fell. "We last attacked the humans five nights ago. We will get more."

Gatak peered up into his face. "Have you fought many battles? Have you driven them out of the mountains?"

Instead of answering, Dotag looked around at the rest of the pack. "Let us talk alone."

That earned a stony silence from Gatak, but she followed him as he strode away. They broke into a run as they left the pack, and Dotag thrilled to be running with her again. Soon they came to a broad cliff that climbed straight up the side of a mountain. Dotag roared and plunged his hands into the stone, grabbing handholds and propelling himself upwards. Gatak followed, but quietly.

Half a span up, they came to a wide ledge that almost looked to have been cut into the mountainside. The ground was soft and overgrown with grass, which formed a soft cushion for them to sit down on. Dotag cast himself down, looking out from the cliff over the mountains as they spun away north. Far away—but not too far—he saw the pall of smoke that marked the humans' city, the one they called Kahaunga.

"We are close now," he said.

"Close, but not there," said Gatak. "Tell me what you have done."

"We have attacked many villages. The humans flee from us. They gather in their city." He drew a crude map of the pact's borders in the turf, digging into it with his stubby finger. "This is the pact line. We are here." He dug a great circle where the pack now resided.

Gatak snorted. "I know where we are. Why have you not attacked the human city?"

Dotag's ears spread wide and began to quiver with his sullenness. "We have been moving closer," he said. "The pack was reluctant."

"When Chok led them," said Gatak. "You lead now. They will follow you."

"They do follow me," said Dotag angrily. He stood and slammed his fists into the ground. His crude drawing was flung to dust.

"How many humans have you killed?"

Dotag almost deflated as she watched. "None," he said. "The others still do not wish to kill. They say there is no reason to. The humans flee whenever we come."

"They flee, but then they gather," snarled Gatak. "And they do not leave the mountains. They infest our land like ticks. They will not flee their city and let you take it. You must kill them. You should have killed many already."

"We will," said Dotag. "I will. And then the others will follow me. We will drive the humans out of the mountains. For you."

That seemed to please Gatak. She pawed the ground. "For the Lord."

"For you," Dotag said again. When she let the matter lie, he went to sit beside her again. "You were right. I lead now. The others follow me. And I can mate as I wish."

Gatak's ears went up. "When did that ever stop us before?"

That very morning, we had set out into the Greatrocks, seeking the weremage.

It did not go well.

Yearsend was almost upon us, and it was the harshest time of winter. We rode out into the snow and the cold, and snowy and cold we remained, day after day. Our first expedition told us nothing. Any clues to the trolls' actions or whereabouts was lost to the winds and a fresh snowfall that started the day we rode out.

Rather than return straight to Kahaunga, we traveled east aways, for I remembered another village in that direction, and I guessed that it, too, might have been attacked by the trolls. I was correct, but it did not help us at all. The attack had clearly happened earlier than the first village, and so the clues were even older. The only thing we could tell for sure was that the trolls had stolen every bit of produce and baked goods from both villages, which was in keeping with what we knew of them already.

We returned to Kahaunga in poor spirits—and

then our mood was worsened further when we heard the news that Dryleaf had managed to gather in the meantime.

"There have been more attacks," he said. "Three of them, and all in villages closer to Kahaunga."

"Dark take me," I said, clenching my hand to a fist. "We should have come home straightaway."

"We should have," said Mag. "But no use worrying about it now." Though her smile was gentle, it put me ill at ease. She had been treating me gingerly ever since our meeting with Ditra, and I was growing sick of it. I would much rather have had her usual teasing.

"There is more," said Dryleaf, his expression grim even as he continued to scratch Oku behind the ears. "The trolls have started killing."

I stared at him, stunned. Mag leaned forwards in her chair.

"How many?" she said.

"Very few," said Dryleaf. "Still, it marks a change. No matter what, they never killed before. It was too obvious to be anything but deliberate. The word around Kahaunga is that they have given up trying to drive humans away from their lands. The people of the city fear they mean to wipe us out."

"And where did you hear that?" I said. "You were supposed to remain safe here in our room."

Dryleaf waved a hand. "One must eat."

I sighed. "Please do not risk yourself. But as long as you are gathering information, I suppose we should use it. You say not many were killed. How many is not many?"

"Less than a dozen, by all accounts," said Dryleaf. "And that tells us something, considering that the trolls have driven hundreds out of their homes. The people are frightened, and that is understandable, but I think fear is making them foolish. If the trolls wished to wipe them out, many more would have fallen."

"It is still too many," I said.

"Of course," said Dryleaf, bowing his head. "I do not mean to make light of those who are lost."

"The ones who died," said Mag. "Did they try to fight the trolls?"

Dryleaf frowned. "Some, yes. Not others. A few were old and frail, and merely trying to escape. Most were simple farmers or craftsmen, without even a weapon to their name, much less in their hands. But . . . but there were also children."

A cold feeling came over me, starting in my gut and making its way up towards my heart. "The trolls have killed children?"

"That is . . . unclear," said Dryleaf. "No one has said such a thing. Not exactly. But children have gone missing. And there was one man . . . I had to ply him with much wine to get him talking, for he was distraught, weeping and rocking back and forth in his chair. But when I finally got him to talk, he told me—and he said as well, mind you, that he had already told others this, but that they had not believed him—but he said the trolls took his children away. Two of them, a son and a daughter. He said that two trolls scooped them up into their great stony paws and carried them off."

Mag and I looked at each other, and I knew she must be feeling the same terror and disgust that I was. The story was all too familiar to us. Children had also been taken from Northwood when it was attacked.

"As if we needed more proof that the Shades are working with the trolls," muttered Mag.

We rested in Kahaunga for one night, and then we set out into the mountains again. Now a fresh urgency spurred our steps. We pushed the horses as hard as we dared, riding for the village that had been attacked most recently. When we reached it, we found all the same signs as before—destroyed buildings, raided storehouses empty of produce and goods, huge footprints tracked everywhere. But now, too, there were bodies. When we could, we burned them, for it was too dangerous for the families to travel out so far and do so.

We kept at it for days. For over a week we explored the mountains, ranging ever farther north, seeking for the trolls while also trying to avoid being seen by them. There seemed to be no pattern to their attacks. First they would strike to the west, and then to the east, then farther north, and then so close to Kahaunga that the refugees reached the city on the same day of the attack. Anywhere humans had been foolish enough not to retreat from the wilderness, the trolls found them. They could travel almost straight across the land, while we had to navigate the roads and paths around the peaks and over the cliffs and crevasses. Whenever we found their trail, it would always lead into rocky terrain and vanish, or straight up sheer cliffs where we could not follow. Still, we made some progress. I began to see a pattern in the way the trolls moved. Always their attacks came from the north, and always they retreated to the east. That was some clue, at least.

But I began to notice something else. Sometimes I would get a sense of being watched. It put Mag and me on high alert, for we were certain that the weremage was stalking us again. But I could never catch sight of anyone, Shade or otherwise, and I saw no ravens in the sky. Then we began to find campsites—but small ones, just a trampled-down area and the remains of a fire, hastily hidden.

"The weremage?" said Mag, when we found the second one.

"I do not think so," I told her. "Why would she leave a campfire? She does not need one."

"Unless she has been remaining in the wilds for days at a time," said Mag.

I frowned. "Mayhap. We should stay wary."

On one of our return trips to Kahaunga, I found a mapmaker and bought a map of the area. I began to plot out where the trolls had struck, and our best guess of where they had run off to. Slowly I began to narrow down the area where I believed we could find them. But the more we searched, and the more I plotted on our map, the more I began to realize something. The noose was tightening. The trolls were massing for an attack. We were hearing reports of dozens of trolls at a time now, swarming from the mountains like an army. The pattern of their attacks seemed to be random, but they were steadily moving in one direction: straight to the heart of Kahaunga.

They were close, and getting closer. And I did not know if Ditra could stand against them. My only hope of helping her was by finding and killing the Shades. And especially the weremage.

"Where are they?"

Maia frowned. "The two from Opara?"

Ditra scowled at him. They were in her private chamber, and she was slouched in her chair at the head of her table. Maia stood in a position of rest at the other end of it. She had not invited him to sit down. "The Shades," said Ditra. "I care nothing for the strangers."

"I have not found them yet," said Maia. "But I believe I am drawing closer. Then again, so are the strangers."

"How?" demanded Ditra. "You are my lead ranger. You were born to this land. How are they keeping up with you?"

Maia shrugged, projecting a nonchalance he did

not feel. "I do not know, Rangatira. They seem to know the area fairly well. Certainly at least one of them has been here before."

Ditra found herself troubled by that, though she did not know why, and she did not greatly wish to speculate upon it. "Well, you must avoid them if you can."

"I have, so far," said Maia. "It has sometimes been a near thing. But I may not be able to avoid them forever. We are on the same trail, after all, and it is leading us both to the same end."

"Then you must beat them to it," said Ditra. "Mayhap you should take others with you."

"No," said Maia. "That would only slow me down."

"You do not seem to be moving particularly fast," snapped Ditra, slamming down her mug. A bit of ale splashed over the side of it onto the table.

Maia said nothing, but only clasped his hands behind his back.

Ditra gave a disgusted snort and stood, making her way over to the window. She stared out into the sky. Another snow was falling, heavier than it had been in the last few days.

"Find the Shades," she said. "Before the strangers can. We have to end this before it begins. We *cannot* engage in an open battle with the trolls."

"Of course, Rangatira." Maia bowed and left the room.

Ditra stayed at her window a long while, looking out into the gusts of white flakes.

I cannot let this come to open war, she thought. But she feared it might already be too late.

THIRTY

I SUPPOSE IT WAS FOOLISH OF ME TO HOPE THAT WE could go on forever without encountering a troll. But I did hold that hope, and it proved to be wrong.

We were investigating yet another destroyed village. This one was only an hour's hard ride from the sight of Kahaunga's walls. The trolls had slain a score of people in the attack, throwing Kahaunga even deeper into panic. It was hard to tell if the trolls were growing more bloodthirsty, or if more people were dying because more people were fighting. Now that the trolls had started to kill, townsfolk were less likely to simply abandon their homes. Many fought to keep them.

Whenever they did, they lost.

We crept up on the village stealthily, though in truth we were not as cautious as we could have been. This was the eleventh village we had investigated, and we had not found trolls in any of them. So although we dismounted a good distance away and approached the village on foot, I did not range very far ahead of Mag to scout the place.

That almost proved disastrous.

Mag and I were picking our way through the buildings when we heard it: the heavy thud of a foot on stone, and a great snorting, snuffling sound. It was close—within half a span, certainly. Terror nearly stopped my heart.

"Oku, kip," I whispered, motioning furiously to the dog as I dragged Mag out of the street and out of sight. We ducked into a half-wrecked home with a massive hole in the wall. Part of the ceiling hung down into the main room.

We waited a long moment. A sharp *crack* sounded not far away—a timber breaking. The troll was digging into another building, likely breaking it apart just like the one we were in now.

"They left one behind?" whispered Mag.

"Or it came back," I whispered back. "From the reports, it sounded as though this raid was quicker than most of the others. This troll might have snuck away from the rest of its pack, hoping to find some foodstuffs the others left behind."

"Mayhap we should ask it."

I stared at her in horror. A smile crept across her face.

"I am joking."

"Do not do that."

Oku growled low in his throat.

"Kip, Oku." He subsided, and I turned back to Mag. "We must get out of here, and as quietly as possible. It sounds as though it is a little distance off. We should be able to get away without it spotting us."

"This could be our chance, Albern," said Mag. "We could follow it back to the others, and from them, to the Shades."

"We cannot risk being discovered," I said harshly, my voice a little too loud. "You do not know these creatures, Mag."

"The entire reason we came out here was to find trolls." Mag pointed through the hole in the wall. "There. I have found one."

"We came to find a trail. Letting a troll see us would be beyond foolish."

"There have been nearly a dozen trails, and they have not led us anywhere. Now we have—"

I covered her mouth with my hand, my eyes wide. She fell silent. I swiveled back and forth, listening, while Oku quivered beside us.

"What is it?" Mag hissed, her voice muffled by my fingers.

"I do not hear the—"

THOOM

The wall on the other side of the building crashed inwards. Shards of wood and plaster showered us. A wooden beam as thick as my leg flew by, missing me by a handbreadth. The troll's stubby fingers reached in, probing for us. It roared in fury.

"Run!" I screamed, dragging Mag out the door. "Oku, kip!"

The hound fled, yelping in panic, and we were just behind him. I heard the troll crash into the building where we had been hiding, but I dared not turn back to look. Mag's arm was still in my clutches. But suddenly, to my horror, she yanked herself free and stopped in the middle of the street.

I skidded to a halt, and Oku did the same. My stomach did somersaults as I looked at Mag.

She had cast her cloak back and off her shoulders. In her right hand was her spear, and upon her left arm was her shield, held up in defense. The troll had stopped thundering after us, coming to a stop several paces away. It seemed more confused than anything as it glowered down at her, showing its teeth. They were mostly grey and blunt, but there were four huge tusks, two on the top and two on the bottom, that jutted from between the lips like latches holding a book closed. It regarded Mag for a long moment, heavy breaths huffing from its nostrils to steam in the frigid air.

"Greetings," said Mag amiably. "I am Mag. We are looking for some friends of yours."

The troll's brows drew close. "You are human," it said.

"And you are obviously a very bright specimen of your kind."

"Mag, you fool!" I cried. "Do not taunt the thing. Run!"

"No, I do not think so," said Mag, before speaking to the troll once again. "You will never have heard of me, I suspect. In many of the nine kingdoms, I am called the Uncut Lady. Though I am not one to flee from battle, I have no wish to fight you. Tell us where we can find the humans who have been working with your pack, and you and I can part as friends."

The troll's scowl deepened. "I am friends with no human," it snarled.

"Except the Shades, I suppose?"

The troll roared and slammed its hands into the earth before storming towards her.

"No chance of peace, then," said Mag. "I suspected as much."

"Mag!"

I was too late. She crouched for a moment and then leaped, spear up and shield forwards.

The troll struck her a backhanded blow. It caught Mag from below and to the left, crashing into her shield. She sailed over the roof of a nearby building like a stone from a catapult, vanishing from sight.

The sight of it froze me in place. I had tried to tell her. I had said she could not treat the trolls like any other foe. And now one of them had dealt with her like she was no more threatening than a gnat. I prayed to the sky that she was still alive, and I could not imagine she was unhurt.

I forced my attention back to the troll. Mag would have to wait for a moment, for I could not help her if I was dead. Like Victon with the bear, I had to survive, and draw the danger away.

The troll had stopped in its advance, shoulders hunched, fists planted on the ground. Its wide, angry eyes fixed on Oku and me. Thc hound had sunk back on his haunches, fur bristling, a low growl in his throat. But he made no move to attack. He wanted to protect me, but I could practically feel the fear radiating from him. I tried to think of what to do.

Fire, I thought. *Dark take me, I need fire.*

I somehow doubted the troll would let me take out my flint and steel to start a blaze. I risked a glance around. None of the buildings showed any signs of smoke—their cooking fires and hearths would have extinguished themselves long ago.

My attention was dragged back to the troll as it took a step forwards. I raised my bow just a touch. But what good was an arrow against its hide?

Mag had tried to speak with it. But she had tried bluster. Mayhap there was another way.

"I do not wish to fight you," I called out.

It gave a sound that was almost a grunt, but closer to a growl. "Get out of our mountains."

"We will leave you in peace. You are welcome to the foodstuffs here."

That was a mistake. My whole body jerked as the troll roared and slammed its fists down again. "You do not give us anything. We have taken it!"

"Of course," I said. "I did not mean to—"

It was too late. The troll charged. I whipped my bow up and fired a shot, aiming for the eye. But it was moving too fast, and the arrow ricocheted from its stony forehead. Oku and I dived out of the way behind the corner of a building just as the troll sped by both of us, slamming its shoulder into another structure. The wooden timbers shattered under the impact, and the roof collapsed.

"Oku, kip!" I said. "Go!"

With a panicked yelp, the hound ran off and out of sight. No use in both of us dying.

I had to decide what my aim was. If Mag was still alive, she had to be hurt. Thus it seemed my best chance of accomplishing anything lay in drawing the troll away from her, and then losing it so I could swing back and find her.

Every part of me screamed in terrified protest as I

turned back to the troll, who was only now emerging from the wreckage of the home it had destroyed.

"All right, then, beast," I called out. "You want a fight? Come and get one."

My heart skipped as it gave another wild roar. I drew and fired just before it charged. But fear made my shot go wide again, and the arrow bounced from its hide.

I turned and fled around the corner of the stone building, thinking that might give the troll pause. I was wrong. Two earth-shattering crashes shook the ground as the troll slammed through the opposite wall, and then the near one just behind me. A stone struck my shoulder, and I stumbled.

I tried desperately not to panic as I turned another corner. I could not outrun the thing, and I could not safely hide behind any of the buildings. I had to make it lose sight of me. But I was nearing the village's edge, and soon I would be in open terrain. My mind whirled, searching for some solution.

Another turn. Another. If I could only stay out of sight a moment longer . . .

The wall to my left exploded outwards, flinging me through the air. I struck the wall of the building opposite and slumped to the ground.

Gasping in pain, I looked up. The troll loomed there, framed in the hole it had put in the building. Its eyes narrowed as it looked down at me, ears angled up. The earth trembled as it stalked forwards on stony fists.

The terror in my heart turned to rage. I struggled to my feet, leaving my bow where it had fallen and drawing my short sword. Sheer disbelief stopped the troll in its tracks.

"If I am to die, then I will die," I said. "But on my feet." *In Tokana. Like my mother. Like Romil.* That was a bitter thought.

The troll snorted. It took another lumbering step forwards.

There came a flash of metal to my right. Mag came rushing at the troll's flank. Her spear leaped, the edge skittering along its stony side. It roared, turning to swipe at her. But Mag ducked with inhuman speed, and her spear slashed up again. This time the tip of it flashed dangerously close to the troll's eye, and it reeled back in confusion.

"Your bow," said Mag. Her voice was toneless, her eyes lifeless with her battle-trance. "That sword will do little good."

I barely heard the words. I could only stare at her in wonder. She was covered in dirt and mud, but she was utterly unharmed. She did not limp, or hunch over like a fighter nursing a broken rib. I could not even see a bruise, though I imagined there had to be many beneath her clothes and armor.

"Mag, are you—"

"Your bow," she snapped.

The words pierced my confusion at last. With shaking hands I stowed my sword in its scabbard and stooped for my bow, keeping watch on the troll. It was staring down at Mag, seemingly just as astounded as I was. But even as we watched, confusion turned to wrath.

"Mag—"

"Aim for the eyes," she said, and attacked.

I was glad to see she had learned her lesson after the last time. The troll tried to bat her aside as it had before, but this time Mag ducked the swing. Her spear flashed up, and the troll recoiled as the blade passed across its cheek—not breaking the skin, but again drawing too close to the eye for comfort.

It took two stumbling steps back, but Mag followed. She slashed again and again. The long, bladed edge of the spear could not hope to pierce the troll's hide, but it provided an ample distraction. I reached to my quiver and drew another arrow. With Mag occupying all of the troll's attention, I had enough time to draw, to hold, to sight along the shaft.

A long, slow breath escaped me.

I loosed.

The arrow sank into the troll's eye, deep enough to strike the skull behind.

It screamed and stumbled back, swiping at the air as if trying to swat away a fly. Black blood dribbled down its face, staining its teeth as it bared them. Mag tried to make another strike, but its flailing arms drove her back.

Something flashed in the sun as it flew towards the troll. A glass vial struck the beast in the face, and dark, oily liquid spilled all over its body.

We froze. So did the troll. It swiped at the oil, black as its own blood, and stared at it in confusion.

"Hail, friend."

Mag and I looked up. Standing on the roof of a nearby building was Maia, Ditra's lead ranger. He had thrown the flask. Now he stood in an almost languid position—but he had an arrow nocked, and its tip was wrapped with a flaming rag.

The troll looked up at him, squinting with its one good eye through the oil.

"Well met," said Maia amiably. "You are covered in flammable oil, and I have a flame to light it. I highly suggest you turn and run."

At first the troll seemed too angry to understand, but gradually it made sense of the words. It looked down at itself, smelling the pitch that covered its body.

It looked back up, and even I could see the fear shining in its remaining eye.

The troll fled from the village, climbing over a hill and out of sight.

THIRTY-ONE

Maia waited until the troll was out of sight. Then he turned as if to leave.

"Wait!" I cried.

He paused. I saw his shoulders heave with a sigh before he turned back and gave Mag and I an easygoing smile.

"Yes?" he said.

"You saved our lives," I said.

"Oh, you seemed to be doing well enough," he said. "I only wanted to make sure."

Mag had let her trance fall away. Now she arched

an eyebrow up at him. "I suppose we are grateful. Though I do question what you are doing out here in the first place."

He gave another sigh and climbed down from the roof. I came over to stand beside Mag. As I neared her, I heard the padding of soft feet. Oku emerged into view, coming to take his place at our side. The poor hound looked almost ashamed, as though he had dishonored himself by fleeing, even though I had told him to.

When Maia reached the ground, he looked us over. "Are the two of you all right?"

"We are fine," said Mag. "Though as I said, I have questions."

"I was simply passing through," said Maia. "I heard the commotion and came to help."

"Are you not in troll territory?" I said. "I am surprised to learn that Ditra—that the Rangatira would send her rangers out this far, when they should be patrolling the lands that you are still trying to protect."

"You yourself are beyond those lands," said Maia.

"And the Rangatira gave us permission to be here," said Mag.

Maia looked slightly uncomfortable. "As she did with me."

"Yet she told us her rangers would be too busy to aid in the fight," said Mag. "What purpose brings you here?"

Maia looked over his shoulder as though searching for aid. "I should be leaving."

A realization struck me. "You are the one I have sensed in the wilderness. I felt as if someone was nearby. We found campfires. That was you."

"I was not actually following you, if that is any comfort," said Maia. "Our paths simply lay in the same direction. Indeed, I did not think I would encounter you at all in the mountains. But you are very skilled. I suspect one or both of you must have spent some time here before, though I do not remember you."

"It has been . . . a long time," I said. "In my youth. I do not remember you either, if that is any comfort."

"No, I suppose you would not," said Maia. "I came to Kahaunga some eighteen years ago as a boy, when my father wed the Rangatira. I became a ranger as soon as I came of age."

I almost did not hear his last words. The realization struck me that Maia was Ditra's son by law, and that made him my nephew. I might have lost members of my family since I left home, but it seemed I had gained others. I wondered what other new relatives there might be within my family's stronghold.

Things had been quiet for too long. Mag was studying Maia as though she were trying to decide if he was a threat. I forced a smile. "That explains why you are so much more skilled here than I am. Though it does not explain what you are doing here, as my friend asked before. I suppose you have been sent to watch us."

"Not at all," said Maia. He gave another heavy sigh, but this time it looked as though he had finally come to a decision. "In fact, I was sent out for the same purpose as you—to track down the Shades. The only problem is that I was supposed to greatly outpace you in the hunt. In fact, I was strictly ordered to."

"We are very sorry to have made your duty so difficult," said Mag, giving him a wry smile.

"I am sure you are," said Maia.

"Mayhap we could work together," I said.

Maia's mouth twisted. "That . . . is not quite possible."

"Because the Rangatira ordered you not to," said Mag. When Maia narrowed his eyes at her, she smiled. "I may not be as familiar with this land as either of you, but I have some understanding of soldiers, and those who order them about."

"Well, you have guessed aright," said Maia. "I am sorry, but I cannot disobey my lord."

"But Ditra—the Rangatira," I said quickly. *Dark take me for a fool, I have to stop doing that.* "She gave us permission to find the Shades. You mean to tell me she did not actually want us to succeed? If we do, we will put a stop to your entire conflict with the trolls."

Maia only shrugged. "I do not pretend to understand everything, nor to be privy to all of the counsel the Rangatira may receive. She is my lord. I do her bidding. Although . . ." His look grew crafty. "Although I suppose there is a way we could both achieve our aims, and better serve the Rangatira at the same time."

"How is that?" said Mag.

Oku had come over to sniff at Maia's boots. He knelt and scratched the hound behind the ears, and Oku stretched up to lick his face. "You mean to hunt down the Shades. I have been ordered to find them, but not to engage with them, and only to relay their location back to the Rangatira. If you can agree to do the same, I would not object to working with you. Our skills would be more effective if we combined them, and I would save myself a great deal of time if I could focus only on the hunt, and not on avoiding you in the wilderness."

"If we find the Shades, you would wish for us to stave off our attack until you have informed your lord?" said Mag. She folded her arms, making their muscular lines more prominent. "That would imperil the success of our attack."

"You would not have to wait long," said Maia placatingly. "My lord wishes to end the threat of the Shades. It is her duty. I am not certain why she wishes to hear from me before she attacks, but she *will* attack. We can join the main Telfer forces in eliminating the Shades. I will have done my duty, and you will have what you want. Everyone's aims will be satisfied."

I thought hard about it, but I could see no reason not to do as he said. It seemed a wise course of action. Ditra was playing some game I did not understand, and it had hampered our search so far. This would solve the problem without harming either party.

"That seems agreeable to me," I said. "Chao?"

Mag was still for a moment before she remembered that I had used her false name. But rather than nodding in agreement, she gave a grimace. "I suppose I might be able to. As long as when it comes to battle, I am the one to kill the weremage."

"The Rangatira might not like that," said Maia with a sigh. "Though I do not know what she could do to prevent you. What is your grudge against Kaita, anyway?"

I froze.

"Kaita?" I whispered.

Maia's eyes went wide, and his face went a shade paler.

Kaita.

THIRTY-TWO

I WAS A CHILD IN MY FAMILY'S STRONGHOLD, CREEPING towards Ditra's room after having a nightmare. Suddenly, the door opened. Out came Kaita, cloaked in shadow. I could scarcely see her in the darkness. I did not recognize her face.

But Kaita saw me, staring at her wide-eyed in the darkness. If the Lord Telfer found out that she had been caught in Ditra's bedchamber . . . no matter how useful Kaita was, she would be flung out into the streets to beg for her food.

She fled in terror. I looked after her for a moment,

before realizing that Ditra now stood in the doorway, and I forgot all about her retainer.

It was the night I fled from home, drunk with wine and pelted by rain. I had left the city already. I had reached the bridge.

I crashed into Kaita, and we both fell to the ground.

The clouds parted for a moment, and I caught a flash of moonslight. I saw Kaita's face, but it swam in the darkness and my own drunkenness. Yet I screamed at the sight of my family's colors on her cloak, and I backed away on hands and knees.

Kaita watched me scramble over the shelf by the end of the bridge. Then she saw me fall off the other side. She barely stifled a cry as she leaped forwards, expecting to see my broken body far below her.

Instead, she saw me sliding away on a steep, rocky surface slick with rainwater.

She looked on in wonder until I turned a corner out of sight. For a moment she debated going after me.

Then she smiled.

I was gone. The youngest Telfer child, and the most useless.

Kahaunga would be well quit of me.

She turned and carried on her way back to the city.

It was the day Romil found me in the mercenary camp.

She stood before me, but behind her, by the horses, was a retainer. Kaita.

Mag struck faster than I could see, flinging my sister to the ground unconscious. I stared at her fallen form in horror and grief. Kaita reached for her weapon, but Mag stopped her with a look.

"That would be unwise," said Mag. "Take your master and ride away with her. Go back to your lord. Tell her whatever you wish, but get this wretch out of my sight before I give her more than a headache."

Kaita did as Mag commanded. I did not even watch them go, for I was sitting on the ground, arms wrapped around my knees, lost in my grief.

I was in the jungle with Victon and Mag. The bear turned and fled, limping on three legs to favor the fourth that Mag had maimed. Mag turned to me, the battle-trance like a mask over her expression. It shook me then, as it always did.

"You are all right?"

"Victon," I gasped. "It is heading for Victon."

She seized my arm and pulled me up, and together we pelted after the beast.

The bear fled from us, bleeding from wounds it had never expected to receive. Suddenly it lurched to the right and lumbered off into the underbrush. It carried on, heedless of the trail it left behind. Even Mag would be able to track it.

But it would not be there when she arrived.

When the bear had lumbered a span away from the main path, it stopped. Without even bothering to look behind to see if it was being followed, it hunched over.

Its eyes began to glow.

In a moment the transformation was done, and Kaita's form emerged from the bear's. She barely stifled a cry as she felt the wounds in her body seal up, lances of pain shooting through her as flesh and skin joined together.

She took two deep, shaky breaths that wracked her body. But she could not remain still for long.

Again her eyes glowed. She shrank, her tight clothing sinking into her flesh. Black feathers sprouted across her skin. In a few heartbeats, she had taken the raven's form. She flapped desperately, winging up and away. She glanced down only once—to see Mag burst into the clearing where she had just been. Panic seized her, and she flapped harder, flying away from the jungle as fast as she could.

It was the battle of Northwood, and I knelt by Sten's side. Across from me were Mag and the medica, whose eyes were glowing as she gripped the torn flesh of his throat, desperately trying to seal the wound. Mag and I held his hands, pulling them away so the medica could work.

And Kaita lurked nearby, hidden just behind the

edge of a building. My back was to her. My attention was all for Sten. I was exposed.

"Try to be silent," said the medica sharply. "It will only be worse."

"Almost, my love," said Mag. "Hold on."

Kaita's eyes glowed. She took the form of the mountain lion. She had made a mistake in the jungles of Feldemar. The bear had been mighty, but it was too slow. In the long years since, she had learned the form of the mountain lion. It was fast. Faster than Mag, or so she believed.

The medica finished her work. "It is done," she said. "He is not out of danger, but—"

Kaita bounded out from behind the building and leaped for me. I saw the flash of movement from the corner of my eye.

"Down!" I dived out of the way, seizing Mag and the medica and taking them with me.

Kaita landed on Sten's chest, her claws sinking into his flesh with a biting *shunk.* His fingers grasped for Kaita's throat. And then he died.

"No," said Mag. "No."

She rose to her feet, and her hands curled to fists at her sides. Kaita growled at her. Mag did not even have her sword. This would be a simple kill.

But it was not. Try as she might, she could not lay a claw on Mag. And as Mag screamed *No!* over and over, she took Kaita apart with her bare hands.

Kaita resumed her human form, recoiling and holding her wounds.

I saw her. And memories tugged at the back of my mind. But there was Mag, and there was Sten's corpse, and the battle of Northwood still raged around us.

"Sow! You feckless sow!" screamed Kaita. Shades came running into view. "Kill her!" cried Kaita, thrusting a finger towards Mag.

She turned into a raven and flew away.

"You knew her!" cried Sun, her voice ringing with something between betrayal and triumph.

"I did not," said Albern.

"You did!" insisted Sun. "You saw her in Tokana again and again, and probably another thousand times that you have never told me about. Yet you told me you had never seen her before."

"I said nothing of the kind," said Albern. "You asked if I knew her. I did not."

"That is splitting hairs," said Sun, folding her arms. "You know what I meant."

"I do know what you meant," said Albern. "But you have been thinking about it all wrong. Tell me: did you know every soldier who served your family?"

Sun frowned. "I knew our master of arms. Her name was Hilde, and she—"

"I said everyone."

It felt as though she was being drawn into a trap, but Sun did not know how to get out. She waved her hands in irritation. "There were dozens of people running in and out of our kitchens," she said. "I did not meet every baker and scullery maid, if that is what you are asking."

"And we had dozens of rangers, of which Kaita was not one, not to mention hundreds of guards, not only in Kahaunga, but all across our lands," said Albern. "And I have told you already that my mother strictly forbid us from becoming too friendly with anyone, least of all those who were not even of the nobility."

Sun huffed and shook her head. "You could have told me about Kaita from the beginning."

Albern grinned at her. "What was it you said this morning? Every part of the story must be told in its proper turn, or the whole thing will collapse. You were quite right, though you hardly knew it."

"Dark take me for a fool," growled Sun. "Had I known you would throw my own words back at me, I would never have spoken them. This conversation is not over, old man, but fortunately for you, I want to know what happened next more than I want to trounce you."

He chuckled and gave a nod. "Very well. Let us return to Tokana."

THIRTY-THREE

I STOOD IN THE RUINED VILLAGE, STARING AT MAIA IN horror and fury. But that only lasted a moment before I turned and stormed off towards the horses, Oku at my heels.

"What is it?" Mag's confusion was plain in her voice.

"Where is he going?" said Maia.

Mag did not answer, but I heard her footsteps behind me as she followed. Soon Maia joined her. He ran up beside me and tried to get in front of me.

"Listen, friend, I do not know what—"

He stopped as Mag snatched his arm and pulled him out of my way. "I do not know what is happening either," she said. "But I would advise you not to try to touch Albern while I am present."

Maia frowned. "Albern?"

Mag floundered for a moment. "Kanohari," she said lamely. "I meant . . . oh, dark take it all, just get on your horse."

I ignored them both, swinging up into Foolhoof's saddle and spurring him south. I rode hard, slowing only just enough for Oku to keep the pace. Soon I heard thundering hooves behind, and Mag and Maia drew close.

"Albern!" she called out. "What is wrong?"

I ignored her, and she seemed to give up on getting an answer. Soon Maia drew near on his own horse, but he stayed a distance back. We rode in silence all the way to Kahaunga.

Farmers in the outlying fields stopped their work and straightened, staring at us as we galloped past. I do not know what went through their minds. Mayhap they thought we were rushing to deliver news of a fresh attack. But I paid them no more attention than I gave to Mag or to Maia. We hit the streets of the outer city. Thankfully they were clear, and I did not have to slow Foolhoof very much. But at last I had to pull to a stop at the gate of the Telfer keep.

"Open the gate!" I called up.

A guard atop the wall peered down at me in confusion. "Who under the sky are you to issue such an order?"

"I am Albern of the family Telfer, and I have returned to my homeland," I answered her. "Open the gate!"

The woman's eyes went wide with shock. She looked past me to Maia, who was just as surprised.

"The family Telfer?" he said to me.

I pulled down my sleeve and showed him our family's mark. He stared at it in wonder for a moment, sighed, and looked back up at the gate guard.

"For good or for ill, I think you had better do as he says."

That seemed good enough, and the guards hastened to open the gate. I spurred Foolhoof forwards as soon as it was high enough for me to avoid hitting my head. Once I reached the keep, I dismounted and left Foolhoof behind as I stormed up the steps. The doors stood open, and I passed through them to stalk down the wide entrance hall.

"Albern," said Mag. It was one of the few times in her life I had heard her sound nervous. "Are you certain about this?"

"More certain than I have been about anything since we got here," I growled.

Two Telfer guards stood at the door to Ditra's audience chamber. They stepped forwards, hands tightening on their spears as I approached.

"Let him pass," said Maia in resignation. "I am with him."

They did not look pleased about it, but they did as he said. I threw open the double doors as hard as I could, and they slammed against the stone walls on either side. Ditra sat on her chair atop the dais, and her head snapped up in shock as I entered. A small cluster of advisors huddled before the dais, and they, too, turned to stare at me in amazement.

"Kaita!" I roared.

Ditra's eyes went wide. The guards at the edges of the room stepped forwards, ready to defend their lord. Among the councilors I spotted a woman in robes of Calentin colors—the king's representative. She studied me with great interest.

"Kaita!" I said again. "She is the weremage. And you knew. You knew! And you sent your ranger after her because you were afraid we would kill her."

The king's representative looked up at Ditra with a faint frown. "Rangatira, who under the sky is this man?"

Ditra ignored her. A flush crept up her neck into her cheeks as she stared at me. "How . . . how *dare* you—"

"How dare I?" I cried. I advanced to stand at the foot of the dais, and the king's representative hastily gave way before me. "You have the gall to ask how dare *I?* You are the Rangatira! You serve the king of Calentin and the High King of Underrealm. And you wanted to let a murdering witch escape justice just because you used to share her bed!"

Ditra's face went from crimson to nearly purple. She looked past me to Maia. "You allowed him in here? What were you thinking?"

I lifted my arm and dragged down my sleeve. The Telfer mark shone against my skin. Ditra stared at it for a moment, speechless. And then I saw recognition flash in her eyes as she looked upon my face. Emotions, one after another, played in her expression. Joy, I think, at seeing me again. Despair that I had discovered her secret. And then, slowly dominating the rest, a cold, mounting fury.

"You return here . . ." she said, the words grinding out of her like a blade on a whetstone. "You return after decades. *Decades.* You parade yourself in front of me, in plain sight but still skulking like a coward. And now you have the audacity to accuse *me?* Arrest them."

The guards began to come forwards.

"We are not your enemies," I said. "Kaita is. You know that, and yet you act to protect her. It is beneath you, Ditra."

"I am the *Lord* Telfer," she snapped, shooting to her feet. "Rangatira of Tokana and servant of the king of Calentin. You are nothing. You gave up any right to speak to me thus when you fled our home. And now you may sit in a cell until I figure out what to do with you."

"That would be a poor idea," said Mag, grip tightening on her spear.

I sagged. All my fury had flowed out of me in my outburst, and suddenly I was very tired. I lifted a hand towards Mag. "No. Do not harm her servants. They are only doing their duty." I glowered up at Ditra again. "Which is more than might be said of some."

While Ditra fumed, Mag spoke to me in a low voice. "Albern. I can keep us from going into a cell in the first place. But if she puts us there . . . no one can bend steel bars. Not even me."

"Then do what you must," I told her. "As for me, it seems I am going to be imprisoned." I raised my wrists, ready for the manacles that one of the guards had already pulled from a pouch.

Mag rolled her eyes and did the same. But she smiled at the guards as they bound her. "You should enjoy yourselves. One day you will be able to brag to your children about capturing the Uncut Lady."

Ditra now seemed to be trying to avoid looking at us. The king's representative now seemed almost amused. "Is this man your brother, Rangatira?" she said. "The one who—"

"Get out," growled Ditra. "I will send for you when I require you."

The representative looked affronted. "But we were discussing—"

"Get out!" roared Ditra. The representative jumped, and then she scurried out of the room like a chastised dog. The other councilors followed at her heels.

I had not looked away from Ditra, and just before her guards dragged us off, she met my gaze at last.

"We do not have endless time," I said, all anger gone from my voice. "You have . . . we have both made mistakes. Speak with me again, so that we can fix them. Do not wait too long."

Her scowl deepened, and she turned it upon the guards. "Take them away. Then go into the city and find that old man they came here with. He can join them in their cell."

The guards spun us around and marched us from the room. Maia gave me a rueful smile just before I passed out of the room.

THIRTY-FOUR

"THAT WAS VERY FOOLISH OF YOU," SAID SUN. "WALKING in there like that."

"It was," said Albern sadly. "I was young, then, and youth comes with many poor ideas."

"You were older than I am now!"

"Well, why do you think I keep such a careful eye on you?" When Sun scowled, he chuckled. "I am only joking. The truth is that it is easy to look back on our past actions—or the actions of others—and see how they were wrong. But we always think we are wise in the moment. No matter how old you get, you will always think you are smarter than you used to be. You will always look back at your younger years and marvel at what an idiot you were—but *now,* of course, you are wise, having learned so much more."

Sun shoved his shoulder. "I am not an idiot."

"And what about when you had seen only fifteen years?"

"Oh, sky above," said Sun, rolling her eyes. "That was different. You would not believe some of the things I got up to."

"And did you think you were a fool, then? Or did you think you were much wiser than you had been when you were ten?"

Sun opened her mouth to reply, but she could think of nothing to say. Her jaw snapped shut, and she glowered at him.

Albern shrugged. "I only tell you the truth as I know it. And I do not excuse myself. I can look back on the events I am telling you about and recognize what a hotheaded young fool I was. If I live another ten years, I am certain I will look back on today and feel the same way."

"Enough idle philosophy," said Sun grumpily. "Where are we going?"

They had passed back out beyond Lan Shui's northern gate, but the town was not yet far behind them. The sun was lowering, nearly kissing the top of the western spur, and just starting to shadow the land. She could see the line of its shade advancing towards them as night approached, a great darkness sweeping over the land. It was a chilling sight.

"Well, it seems there are some less-than-gentle folk plaguing Lan Shui again," said Albern. "This time, though, they seem to be operating somewhere outside the town's borders. We are not exactly certain where."

Sun frowned at him. "We?"

"Why, you and I," said Albern, cocking his head at her. "I apologize—I did not mean to dictate your own uncertainty to you."

"Oh no, please feel free," said Sun, arching an eyebrow. "So how do *we* mean to find them?"

"I do not know if you have heard, but I am something of a good tracker," said Albern. "A wagon was ambushed not far from here just the other day, and I think we will be able to find our foes' hideout by following the trail away from it."

"Why did we not see thc location of the attack when we approached Lan Shui?"

"There is more than one road leading into town. I wanted to see Dawan before I went to investigate the caravan."

"And who are these people, exactly?"

He sighed. "Hopefully they are bandits."

"You do not sound very hopeful."

"That is because I do not think they are bandits."

Sun gave a small but very frustrated growl. "What *do* you think they are?"

He seemed to be struggling for an answer, pursing

his lips and looking around, as though he was searching his own mind for the right words. When he did speak, it almost sounded as if he was ignoring her question. "Do you remember the tree from my youth? The tall kauri?"

"I . . . do," said Sun, confused.

"When I was young, I paid little attention to the lands of my home. I only watched the tree. It was always there. It changed slowly. It was a landmark, in more than one sense. Only when it was torn down was I finally able to look around and see how all the dale had changed around it.

"The people of Lan Shui are the same. In fact, most people are. If one thing remains the same—a tree, a nation, a king—and if that thing is important enough to them, they think the world is hardly changing at all. Until one day their landmark changes at last, and they realize that things have been happening all along that they paid little heed to. It can be helpful to focus on one thing, one place, one person more than the rest. It anchors us. It can help us find ourselves when the world seems too chaotic, too frightening. But we must remain at least brave enough to keep *looking* at the world beyond our landmarks, to ensure that no danger threatens them—and that the landmarks themselves are still as we imagine them to be."

"And what does this have to do with my question?" said Sun.

Albern pointed. "Look for yourself."

By the side of the road lay the remnants of a destroyed wagon. Sun had been so absorbed by Albern's words that she had not noticed it. The planks looked to be scored and gouged by weapons, and Sun saw at least three arrows sticking out of them. Worse, there were several dark streaks in the dirt of the road. Sun was certain they were blood.

Albern knelt to inspect the dark streaks. Then he went to the wagon, pacing all around it. At first he only looked without touching, but then he stepped closer, running his hand along the wood, peering closely at the grain, the gouges, the arrows. Sun did not know what he was looking at, but there was no hint of uncertainty in his movements.

Then he stopped short, eyes narrowing. He knelt and leaned under the wagon. When he emerged and stood, he held a small piece of brown cloth, hardly any bigger than his hand.

"What is that?"

"It *was* the wrapping of a small packet," said Albern, his tone grim. "They took what was inside."

"Or destroyed it."

"No, they took it." Albern pointed. "The attackers fled that way. Do you see their tracks there, leading off into the foothills of the Greatrocks?"

Sun stared at the spot. She could see nothing. She came to stand beside Albern, trying to view the spot from the same place.

"I do not see any such tracks," she said at last.

Albern sighed. "Mag never did, either. Come along."

He set off in the direction he had indicated. Sun trailed along behind him. It was only then that she realized Albern had not brought his horse from the Sunspear. She guessed that he had left it behind so that the noise of its hooves would not betray their position. She began to walk more slowly, trying to make her footfalls as quiet as she could.

Albern glanced back over his shoulder. "What are you doing?"

Sun felt a blush creep into her cheeks. "I am trying to be quiet. I thought that was why you left your horse behind."

Albern smiled. "It is, but such measures are not yet necessary. Our prey is still a fair distance away. We can talk, if you wish."

"I do," said Sun. "You keep hinting at these people and expecting me to assemble the hints into an answer. I would rather just hear it plain. Who are they? What are they after?"

Albern shook his head. "I am not trying to trick you or deceive you, but to teach you. However, if you wish for an answer, here is the best one I have. They do not have a name that I am aware of. But they have some purpose here. I think, but do not know, that it is something evil—more evil than mere banditry. But because they are hiding it, because it is happening in the shadows and the silence, no one in Lan Shui is paying too much attention. They think they face only bandits. Bandits, themselves, are their own sort of landmark in the lives of the people of Lan Shui. That is an evil they can face, and so they would rather believe in bandits than seek the truth. 'Only in watchfulness lies safety,' said a Mystic to me once. But people do not remain watchful forever, and when they lapse, darkness gathers."

"That is not exactly an answer," said Sun.

"I wish I had a better answer to give you," said Albern. "But failing that, I will continue the tale."

Dryleaf did not seem particularly annoyed when they brought him to our cell, which was a courtesy I had no right to expect of him. He settled quite easily down onto the bench against the back wall, resting against the stone with a sigh. I sat opposite him, on the ground, my back against the iron bars. A quick glance around had told me that the rest of the cells were empty. I took that as a good sign. Ditra did not seem overly fond of jailing people for little reason, it seemed. I wondered if my mother had been any different. I had never bothered to spend much time inspecting the dungeons.

"Well, this is all a great deal of foolishness," said Mag lightly. She stood at the other end of the iron bars from me, leaning against them with her arms crossed, as though she were awaiting a delivery of barley to her inn.

"Yes," I said.

"Unabashed, reckless foolishness."

"It is."

"Now, Mag," said Dryleaf kindly. "Do not be too unkind. Tomorrow is the first day of Yearsend, after all. A time for forgiveness."

"I find her words comforting, actually," I said. "It is when she gets quiet, or tries to treat me too delicately, that I grow worried."

"Then I suppose I retract my scolding."

"So your sister and the weremage used to bed each other, did they?" said Mag.

"They did," I said. "They were young. Kaita started as Ditra's retainer when she had seen only eighteen years, freshly returned from the Academy, and she is only a year or two older than Ditra. I cannot believe I did not recognize her in Northwood. There was a twinge at the back of my mind, but I never—"

"None of that," said Mag. "It was long ago. Your sister did not recognize you, her own brother. Why should you recognize someone you barely even knew?"

I shook my head slowly. "Mag, I . . . this means something."

"I know."

"No, I mean . . . in Northwood. We both thought Kaita was after you. We thought she bore some grudge against you, though we did not know what. But she was never after you. She was trying to get to me. When she attacked, I shoved you out of the way, and she killed Sten instead." I looked up at her, tears shining in my eyes. "But she was never aiming for you. It was me all along."

"I know," said Mag. "I worked that out for myself. I am actually rather clever, as well as being mighty."

"And humble," said Dryleaf.

"Sky above, Mag," I whispered. "I am so sorry."

"You should not be," she said brusquely. "Your actions change nothing. It was not your fault. I would have thrown myself in her path to protect you, and Sten would have done the same. And the only reason he died was that you were trying to protect me. None of us did anything wrong. No one but Kaita."

Her words were little comfort. I bowed my head into my hands.

"We had a sense that she was stringing us along," said Dryleaf quietly. "Now we know why. She wanted to draw you here. To your home, and hers. But why? Why not strike at us on the road?"

"Because of Mag," I said quietly, looking up.

Mag frowned. "Me?"

I nodded. "Do you remember that time we saved Victon from the bear in the jungle?"

Her frown deepened. "I do, but I fail to see what it has to do with anything."

"That, too, was Kaita."

Her eyes went wide. "How do you know?"

"You were confused by how it seemed to vanish. I was, too. It stuck in my mind, so that I still remember it all these years later. That was Kaita. I believe she turned into a raven and flew away, which is why the trail ended so. That was the first time she tried to kill me, I think. But you were there to protect me, and we remained by each other's side for years. She must have given up. And then one day she joined the Shades, and that must have occupied her time too much to think of hunting me down. But then, when she learned that we were together again, and in Northwood . . . she had the strength of an army behind her. She thought she could try again. But even then, you defeated her. She must have realized that she could not defeat you, that no human could. No *human.*"

"The trolls," said Dryleaf suddenly. "She hoped the trolls could do it."

"Sky above," breathed Mag. "And it seems she might be right. I was almost as helpless against the troll as you were."

That drew me just enough out of my dark mood to scowl at her. "If you will remember, it was I who wounded the troll."

She gave a dismissive wave of her hand. "I kept its attention so that you could."

"In any case," I said, soldiering on, "she knew she could lure us here, because I would not let her harm my family. And here, she has a chance of defeating you. Once you are out of the way, she can take her revenge on me at last."

"And your sister."

I frowned at her. "My sister?"

"Of course," said Mag. "If she only wanted to draw us into conflict with the trolls, she could have done that in the mountains farther south. But she and the Shades have driven the trolls into a war with the family Telfer. She cannot think your sister will emerge from such a conflict unscathed. Whatever grudge she bears against you, she includes Lord Telfer in it as well."

That detail had escaped me. But just as I was beginning to mull it over, there came the high squeak of a lock turning towards the front of the dungeon. I made my way to my feet as we heard boots approaching. Two of my family's guards appeared outside the cell, their faces grim. Behind them was Ditra.

"You wanted to talk," she said.

"Did you think you needed these guards?" I said, pointing to them.

"They are not for you," said Ditra. Her gaze shifted to Mag. "They are for her. We have heard of the Uncut Lady even this far to the north."

"Then you know your guards are useless," said Mag with a smile.

An angry flush crept up into Ditra's face, and I raised a hand to pacify Mag. "It is fine. Please, sit, and wait for my return." I glanced at Ditra. "Assuming I *will* return?"

"As long as you do not do anything stupid," she growled in irritation. "Stupider, I mean."

Mag shrugged and went to sit beside Dryleaf. The

guards unlocked the cell door, and I joined them in the hallway. We waited while they locked it again, and then I followed Ditra and her guards out of the dungeon.

THIRTY-FIVE

DITRA LED ME UP TO THE ENTRY HALL, AND THEN through the large door to her audience chamber. But she did not stop there. She took me to the back, to the doorway hidden behind a stone wall that led to a narrow stairway. I knew that stairway led up to her personal chamber. It had once been my mother's, and I had no fond memories of it. But I followed her up.

The two guards remained downstairs. But when we reached the upper hallway, I found Maia standing at the door to Ditra's chamber, his hands clasped behind his back. As I emerged from the stairwell, he gave me a nearly imperceptible nod. Ditra ignored him, striding through the door into her room. I paused for a moment.

"Will you be joining us?" I asked Maia.

"Do I need to?"

That made me deflate a bit. "Of course not. I would never harm her."

"So I thought," said Maia. "I will remain outside."

"Actually, you will fetch us some food and wine," said Ditra sharply. It appeared she had not entirely gotten over her annoyance at Maia for the earlier spectacle. After a moment she added, "And have some sent to the others in the cell, while you are visiting the kitchens."

"Of course, my lord," said Maia. He gave a little sigh and left.

I steeled myself. Painful memories swam to the forefront of my mind, of so many times I had stepped into this chamber and left it in despair, or in tears. But that had been a long time ago. I shook off my thoughts and stepped into the room, closing the door behind me.

To my surprise, Ditra had not taken her seat at the head of the table. Instead she leaned against the nearest edge of it, her hands probing its corner idly. The posture was so unlike our mother that for a moment I could see only the sister of my youth.

"So," she began. "Tell me about your friends. The truth, please, and not the lie you fed me earlier."

"Mag was my friend in the Upangan Blades," I said. "We have been close ever since. Dryleaf is an old man we found in Dorsea not long ago."

"Very well." She took a long breath and loosed it through her nose. "There is one matter we must tend to before any others. How are you?"

I stood there for a very long moment, and I am certain I had an utterly buffoonish look upon my face. When the words finally registered, I shrugged. "I . . . I am all right. I suppose."

Her jaw clenched, and she shook her head. "I mean after the wending."

Suddenly I realized what she was doing, and for a moment I could not speak. There is a conversation the family of an ander person is supposed to have with them after their wending, a ritual of long custom, stretching back to the time before time. She was having it with me now.

"Ditra, that was twenty years ago." I could barely choke the words out. My throat had grown tight.

Her nostrils flared. "And you were not here. How are you?"

I could not hold her gaze any longer. I stared at my feet and shook my head, feeling tears close to bursting. "I am fine," I whispered.

She came forwards and put her hands on my shoulders. "You look wonderful. Graceful. Like an adult, and not just for the grey in your hair. You were so very awkward as a child."

Still I could barely choke my answers out. "I had good reason to be."

From the corner of my eye I saw a smile on her lips, and I saw how sad it was. "You did. I wish to be certain—it is Albern now, correct?"

"It is."

"Albern," she said. "As your sister, I am overjoyed. Come, brother. For the first time, let me greet you as the man you are."

She took me into her arms, and I could not withhold myself any longer. I did not fall sobbing into her grip, as I had done to Mag when I learned of my mother's death. But still my tears slipped from me, and I held her hard, pressing my face into her shoulder, the way I had done so many times in my youth, when a nightmare had woken me in the middle of the night. And when at last we drew back, I saw tears shining in her eyes as well.

But then she took another step back, and I saw her emotions fade away, not unlike when Mag's battle-trance slid into place. In that moment she became not my sister, but the Lord Telfer, Rangatira of Tokana. I, too, pushed my emotions to the side.

"Now. I am not only your sister, Albern. I am lord of these lands, and it falls to me to protect them. What is Kaita doing here? And what brought you here to hunt her?"

"I have only guesses for the first question, though I can answer the second easily enough. I am here to kill her. And I know she wishes to kill me as well. But I think she came here because she wants to kill you, too."

Ditra frowned. "Me? What makes you think that?"

"Many things," I said. "Chief among them being the fact that she led me across three kingdoms to get here."

She shook her head. "Kaita is not trying to kill me."

I was flabbergasted. "You cannot be that naive," I said. Her eyes flashed, and I went on quickly. "Ditra, I know you and she used to share a bed on occasion, but that was—"

"It was more than some idle tryst," said Ditra. "She risked her life to be with me."

"She . . . she what?"

A knock sounded at the door. Maia opened it, bearing a tray with food and wine.

"Thank you," said Ditra briskly. "Give it to him, and then leave us be."

"Of course, Rangatira," said Maia. He gave us both a quick, surreptitious glance, but he did as his lord bid him. When the door closed again, Ditra motioned me over to the table. We both sat, the tray between us, but neither of us touched anything upon it.

"When you . . ." Ditra's nostrils flared again, and she took a moment to master herself. "When you left. Mother sent Romil to fetch you back. She sent Kaita along with her, as a retainer and a bodyguard. Of course, we both know that Romil failed. But on her journey back here to Tokana, she was attacked by Feldemarians. They killed Romil. Kaita tried to protect her, but she barely escaped with her own life. And when she finally returned home, Mother tried to have her executed."

"What?" I exclaimed. "Why?"

"For failing to protect Romil." Ditra's expression had gone dark. It was plain that she thought Mother's decision was wrong, even barbaric. "Mother was enraged. Kaita, who had barely survived the Feldemarian attack, was nearly killed again. But she escaped, and then she came to me, and asked me to leave with her, if you can believe it."

"She thought you would go with her?" I said. "What kind of fool did she—"

Ditra waved a hand in dismissal. "We were in love, Albern. Or we thought we were, the way people do at that age. But of course I told her not to be ridiculous. Mother's decision might have been wrong, but I would not betray our family. I promised I would keep her visit a secret, and then I told her to go."

I shook my head. It seemed I understood at last.

"Ditra," I said slowly, wondering how I could make her see it. "Kaita lost her position in our household because of me. And then she lost you, her lover, when she tried to run."

"She should not have had to run," said Ditra. "If I had been Rangatira, it would never have happened. What Mother did was evil. You should understand that better than most. Kaita was her victim, just as you were."

"You cannot fix all of Mother's wrongs," I said. "If you try, you will doom yourself. Mother was cruel to me, and it made my life miserable—but I shed her cruelty as soon as I could, and I purged it from my life. Kaita has taken that cruelty and made it her own. Now she means to tear the family Telfer down, to raze Tokana and leave no one here to contest her. It is part of the Shades' strategy in their war against the High King. But for Kaita, it is more than that. She is going to destroy everything we have, and she is going to use the trolls to do it. You have to stop her. You must let Mag and me help you."

"I did only my duty," said Ditra firmly. "Kaita was distressed. She might have thought, in the moment, that I would abandon my family, but she could not have truly believed it. This matter between the two of you is something else."

"She is a Shade," I said. "I have faced her on the battlefield. She is a high captain in their ranks. They are the ones behind the troll attacks."

Ditra's nostrils flared. "You did not know Kaita as I did. You barely knew her at all."

"Do you honestly think she still—"

"You never knew her, Albern," snapped Ditra. "You only cared about yourself when you lived here."

I felt my own anger rising to meet hers. "Well, someone had to."

"No!" Ditra's bark made me jump. She stood from her chair, planting her hands on the table as she leaned over me. "You do not get to speak to me that way. *Me,* of all people. Not after you abandoned your duty to our family."

I felt like a pouting child again, but I could not help the sullen expression on my face. "What duty is that?"

"You know what. Maia is a fine man, but you should be my lead ranger."

"I grew up thinking you would be lead ranger, and Romil would be the Rangatira after Mother."

"So you left because you would not have a title?" said Ditra, staring at me wide-eyed. "You were unsatisfied with—"

"I left because I had no reason to stay!" I snapped. "I had nothing here!"

"You had me."

"You were my sister," I said slowly, trying to master my temper. "Yes, we had each other. But Mother . . . Romil . . ."

"They are dead, Albern." Her voice caught. "They have been dead a long time. Yet you never came back."

I could scarcely speak above a whisper. "I did not know Mother had died until I stood in your council chamber a few days ago."

She dropped her gaze from mine and stepped away from the table. Scooping up her cup of wine, she went to the window, raising one arm to lean against it, picking with her nails at the diamond-shaped bolts that held the glass in place. "I know. We tried to send word, but we had lost track of you. And there was so much to do, so much expected of me . . ."

Her voice trailed away. I shifted in my seat. "You do not have to explain anything," I said. "You were—"

"Mother?"

I stopped, frowning. "What?"

She turned to me slowly. "You said you did not know about Mother."

My throat had gone dry. I tried to speak, but I could not.

"You said you did not know about *Mother,"* she said again, fury rising in her tone. "What of Romil? Did you know? Did you receive our letter?"

I could not meet her gaze. I took one of the goblets of wine from the tray and sipped it. "I did."

"You knew," said Ditra, her voice toneless, like Mag's trance. "You knew your sister had died. Yet you stayed away."

"Whose sister?" I demanded. "How was she my sister? She did not help me. She did not comfort me. She did not care a whit whether I lived or died."

"She was our sister regardless," said Ditra. "Or do you think that Thada was not our mother?"

"I do not know what she was to you, after I left. She was never a mother to me."

Ditra scoffed. "You are being ridiculous. She raised us, she—"

"Raised us? What does that mean to you? She never even noticed my existence until she needed me. Until I was *useful* to her." I spat the word. "She never cared about anything we did, anything we wanted, unless it was in her service. You have seen this already."

I lifted my arm and dragged down my sleeve again to show the family mark. Ditra's sleeve was tighter than mine, but she ripped it open to show her own mark.

"We both have one," she said. "But I have not forgotten what mine means, as you have."

"You were away when she gave me the mark," I said. "It was during the same trip you were on when I left. Mother decided it was time for me to receive it, whether I wanted it or not. And indeed, I did not want it. So she forced me. She summoned soldiers and had them *hold me down* so she could carve it into my skin herself. When I fought, she slapped me. No, she was never a mother to me. You were the closest thing I ever had to that."

But that only made the dam burst. Ditra seized the tray of food and threw it against the wall.

"And I *needed* you, Albern!" she screamed. "I had *no one.* No one at all. When Romil died, do you think Mother was there to comfort me? Do you think she took care of me? Consoled me? Do you think she even gave me the cold comfort of allowing me to weep in her presence? After we laid Romil to rest, she called me to this chamber. Do you know what she said? 'You will be my new lead ranger, of course. Someone will be along to show you your duties.' Then she dismissed me. That was all. What did you think would happen? Did you think she would see the evil of her ways, and finally love me the way she always should have? You have never been that great of a fool."

I could not answer. I had no answer to give. This was the true burden of guilt that had hung over me all the long years since I left home. This was what I had never been able to tell anyone, not even Mag. I knew Romil had died, and I knew I should have gone home—not for myself, and certainly not for Mother, but for Ditra. So that she would not be alone.

Ditra's fury now was more than I could bear. I cast my gaze to the floor, unable even to look at her.

She straightened. "I am done with you. Tell Maia to return you to your cell."

You might think it was a strange command—ordering someone to have themselves put back in prison. But I did it. I rose, left the room, and said nothing as I let Maia lead me back to my friends.

THIRTY-SIX

Dotag came to speak with Gatak again that night. They were on a ridge towards the north end of the Kahaunga valley. Gatak had found another cliff to sit on, a place to look out over the lowlands, a place with a good view of the city. Dotag strutted up to her, puffing his chest and rolling his shoulders. Gatak did not look at him right away. Her gaze was fixed on the smoke of the humans' city.

Close now. So close.

After a moment of waiting for Gatak to look at him, to no avail, Dotag finally spoke. "It is nearly done," he boasted. "No humans still dwell in the mountains. Only in their valley. I have sent the gifts we stole from them to other packs, and many of them have joined us. We are ready."

Gatak looked over at last. "Are you?"

"We are many. We are strong. Their homes will not stand before us. They will flee. Any who stand and fight will die."

"Then I hope none of them try to flee," said Gatak. "I hope you kill them all."

Dotag showed just a bit of his teeth. Gatak stepped closer and pressed her forehead to his. They both closed their eyes for a moment and shared a breath. When they pulled back, Dotag's ears were back in pleasure, and he viewed her with a hungry look in his eyes.

But she had other things to see to.

"I must go for now," she said.

Dotag's face fell, and his ears came back up. "Go?" he said. "Go where?"

"To speak with the Lord," she said. "And to ensure our victory."

"We will win," insisted Dotag. "The humans cannot stop us."

"I believe you," said Gatak. "Do not worry. I will return soon."

"You said that before," said Dotag. "You did not come back for a long time."

Gatak lowered her ears and pressed her head into his chest. "A few months are nothing. There are many years ahead of us. But I will not be gone that long this time. I promise I will return to you before the attack."

Dotag seemed comforted at that—and at the feeling of her pressing into him. "You vow it?"

"I vow it," she said. "Watch for my return."

She made her long, slow climb down the cliff. She hated coming down. It always took so much longer than climbing. But it was worth it to view the world from those lofty heights—not as high as a bird, but with solid ground underneath you, like a throne from which you could view the world far below your feet.

Gatak reached the bottom and lumbered off into the darkness, to a place she knew was well out of sight of Dotag, where no troll had any hope of seeing her.

Once she was certain she was alone, her eyes began to glow.

Her form shrank. Her limbs grew slim. Tight clothing sprang from where it had been wrapped deep within her form.

Kaita emerged into the night. She took a deep breath of the air, reveling in her returned sense of smell. Trolls could smell almost nothing, and she always felt like she had a wolf's nose after she resumed human form.

But she had little time to enjoy herself. Her eyes glowed again. She took her raven form and flapped up into the air. The mountain winds were with her, and in no time she had reached the Shade encampment. They had set themselves up in rows of tents, buried deep in the mountains where few had any hope of finding them. Even rangers would not have drawn near to the camp, for the trolls were between them and the city.

She landed in their midst and resumed her human form again. A wave of fatigue struck her, but she shrugged it off. There was a moment's shock among the Shades, but it did not last long. Their commander's habits were well known, and they relaxed as soon as they recognized her. Phelan stepped up, bowing low before her.

"Order everyone to be ready," said Kaita. "The trolls will attack soon. When they do, we shall fight beside them."

"Of course, Commander," said Phelan. "We are prepared to strike at a moment's notice."

"And the special team I tasked you with putting together?"

Phelan hesitated. "They, too, are prepared. Eleven of our best soldiers. They will infiltrate the keep and kill every Telfer they can."

Kaita fixed him with a look. "You have doubts?"

"The Telfer keep is well defended, Commander. I worry for the success of their mission. But I have faith in your plan."

"You should," said Kaita. "I myself will be on that mission."

His eyes widened. "That is too dangerous."

"It is necessary," said Kaita. "I know the keep. I

know all of its secret ways, the passages in and out. Do not trouble yourself over my safety. The Telfers are the ones who should be worried."

"As you say, Commander." Phelan did an admirable job of trying to hide his doubt. He bowed again and left her.

Kaita spent a little while longer patrolling the camp, ensuring that everything was prepared and that her soldiers were ready for the battle. Finally she accepted that things were as prepared as they were going to be, and she made her way to a tent to sleep. But she lay awake a long time, staring at the top of her tent, fingers playing at her braid in the darkness and listening to the gentle nighttime sounds of the camp.

Close now. So close.

Maia led me back to my cell. But when we reached it, I found a surprise. Mag stood against the bars, her arms passed through them and her wrists manacled. Two guards were moving a mattress into the cell.

I looked at Mag. "What did you do?"

"Nothing," she said, sounding almost disappointed. "Dryleaf said his cot was too hard for his old back. He asked for a softer mattress, and the guards would only provide it if I let them truss me up. I agreed for his sake."

"And I cannot tell you how much I appreciate it,"

Dryleaf piped up from the back of the cell. He sat on the cot, smiling broadly, as the guards wrestled the new mattress in and placed it on the floor to the right.

Mag studied my face. She must have noticed my red, puffy eyes, for she frowned. "You look a bit worse for wear. Did she hurt you?"

She had, of course, though not in the way that Mag meant. So I forced a chuckle. "We did not have a brawl in her chambers, if that is what you mean."

"Hm," said Mag.

Dryleaf found his way to his feet as he heard the guards retreating from the cell. He probed at the air, and when he found one of them, he patted her on the back. "Thank you again, very kindly. It is good to see that even in dire times, the hospitality of Calentin knows no bounds."

"That is kind of you to say," said the guard. She looked a little ashamed, as if she had not expected her duties to include imprisoning such an old and frail man.

"Not as kind as you have been," said Dryleaf, his smile widening.

Once they had left the cell, I walked myself in. Maia shut the door behind me, and when I turned, I saw that he was eyeing me carefully. But he said nothing as the guards locked the door again, and he turned to go, along with one of the guards. The woman Dryleaf had spoken to went to unbind Mag's wrists.

"Thank you for not making this difficult," she said.

"Think nothing of it," said Mag. "I told you it was for the old man's sake."

The guard smiled and unlocked the manacles. She glanced up the hallway where Maia and the other guard had retreated. When she spoke again, her voice was soft. "I . . . I wanted to let you know. I have heard many tales of you, and I know you are no evil person. I hope the Lord Telfer does not treat you too harshly. She is a fair woman."

"You would know better than I," said Mag with a smile.

The woman stepped a bit closer. "I heard a story once . . . is it true that you once held a breach in a keep wall for four hours, alone?"

Mag's smile dampened. "It is. That was not a good day. I was only alone because all my companions had died."

The woman's face fell at once. "I . . . I am sorry to bring an old grief to mind."

"Do not trouble yourself." Mag smirked. "And, if I may offer a word of advice?"

She had not yet pulled her hands back within the cell. Now she seized the front of the girl's shirt—quickly, but gently.

"You are a little too close. I could seize you, smash your head into the bars, and steal the keys to escape."

The girl's face flamed as Mag let go of her shirt and gave her a little pat on the cheek. "I . . . will keep that in mind. But I do not think you would do such a thing." She reached to put the manacle keys on her belt—and then she frowned. "Dark take me. It would not have helped you, anyway. I must have put the cell key somewhere . . ."

She froze and looked up at Mag suspiciously. Mag smiled broadly and raised her hands.

"You took all my pouches. I could not hide a key on myself if I wanted to."

The guard sighed and rolled her eyes. "Very well. I believe you. I wish I could say this was the first time I had lost it." With a rueful shake of her head she left us, grumbling under her breath.

"They brought you food?" I asked, once she had gone.

Dryleaf nodded. "They did. And fine fare it was, for a prison. It was when they brought our meal that I asked for the mattress. Thank you for seeing to our arrangements."

"I did nothing," I told him. "Ditra thought of it on her own."

He nodded. "It is as the girl said—she sounds like a fair woman."

"She is, I suppose," I said. "Though just now she is trying a bit too hard to be like our mother."

"That displeases you, I gather."

"My mother was a hard woman. So hard, for so long, that she forgot how to be gentle. And that is all I wish to say about her for the moment."

Dryleaf nodded. I went and sat on the floor by the

cell door, just where I had rested the last time I was in here. Mag, too, resumed her position, leaning against the other end of the bars. But when I glanced up, I found her studying me. I did not wish to speak with her any more than with Dryleaf, so I avoided her gaze.

"This is a nice jail," said Dryleaf, not seeming to mind our silence. "I have been in far worse."

That drew me somewhat out of my dark thoughts. "You? In jail? What for?"

"I assure you, only for other misunderstandings like this one," he said, chuckling. "I may be old now, but I have gotten myself into a great deal of trouble under many names. Good people end up in prison all the time. Some of my most popular stories are about just that thing."

"Well, let us hope that your luck holds out," said Mag, "and that this trip to a cell is no worse than your previous ones."

"No, indeed," said Dryleaf. "Already it is a good deal more pleasant. Fear not, my lord of Telfer. I have a feeling this will all work itself out in the end."

"I am not the Lord Telfer," I said quietly, turning away from him.

THIRTY-SEVEN

DITRA SAT IN HER CHAMBER A LONG WHILE AFTER I left. She stared long out the window, at the gentle snows that fell outside it, into the darkness that was gathering to the north. Then she roused herself and went to bed. The tray of food lay where she had cast it on the floor, untended.

She went through her morning the next day in a dark mood. Again and again she tried to put me from her mind, but again and again her thoughts returned to me. She could sense it affecting her decisions, creating long silences before she realized someone had spoken to her, and that she had to answer. It was hard to concentrate, hard to focus.

During her midday meal, she finally threw her knife down onto her plate and abandoned her pathetic attempt to eat.

She rose and went to the door of another chamber down the hall, knocking at it twice.

"Yes?" came a soft voice from inside.

Ditra opened the door. Her daughter sat at a desk across the room, her quill out, a stack of parchment in front of her. She had been copying from a tome of history recently—a pursuit Ditra did not particularly understand, but it took up her daughter's time and kept her from getting underfoot, for which Ditra was grateful.

"Mother," she said, beaming. She rose and ran to her in the doorway, throwing her arms around Ditra's waist.

"I have not been able to visit you of late," said Ditra, trying to maintain a regal tone. "I thought we could speak for a moment, in this brief calm between storms."

"Storms?" Her daughter looked up into her face. "Is something the matter?"

"You have heard about the attacks in the mountains," said Ditra sternly. "It ill behooves you to play at ignorance, V-Vera."

Ditra stumbled over the name, her throat suddenly dry. It had been my name, of course, before my wending. She had meant it as a tribute to me, especially because she had not known I was ander. But it seemed a poor decision now.

Vera, for her part, looked chastised. It hurt Ditra to see it, but she steeled herself. She had not even been particularly harsh. Vera would need to withstand much worse than this, when she one day took Maia's place as lead ranger, after he became Rangatira.

"Come," said Ditra. "Sit."

She guided Vera back to her chair by the desk, and then she sat on the girl's bed. For a moment they waited there in silence, both staring at their hands, which each of them had folded in their lap. The silence drew on, long past awkwardness and into discomfort.

"Do you . . . do you want to be a ranger, Vera?"

Vera looked up at her, eyes wide. "Why, yes, Mother. Of course. You know that."

"You have said so," said Ditra. "But I have often told you that it is what I expect. I mean to ask . . . do you *want* to be a ranger? Would you, if I were not Lord of Tokana?"

It was clear the girl had not considered it before. Now she frowned and looked away, her eyes growing distant. "I think so. All of our rangers are certainly very dashing. And I am always happiest out in the wilderness." She flushed and looked quickly at Ditra. "I do not mean to say I am not happy here—"

Ditra forestalled her with a raised hand. "I understand what you mean." *Better than you can know.* "Go on."

Vera frowned again, and she began to twist her hands. "I have never fought before, of course. I like my training, but I do not enjoy the thought of . . . of killing. But I know we never do it without reason."

Do we not? thought Ditra. *I always thought Mother was too careless of others' lives.*

She closed her eyes and steeled herself. *Enough.* She had become a confused mess, and she would not serve her people well in this state.

"There have been some . . . arrivals, to the keep," she said to Vera.

"Guests?" said Vera, frowning.

"No," said Ditra. "Prisoners. They may be here on dishonorable business." The words tasted bitter in her mouth. Even she barely believed them.

"I cannot remember the last time we had prisoners in the dungeons," said Vera, her voice suddenly small.

Ditra could not help a snort of laughter. "I could not have said that when I was your age."

Vera smiled at Ditra's laughter, brief and grim though it was. She had always loved it when they laughed together, and loved it all the more for how rare it was.

"I . . . I have something I think I should tell you," said Ditra. "But it is a long tale, and a difficult one. Do you remember—"

A horn sounded. Ditra shot to her feet.

"Mother?" said Vera.

"Stay here," said Ditra. She almost left, but at the last moment she stopped. Turning, she embraced Vera, holding her tight. "Be strong. I will return when I can."

She ran from the room. A door at the end of the hall led her into a passageway onto the walls. Soldiers of her house started in surprise as she emerged into the open and marched down the ramparts. She stopped at the first person she saw—and suddenly she realized that she knew the woman. It was Whetu, the former ranger whose family had narrowly escaped their village's destruction a few weeks before.

"Whetu," she said, nodding. "I am somewhat surprised to see you here."

"Rangatira," said Whetu, bowing with a fist to her forehead. "It seemed clear things would come to a fight before long. I took up your service again, for that seemed better than waiting idly for the trolls to come to us."

"Maia assigned you?"

"He did, Rangatira," said Whetu.

Ditra's mouth gave a wry twist. Maia had not mentioned it, but then, he had been rather preoccupied lately. "I am glad you are here. I am assigning you to guard my daughter's chamber. Find two others on your way and bring them with you, on my authority."

"Yes, Rangatira," said Whetu. "No harm will come to her."

Ditra nodded and walked on while Whetu ran to do her bidding. Ditra stalked up to the short tower overlooking the east gatehouse, and there she found Maia.

"Report."

Maia turned at the sound of her voice, and though he kept a passive expression, Ditra could see the relief in his eyes. He was obviously struggling to maintain his customary good humor, but it was overpowered by a worry he could not entirely hide.

"Rangatira," he said. "Trolls have gathered at the north end of the dale."

Ditra suppressed a shudder. They had all known that Kahaunga was the trolls' eventual aim, but her scouts had guessed that any attack would not come for several more days. Ditra had thought they would have more time—time for the king's reinforcements to arrive, time to work out another solution. Time to find and eliminate the Shades, mayhap.

A thought came to her briefly that that might have happened, if she had ordered Maia to work with us, as he had wished to. But she quashed that thought immediately. This was a time for action, not doubt.

"How many?"

"Many," said Maia. "More than two hundreds."

Ditra's eyes shot wide. "Two *hundreds?*" She realized that soldiers all around them were staring at her, and she forced her expression back to one of impassive calm. "What are they doing?"

"They are holding their position for now," said Maia. "But they may only be waiting until they finish gathering their forces." He paused. "I did not even know there were that many in the mountains."

"Of course there are," she snapped. "The Greatrocks stretch for hundreds of leagues."

"I mean the mountains of Tokana," said Maia. "We have never glimpsed a pack even a fraction of this size."

"Why would you? They have always observed the pact. They have kept to themselves for more generations than the years in your life."

"That seems to have changed."

Ditra frowned slightly. "And we will deal with it."

Maia paused, glancing around. Ditra was grateful that at least he, too, was aware that everyone was watching them, and that morale might depend a great deal on the words the others heard them speak. He leaned close and dropped to a whisper.

"I respect that you must keep a strong front, Rangatira," he said. "But are you not worried? Should we not retreat?"

Ditra leaned on the wall and looked into the dale far below. The mountains hid the northern end of it from this position, but she could almost imagine them there, gathering, milling about.

Preparing to sweep down upon her people and kill them all.

"We do not retreat," she said loudly. "Kahaunga is our home."

Maia looked frustrated, but still he kept his voice low. "A corpse is not comforted that it lies in the same place it dwelled when alive. We cannot hope to hold against a pack so large."

Ditra looked to him. "Do you not see?" she said, lowering her voice to match his. "It is too late for that. Kahaunga is not only our home, it is our best hope. We can defend ourselves on these walls. If we retreat, and they attack us on the road, we will be helpless. We will fight here, and we will win here, or we will die here."

He looked away, eyes flicking back and forth as he surveyed the dale. "What if we order an evacuation of the most vulnerable? Tell all those who cannot fight to leave, while the rest of us hold off the trolls to cover their retreat."

Ditra considered it. The Telfer stronghold could hold a third of the city at most, and that would be an exceptionally tight fit. There would be folk on cots in the cells of her dungeon.

The dungeon. Mag and I crossed her mind. She forced the thought away.

"Do it," she said. "Everyone in Kahaunga who can pick up a weapon must join us here in the stronghold, especially those who can shoot. We will hold against the trolls as long as we can. All other citizens must make for the pass west out of the mountains."

He straightened, relief plain on his face. "Yes, Rangatira." He turned to the others. "You heard her. Order the evacuation."

Ditra turned her attention back to the city below. *This is why Mother was so cold,* she thought. *One must be hard to be a Telfer.*

But as she saw Maia looking at her out of the corner of his eye, she felt a flicker of doubt that she did not think our mother ever had.

Dotag stood on a hillock, observing the trolls as they gathered before him.

Two hundreds. No one had ever commanded a pack so large.

He felt nervous. He felt sick. A doubt was in him now, one he could no longer suppress. No one had ever commanded this many trolls—and no trolls had ever attacked human lands, as they were about to do. Not since the days trolls first came into these mountains.

That should have been a comforting thought—that he was following in the footsteps of his ancient forefathers. But it only made him more nervous, increasing his misgivings until he felt as though he wanted to vomit.

He looked down and saw Apok. She was staring up at him, not moving, not blinking. His doubt increased tenfold, fear creeping in at the edges of it. He thought of Chok's broken body as he dragged it out of the Shade stronghold, and quickly he tried to think of something else.

Then a commotion caught his attention. As the

trolls milled about, moving in great swirls and spreading out across the open turf, a path opened between them. Down that path lumbered Gatak. Trolls gave way before her, and the pack closed again behind her. She was headed straight towards Dotag's hillock.

All of Dotag's fears vanished in an instant. Gatak had come. Just as she had said she would.

Mayhap everything else she had promised would come true as well.

Gatak joined him on the hillock. She turned back and looked over the trolls. They covered the ground, a small plateau at the northern end of the Kahaunga valley.

"I thought there would be more," she said, sounding vaguely disappointed.

Dotag felt somewhat crestfallen. "We are enough. We will drive the humans out. And then all the mountains will be ours."

Gatak turned to him, her ears rising in anticipation. "Then do it."

We had spent an uncomfortable night in our cell—or at least, Mag and I had. Dryleaf, of course, had his mattress. But his snoring had kept the two of us awake, which had not been helped by our hard cots. I understood why the old man had complained. I had spent much of the day dozing, trying to gain what extra rest I could.

But I shot awake when the horns sounded.

"What was that?" said Mag, looking towards the ceiling.

"You have never heard horns before?" I said.

"Is it the trolls?"

"It has to be."

We sat in silence. I did not know what to do. Dryleaf bowed his head with a frown, seeming deep in thought. My hands clenched into fists and then relaxed, over and over. Mag's gaze wandered as though she was considering something, replaying events in her head.

A door crashed open at one end of the hallway, and a guard rushed past us. At the last moment I recognized her as the one who had spoken to Mag yesterday.

"Wait!"

She skidded to a halt, looking at us with wide, frightened eyes. "I cannot—"

"What is happening?" I said, gripping the bars.

"Trolls," she said. "They have gathered in the dale to attack the city."

"How many?"

Her face went a shade paler. "Many."

"Let me out," said Mag. "You know who I am. My friend here is just as remarkable."

I thought privately that that was a tremendous lie, but I was not going to countermand her just then. The guard hesitated. But she shook her head. "I cannot. I am sorry."

"But if you—"

She ran on, rushing through the door at the other end of the hall.

Dryleaf sighed and stood. He shuffled towards the two of us, hand outstretched. "It sounds as though things are getting most dire. I suspect the Lord Telfer could use the two of you."

I slammed my hand against the cell bars. "She could, though she will never admit it."

Dryleaf pulled a key from his sleeve. Mag and I froze. He groped the air for a moment before finding the door handle. Reaching through the bars, he inserted the key and turned it.

Click

The door swung open.

Dryleaf held the key up, dangling it before us.

"I took it when the guards brought the mattress. You should return it to them on your way out."

Mag could barely contain herself. "Why under the sky did you not tell us this before," she growled. It was far more of an accusation than a question.

Dryleaf frowned and held up an admonishing finger. "The guards brought me my mattress because I was old and infirm and blind. It is not right to betray the kindness of anyone who would do that, even if they are imprisoning one. Unless, of course, one does so to save their lives. Just as I am doing now."

Mag and I stared at him. "You have a very strange sense of right and wrong, old man," I said.

Dryleaf's frown cracked, becoming a grin. "I suppose some might think so. Take care of yourselves. I believe I will remain here. The mattress is *very* comfortable."

We rushed out of the cell and down the hall where the guard had gone. Mag threw the door open to the small guard room. At the other end, the guard stood by another door leading up into the keep. She stared at us, frozen in shock.

"We are going to help in the fighting," said Mag matter-of-factly. "And if you give us back our weapons, we will be much better at it."

The girl's mouth opened and then closed again. Her hand twitched as if to reach for her weapon, but she looked at Mag and thought better of it. Finally she sighed and pointed to a wooden locker across the room.

"They are in there," she said. From her pocket she fished a small iron key and threw it into my hand. "At least I did not lose *that* key."

THIRTY-EIGHT

We emerged into the stronghold's main bailey to find chaos.

A mass of people had pressed into a great throng before the keep doors. When I first emerged into the open, I thought they were pressing forwards, seeking safety in the keep itself. But after a moment I realized that these did not look like refugees. They were young and hale people, and they were listening attentively to commands shouted at them by Telfer soldiers in armor, standing on whatever platform they could find, desperately barking orders.

Mag seized the arm of a passing guard. "Where is the battle?" she demanded.

The guard stopped looking her up and down for a moment. "In the city, of course," she said.

"The dale?" I said.

"Yes. Lord Telfer led her forces into the streets. They are trying to slow the trolls' advance while the rest of the city escapes."

"If these people are trying to escape, why do they look like they are forming for battle?" I said.

"These ones are," she said. "Everyone who can fight has been commanded to do so. The rest are taking the western pass out of the mountains."

I took Mag's arm. "To the city with us, then."

We ran for the main gate. It stood open, and more people were still pushing their way through. We had to force our way through the crowd. Mag led the way, for as with so many things, she seemed to have a particular knack for threading through the mass. But once we were in the open again, we stopped to take in the sight before us. A mass of people was making its way up from the dale, clogging the roads. When they reached the Telfer stronghold, they split into three columns, one passing in through the gate, and the two others curling around it to keep traveling west.

"I wish we had our horses," said Mag.

"They would not help us," I said. "We cannot ride through the crowd and trample these people, and besides, they would bolt at the first sign of the trolls. I will take us on the side streets."

A peal of overjoyed barking drew our attention. We turned to see Oku streaking towards us. He leaped around our feet, yapping and licking our hands and then retreating to bark some more.

"We are glad you are here as well, Oku," I said. "Even Mag."

"Hm," said Mag, who had scratched Oku behind the ears just as much as I had, though she tried to look aloof while she did it. "Let us not waste any more time. If our last tumble with the trolls was any indication, your sister is not having an easy time of it."

I nodded and led the way into the city. We avoided the main roads, and I took them down any side streets I could remember. But even those avenues were full of people, Kahaunga natives who knew their way better than I did and who wanted to escape. We pressed through them as quickly as we could.

It was quite clear when we reached the battle at last.

We slid to a halt in the center of a wide square as a roar ripped through the air. Mag lifted her spear, and I raised my bow. A squadron of Telfer soldiers came pelting into view, fear on their faces.

A troll was just behind them.

I fired as Mag leaped to the attack. My arrow bounced from the troll's shoulder. It did not so much as flinch. But it did stop in its pursuit of the soldiers and focused on Mag, who stood firm before it, her feet wide, her weapon ready. Oku joined her, bristling and growling.

"Albern," called Mag. "Do you have any ideas?"

"Try not to die."

The troll snarled and swung for her. Mag dived to the side. Oku snapped at the troll's massive fist, but darted out of the way as it pressed forwards.

I turned to the soldiers. They had stopped in their flight and now stood in a cluster around me, staring in wonder at the sight of Mag facing the troll with only a wolfhound to join her.

"Oil! Who has oil?"

One of the soldiers blinked at me as though she did not understand. But finally she pulled a flask of it from her belt. "This is the last one we have."

"Someone give me a torch!" I barked.

"We lost them," said one of the soldiers. "We would not have retreated if we had fire."

Growling in frustration, I spared a glance for Mag. She had the troll chasing her all around the square, always staying just out of its grasp. Her flight looked desperate, but I could not tell if she was merely leading it on. Oku trailed behind the troll, sometimes snapping at its ankles, but he did not distract it at all.

"We have to get fire," I said. "Now."

"The . . . the buildings," said a soldier. "Some are—"

I looked past him. To the north, where the battle

was thickest, smoke rose into the air. I shoved the flask of oil into his hand.

"Land this on that troll," I said. "Do not miss."

Several of them had arrows wrapped with pitch-covered rags. I snatched two up and sprinted for the smoke.

Three houses down, I found one with flames licking at the outer wall. I thrust the arrows into the flames, and they caught at once. Turning, I sprinted back for the square.

The troll no longer pressed Mag so closely, but I soon saw why. The soldiers had fanned back out around the two of them, trying to distract it so the one with the flask could throw it. Two had been killed. Their bodies lay at the edges of the square, limbs twisted at odd angles.

I readied one of the arrows. "Do it!" I roared.

The soldier looked back at me. In his terror, he almost dropped the flask.

"Now! What are you waiting for?"

He looked ready to faint. But he turned and threw.

The flask sailed over the troll's head. It shattered against a distant wall, the oil splattering over a square area three paces wide.

The soldier turned to look back at me in horror. I was just as shocked as he was.

"It is the size of a house!" I cried. "How could you miss?"

His limbs shook, but he gave no reply.

"All right, all of you, get out," I commanded. "If you can, find another unit and join them. If you cannot, retreat to the keep."

They ran to do as I ordered, scooping up their fallen comrades and carrying them off. I still held my arrow ready, but the flame was useless now. It would not pierce the troll's hide, and without oil, I could not hope to catch it in a blaze.

Mag's desperate turns and dodges were bringing her closer to me with every step. I edged backwards. I could not abandon her to fight alone, but I was out of ideas. In the heat of battle, I could not hurt the troll any more than Mag could, and neither could I dodge its wild blows as well as she.

She glanced over and seemed to notice me for the first time. "Where is the oil?" she called out, ducking the troll's huge fist as it whirled through the air where her head had just been.

"All over that building," I said, pointing. "The fool missed."

Mag had to leap backwards as the troll's hands crashed into the street with a punishing blow. "He *missed?"* she cried. "It is as big as a house!"

"I told him."

She looked over at the building again, and then at me. The troll paused for a moment, eyes narrowing, looking for an opening.

"Light it," said Mag.

The troll snorted and stepped forwards.

"What?" I said, incredulous.

"Light it!" she said, running for the building. The troll screamed in rage as it went after her.

I understood almost too late. Raising the bow, I drew. The flames danced in front of my eyes, almost obscuring Mag with waves of heat. She skidded to a stop in front of the building and turned to face the troll head-on. It was in a full charge now, thundering straight for her.

I loosed. Mag dodged aside at the last possible moment.

The troll and the arrow hit the oil at the same time.

Flames erupted all over the building, just as it collapsed inwards with a crash that shook the ground. Oil from the timbers spread all over the troll's body, covering it with flames. The troll's furious roaring turned to panicked bleats of fear. It slapped at itself, trying to put out the flames. But the folk of Tokana had had centuries to perfect their craft, and the oil continued to burn.

Shrieking in terror, the troll turned and ran from the square. Mag looked very much as though she wanted to pursue it, but she stayed put. The building continued to burn, the flames gradually climbing higher until the roof caught as well.

"Are you all right?" I said.

"It did not touch me. Some of your sister's soldiers were not so fortunate."

"Speaking of which," I said, "we should get moving. The battle goes on without us."

Mag nodded, and we turned to head north. But suddenly there came the sound of tramping feet down the city street towards us. A company of Telfer soldiers came into view. They were not exactly running, but they were clearly in retreat. At their head was Ditra. Her face was smudged with soot and sweat, and there was an ugly cut on her cheek. Her armor was dented in several places, and I thought I detected a limp in her step.

Her steps faltered as she caught sight of us, and the company ground to a halt. I could see the fury rising in her, and her hand tightened on her axe.

"What in the dark below—"

"We heard there was a battle," I said. "I thought you might be able to use us."

"You broke out?" she said. "Who did you—"

"We harmed no one, I promise you," I said.

"And we just saved a squadron of your soldiers," added Mag.

Ditra's gaze flashed to her. "What?"

"A troll pursued them into this square," I said. "Mag held it off while I used oil and fire upon it."

Sheer shock seemed to wipe the anger from Ditra's face. "You faced a troll alone?"

I watched as Mag struggled not to look haughty, and she almost succeeded. "You said you have heard of me."

A crash sounded from behind the soldiers—a fair distance away, but not far enough for comfort. Ditra glanced back for a moment, and when she turned back, there was a resigned look upon her face.

"If you are willing to aid our fight against the trolls, I suppose I cannot turn you away," she said. "But you will do exactly as my officers and I command, when we command it."

"Of course." I bowed low, and then remembered my decorum. "Rangatira."

"Then follow us. We are pulling back to the stronghold."

"But the trolls—" Mag began.

"Mag," I said. She stopped short. "Do as she says."

She cocked her head, and the corner of her lips twisted. She nodded to Ditra. "Very well, Rangatira."

Ditra nodded and started off, and we fell into step beside her. "We cannot stop the trolls in the city," she said. "We have given our people enough time to flee to the keep, if they mean to fight, or to the pass, if they do not. Our duty now is to consolidate our forces and hold the trolls."

"How long do you mean to hold them?" I said.

Her eyes were grim. "As long as we can."

Dotag stood in the middle of the burning city, his chest heaving, his breath coming out in loud snorts that turned to mist in the air. The humans had fled from their city. He had walked such a long road to get here, and now it was almost over. He could hardly have dreamed that he would be here one day, standing triumphant among the wreckage of the humans' homes, leading a pack greater than any troll had ever commanded.

He roared, throwing his head back and slamming his fists into his chest. Several trolls around him recoiled at the sound of his voice, but when they saw him celebrating their victory, they raised their voices in chorus with his.

At last he subsided as one of the trolls brought him a handful of crops pillaged from one of the human's homes. It was only the first of many tributes he would receive tonight. With a pack of two hundreds, Dotag could hardly imagine the mountain of goods that would be brought before him, for him to pick and choose from, sharing the tastiest morsels with—

Dotag stopped. His brows drew together, lowering over beady eyes as he swung back and forth, searching his surroundings.

Where had Gatak gone?

THIRTY-NINE

We made our way to the stronghold and found the gates open. Ditra's company was the last to return, and the guards on the wall looked relieved when she ordered them to close the gates after we had entered. She had ordered the rest of her troops to divide and make their way back through the city piecemeal, like the squadron we had rescued before meeting her. The rangers had held the trolls off as long as they could to give the rest time to get away.

The moment we had entered the keep, Ditra

turned to Maia. "Summon my councilors to the audience chamber immediately."

"At once, Rangatira." Maia gave us a half-smile and a quick nod before darting off to do as she said. It left the three of us standing in the center of the bailey, crowds milling around us, while Ditra studied Mag and me.

"If you would like—" I began.

"What? You could attend my council?" said Ditra. "How very magnanimous of you. But I do not require the advice of prisoners pressed into service for battle."

"We could save lives." I pointed back towards the city. "We already did. Rangatira," I added, after just a moment's too much hesitation.

"Then when it comes to battle again, I will summon you," she said. "But you will pardon me if I do not consider your advice more useful than my advisors who have lived here their whole lives, and know our situation better."

I bit back the argument that sprang to my lips. She was not wrong. I might have been her younger brother, but we were no longer children, and it was not my place to countermand her, no matter how I hated to hear the word *useful* on her lips. "As you wish, Rangatira."

For a moment I thought I saw her expression soften. But she only turned away to stride off towards the keep.

"A shame," said Mag. "I had hoped the prospect of

nearly dying in battle might have bridged at least some of the rift between you."

"Believe me, that was a far more civil conversation than our last," I said. "Let us find Dryleaf and wait. Ditra may not want us to attend her council, but I want to know what is going on the second she comes out to tell everyone."

Ditra strode into her audience chamber, pulling her leather gauntlets off. She winced as she flexed her fingers. They had gripped her axe and shield so tightly that she could hardly feel them now. For a moment she bent and uncurled them while she looked around the chamber. It had been empty of guards, but they were filing back in now as their lord prepared for her meeting.

She noticed something odd. The guards were filing in from the back of the room, from the stairway leading up to the nobility's living quarters. They should have been out in the main bailey, directing the influx of citizens being pressed into fighting service. Ditra supposed they must have been drawn up to the walls to coordinate their defense, and taken the shorter route down to the council room. But she shrugged off such thoughts as Maia came hurrying up, nodding briskly to her.

"Everyone—"

"Vera," said Ditra. "Did you check on her?"

He nodded. "She is safe. Her guards have not left their post since you sent them there."

"Good. What else?"

"Everyone is here. All the captains, and the king's representative."

"Is she still here?" said Ditra with faint surprise. "I half thought she might try to sneak out with the refugees."

Maia hid a smile, though it seemed a near thing. "She still has time. Many are still gathering to flee the city."

Ditra nodded and went to her chair. The councilors gathered around the dais, looking up at her with stern, impassive faces. She saw no sign of eagerness in them, but neither did she see any doubt. They were ready to serve their lord.

"The trolls will not give us much time to rest," said Ditra. "They are looting the lower city now, but it is only a matter of time before they push towards the stronghold. We must discuss the strategy of our defense."

Callen, the king's representative, took a hesitant step forwards. Her tongue crept out to moisten cracked lips. "Can we even hope to defend against them?"

"We have no choice but to do so," said Ditra.

"Your forces have never faced so many," said Callen. "Without reinforcements from the king—"

"The king has sent soldiers and oil in support," said Ditra. "But the trolls attacked earlier than we thought they would, and it seems their strategy is to overwhelm us before any help can arrive."

"Strategy?" scoffed Callen. "They are trolls! They barely have—"

Ditra stood from her chair. Every ranger in the room bowed their head. Callen fell silent, eyes wide.

"They have pushed into our territory. They have avoided our rangers at every turn. They even misled our scouts into believing they would attack at least a week later than they have. You do yourself no favors by assuming them to be mindless beasts, and you serve your Rangatira not at all."

"O-of course," stammered Callen. "Forgive me, Rangatira. But if the king's forces may not even be coming, mayhap we should flee with the rest, for I do not see how we can defend Kahaunga forever."

"The king has sent their army. We might be able to hold the walls until it arrives, or we might not. We cannot know for certain. But we do know that we cannot abandon Kahaunga. If the trolls face no opposition here, they will simply chase our people into the pass, where they will find them defenseless, and slaughter them. We who remain here are a rearguard, to ensure that does not happen."

"You mean we remain here to die!" said Callen. "You have no hope or plan of escape!"

Ditra's anger bubbled up, threatening to burst. But before it could, Maia stepped from her side to face Callen from a pace away.

"I have no intention of dying in Kahaunga," said Maia. "But I will happily throw you over the wall to our enemies, if you see nothing but death in your future."

Callen took a step back. Ditra noticed that the guards at the edge of the room had pressed forwards, as if they were ready to intervene if things should come to a fight. *Fools,* she thought irritably. *Callen would never dare to raise a hand against Maia—and if she did, he would have her on the floor faster than blinking.*

"I have no wish to die," said Callen, making an impressive attempt to rally. "That is why I counsel against this foolish course."

"You serve me, and through me, the king of Calentin," said Ditra, letting an edge creep into her voice. "If you think you serve us best by fleeing with the rest of the city's people, then by all means, do so. Return to the king in Tara and tell them what transpired here. But if you do not wish to die, you might find that a foolish course of action. They have no great love for cowards."

Callen took several deep breaths, each time seeming as if she was about to say something. Her eyes flew wildly about, as if searching for any words that she thought might spare her. At last she shook her head and gave a hasty bow with her fist raised.

"I . . . I think I will retire to my chambers. A new missive must be written and sent to the king about our situation, and I should send it along before all the city's residents have passed us by."

Ditra nodded in approval. Callen turned and began to push through the rangers on her way to the door, while Maia looked up and gave Ditra a wry look. She knew they were both thinking the same thing: Callen would doubtless decide at the last minute to deliver the message herself. She would be gone before nightfall.

Callen reached the back of the crowd, but suddenly she pulled up short before two of the room's guards. Ditra frowned as she realized the guards had come even closer than before. Now the twelve of them nearly surrounded Ditra, Maia, and the six ranger captains that served on her council.

"What in the dark below are you doing?" Ditra barked. "Move aside and let her pass."

The air filled with the hiss of drawn steel as the guards unsheathed their weapons.

FORTY

MAG AND I WAITED IN THE ENTRANCE HALL OUTSIDE. I paced back and forth in front of the doors, while Mag stood stoically, watching me walk by her each time. The hall was in chaos around us, with guards trying to give orders to their new army of recruits, while the new arrivals roved back and forth in great groups, trying to obey those orders but mostly just colliding with each other. Two guards were posted at the entrance of Ditra's council chamber, and they eyed us suspiciously as we walked back and forth. Mag gave them a smile.

"Greetings, friends," she said. "How are you on this fine day?"

Neither guard answered her.

"The Rangatira's council should not take long," I told her as I walked by on my next pass. "Once she has decided what she wants to do, we can determine how to help her."

"I hope it is as quick as you say," said Mag. "Or she will come out here to find a trench where she once had an even floor in her hall. Stop pacing."

I stopped, but I glared at her. "I will, but only because I want to."

"Of course," said Mag.

"This is no time for jokes, Mag. People are already dying, and—"

From Ditra's council chamber came shouts and the clashing of steel.

As one, Mag and I and the guards turned towards the door. But while the guards were still staring in confusion, Mag and I sprinted for the doorway. At the last moment, the guards turned and crossed their spears to bar it.

"No one is permitted to—"

"Oh, be silent," said Mag, snatching one of the spears and slamming the haft into the guard's head. The woman reeled backwards.

"My apologies." I struck the other in the face. He slammed into the door. With two quick jabs, Mag knocked her guard to the ground, senseless, and then took mine to the floor with a swift kick to the side.

We threw open the doors and rushed inside to a scene of chaos. Ditra's ranger captains stood at the foot of her dais, facing outwards, blades in their hands. Only four remained, including Maia—three lay on the floor in swiftly spreading pools of their own blood. There, too, lay two people in guard uniforms. But ten more guards remained on their feet, and they were pressing in towards the rangers with blades drawn.

"Ditra!" I cried.

Her gaze snapped up over the combat to see me. But she could not spare more than a glance, as the guards pressed forwards and the rangers tried desperately to hold them back.

Mag threw her spear before we reached their line. It impaled one guard straight through his chainmail. His hands scrabbled at his back, trying to grasp the thing. Mag reached him a blink later, planted a foot on his back, and dragged the spear out with both hands. Oku lunged, latching onto the leg of one of the other guards. The woman fell, and Oku's jaws crushed her throat.

I had nocked an arrow. As Mag did her bloody work, I fired as fast as I could. Two of the guards fell to my arrows. Maia joined his lord on her dais and found his own bow, and he sank a shot into the eye of a third.

But the other rangers had fallen now. One of the

guards leaped for Maia and swung her sword for his face. He managed to block it with his bow, which snapped in half.

The guard dragged a knife from her belt and plunged it into Maia's shoulder. Then his gut.

His eyes went wide. His hands scrabbled for the guard's face. But he only succeeded in gripping her helmet and pulling it off.

Kaita. It was Kaita.

Ditra and I froze in horror at the same time. And then Kaita plunged the dagger into Ditra's chest.

She fell back, striking the chair and then the ground.

"No!" I screamed.

Kaita stepped forwards. She raised her dagger to strike again, to be sure.

The arrow flew from my bow. It pierced straight through her forearm. She cried out and dropped the dagger.

In shock, she looked up and noticed me for the first time. Then her gaze fell upon Mag closer by. There were only four guards left, and even as Kaita watched, Mag slew one of them.

Oku lunged at Kaita, bowling her over, and I heard her scream as his fangs sank into her already-wounded arm. Somehow she managed to throw him off. It gave her just enough time to rise and flee. One of the Shades saw her go, and he tried to follow. Together they ran for the back of the room, to the staircase that would take them up into the keep. Oku went after them, silently, hunting.

I sprinted forwards, already nocking another arrow. I loosed it at a Shade on the dais from only two paces away. Distracted as he was by Mag, he never even saw the arrow that killed him. Mag slew the last one a moment later.

"Ditra!" I cried, falling on my knees beside her. I seized her shoulder and pulled her up.

She gave a deep gasp, fingers clutching the front of my jerkin.

"Ditra!" I said again, my voice breaking. Sky above, she was alive. I seized her tabard and pulled it aside, trying to see her wound.

I saw only metal glinting up at me. Chain mail. Several of the links were bent and pressed into her flesh, but she would survive.

Lost for words, I could only take her shoulders and pull her into an embrace. But Ditra pushed me away.

"Maia," she said, wincing as she clutched at her chest.

Panic had driven him from my mind. I looked over. He lay on his back, hands and arms twitching as he held the wound in his belly. I helped Ditra over to him.

"Albern," said Mag, her voice toneless. "The weremage."

"Go," I told her. "Find her if you can."

Mag started off as I joined Ditra by Maia's side. But he looked up at me with wild eyes. "Vera."

I felt a sickening lurch in my gut. "No. It is Albern. We are here."

"No," he said. His voice shook with pain, grunting between gasped words. His eyes found Ditra's. "My—lord. Vera."

All the blood drained from Ditra's face. Her hands twitched, wanting to hold Maia, wanting to pull away. She looked wildly from him to the doorway through which Kaita had fled. Still unsure, she looked back down at him.

"Maia—"

"Go!" growled Maia, glaring up at her in fury. "Get—out—of here."

I wagered it was the first time in his life he had ever dared to give her an order. But Ditra obeyed it, bolting for the back of the room. Mag hesitated, looking down at me.

"Go," I said. "Guard her with your life."

Mag nodded and vanished.

The room settled to silence as I knelt by Maia's side. A cloak close at hand was free from bloodstains. I ripped it from the corpse it had adorned and began to tear strips off it.

"Keep holding that wound," I said. "I will stanch the bleeding from your shoulder."

"Vera," he gasped.

Another sickening lurch in my gut. "My name—"

"Not—you." For a moment the pain increased, and he only winced and sucked in deep, desperate breaths. "Vera. Ditra's—daughter. Forgive—me."

My hands stilled, and I could only stare at him for a moment. But I forced my mind back to the task, trying to find any way I could to stop him from continuing to bleed.

"Never mind that now," I said. "Just keep pressing that wound."

"No—good," said Maia, managing a smile. His teeth were bloodstained, and each breath came in a deep, hissing gasp. "Too—deep."

"Stop talking," I ordered.

"Seen—it," said Maia. "Many—times. Too—many." He gave a rasping breath that might have been an attempt at laughter. Flecks of blood came out.

"Dark take you," I growled. The cloth I pressed to his shoulder soaked through with blood in an instant. I turned my attention to his gut wound. "A Rangatira needs her lead ranger. You are not relieved of your duty."

"No—choice," said Maia. "She—needs—"

"What she needs is for you to stop talking," I said. "Lift your hands when I say. Count of four. One—"

He lifted one hand from the wound and seized my wrist, staining my skin red. I met his gaze. His skin had gone deathly pale. A thin bubble of blood protruded from his lips and then burst. Each gasp was shallower, but he forced the words out regardless.

"She—she needs—you—to save—her."

"Mag and the Rangatira have gone after her," I said. "They will see to—to Vera."

He shook his head—he could only move it a finger in each direction. "No. Ditra." I felt his fingers slacken on my wrist. "Ditra."

Slowly, as though he were relaxing into sleep, his head sank back. But his eyes never left me. Not even as I bowed my head over him, and the hall around us settled to silence.

FORTY-ONE

"She killed him?" said Sun.

Albern nodded slowly. "She did."

"Did Mag catch her?"

He shook his head, never taking his eyes from the trail they were following. Or rather, that *he* was following, for Sun could not see it. "She did not. Not then."

"She escaped again?" said Sun, incredulous, her voice rising. "Mag was just behind her!"

"We hesitated a moment too long, after Maia," said Albern. "Mag caught the other Shade that tried to flee. But Kaita took her mountain lion form as soon as she could. She was on the wall and in her raven form before anyone knew what had happened, and then she took wing."

Sun glared into the grass, picturing it in her mind, running it over and over as though by sheer force of will she could change what had happened. "I cannot believe how she kept getting away from you. Did Mag not wish to catch her?"

"Oh, she did," said Albern. "More than you can believe. More than she wanted to save the lives of the people of Kahaunga, certainly. Every time Kaita escaped us, it was sheer luck. If I had not lived it myself, I would not believe it. And though I do not mean to cast an even darker pall over what is already an unhappy tale thus far, I will say this: many, many times have I seen evil people escape judgement, while good people meet an early end. The world should not be that way, but sometimes it is."

"I am no child. I do not believe that everything is always just and right. But dark below, at least tell me that she did not kill your—"

Albern raised a hand. Sun stopped short, glaring at him. "Are you shushing—"

"Please," whispered Albern. "Do not speak for a moment. I think we are drawing close to the end of the trail."

Somewhat mollified, Sun fell silent. Albern's bow was in her hand, and his quiver on her belt. She drew an arrow, holding it nocked and ready.

"Where?" she whispered.

"Not far," he said. "Come. Off the beaten path for a little while."

Sun's face twisted. She could see no trace whatsoever of their prey, and certainly not a beaten path. But she followed Albern as he cut suddenly right, working his way around the southern side of a great hill that rose to a cluster of reddish boulders at the top. It brought them to another hill, which Albern circumvented again. But when they came to a third hill, this time he began to climb. Sun followed, and when Albern began to walk in a half-crouch, she did the same.

They reached the crest of the hill. Two trees grew towards the north end of it, and they snuck up to one of them. A few paces from the edge of the hill, Albern lowered himself to the ground, creeping forwards like a jungle cat stalking through grass. Sun did the same, though she had to restrain herself from moving too quickly—it was easier for her than for Albern, with his missing arm.

Together they sidled up to the edge of the hill and looked down into a small dip in the land. Sun barely restrained a gasp.

A camp sat in the lowest flat point in the land. A motley assortment of disheveled individuals lounged about in various positions of rest, many of them near a campfire with some meat suspended above it. There looked to be a few guards posted, but they were scant paces away from the others, and they sat on rocks or the flat ground. They hardly seemed to be looking out for a squirrel to shoot, much less intruders.

But the center of the camp drew Sun's attention immediately. There she saw a sizable cauldron made of black iron, and full of an even blacker liquid. The sun's final rays only gave it a few hints of any color, and that was a dark red. Beneath the cauldron burned a flame—a flame like Sun had never seen before, black instead of red, with the barest hints of blue and grey flicking at the top of it. A flame that seemed to draw light from the air rather than bestowing it.

"Dark below!" hissed Sun. "That is—"

"Please do be quieter," said Albern.

"That is a cauldron of blood," whispered Sun. "And is that . . . is that darkfire beneath it?"

"It is," whispered Albern.

"Then those people are Shades?"

"No," said Albern. "Not quite. But they have some idea of what the Shades were, and despite that, they are trying to emulate them."

His gaze flicked back and forth across the scene before them. He was surveying the scene, taking stock of the people and the layout of their camp.

"Do . . . do you mean to fight them?"

"Fight might be a strong word," said Albern. "But I do mean to stop them."

"But there are so many. I have never fought in a battle before. I cannot defeat a dozen foes. And you . . ."

"Yes," said Albern, shrugging his right shoulder to

highlight his missing arm. "Not exactly the stalwart battle companion you might hope for."

"Then you do not think we can defeat them?"

"Look there." Albern pointed to a crate, close to both the cauldron and the campfire. "A guard on either side of it. And they are the only ones in the whole party who seem alert. I would wager that is where they keep the rest of their magestones."

"We should tell the constables," said Sun.

"Hm," said Albern. "I have another idea. Let us get out of sight and wait until sundown."

They slid back, away from the edge of the hill. Once they were out of sight, Albern rose and walked down the other side of the hill, Sun just behind him.

"The two of us cannot hope to win against them."

He smiled back over his shoulder at her. "There are many ways to win. In Kahaunga, we were well outmatched by the trolls. Yet we had an advantage. One we did not yet realize."

"An advantage?" said Sun.

"Oh yes. If you know something your foe does not, you always have an advantage. Let us get somewhere more private and have a bite to eat. We will take care of these conspirators at dusk. That should give us just enough time to finish this part of the tale. That is, if you want me to go on?"

Sun rolled her eyes and reached for the pouch of food at her belt. "You already know the answer, old man."

FORTY-TWO

After chasing Kaita out of the stronghold, Ditra and Mag returned to the council chamber. When she saw Maia lying dead at the foot of her chair, Ditra looked ready to collapse.

"He died bravely," I murmured.

"Who cares for that?" said Ditra, her voice cracking.

She sank to sit on the stairs of her dais, and I sat close beside her. I wanted to ask about her daughter, but I could not quite bring myself to name her. Not yet. "Did you . . . did you and Mag . . ."

For a moment she only stared at Maia's body, but at last she looked up. "We went after my daughter. Albern, I . . . I named her Vera. I wanted to tell you when . . . you should not have found out like that."

"It is all right," I said at once.

"I missed you," she said, her voice cracking. "And I thought . . . after Romil, and Mother, and when you still did not return . . . I thought I would never see you again."

"Ditra," I said, reaching over and taking her shoulder. "It is all right. I am honored."

She bowed her head. "Well. She is safe. The guards outside her room never even saw the commotion. Kaita may have had plans for her, but she had to abandon them after you showed up."

"That is a comfort, at least."

Ditra looked at Maia's body. "I will call nothing a comfort today. Not today."

Two of her ranger captains had been slain, and the other four had been wounded—two of them grievously. They had been carried off to be attended by healers. That left two in the chamber. They knelt beside Maia's body like an honor guard, their heads bowed over him. Now they tried to rise, but they swayed as they did it.

"No," snapped Ditra. "Sit. I will not have either of you fainting in my council chamber."

The rangers settled back down at our feet, grateful looks upon their faces.

"Thank you, Rangatira."

Ditra rose and went to her chair, bowing her head and covering her eyes with one hand, her elbow resting on the chair. I looked to Mag, who stood a few paces off. Her expression was stony, but not emotionless. The battle-trance was gone. The look on her face was one of disappointment, of frustration at losing Kaita yet again.

"This is not over," I told her.

"Well do I know it," said Mag.

I nodded and looked up to Ditra. "If you still mean to hold council, might I fetch our friend, Dryleaf? He bears the wisdom of many years, and might have valuable advice."

Ditra did not look up. "Why not? I seem now to have a dearth of councilors." She looked up suddenly. "Where is the king's representative?"

"The thin woman wearing robes of the king's colors? Dead."

"First to fall to the Shades," growled one of the remaining rangers.

"Of course she was," said Ditra. She waved a hand at me. "Go and fetch the old man."

I bowed to her and went to retrieve Dryleaf. By the time I returned, Maia's body had been removed from the council chamber. Servants had removed many skins from the floor that had been stained with blood, and they were scrubbing at the stone beneath, trying to remove the stains. Dryleaf bowed low to Ditra with a fist on his forehead.

"Rangatira," he said. "My most grievous condolences for your loss."

"I thank you for them," said Ditra. "And if I was less courteous the last time you offered such graceful sentiment, please forgive me. Fetch him a—" She looked around the chamber for a moment, seeming lost. "Dark take me, I have no one left to fetch you a chair."

"A moment," I said, ducking out of the room again. I went to the first guard I saw. "The Rangatira needs new guards in her council chamber. Choose half a dozen of them—but make sure you know them intimately well, and ask them questions only they would have the answer to. We have already been infiltrated today."

Rumor of the Shades must have spread fast, for her face went pale, and she nodded. "As you say." She turned to run off. I pointed to the next guard, just a few paces away, who looked as though he had been trying to overhear us.

"You. The Rangatira requires chairs for her council. Fetch . . ." I counted us off on my fingers. "Five of them. The most comfortable ones you can find, but do not take too long."

He nodded and ran to do my bidding at once. I realized in that instant that I had begun talking to the guards as I had spoken to them in my youth. That was a disconcerting thought.

I returned to the council chamber. No one seemed to have moved or spoken since I had left. We waited in silence a while until guards filtered into the room, bearing chairs for us. They set them in a semicircle facing the dais, and then they retreated to stand at the edges of the room. Ditra studied them, likely inspecting their faces to ensure she knew them.

"Very well," said Ditra, leaning forwards. Her rangers straightened where they were sitting upon the steps. "I suppose we had better begin. These are my ranger captains, Huia and Ihaia, both of the family Taumata."

They rose from their chairs and bowed to us. I rose and bowed in turn, and then gestured to myself and my companions. "I am Albern of the family Telfer. This is Mag, the Uncut Lady, and Dryleaf, our friend."

"Well met. We are honored to meet the Uncut Lady," said Huia. She was a thin but wirily muscled woman. The sides of her hair were trimmed to stubble, while the top was gathered into a tail that ran back and hung down to her shoulder blades. Her face was more tattoo than unmarked skin. She gestured to Ihaia. "My cousin and I were little more than whelps when last you were home. I am glad to see your return."

That put me off for a moment, but I managed to nod. "You have my thanks."

"With that out of the way," said Ditra. "Let us begin. We must defend Kahaunga as long as we can. To do that, it would be helpful to know when the trolls mean to attack."

"Our scouts have been returning with regular reports," said Huia. "The trolls are still looting the city. We think it will be some time before they finish and start to climb the western side of the dale. Normally, I would say we could expect their attack tomorrow, or the next day. Of course, they attacked the city sooner than we expected, so we cannot be certain."

"I suspect they will be spurred to action when the weremage returns to them," I said. "She will be incensed by her failure to kill the Rangatira, and since she has ordered the trolls' attacks thus far, fury might lead her to order them to attack at once."

"How do you know that she—" Ditra bit her own words off and shook her head. "No. You have been right about the weremage thus far. I will trust your council in this."

"Your soldiers know how to fight trolls?" said Dryleaf.

"Our trained soldiers, yes," said Ihaia. "The new arrivals from the city . . . well, they shall have to learn fast."

"It is not too difficult," I said. "Cover the trolls with oil, and use flame upon them. We should tell every guard to repeat those words until they are blue in the face. I wish we could drill it, but I think we will not have the time."

"And we cannot waste any oil," said Ditra. "Our stores are low. The king's army will bring more, but who knows when they will arrive? Our new recruits shall learn it as they do it."

"A trial by fire," I said. The moment the words were out of my mouth, I regretted them—it was just the sort of flippant joke I would have made to my mother when I was a child, inviting her wrath. But to my surprise, and not inconsiderable joy, Ditra gave me the tiniest smile, just as she had when we were young, and she did not want Mother to notice.

"You should send scouts to the north and south as well," said Dryleaf. "Just in case the trolls try to maneuver around Kahaunga and attack your folk who are fleeing upon the road."

"But not too many," I said. "I doubt it will be necessary, for I hardly think that even the Shades could influence the trolls in so subtle a way. They will almost certainly attack the walls. Send your scouts, but only two in each direction."

"As you say," said Ditra. She glanced over at Mag. "You are very quiet. More so than the last time you stood in this chamber. Have you no counsel to give?"

"I think these two have the better advice," said Mag. "I came to Tokana for the weremage, and nothing else."

Ditra's mouth set in a thin line. "Then that is your task in the battle. Kill her, if you get so much as half a chance."

Mag bowed. "As you command, Rangatira."

Ditra nodded. "Very well. That is all for now. Go and see to the orders I have given." She turned to me. "Albern. I wish to speak with you privately."

I hesitated as the others rose and prepared to leave. Ditra must have seen the apprehension on my face, for she shook her head.

"That is not an order. Please, brother."

I relaxed. As her rangers went to issue her orders, and Mag remained with Dryleaf, I followed Ditra up the stairs to the same chamber where we had met last. There was a new bottle of wine on the table, and two cups. She stopped in the middle of the room, staring at them.

"One of those cups was for Maia," she said. "I suppose it is yours, now."

"Thank you," I said. I poured for both of us and sat back, but I did not touch my wine. Ditra, on the other hand, drank half of hers in one gulp. She put it back down upon the table, staring at her own hand as it gripped the glass.

"You were right about Kaita."

"I wish I had not been."

"The past is barren ground for sowing wishes," she said, "and the future is fertile for nothing else."

My brows rose. "I have never heard that wisdom. I doubt you learned it from Mother."

"I did not. It came from my late husband." At last Ditra looked up at me. But far from the pain I had seen there last time, her eyes were filled with a profound sadness, almost mourning. "You should have come back, Albern. When Romil died. You should have come back."

"And what would Mother have said?" I asked her quietly. "How could I have faced her? She, who I could never quite say hated me, but simply . . . did not seem to care. Yet she would have cared, had I returned. Romil would not have died, if not for me. She was only on that pass because she was returning after seeking me out."

"Yes, she was," said Ditra. "That does not mean it was your fault."

"I know that. But Mother . . . she would not have seen it the same way. She would have hated me, then."

Ditra nodded slightly. "You are right. She would have. She did. And without you there to turn her hatred upon, she turned it on me instead, and on herself. She spent nearly every waking moment in the pass, hunting down any Feldemarian who dared to enter our domain, until in the end, they killed her. But not before she had let me know just how useless I was to her, in her time of loss."

I shook my head. "Ditra . . . no one should have suffered that. Least of all you. I am sorry."

"No. That was not your fault, either." She sighed and pushed her chair back a few fingers. "And we have no time to worry about it now, in any case. Kaita will be back. I doubted you before, but no longer. If we are to die here, as might well be the case, I would sooner do it by your side than alone. Will you stand with me?"

I nodded. "I will help you save your people."

"Thank you." It came out as a whisper, though I do

not think she intended it to. She took a deep breath, obviously steeling herself. “Albern, I . . . my daughter. Vera. I never knew that you were ander, I would never have . . .”

She trailed off. The sound of the name caused my chest to grow tight. But this was nothing like when Romil had said it to me, on the edges of that sellsword camp, or when I thought Maia had said it to me. This feeling was strange.

Because never, in all the early years I had spent in Tokana, had I ever dreamed that someone would be proud to name their child after me.

“It is a perfect name,” I managed to say. “I am sure it suits her beautifully. Better than it ever suited me.”

Ditra gave the first full, genuine smile I had seen since my return to Tokana. “It does, at that. I am going to send her with the rest of the refugees, and I must do it soon. But before she goes, would . . . would you like to meet her?”

I felt dangerously close to shattering, so I remained silent. But I nodded. Ditra rose and left the chamber. When she returned, she brought a little girl who could not be older than twelve. The girl’s eyes were wide and wonderstruck as she looked up at me.

It was like looking at a painting of myself at her age.

Ditra kept her hand on Vera’s shoulder, looking at me with obvious apprehension. I smiled and held out my hand.

"Hello," I said. "I am Albern."

Vera's eyes went wide. She looked up at her mother, who nodded, and then back to me. "You are my uncle," she said in a quiet voice, putting her hand in mine.

"I am."

"Mother says I look just like you used to."

Ditra's hand clenched on her shoulder. "Vera—"

"It is all right," I told her quietly, before smiling at Vera again. "Your mother could not be more right. I only wish we had more time to talk. But you have somewhere to go."

Vera's smile dampened, and her eyes filled with doubt as she looked up at Ditra. "I told her I did not want to leave."

"Yet you must. Your mother is doing what is best for you." I met Ditra's eyes. "Parents always try to do that. Some of them fail. But not your mother."

Vera frowned. But she took a hesitant step forwards, and then another, and then she hugged me about the waist. It startled me, and a long moment stretched before I thought to embrace her in return.

"I am glad I met you, at least," said Vera quietly. "Might we talk more, when we return?"

"I hope so, child. In fact, I promise that we will."

FORTY-THREE

Kaita flew towards the northern edge of the city. Great swells of warm air rose before her from the flames of Kahaunga's burning buildings, but she flapped anyway, powering her wing muscles with sheer fury.

Why in the dark below was Mag there? she raged in her mind. *They were in prison. Both of them. Again, always again, she robs me of my victory.*

At last she reached the city's northern borders. The Shades had gathered there, only showing themselves after the trolls pressed deep into the city streets. Now they waited, unwary, for the fighting had moved far away. Kaita landed in their midst and shed her raven form, even as many Shades stepped away from her in alarm.

"Report," she snarled, as soon as she had the mouth to speak the word.

Phelan, her captain, stepped forth, looking only slightly unnerved by her transformation. "We are ready to strike on your order, Comm—"

"Not my order," snapped Kaita. "I will not be here to command you, and so I leave it to you. Take our forces to the western end of the city. The moment you see the trolls attack, join them at once. You know where to strike to put our numbers to best effect."

"Yes, Commander," said Phelan. "Our soldiers are prepared. We have brought ladders and—"

"I *know* what you have brought!" roared Kaita. "I created the plan, and it is almost complete. Tonight we wipe the family of Telfer from the face of the world. Now move!"

His face reddened, but Kaita had ceased paying attention. She stalked south, away from the camp. Before she had even finished passing through their ranks, her eyes glowed, and her form began to shift again. Shades cried out and dived aside as she suddenly grew gigantic. Grey, stone-solid skin swept across her, and her ears turned to giant flaps that swept out from her head.

In a moment the transformation was complete,

and she had taken Gatak's shape. She broke into a troll's gallop, thundering out of sight of the Shades on all fours to vanish into the city. She had never taken her troll shape where the other Shades could see. If the trolls ever discovered her secret, the whole plan would come apart. But everything was nearing completion now. Even if there was a traitor among the Shades, they would not have enough time to tell the trolls before the battle would be over.

She began to spot trolls amid the wreckage of Kahaunga's buildings. They were picking through the destruction, searching for food. The first time she spotted one, she stopped and bared her teeth at him.

"Come. We are readying for the attack. Dotag needs all the pack."

The troll scowled at her, its ears rising. "He said we could rest and eat."

"And now he needs us," said Gatak. "You are of his pack. Come."

She gathered every troll she could find as she went, until soon there were at least two dozen trailing along behind her, though none walked with quite her speed or purpose. She searched for the front lines of the gathered pack. There she would find Dotag. A pack leader had to *lead.* Dotag had been in the thick of the fighting when they had attacked the city, and he would be there again when they assaulted the Telfer stronghold.

At last she spotted him, in a large square towards

the city's western end. A great pile of produce and bread had been put before him, tributes from trolls in the pack who looked to curry favor. Dotag was picking at the pile, searching for the choicest morsels to eat first. He looked rather ragged—there was a tear in his left ear that had not been there that morning, and there were burn marks on his right flank. Kaita even saw some broken skin on his right shoulder. A very large building must have fallen on him for that to happen. Kaita ignored it and stalked up to him. Dotag noticed her at the last second, and his ears dipped in pleasure—but they flew sideways in alarm as Kaita pressed her face close to his.

"We have rested long enough." She thrust a stubby finger up the long slope rising to the west. "The humans have gathered in their fortress. Now is the time to tear it down and kill them all."

Dotag very nearly looked frightened of her. "We do not need to attack now," he said. "They have run from their city. They know we have won."

"We have to kill them!" roared Kaita. "They have broken the pact!"

"So have we," came Apok's voice.

Kaita snarled and turned. The younger troll stood at the edge of the square, her stony, angry gaze fixed on Dotag.

"I speak to Dotag," snarled Kaita. "Not to you."

"And you tell him that the humans broke the pact,"

said Apok, stalking forwards. "Yet we have attacked their city. We have killed them. That, too, breaks the pact."

"Only after they did it first."

"What, then?" said Apok. "Do we kill more? They will bring their armies. They will bring oil and fire. Already today they killed many of us. The pack lost more trolls today than it did in all the years Chok led us."

"Because more trolls follow Dotag than ever followed Chok," said Kaita. "Dotag is a great leader."

"He leads more of us, and he leads more of us to die," said Apok. "The humans will drive us out of this city, and then they will drive us farther. Beyond the bounds of the pact. Even out of the mountains. Will you call that victory?"

Dotag looked more uncertain than ever. Kaita whirled on him. "The Telfers," she said. "They are the ones who broke their word. Do whatever you want after they are dead. But you cannot allow them to live after breaking the pact. The Lord wishes them to be dealt with."

"Trolls do not follow your human lord," growled Apok, taking another step forwards. "Trolls fight for ourselves. We follow ourselves. I think you have left for so long that you have forgotten."

Kaita could feel herself close to the breaking point. But if she attacked Apok, even Dotag would not be able to protect her from the other trolls in the pack.

The pack. Inwardly, Kaita grinned. Apok might

speak against her, but she could not speak against Dotag without repercussions.

"I follow Dotag," said Kaita. "He leads the pack, not I. Do you challenge him?"

Apok hesitated. It was a long, uncomfortable moment in the square before she spoke, but Kaita knew she had already won.

"No," said Apok.

"Then be silent." Kaita turned back to Dotag and lowered her voice. "We have the Telfers trapped. Apok is right about one thing. The humans will bring their armies. They will bring their fire. But if we kill the Telfers, no human will ever dare to break the bonds of the pact."

Still Dotag did not look entirely convinced. He pawed at the pavement of the town square, eyeing the pile of bread and produce before him. "We have gone far enough for now. Many have died. More are hurt. We need to rest."

"We *need* to kill them," said Kaita, her voice rumbling with fury. "They will never leave these mountains until we throw them out. You lead this pack now. You must be strong. You must protect us from the humans. And you must do it *now*. The Lord will reward you for it."

Dotag looked more reluctant than ever. But he tore his gaze away from the pile of food before him, looking up towards the western rim of the valley. At last he turned to the other trolls in the square.

“We attack.” Dotag tried to make his voice loud and commanding, but it rasped, weary from all his roaring during the battle earlier. “Gather the pack. We will destroy the humans’ home. We will rest when they are all dead.”

The trolls lumbered off to do his bidding. Dotag turned to Kaita, his expression full of doubt. But Kaita only smiled.

FORTY-FOUR

Maia's body was burned in the center of the stronghold's bailey with everyone in attendance. Ditra had Vera to one side of her, and I stood to the other. When the flames began to subside, Ditra sent Vera away to join the rest of the refugees. With her went a dozen guards for protection. I could not help but think that a dozen more soldiers would be useful in the coming battle, but I said nothing. Ditra had to know it. But if we died in the coming battle, then Vera would be the last remnant of our line.

Not that it seemed to make much difference to Ditra's soldiers. At first she asked for volunteers, but no one stepped forwards. I was shocked, until I realized the soldiers did not see the assignment as an honor—they saw it as fleeing from the battle to come. It astounded me, and I could not help but wonder if they would have been so eager to stay and die at their lord's side if my mother had still been the Rangatira.

In the end, Ditra had to order a dozen of them to leave with Vera. The first tried to argue. She subsided when Ditra asked her if she thought Vera's life was not worth saving—in which case Ditra would happily strip her of rank and send her out to face the trolls first. After that, she and the others went along quite meekly, if not exactly willingly.

Mag and I faced much the same resistance when we told Dryleaf to leave the city as well. The old man flatly refused until we threatened to tie him up and stick him in the back of a wagon. He could not help in a fight, and though his counsel was valuable, the time for advice was long past. We sent Oku with him. The hound trotted along at the heels of Dryleaf's horse, looking back at Mag and I often. For once, he did not seem to understand what was going on, and it nearly broke my heart.

With Vera seen to, and all the other preparations at the stronghold underway, Ditra's remaining rangers and I convinced her to rest. She retired to her chamber to sleep, but not before assigning a servant to find lodgings for Mag and me. "If I am being forced to sleep until the battle, then I will force you to do the same," she said.

I was more than happy to obey. The battle in the city had not lasted long—certainly not as long for me as it had been for Ditra—but I was exhausted to the point of collapse. When they showed me to my bed, I paused only long enough to stow my bow and sword before I fell upon the mattress, fully clothed. I have some vague sense that Mag came into my room just before sleep claimed me. If she meant to talk, she left disappointed.

The blast of a horn woke me in an instant. I had slept for three hours, but it felt like no time at all. Groggy, I belted my sword on and slung my bow across my back, stumbling from the room to find Mag waiting for me.

"Did you sleep?" I said, my speech slurred with weariness.

"A bit," she said. Her words were clear, and her eyes looked as sharp as ever. "Less than you, though yours looks to have done you less good."

I waved her words away. "Leave off. Let us go to Ditra."

We found her on the eastern wall, looking into the dale below. The night sky was dark above us, but the landscape was fairly well lit by the fires that still burned in the city, which reflected off the pall of black smoke hanging in the air. A chill wind blew hard into our faces, and I pulled my cloak tighter as I shivered. Ditra looked up at our approach and gave us a stiff nod.

"They are coming."

I squinted down into the darkness. The burning city cast a tint across the world, so that everything was only visible in shades between black and crimson. But I saw no signs of movement down below, no indication of the trolls at all.

"Where?" I said.

"My scouts reported it," said Ditra. "Rest assured, they will be here soon."

"That prospect urges neither rest nor assurance."

Mag laughed and clapped my shoulder, probably a bit harder than she had to. "Relax, Albern. I will be here to keep you safe."

Despite herself, I saw a smile tugging at the corner of Ditra's mouth. "Yes, see that you do, will you? I have waited for the fool to return home for quite some time. It would be a tragic shame to lose him now."

"Like an old pet," said Mag, brightening immediately.

"I am *not—*"

"Yes, exactly," said Ditra, and now she could not stop the grin from spreading across her face.

I subsided, glowering into the darkness of the dale. But despite my objections, the smile on Ditra's face was worth any amount of jibes aimed at me.

Her good mood faded as she returned to business.

"You will want pitch arrows," she told me. "There are many stored along the wall. Fill your quiver. There are torches and braziers, too, which you can use to light them." She turned to Mag. "I take it from the spear in your hand that you are not much of an archer."

"Not much of one, no," said Mag.

"You will want oil, then," said Ditra. "Your spear will be little help other than as a distraction. Carry a few flasks on your belt. If you can soak a troll with oil, that will let the archers take care of them. The flasks are stowed near the arrows."

"As you say, Rangatira." Mag bowed to her and went to fetch them. I stared at her retreating back, scowling. Finally I caught Ditra giving me an amused look, and I turned the scowl upon her.

"She keeps bowing to you."

Ditra smirked. "She bowed to me when you all first arrived."

"When she was trying to deceive you," I said. "The last few times, it has been genuine."

"I consider it a great honor to receive such courtesy from the Uncut Lady herself."

Together we peered out into the darkness, searching for the first sign of our foes. "They are coming sooner than we thought. I had hoped they would rest."

Ditra shrugged. "We did not think they would attack the city at all for at least another week. It is the Shades' doing." Her expression grew grim. "It is Kaita's."

"We must look for her in the battle," I said. "If she falls . . ."

Ditra shook her head. "I have little hope that that will stop them. She may be spurring the trolls on, but she seems to be doing so from the rear. And even if we fell her, the trolls do not follow humans. They have been persuaded to make up their minds, and that will not change simply because one human dies on the battlefield."

"It might make me feel better, at least," I muttered.

She sighed, frowning down at her feet. "I suppose I agree."

"Her actions were not your doing," I said.

"I kept Maia from working with you, as he wished to do. I wanted to make it right with her somehow . . . after what Mother did, I mean."

"That was a kind and just thing to do."

"But not a wise thing to do," she said.

"I doubt we would have found her even with Maia's help. And I would not have trusted unsworn strangers from another land any more than you did."

Ditra considered that for a moment, and then she shook herself. "Well, we can never repeat the past. There is only the present, and whatever future remains to us."

"If we can hold until the king sends their army . . ."

"That is doubtful. We have never seen more than a dozen or so trolls at a time. We managed to kill a few in the city, but there are still nearly two hundreds of them, and I have scarcely twice that number of soldiers at my command."

"But you have your walls," I told her. "They were built to withstand trolls."

"Nothing can withstand them forever."

Something in her tone worried me. For a moment I forgot that she was the Lord Telfer, that she was, by rights, my Rangatira. For a moment I saw only my sister. I reached out and gently took her shoulder.

"Ditra. You cannot give up."

She did not look at me. "I will not surrender to them, if that is what you mean."

"I mean you cannot give up hope."

"Hope," she snorted. "I have been so ill acquainted with it for so many years that I no longer know what it looks like. And how am I to be reminded now, when the night is dark and an unstoppable foe lurks just beyond the doorstep? I am Lord Ditra of the family Telfer, Rangatira of Tokana. It looks as though we will be the last of Mother's children to fall. If you had remained in Strapa, that might have left me with some small hope—the idea that you could return and take my place. But if one of us falls tonight, we both shall."

"There is always Vera," I said. "And I never thought I would return here at all. No one knows what fortune may bring."

"Nor whether it will be kind or cruel." At last she met my eyes and smiled, but I could see that it was mostly for show. She reached out and gripped my shoulder. "Go and fetch yourself some arrows. Be ready for the call to retreat—if they take the walls, we will fall back to the keep. Above all, look after yourself. I do not know if we can survive this battle. But if we can, I expect you to emerge on the other side of it."

"I can only promise that I will try," I told her. "But then, I have been trying to stay alive for a good long while now, and I have managed it so far."

"Then take this as an order from your Rangatira: stay alive tonight."

"Only if you do the same." I bowed, and then I stepped forwards to place my forehead against hers, the act of greeting and parting between family.

We parted, me to fetch my arrows, and her to see to the last arrangements of defense. Soldiers gathered atop the eastern gate and all along its wall, with only a token force left to the western defenses. Shades or no, we did not suspect the trolls would suddenly show a gift for strategy. They had not done so in any of the towns they had attacked. They would throw themselves at the first thing they saw—the eastern wall—and break it.

And why not? We cannot stop them. We cannot even hold them back for all that long.

I stamped that thought down at once. One thing I knew, at least, from my many years as a sellsword: things only become hopeless when you decide to abandon hope.

FORTY-FIVE

THE TROLLS APPROACHED THE STRONGHOLD OUT OF the darkness, silhouetted by the fires in the city. They gathered well within arrow range, but we loosed no shots. Arrows would be pointless against their stony hides—pointless until they approached close enough to strike with oil, and then flaming arrows.

Every soldier on the wall remained stock still, gazing out at our gathering foe. I cannot speak for the rest of them, but my heart was filled with fear. Trolls had been a story of terror for me since I was a child. They had killed many of the people I had once called mine.

And before the night was over, I was sure they would kill many more.

Nearly a hundred archers lined the wall. Besides the bows in their hands, they had stores of oil flasks ready to throw. We expected the gatehouse to be the focus of the trolls' assault. There were two gates, both made of wood reinforced with a grid of thick steel bands. We would defend the outer gate as long as we could, but that would not last long. Once the trolls broke through into the gatehouse, there were great cauldrons of oil ready to pour atop them through murder holes. The second gate would be sturdier, for there were three dozens of soldiers in the bailey ready to bolster it. They were each equipped with bracers, long iron poles like spears, but with flat metal plates at the end instead of pointed spearheads. They would hold the plates against the gate and step on the other end, like infantry preparing for a cavalry charge.

As I looked upon the massive limbs of the trolls arranging themselves before us, I wondered how long the second gate would last.

Ditra joined me above the gatehouse as the trolls looked to be finishing their preparations. Her expression was grim as she surveyed them.

"There is the leader." She pointed to a large troll at the head of the pack. He was not quite so large as I had feared, but he was clearly in charge. The other trolls moved around him, keeping an eye on him if they were close, as though ready to move out of his way, or to follow him if he began the advance. As I watched, he slammed his fists into the ground and gave a loud, barking command.

But then my eyes were drawn to the troll just beside him. I did not know trolls very well, but I thought this one was female. And she did not treat the leader like the others did. She barely seemed to notice him. Instead, her gaze was fixed unswervingly upon the wall, and upon the keep behind it. It seemed strange behavior, and it stuck out in my mind.

My thoughts were pulled back to the present as the trolls charged. Roaring with fury, they crossed the open ground with great, bounding leaps. I could feel the thunder of their coming reverberate through the stone wall beneath my feet. My fingers tightened on my bow, and I fingered the oil flask in my right hand.

"Ready!" Ditra's sergeants echoed her cry along the wall. The troops held their flasks aloft.

The trolls drew close. Now we could see the rage in their eyes. They drew within thirty paces of the wall. Then twenty. I wagered I could throw that far, but no command came. I glanced at Ditra from the corner of my eye. She held steady. The trolls drew within ten paces.

"Throw!"

A hundred flasks of oil arced through the air. Their glass glittered in the light of our braziers.

"Loose!"

I had nocked the second I let go of the flask, and

now I fired my flaming arrow straight at it. It shattered, flinging its flaming contents straight into the face of an unlucky troll right next to the leader. The troll stumbled and fell upon its face, screaming. His fellows ran straight over him, pressing him deeper and deeper into the snowy mud. It did not seem to harm him, but only to stifle the flames.

Fire had ripped into the troll's front line. Dozens of them reeled away from the wall. They screamed in pain and tried to batter the blazes that roasted them. But more trolls pushed forwards, slamming into the wall. Fists as large as my torso slammed into the stone. The wall shook, but it held.

Some trolls scrambled up the backs and shoulders of their companions, leaping for the ramparts. Soldiers dropped their bows and hacked at the trolls' hands with steel. Ditra gave a great cry and raised her axe as a stubby hand appeared in front of her. The weapon was called Uira, and it was an heirloom of our house. It flashed with runic light as she brought it down, cleaving straight through the troll's forefinger. The creature fell back to the ground with a roar.

They had massed below us at the front gate. Their leader was off to the side, fighting to push through his pack and reach the gate. I threw a flask at him, but he saw it and batted it aside, where it shattered over the face of another troll. Flaming arrows streaked through the darkness, and fresh bursts of fire exploded over the trolls' heads and shoulders. They surged back. For a moment I thought they might turn and run. But their leader gave a great roar and pressed forwards, slamming his fists into the gate. The others gained new heart, and they crashed into it with all their fury.

It shattered with the sound of splintering wood and rending metal. The trolls poured into the gatehouse and straight into the second gate. It rocked on its hinges, but the soldiers in the bailey held. More trolls crowded into the space, though only a dozen could fit. The leader held his ground rather than enter the gatehouse.

Ditra turned to her soldiers atop the barbican. "Oil!" she roared.

The soldiers seized their cauldrons and heaved. The iron turned on great wooden wheels. I ran forwards to lend a hand, seizing the bottom of a vat and lifting with all my might. Soldiers thrust torches into the oil as it came pouring out, and a wave of blistering heat washed across my face.

Flaming oil poured down over the trolls like the spewing of a volcano. I saw one of them look up just as it came pouring down. Oil flooded her face, pouring down her throat. She fell to the ground, clawing at herself. It lasted only a moment before she stilled forever.

The oil coated everyone else who had entered the gatehouse, killing most in seconds. The others fled back into the open air, slamming into the rest of the pack, smearing them with flames. The trolls' lines shuddered and began to draw back. I saw the first few begin to turn and run, and then it was like a bursting dam. As one they pounded away from the wall, separating themselves to avoid spreading the fire any more. Some did not make it back, the oil and flames claiming them before they could make it more than a few paces away from the wall. The trolls ran out to beyond throwing range again, lurking on the edge of darkness, pacing back and forth and licking their wounds.

Ditra was only a few paces away. Both of us were covered in sweat, leaning heavily against the wall. Her helm had come off sometime during the battle. I saw it two paces away and went to fetch it for her.

"Thank you," she gasped as I placed it in her hand.

Mag approached. She strode between the soldiers who had collapsed in exhaustion against the wall, and she looked for all the world as if she were taking a stroll through the woods. She raised two skins in her hands. "I have brought water."

Ditra and I each took a skin from her and drank greedily. It was not quite cold, but it was a good deal cooler than the heat atop the wall, drifting up from the pools of burning oil and the flaming corpses of trolls below the wall.

"How did the gatehouse fare?" said Mag.

"Better than it could have," I said.

Ditra's mouth gave a grim twist as she pulled the helm on. "We do not have enough oil to refill the cauldrons. We will have only flasks and arrows when they return. How did the fighting go farther along the wall?"

Mag frowned slightly. "We lost some soldiers. The trolls flung rocks at them from below. I feel useless up here. All I could do was stab their fingers when they tried to climb up, like a wasp attacking a bear."

"Enough wasps can ruin a bear's day," I said.

She pointed out into the darkness. "That only works if there are many wasps and just one bear. This is quite the reverse."

"Yet even one sting can hurt. Mayhap they will give up and flee home."

Ditra arched an eyebrow. "That is a poor joke, brother."

I shrugged. "What other kind is there, on a night like tonight?"

Kaita, still in the form of Gatak, stalked up to Dotag. His right arm was curled up to his chest, and he probed gently at a nasty burn he had received in the fight around the gatehouse. As she approached, Dotag looked up, and Kaita was troubled by his resentful look.

"We have rested long enough," she said. "We must attack again, before they have time to regroup."

"Many died," said Dotag. "We are not ready."

"They cannot stop us," said Kaita. "Some died, but we have many more."

"The gate," said Dotag. "They burned us. None will go back in there again."

"That was most of the oil they had," said Kaita. "They will not be able to pour such fire down upon you again."

"How do you know that?" said Apok, whom Kaita had not noticed standing close by. Burns covered most of her chest, but her eyes were sharp, and she looked upon Kaita with suspicion.

"What?" snarled Kaita.

"How do you know of the humans' oil, Gatak?"

"The Lord has told me," said Kaita. "He knows many secrets. He has much power. He knows we will win."

"I think your Lord is a meddling human," rumbled Apok. "A human who wishes to control us."

Kaita took a lunging step forwards and smashed her fists into the dirt. "You dare to speak ill of him?"

"Gatak!"

She froze at Dotag's voice. He was scowling when she turned back to him. Immediately Kaita dropped her ears and stooped, making sure she stood almost a pace shorter than he.

"You may trust my words, Dotag," she said soothingly. "The Lord assures our victory."

Dotag gave a *snuff.* He looked uncertainly up at the stronghold wall, and then looked past Kaita to Apok.

"Why do you look at her?" said Kaita. "She would have us all turn and flee from this place. She would not have us take these mountains for our own. Does she lead the pack, or do you?"

"He does," growled Apok. "Not me. Not you."

But this was too much for Dotag. He pounded a fist on the ground. "I lead. We attack again." He glared past Kaita to Apok. "I will attack the gate myself. And you will come with me."

Apok's nostrils flared, but she ducked her head and turned away. Dotag grunted and turned to Kaita. He spoke in a lower voice, so low that only she could hear.

"You said the other humans would help us. Where were they?"

Kaita ducked her head. "They could not reveal themselves. We had to break the outer gate. Now that that is done, they will lend their strength to ours. You will take the wall, and then kill everyone inside."

Dotag's eyes narrowed. "You did not say that before."

Kaita suppressed a momentary surge of anger, that a troll would think himself worthy of questioning her counsel. But of course she could not say that. "I told you they would help us take the inner gate. That is what they will do."

He stared at her a long moment. Kaita met his gaze, unflinching. At last Dotag snorted and turned away.

"Tell the others. We attack. Now."

FORTY-SIX

It felt as though we had had barely a moment's respite before the trolls charged again. New soldiers had taken the place of those who fell on the wall, but everyone looked weary enough to fall over. I felt the same.

We rained oil and fire down upon the trolls as soon as they came in range. But they were better prepared this time, and they leaped aside or batted at the vials. Still we scored many hits, and their rending screams cut the air.

Once again they swarmed the gatehouse. This time

Mag had joined us atop it. She flung a perfectly timed vial of oil, and I lit it, and our unlucky victim's wild flailing stalled the charge of many behind him. Even so, half a dozen trolls burst into the gatehouse. We ran to the murder holes, throwing flasks and firing flame at them as best we could. Their roars of pain shook the wall, but without the overwhelming torrent of oil we had had last time, they only seemed spurred to greater fury. They flung themselves at the second gate like mad beasts. Dents appeared in the solid steel banding.

One of the trolls at the back of the group could not reach the gate. She looked up through the murder holes with eyes full of hate. Then a soldier leaned too far over. The troll vaulted upwards. Her hand reached through the opening to seize the guard's head and drag him down into the darkness. His body cracked and popped sickeningly as it was forced through the narrow gap, but his screams were swiftly cut off as the troll battered him against the ground below.

"Stay back!" commanded Ditra. She ran to the back of the barbican, looking down upon the soldiers in the bailey who were still bracing the second gate. "Hold! Hold them! They cannot—"

I heard a whistling on the air. The sound of many arrows. On instinct, I shouted, "Down!" and dived to tackle Ditra to the floor.

But the arrows had not been aimed at us. They fell upon the soldiers in the bailey. I looked up in confusion, and then I heard shouting from the west wall.

Peering through the gloom, by the light of torches I saw soldiers in blue and grey swarming along the ramparts there. They had swords on their belts and shields on their backs, but in their hands were bows. Even now they were preparing another volley to loose upon the soldiers in the courtyard. Behind them, I could just glimpse bits of shining metal—grappling hooks, and the tops of siege ladders.

"They have flanked us!" I cried. "Shades from the west!"

Ditra looked down. Corpses littered the stone. Barely a dozen soldiers still braced the second gate, and they were wavering.

She cried out to the soldiers around us. "The walls have been taken, and the gate will follow! Back! Back to the keep!"

They took up the cry all up and down the wall, and the soldiers turned in a rout. I stayed by Ditra's side, wishing she would move faster. But she pushed everyone else ahead of her, determined to be the last to leave the wall. We ran down the southeast battlements and turned down the stretch that would lead us to the keep door. Every living soldier in the bailey had fled, and now the second gate was crumpling under the trolls' onslaught. Even as I watched, it shattered. In three pieces it fell, skittering away against stone that was slick with melted snow, now tinged red with blood.

"Albern!"

Mag's cry brought my attention back to the wall. I

heard a coarse rasping, like two stones grinding against each other. The hand of a troll had appeared over the top of the ramparts. They had circled around to the south, and one was climbing up now. A huge, stony head appeared before us.

We attacked it at the same time, but Mag got there first. Her spear plunged into its eye socket, and I saw the jolt in Mag's arm as she struck the skull. As the troll screamed, I hacked at its hand with my sword. Still it did not let go—not until Ditra brought her axe down, and its enchantments hewed the troll's hand in half. The creature roared as it fell away into darkness.

"Thank you," I said, gripping Ditra's shoulder.

"You would have done it yourself, if you held the axe," said Ditra. "But you are welcome."

"I had *some* hand in it as well," grumbled Mag. But her words were lost in the din as we passed through the door and into the keep. The door was iron, and inside it had great iron bolts, thick as my arm, which we slid into place. Not even a troll would be able to break them down, and they were unlikely to try, since they could not fit inside.

We made our way quickly to the main entry hall. Some wise soul had gathered as many bracers as they could from the bailey, and now a dozen Telfer guards stood at the great main doors, bracing them against entry. But I heard no sounds of assault from outside.

Ditra caught sight of Captain Huia. "Have they moved towards the keep yet?"

Huia drew up straight, though she looked ready to fall over from both weariness and the nasty cut below her temple, slicing through her close-shaved hair and soaking her short braid with blood. "No, Rangatira. We are mustering every soldier we have left into this room."

"Post two at each wall door," said Ditra. "The trolls cannot break them, but the Shades may have some trickery left. And see to your wound." She turned to Mag and me. "With me."

We followed her to a circular side stairway that led to the keep's upper floors. She passed them one after the other until we finally emerged onto the roof of the keep, more than fifteen paces above the floor of the bailey—too high for the trolls to throw stones at us. We went to the battlements and looked down.

The trolls were again regrouping, nursing their wounds and preparing for another charge. They were close, pressing together in the bailey, while still more tried to force their way in through the gatehouse. Our only way out was through the keep's front door, and they had it blocked. They were close to victory now, and they knew it. They growled and roared, slamming their hands into the ground and cracking cobblestones.

"They will not wait as long this time," I said.

"They did not wait very long last time," said Mag.

"Their leader," said Ditra. "Where is he?"

I pointed. "There." He stood in the midst of the pack, pacing back and forth, a few steps each way, growling and leering at the keep door like it was a rival come to challenge him.

"Out of our reach, from up here," said Mag.

"I could stick him with an arrow," I said. "It might annoy him."

"Yes, it would please me to know he will be irritated when he breaks in the door and kills us all," mused Ditra.

Mag met my gaze. "What would happen if we brought him down? When they break down the door, you and I try to slay him. I can land the oil if you strike him with the arrows."

I looked to Ditra. "Rangatira?"

She mulled it over. "Even if he dies, I do not think they will simply turn and walk away from the city. But if they at least withdraw from the keep, and take the time to establish a new pack leader . . . it could delay them a day or two. That might give the king's army time to arrive, if indeed they are on their way."

"And if they are not?" said Mag.

Ditra looked grim. "It might give us time to withdraw. We have given the refugees enough time. The trolls care only about the mountains. They will not chase us into the lowlands. It would mean giving Kahaunga up for lost, but that is better than letting everyone die."

Only a week ago, I would have agreed without question. But now, the prospect of retreat filled me with a wild, unreasoning rage. If we fled, we would not only give up the city. We might lose our best chance to kill Kaita since Northwood. I strode to the edge of the balcony.

"Albern?" said Ditra, alarmed.

I drew an arrow, nocked, and loosed. It plunged through the air, striking the line between stones in the bailey just at the foot of the troll's leader. He jumped at the sound, looking down at the arrow in confusion. It was a long moment before he put it together, and his gaze snapped up to see me atop the keep.

"I am Albern of the family Telfer!" I called down to him. "Turn away from here. Go back to your homes. Go back to the borders of the pact."

He bared his teeth at me. "I am Dotag!" he roared, standing to his full height. "I lead the pack. I do not listen to humans."

"Your pack did once," I said. "Go back to the border."

"You broke the pact long before we did," said Dotag. "I will not listen to you now."

"Humans did break the pact, but we never harmed your people. And you do not fight us now because of the pact. You say you do not listen to humans, but you are spurred on by the Shades. They are treacherous. They have used you to attack us, but they will betray you, as they have done to others. I have traveled three kingdoms in pursuit of them, and you cannot trust them."

"We serve no humans!" roared Dotag. "We will never listen to you! Your words mean nothing to us!"

I frowned—but not at Dotag. My attention had moved past him, to the female troll who still lurked by his side. She was not paying the slightest attention to her leader, as the other trolls were. Instead she looked straight at me. The look of hatred upon her face was almost human.

But my thoughts were pulled back to Dotag as he rounded on the rest of the pack. "We will never serve humans!" he bellowed. "Tear their home to the ground! Kill all you find inside!"

They stampeded towards the door, Dotag leading the way. The female troll was swept along in the tide. They pressed up against the sides of the keep.

"Dark take them," said Ditra. "To the hall! We must try to bring him down."

She ran for the trapdoor leading back into the keep, and Mag was just behind her. But I paused at the battlements for a moment, looking down. To this day, I could not tell you what made me stay, but I did.

A hail of oil vials crashed along the troll's ranks, flung from arrow slits. Flaming arrows came just behind, sending a blast of fire across them. The trolls recoiled, stumbling back from the keep for a moment.

I seized the merlon, leaning forwards, my eyes wide.

The flames struck the troll by Dotag's side, and she

recoiled with the others. But she bent her head away, out of sight, and I saw a flash. Magelight. And the flesh that had been struck by flames now stitched itself together before my eyes.

I turned and ran from the battlement. The trapdoor still hung open, and I dived into it, running down the stairs and through the rest of the keep. At the front of the main hall, soldiers were leaning on the bracers, holding the door shut as long as they could. There came a great, shattering crash as a troll threw itself against the doors. I reached Mag and Ditra just at the entrance to the main hall, and I seized Mag's shoulder to pull her around.

"Kaita!" I cried. "The female troll lurking near the leader. She is Kaita in disguise."

Mag stared at me in wonder. Ditra turned at my words, astonished.

"How do you—"

"Fire struck her, and she used her magic to heal herself," I said. "It was only a flash, but I saw it. It is her."

There came a great *crack* as timbers began to splinter on the keep door. Through a hole in the iron grid, I saw a troll's eye peeking through.

Mag's face went stony as the battle-trance settled over her. "Then I will kill her."

"We cannot. You have to expose her."

"Killing her *will* expose her, Albern," said Ditra. "If a weremage is killed, they take their true form."

"She hangs back from the fighting," I told Mag. "You

might get close enough to strike her, but I cannot. But there is Tuhin's trick. The one they showed us in Opara."

Mag's face remained impassive. "I remember."

"Use it. Force her to resume her human form in front of the trolls. She has been goading them all along. They have followed her advice because they think she is one of their own. When they realize a Shade has been deceiving them the whole time—"

A thunderous crash rocked the keep as the doors shattered inwards. Timbers and bands of iron went flying, flinging soldiers away from the door. Dotag flew into the open space at the front of the hall, roaring his hatred. Trolls tumbled in behind him—and among them was Kaita.

"Push them back!" cried Ditra, raising her axe and running forwards. "Fire! Fire!"

Flasks of oil came flying from all directions. A brazier stood next to me against the wall, and I lit and loosed. Flame erupted among the trolls. But they were too enraged now to let that stop them. They seized any Telfer soldier they could get their hands on, flinging them into walls, smashing them against the floor, or simply squeezing them until their bodies broke.

But they could not touch Mag.

She had sprung towards them as soon as the doors caved in. Now she vaulted and leaped off a woman's shoulders. Dotag froze in shock as she flew straight towards his massive head. But she landed on his shoulder and jumped again.

Kaita saw her at the last instant. Her wide troll's eyes filled with fear, and she scrambled desperately to try and escape the keep. Even in a troll's form, she was too afraid of Mag to face her in battle. But the crowd of trolls was too thick, and she could not flee.

Mag landed in the midst of them. A troll attacked from either side, trying to seize her, to smash her, to fling her away. She rolled under the grasping hands of one, and leaped over the swipe of another.

She cast aside her spear and shield, landed on one of her assailant's oak-thick arms, and jumped straight for Kaita's terrified face.

I could see nothing else in the hall. The world seemed frozen for a moment. I can remember it now as clear as anything—Mag's fluttering cloak, and Kaita trying desperately to evade her.

Then Mag swept her fists forwards and struck. One fist crashed into each temple, just where Tuhin had showed us in Opara.

Kaita screamed, a deep, guttural roar that echoed through the hall. Magelight poured from her eyes, bright as a beacon fire, lighting the ceiling and walls.

The trolls' assault shuddered to a stop. At their head, Dotag turned and looked upon Kaita in confusion. And as trolls and humans alike watched, frozen in place, Kaita shrank, withered, and became human once more, to fall stunned at Mag's feet.

FORTY-SEVEN

Everyone in the hall, troll and human alike, seemed to be waiting for someone to say something—to explain, to denounce Kaita, anything. Instead, the only sound was a slight scrape of metal on stone as Mag fetched her spear, and then stooped to haul Kaita up by the back of the neck. She turned the weremage to face Dotag, holding the haft of the spear across the weremage's throat.

"A weremage," she said loudly, so that every troll could hear. "A human. She has prodded you into this fight. She has led you to go far beyond the pact boundary, to attack the family Telfer. She has been using you."

Ditra saw her chance and stepped forwards. "This was a base, dishonorable trick," she said. "This woman has harmed both our people equally. We have both lost many of our own here today. But we need not fight any longer, now that we see our common foe."

But Dotag ignored both of them. He only stared at Kaita in shock, his shoulders drooping, his mouth hanging agape. He took one slow, hesitant step forwards. And then he spoke, in the troll's language, which I could not understand. But others in the hall knew it, and they told me later what he and the other trolls said in the moments that followed, and so I will render it to you now.

"Gatak," he said. "Gatak, what trickery is this?"

"Not Gatak," said Ditra, for she knew the troll tongue. "Kaita. Her name is Kaita."

Dotag barely seemed to hear her. "You pretended. You pretended to be one of us."

Kaita, for her part, did not seem to be even slightly interested in Dotag's horror. Her eyes darted everywhere, wild, terrified at Mag's grip upon her, desperate to find some way to escape.

"Answer me!" roared Dotag, so loud that I jumped.

That seemed to snap Kaita's attention back to him. She looked up into his enraged, bewildered expression, and she forced a smile upon her face. "You are so close, Dotag," she said eagerly. "You have come so far. The humans cannot hope to stop your pack now. Finish it. Kill them!"

She struggled against Mag's spear, but Mag, expressionless, only squeezed tighter. Kaita began to gag, the wood pressing into her windpipe.

"You . . . you did this," said Dotag. His shoulders heaved. "You . . . you—"

He straightened and threw his fists wide, unleashing a roar that startled everyone in the hall. Then he charged. I saw Mag hesitate for just a heartbeat, and for a mad moment I thought she was going to let Dotag crush her and Kaita together.

Instead, she wrapped an arm around Kaita's neck and leaped to the side, dodging just as Dotag's fist came crashing down where they had just been standing. Both women fell. Mag tried to get back up, but Kaita was fighting her now. She could not free herself from Mag's grip, but her struggles kept either of them from getting to their feet.

Dotag roared and attacked again. Mag had to roll away. Without Kaita to hamper her movements, she was able to shoot to her feet and strike. Dotag screamed and reeled away. Mag had sliced his right ear clean off.

But Kaita had been given the reprieve she needed. Her eyes flashed, and even as Ditra cried out for archers to stop her, she took her mountain lion form. I was the only one who managed a shot—it flew straight through the crowd, piercing her flank. She yowled, but she did not stop. In a blink she had slithered through the press of trolls, out the door and into the bailey beyond. Another flash of magelight, and then I saw a raven wheel away above the heads of the trolls, screaming in frustration as it vanished into the sky.

Mag stood stock still, watching. Had it not been for the battle-trance, I am sure she would have been shaking with rage.

Dotag hardly seemed to know what to do with himself. His thick fingers probed at the wound in the side of his head. I thought it would enrage him further, but instead he only seemed confused. He looked down at Mag, but he did not try to attack her. He looked at the rest of us in the hall, taking in the many flaming arrows raised and flasks of oil ready to throw.

At last he turned back to his pack. "The mountains are still ours! Fight! Kill them!"

He whirled back, ready to plunge into the midst of Ditra's troops. But he only got two steps before he realized that not one troll had moved to follow him. They were looking at him instead, their faces impassive, studying him like a beast in the mountains. He stopped and turned.

"Fight!" he roared, louder than before. Still they held their ground. Dotag snarled and lunged towards them, smashing his fists against the floor. "I lead this pack. I lead! Challenge me, or obey!"

"I challenge you."

One of the trolls—another female—stepped forwards. She was thick and tall, and imposing despite the small burns on her skin. And I did not need to speak the troll's language to hear the hatred thick in her voice.

"I, Apok, challenge you. You let yourself be tricked by the humans. You followed their counsel when Chok told you not to. You killed Chok to serve the humans. You will lead us to ruin. I, Apok, challenge you."

Dotag looked truly terrified now. But he stumped towards her, spreading his shoulders to appear thicker and bigger than before.

"Get back!" called Ditra. Her soldiers needed no second urging; they backed as far from the two trolls as they could, pressing against the far edges of the hall. Only Mag remained where she was, still staring off where Kaita had flown. I pushed through the crowd and seized her, drawing her away from the trolls.

"Come," I murmured. "We will find her again."

We barely got out of the way before Dotag snarled and charged Apok. He leaped at her, swinging both fists with all his might. But Apok stepped out of the way and used his own momentum to slam him into the ground. She struck him twice before he managed to roll away—but when he came up, it was with a powerful blow that flung her back into the wall. She slumped down, and I saw cracked stone behind her.

Dotag pressed his advantage. As Apok fought for her feet, he struck her once in the face, sending her head crashing against the wall again. He struck her twice more, both in places on her torso that had been badly burned in the battle. Apok roared with pain. She lashed out, the nails of her stubby fingers raking the place where Dotag's ear had been. He recoiled, falling back a few steps and giving her the chance to gain her feet again.

Mag's arm tensed in my hand. I gripped her tighter, and she turned to look at me. "Leave it," I said quietly. "This is their affair, and they will brook no interference."

"If that one wins . . ." she tilted her head towards Dotag.

"I know," I said. "But we have no choice."

Apok approached Dotag cautiously. They were both grimacing, showing each other their teeth. But Apok held herself firm, her gaze fixed on Dotag, whereas he was shifting back and forth, looking about. He might have been searching for some advantage, but he looked like he was trying to find an escape.

Finally Apok attacked again. Dotag ducked her first blow, but her second crashed into his jaw. He went sliding back across the stone floor and came to a stop amid the wreckage of the keep door, curled up like a babe in a cradle. The Telfer soldiers in the room gasped, and there was a murmur among the trolls.

But it was a ruse. As Apok approached, Dotag struck. He had snatched up a piece of the broken iron grid that had held the door, a shard of metal almost two paces long. He thrust it into Apok's chest, and almost two handbreadths of the metal sank into her flesh. She clutched at it with both hands, falling back on her rear, roaring. Dotag stepped closer, trying to jam it deeper, a low growl issuing from his throat. The rest of the trolls shifted. Some of them gave angry, rumbling shouts, and nearly all of them glared at Dotag. It seemed clear they did not approve of his cowardly trick.

Apok's eyes widened, and she bared her teeth again. She let go the iron shard, and Dotag's weight pressed it deeper into her chest. But Apok's hands rose and wrapped around his throat. She squeezed. Dotag's hands slackened on the iron, and he seized her wrists, trying to pull her away. But Apok had him now. She heaved, throwing him off balance and bringing him crashing to the ground. Apok pulled him up just enough to slam his head back into the stone. Dotag's nails dug into her forearms, but she did not relent. Again and again she sent the back of his head crashing into the floor. A black stain of blood appeared on the ground beneath him, and his arms fell away from her wrists.

Apok stopped. She straightened. With one massive hand, she dragged the iron shard from her own chest. Dotag stirred. His eyes spun in their sockets as he tried to sit up.

Apok rammed the iron shard into his mouth. It pierced straight through the back of his head, pinning him to the stone floor.

Dotag jerked once and then lay still.

The hall fell quiet, save for Apok's great, heaving

breaths. She tossed her head as though shaking away a dizzy spell. My gaze shifted to Ditra. She stood near the front of her soldiers, her mouth slightly open, waiting.

Apok turned to her, eyes narrowed. I gripped my bow.

"I lead the pack now." Apok's growl echoed around the hall. She spoke in the common tongue of Underrealm. "Our fight is over."

I nearly sagged with relief, as did most of the Telfer soldiers I could see. But Ditra stood straighter, stepping forwards to separate herself from the crowd. She inclined her head.

"Then we shall part," she said. "And you will leave here pursued by no ill will of my family or our warriors."

Apok nodded slowly. Then, "There is still the pact."

"Yes," said Ditra. "I am Lord Ditra of the family Telfer, Rangatira of Tokana, and descendant of the first Albern of the family Telfer. My ancestor forged the pact with your people. But it has been neglected for so long that it has grown rusted and damaged, like a blade unused. It must be reforged. You and I can do so, as our predecessors did long ago."

That produced a long moment of silence. At first I thought Apok might not have understood. But then she snorted in what seemed like amusement.

"Tomorrow, then," she said. "We do not love many words, as humans do. But you and I will use as many words as we have to, in order to return peace to the mountains."

Ditra seemed taken aback. But at last she smiled. "Tomorrow, then."

Apok turned to her pack. "Leave," she said. "Back to the mountains, and away from the city."

The trolls did not make a sound, but turned as one to obey her. We stood there, all of us, and watched their giant, lumbering forms stalk away into the night. No one moved until the last one was gone. When the hall had settled to silence once again, I turned to Mag. She was staring out into the darkness—out the shattered door through which Kaita had escaped.

I let go her arm and gripped her shoulder. "We will find her."

Mag smiled—but it was a smile of such sadness, and such bone-deep weariness, that I felt my eyes sting.

"I know," she whispered. "I know we will."

FORTY-EIGHT

THERE WAS STILL MUCH TO BE DONE THAT NIGHT. Ditra sent the fastest messengers she had left to find the refugees on the road and order their return. She then sent a small contingent of soldiers to meet them on the road and provide protection from ambush. The Shades had vanished after the small part they played in the battle, and Ditra feared further mischief from them.

After that she retired at last, ordering us to do the same. Mag and I collapsed in our beds the moment we saw them. We slept well past midday and rose to find

Kahaunga had begun the long process of rebuilding itself. We helped where we could, and spent our time in rest when we could not.

True to her word, Apok returned the next day, and she met with Ditra on the slopes north of Kahaunga. They discussed the pact again, redrew the boundaries, and pledged that their descendants, and those they commanded, would swear by the new pact from that day forth. Then the humans and the trolls joined each other in rebuilding their lives, with the trolls helping Telfer subjects reclaim and rebuild their homes in the mountains, and the Telfers providing the trolls with great stores of bread and crops, which were gratefully (if messily) devoured.

Early on the third day, Dryleaf and Oku returned to us, along with the rest of the refugees. Oku barked madly as he leaped around us, and Dryleaf beamed.

"I knew somehow that you two would come out all right," he said, "yet I am glad to see myself proven correct."

"I think you had an almost foolish confidence in our success, then," I told him.

"Someone had to."

"Albern may speak for himself, but not for me," said Mag, in a light mood that I doubted was genuine. "If our foes wish to rid themselves of me, they shall have to do better than trolls."

"And speaking of your foes," said Dryleaf, "what of Kaita?"

Mag's false cheer vanished.

"She escaped," I said. "She was last seen fleeing southwest, as fast as her raven wings would carry her."

Dryleaf gave a tired sigh. "I suppose you wish to strike out upon the road as soon as may be, without even giving an old man a night to rest?"

Mag paused for a long moment. Her mouth worked, her lips twisting around each other, as though words were fighting to escape.

At last she simply said, "No."

I gaped at her. "No?"

"No." Mag shook her head. "Kaita led us here step by step. Always she left us a clue, pulling us along until we reached Tokana, where she hoped to have done with us. That game has finished, and she has lost. Now we have no more clues, no signs by which to pursue her. So why should we hurry back to the road? Besides"—and she gave me a gentle smile—"you have returned home after far too long. You have reunited with your family. You should take the time to enjoy that."

"I will," I said. "But my aims have not changed. In Northwood, you and I said we would make Kaita pay. I said I was with you. That promise still stands."

"I am glad to hear it," said Mag, and I could hear how deeply she meant it. "Then enjoy your return to your homeland. Kaita will still be out there when you are done, and we will find her together."

"I, too, am still with you," muttered Dryleaf from

his chair. "Though I suppose it sounds less heroically inspiring coming from me."

The rest of our Yearsend was rather pleasant. Ditra's rangers were kept very busy hunting down the Shades in the mountains. When Kaita abandoned them, they melted into the wilderness, trying to hide from all sight and retribution. Most did not succeed. Ditra's forces hunted the Shades down in every hole where they tried to hide. And those who passed farther into the mountains, and were discovered by trolls . . . well, I did not like to imagine their fate then, and I still do not.

We stayed in Kahaunga for more than a week. When Ditra was not too busy rebuilding her city, I spent most of my days with her, and when she was, I would visit Vera instead. Sometimes I would take her riding beyond the walls of the stronghold, and I discovered to my great delight that she seemed to love the mountain wilderness almost as much as I had when I was her age.

My time spent with Ditra was mostly pleasant. In the very first days, we were so thrilled at Kahaunga's salvation that we thought of little else. After that, our conversations turned back to our past and our family. We still had some angry words to say to each other then, things we had not had time to say before the trolls attacked. But I will not repeat it all here, for it worked itself out in the end—the way it usually does, with family. One's true family, at any rate. We found peace with each other, and I took every meal with her and Vera, with Mag and Dryleaf joining us more often than not. Ditra had, you remember, been rather cool towards Mag when she thought she was a sellsword. That was no longer the case, and they grew to like each other greatly in a very short time. Ditra found great amusement in Mag's frequent jokes at my expense, and sometimes the two of them would join forces against me, doing their utmost to make me blush, and falling into peals of laughter when I retreated, muttering, into my wine. On one such occasion, Dryleaf gave a sudden, barking laugh.

"Sky above, I have just realized it." He reached over and patted Mag's arm. "Mag has become your new Ditra."

That sobered both women up rather sharply, and they glared at him. "I certainly have not," said Mag.

"She certainly has not," said Ditra, at the exact same time.

This, of course, sent both Dryleaf and me into hysterics, and Vera giggled at her mother's side. When I had recovered enough to talk, I patted Mag's hand.

"I think he is wiser than either of us, my friend."

It was Mag's turn to retreat to her cup of wine.

Ditra and Vera got to hear Dryleaf sing often during that time. We would sit in her chamber, Vera on my lap or her mother's, Mag by the window with Oku curled at her feet, and listen as Dryleaf shared songs we had never heard before. I never failed to marvel at how many he seemed to know. I thought I could learn a new one every week for the rest of my life and still not match him. The years seemed to fall away from him when he performed; his face shone in the firelight, his stance was firm, his shoulders straight. And as I watched him, and listened, I reflected on a conversation that he and I had had more than once in the last few months.

One day, nearly a week after the battle with the trolls, I saw him alone in his chamber after the others had gone to bed. I had just helped Ditra put Vera to bed; she had fallen asleep on her mother's lap, and I carried her to her room while Ditra tucked the blankets in around her.

"What is it, my boy?" said Dryleaf, brows raised in curiosity.

"I . . . I wanted to share something with you, if you do not mind staying up a while longer."

Dryleaf frowned. "Of course. Is everything all right?"

I took a deep breath. "It is. I have . . . this is still dear to me, and I am reluctant . . . it is the song. Jordel's song."

Dryleaf understood at once, and he nodded solemnly. "Ah."

"I told you of my journey with Loren in the Greatrocks. I spoke more of her than of Jordel, but Jordel was dearer to me, and I promised that I would make a song for him. I . . . I would be honored if you were the first to hear it."

I did not look up at him, even though he could not see me, for I suddenly felt like a very foolish child. But Dryleaf reached over and took up my hand and squeezed it between his leathery fingers. I looked up to find him smiling gently, his gaze seemingly just over my left shoulder.

"The honor would be mine," he said.

And so, in hesitant, stumbling tones, I sang him the song I had spent the last few months writing.

What sorrow feel we
Who mourning raise our hands
To farewell bid to he
Who watchfully guarded the nine lands

Stranger, will not you weep
Do you know he who fell from high
In a bed of stones and there to sleep
And ages will pass him by

Do you know Jordel of Adair
Who walked miles long
His mighty arm, his silver hair
His shining blade, his armor strong

For none could meet one so bold
Or kindness in such measure great

Without weeping when he lay there cold
The master of his own fate

He saw along his own trail
And knew the fate that loomed
With his head high, in shining mail
Jordel rode forth to meet his doom

Our tears we must bring to close
And bitter our grief we must allay
Jordel his own resting place chose
To bring us all through night to day

My voice faded in the chamber, and Dryleaf sat nodding in the firelight, his head bobbing in time with the pace at which I had sung. I could not even look at him, such was my embarrassment.

"You can tell me," I said. "It is not very good."

"I can hear the heart of it. You have done a rare thing. A fine thing."

"How very diplomatic of you," I said, with an embarrassed snort. My face was beet-red. "But those are fair words holding little substance. You are trying to try to make me feel better."

"Stop it, boy," said Dryleaf. It was one of the only times he ever spoke sharply to me. "You think it will make you feel better to hear it, so let me make it plain that you are wrong: No, your song is not very good. Of course it is not. You said you have never written one before, and you have been trying to do it all on your own. And it is not even finished."

"No, just a great deal of time wasted, it seems." I already knew the song was poor, but hearing it from the old man, who was always so kind, was like a knife in the gut.

"Wasted?" said Dryleaf incredulously. "No. You could have brought it to me sooner, and then things might have gone a bit faster. But no work upon a song is wasted. You have done the important work, my boy, you have the most important piece. You have the *heart* of it. Your language is off, the poetry lacks, and your rhythm . . . well. But these are dressings. These are the niceties you drape atop the soul of the song itself. If the soul is weak, all the dressings in the world will yield you nothing. You have spent your time wrestling with the hardest task, the part that too many bards eschew. But your work has borne fruit. Now it is ready to be honed, like a blade on a whetstone."

"I will work on it more, then," I said. "Thank you for your advice." I made to rise, but Dryleaf reached out suddenly and seized my hand.

"Sit down, boy, sit down," he said. "You have struggled too long at this alone."

"It is mine." I could hardly understand the sense of jealousy and selfishness rising up in me, and I did not enjoy it, but neither could I rid myself of it. "I have to do this on my own. It is important to me."

He released my hand and leaned back in his chair with a sigh. "I am sure it is. It is clear you loved him."

My anger abated somewhat, and I spoke softly. "I did."

"Then do him justice, and let the song become something great. You feel you must do this yourself, because you think it would be weak to beg help from another. Forgive me, but it is very like Mag."

I scoffed. "Mag? Mag has no interest in songs."

Dryleaf shook his head. "Not in songs. But in other things. She is the greatest warrior of her age. Everyone knows it. She feels the weight of it. It makes her feel that she must always take on more, and do it alone."

"She fought beside us against the trolls."

"I have no doubt," he said, "that if she thought you would have stayed behind and let her face them alone, she would have. And she took it upon herself to slay the pack leader, and to subdue Kaita."

I looked down at my hands in my lap. "She asked me to come with her, when she left Northwood."

"Did she?" said Dryleaf. "That, then, was a rare moment of wisdom. I think that, if you do not want both your roads to end in tragedy, you must teach her to show such wisdom more often. You should not learn her way of doing things, but persuade her to a wiser course instead. She needs your help if she is to accomplish her aims. If she tries to do it alone, she will fail, Uncut Lady or not." He took a deep breath. "It is a lesson many never learn. Your sister thought she could succeed on her own. But look how she fared here, before you came. In the end, only you and Mag brought even the faintest hope of success."

We fell silent. I thought upon what Dryleaf had said, and I saw, swimming before me, the face of Maia. *She needs you to save her,* he had said to me.

After a little while, I stood and made for the door. But I stopped by Dryleaf's chair and reached down for his hand. He squeezed my fingers again, gently.

"Thank you," I said quietly. "It is late now. But we will speak of the song again soon."

"I cannot wait," he murmured.

FORTY-NINE

After a week and a half of rest, we left Kahaunga at last.

When Mag and I told Ditra of our intention to leave, she went very quiet. We were in her chamber eating our evening meal, along with Dryleaf, but I had made sure that Vera was not in the room. As the silence stretched on after I had finished speaking, I looked uncertainly at Mag, but she never took her gaze from Ditra.

"I had meant to discuss matters with you before now," said Ditra softly. "I thought to ask you to be my new lead ranger. I can think of no one else more suited to take Maia's place at my side."

"And I expected you to say so," I said. "But I have been away from Calentin a long time, and I am happier wandering the nine lands than I ever was here." She began to object, but I raised a hand to forestall her. "It was not only Mother who made me unhappy here. It is the life I was expected to lead. The one you want me to lead now. I am not suited to a noble's life, Ditra. I never was."

She sighed and shook her head. "No. I suppose you are not. I will not pretend I am happy with your answer, but neither can I say truthfully that you are wrong. Mayhap that is why I waited so long to raise the subject." To my surprise, she turned to Dryleaf. "And what of you, Grandfather? You have ridden a long road to reach us, and a longer one stretches before you still, unless I miss my guess. Would you rather remain? I would treasure your presence as an advisor, not to mention your singing voice."

Dryleaf bowed in his seat. "You are very kind, Rangatira. But my road does stretch on a long way, as you said, and there is an old friend at the end of it, unless I miss *my* guess." He grinned and turned, so that his blind eyes seemed to gaze somewhere between Mag and me. "And besides, what hope do you truly think these young ones have without me at their side?"

That made us all laugh, and our talk turned to other things. With the matter settled, over the next few days Ditra commanded her servants to help us ready for travel. They provisioned us well, and groomed and re-shod our horses. And in those two days, we spent more time with Ditra and Vera than ever, and our meals were all the sweeter for our knowledge that our time together would soon end. Kaita had been seen flying away southwest, and there were some vague reports of strange things happening in that direction. Mag, Dryleaf, and I spent many days holed up in council with Ditra, poring over maps and determining our best course south. She sent word to the Calentin king, to be sent to all their Rangatira, that a rogue weremage allied with the Shades was passing through the kingdom, and that they should be on watch for her. At last we settled on a road that would bring us back to Opara by much the same route we had taken to get to Kahaunga, but with frequent stops along the way to search for any rumors of Kaita's passing. Ditra gave us a new writ, of course, granting us broad, sweeping powers to aid us in our search.

At last, our time came to depart. We rose before dawn on the thirteenth of Martis to find our horses ready by the stables. Ditra was there to bid us farewell, and she had brought Vera with her. The poor girl was still blinking sleep from her eyes. But she came alert and ran forwards as soon as she saw me.

"Tell me you are not really leaving," she pleaded.

"I am," I said, ruffling her hair. "But not forever. We will meet again. And in the meantime, I have taught you much of the wilderness. I will expect you to know much more when I return. I think your mother needs another ranger, if you are willing to be one."

Her eyes shone, and she smiled. "Of course I am!" she cried.

I smiled and patted her cheek. So like me in some ways, and so different in others. She stepped away to bid Mag and Dryleaf farewell, and especially to scratch Oku's belly, while I went to Ditra. She had put on a stern look, very reminiscent of our mother. But her eyes gleamed with love, and with mischief.

"You will write me, of course," she said sternly. "You have no excuses this time. If I do not receive any word from you, I will send all my rangers out to hunt you down, leaving Kahaunga defenseless."

"I promise I will not make you take such drastic measures," I said. "I will write as often as I can. To Vera, at least."

Her mouth twitched, and she slapped my arm. Then she pulled me in for an embrace. "Fare well, brother. Take care of yourself, and your friends. I owe you everything. If ever I can be of service, I will."

I clutched her tight, closing my eyes, trying to freeze the memory in my mind forever—and I succeeded. Even now, I can smell the scent of her hair, feel the smooth weave of her cloak against my cheek, shiver at the cold winter air that blew against my back.

"Thank you," I said. "For your offer, and for all else you have done. I will not stay away so long this time."

"You damned well had better not," she said gruffly, pushing me back to hold at arm's length. "You may think I am joking, but you *will* find rangers on your doorstep if you defy me."

"I will remember it. Fare well, dearest sister. Protect our home."

Tears came to her eyes at that, and the sight of it finally sent my own spilling down my cheeks. It was the kind of weeping that you do not mind, that stems from joy rather than pain, and is sweeter even than laughter in the sunlight.

We mounted soon after, and rode through the rebuilt gate. I looked back often, until the road turned and we lost sight of them at last. I faced forwards then, and heaved a deep breath as I gazed upon the road that would take us west and out of the mountains.

"Are you all right?" said Mag. "You could have stayed, you know."

"I could have," I said. "But then what hope would you have?"

She rolled her eyes. "I am going to trounce you."

I chuckled, but after a moment I looked her steadily in the eye. "I am with you, Mag, until the end of this road. You may be the Uncut Lady, and I may be only a simple bowyer, but you may count on my help, whether it be through my counsel, or my presence at your side in a fight. To whatever end."

She smiled. "Of course I know it. Do you really think I would let you leave, even if you wanted to?"

"I am serious."

"Do you think I am not?"

I shook my head. "Have your jests, then. But let us speak of Kaita. How do we plan to find her?"

Mag shrugged and nudged Mist to trot a little faster. "I do not know. But we *will* find her. After all, I have nothing better to do."

I nudged Foolhoof to catch up. "Nor do I."

FIFTY

Albern's timing was impeccable. The first edges of dusk were just creeping into the sky as he quietly finished his tale. Sun took a deep breath and released it in a sigh, just as she had the first night, before the vampire had attacked.

"I am glad you fixed things with your sister," she said. "Is she still alive?"

"She is," said Albern, grinning hugely. "She survived the War of the Necromancer, and everything that has come since. Old age has left her slightly less healthy than I am, if you can believe it, and Vera rules

Tokana in her stead. She is an excellent Rangatira, well respected by her king, as well as the other lords, and beloved by her people. She has two sons of her own now. I still go to visit them every once in a while. Mayhap you will come with me next time."

"I would love to," said Sun.

Albern nodded. Then his smile died. "Another day, then. For now, we have work to do."

"Yes," said Sun. "Though I am still unclear about just what exactly it is that you *want* to do."

"Our friends over the hill are trying to perform the same ritual the Shades performed in Lan Shui years ago," said Albern. "But they are disorganized. They have neither the reach nor the resources of the Shades of old. If we brought this information to the King's law, they would certainly stop the ritual. But, too, they might claim the magestones for themselves. And in any case, some officers of the law might be killed in the fighting, and likely all of the criminals. I think we can put a stop to their plans without anyone dying tonight."

"A noble goal," said Sun. "But you did not answer my question: *what* exactly do you mean to do?"

"First, you will sneak into position on the other side of their camp," said Albern. "I will distract them and draw them away from the cauldron, and their store of magestones. You will take the stones and fling them into the fire, and then steal one of their torches to throw into the cauldron itself. We will burn away their contraband, and their plans, all at once."

Sun's throat had gone quite dry. "You mean for me to sneak in among them?"

"Only if you are willing," said Albern. "I pitted you against the vampire all unawares. I did it to teach you your worth in a fight, but I will never do that again. If you help me with this now, I want you to do it with both eyes open, and with both of us agreeing to what we do before we do it." He smiled and held forth his left hand. "As partners."

Sun returned his smile, though in truth she felt far less confident than he sounded. She gripped his wrist and shook. "Partners, then."

He pulled his sword off his belt and handed it to her. "Here. I do not mean to let them draw close enough for this to be of use to me."

Sun could not help a moment's trepidation as she accepted the blade. "Do you think I will need it?"

"Not if all goes well, but there is no guarantee of that."

"How comforting."

At Albern's direction, she slipped away down the other side of the hill, circling wide around the camp, out of sight. The day's fading light was just enough for her to see by. She kept a careful eye on the glow of the campfire that shone above the tops of the hills she passed. As she went, she tried her best to silence her steps, though she did not have Albern's gift for it. Hopefully the activity of the camp would be enough to keep them from noticing.

Finally she spotted the gap between the hills that would let her draw as close as possible to the chest where the magestones were being kept. Crouching so low she was almost crawling, Sun edged forwards. Soon she could see the tents. She stopped as soon as the first person came into view. It was a woman, facing away towards the campfire. That was a good thing—it would ruin her night vision. Sun peered through the darkness, searching for the shape of Albern atop the hill on the other side of the camp. At last she caught sight of him—a small black form moving against the stars. She hoped he could see her as well. Then, even as she watched, she saw him raise his arm, and then bring it down swiftly.

Thwack

The sound of a stone striking flesh echoed in the night.

"What in the dark—"

The guard Sun could see shot to her feet. She was looking at something Sun could not see.

"What happened?" called a voice.

"Something hit Wen."

"What do you mean 'some—'"

Thwack

The voice died abruptly.

"Attack!" cried the woman in Sun's view. "We are under attack!"

She ran off out of sight. Someone came and threw open the flap of the tent closest to Sun, and a figure stumbled out of it into the night. Sun ducked back until the figure was out of sight.

Trotting, but still trying to remain silent, Sun crept up behind the tent. She stuck one eye out around the edge of it, but it seemed she need not have bothered. Ten or so people were gathered at the other end of the camp, but they were staring in Albern's direction, away from Sun.

Thwack

One of the figures fell poleaxed to the ground and did not move. A stone bounced away from his limp form.

"There!" A man thrust his finger up towards the hill where Albern was hiding. "I saw something!"

"Find them!" barked another. "We cannot let them bring word of us to Lan Shui!"

Most of them attempted to climb the hill, while two circled around the base of it, likely hoping to cut off Albern's escape.

Sun moved. Her heart thundered in her ears as she reached the chest holding the magestones and threw herself to the ground behind it. Only then did she see the heavy iron lock that held it shut.

"Dark below," muttered Sun.

She risked a glance at the hill. The Shades—or whatever they were—were not paying any attention to their own camp. After a quick search, she found a large rock, half as big as her head. She hefted it high and slammed it against the lock. The iron held for two strikes, but on the third, it fell open.

With shaking fingers, she pulled the lock out and opened the chest. It was packed to the lid with packets wrapped in brown cloth. Sun pulled one open to find black, semi-translucent crystals. Magestones.

She scooped all the packets up into her arms and dashed towards the cauldron. She threw them into the flame beneath it, but it was an awkward throw, and half of them fell upon the ground next to the fire. She fell to her knees and tried to scoop them up, wincing at the heat of the darkfire that leaped up, licking at the sides of the cauldron.

A hand seized her hair and threw her backwards.

Sun's head struck the ground hard, and she rolled away, stunned. A heavy boot struck her in the ribs. She had just enough presence of mind to roll away from it.

"Glad I came back to make sure the camp was safe," snarled a woman's voice.

Sun heard her foe's footsteps approaching. She threw herself to the side as the woman aimed another kick. Fighting to her feet, Sun backed away, trying to take stock of the situation.

One woman had returned to the camp—the one

Sun had seen as she approached. Her face was gaunt, with high, sharp cheekbones, and her head was shaved to stubble. Her clothes were all of thick leather and fur, far too hot for the weather recently. It looked as though she had dressed to be more impressive than practical. But the others were all gone, vanished over the top of the hill. Sun hoped that Albern was all right.

Sun shook her head to clear it. She needed time to figure out what to do. "What are you doing out here?"

"You are not that ignorant, or you would not have thrown the stones into the flames," snarled the woman. She took a step forwards.

Sun drew Albern's sword and held it before her, the tip a pace away from the woman's chest.

"Stop."

The woman paused, but only for a moment. A cruel smile played across her lips. "Do you even know how to use that, girl?"

"Trust me, I do. I am older than I look, if not nearly as old as you."

That earned Sun a snarl. The woman drew two long daggers from her belt and lunged forwards, trying to batter Sun's weapon aside. But Sun had spent many hours training in her family's yard, and she retreated, using her own weapon to block the woman's slashes and thrusts.

Knives, knives, she thought. *What do you do against a foe with knives?* She knew she had learned it, but all thought had fled her mind, and she was moving on instinct. It was harder to remember her lessons when she knew her foe wanted to kill her.

She stepped forwards with a wild swing. The woman took two steps away, breathing heavily. Sweat beaded her brow, made all the worse by the heat of the darkfire behind her. Sun hoped she regretted her choice of clothing.

"You do not look like a killer," growled the woman.

"There is a first time for everything, I am beginning to learn."

"Walk away. What we are doing here does not concern you. And it will make Underrealm a better place in the end."

Sun loosened her grip on her sword for a moment, flexing her fingers. "I am told that your sort always thinks that. But I have learned another lesson. It does no good to ignore evil done in the shadows, no matter how much people would rather do so."

The woman lunged. Again she tried to slap Sun's blade aside—but this time Sun let her. She spun with the blow, sidestepping as the woman's other dagger plunged through the space she had been standing.

Sun brought the sword arcing back around, and with the flat of the blade she slapped the woman's hand. The dagger slipped from her sweat-soaked fingers to the ground. When she stooped to retrieve it, Sun sliced a thin cut on the back of her thigh. The woman's back arched as she cried out. Sun stepped in close and struck her in the neck with a fist, making her cough and fall back, dropping her other dagger.

She stumbled on the rock Sun had used to break the lock, falling on her back. Before she could rise, Sun stepped up, blade pointed straight at the woman's face, now only a finger's breadth away.

"Please," the woman whispered. "Please do not kill me."

"As I said, there is a first time for everything," said Sun. "But not for this. Not tonight."

She flipped the sword and fell on the woman's chest in one smooth motion, bringing the pommel crashing into her head. The woman's head snapped back and her eyes rolled up, showing their whites for just a moment before they closed.

Breathing heavily, Sun stood again and sheathed the sword. She looked at the hill. The rest of the would-be Shades were nowhere in sight.

Quickly she ran back to the cauldron, scooped up the rest of the magestones and flung them into the darkfire beneath. The flames sprang still higher. They had caught on the sides of the cauldron, though they had not burned through it yet. It was only a matter of time, but Sun found a torch and plunged it into the cauldron anyway. Albern had said to do it, and she guessed he had a reason.

Darkfire sprang up from the top of the cauldron, mingling with the black flames that crept up from the bottom. It began to consume the metal at last, creating holes that sent black blood pouring out into the flames. But Sun did not stay to watch. She sprinted off in the direction she had approached the camp—when she ran head-on into a figure in the darkness. They both grunted and fell to the ground beside each other.

Sun scrambled away from the figure, grasping for the sword at her belt—but then she heard Albern's deep voice in the darkness. "Sky above, that hurt."

"Albern!" Sun whispered. "I am sorry. Are you all right?"

"Well enough, I suppose." He accepted Sun's hand, and she pulled him to his feet. "Is your task done?"

"It is," she said. "What of the other Shades? Or whatever they are."

"They are gone," he said. "I led them on a merry chase south and then lost them as soon as I could. One slipped away from the others, and I feared she might return here."

"She did," said Sun, pointing to the woman's unconscious form. "I dealt with her."

His eyes shot wide. "Did you, now? Well done."

"I will tell you honestly: after fighting a vampire, I found myself rather unimpressed with her."

That made him laugh, though he quickly stifled it. "Well, we should be going. We have done a good thing here tonight—another good deed no one will ever hear about."

"Just as I want it," said Sun.

She followed him as he crept away from the camp

and began a long westward loop that would bring them back to the road. Soon they had come out of the hills and begun to walk on open, grassy ground under the light of the stars. The moons had risen as well, and they cast all the world in a silvery pale glow. Sun looked up at them, her heart full, her mind replaying her brief scuffle with the woman in the camp.

"What of the rest of them?" she said. "They got away."

"They did, but it is of little consequence," said Albern. "It took them a very long time to gather the information they needed to steal those magestones. It will take them longer to do it again, if they even have the nerve for it. And if they should do so, well, then, someone will stop them. Mayhap it will be us."

"How do you know how long it took them?"

He grinned at her in the moonslight. "You are welcome to join my adventures, Sun, but you cannot expect to learn everything all at once. I have many friends in many lands who send me much information. And I told you I reserve the right to keep *some* things a surprise."

Sun shook her head. "Then what is our aim now?"

Albern stopped and turned, surveying her in the moonslight. "That is up to us. We are partners now, or so you said you desired."

"I . . . I did," said Sun. "I do. Yet I . . . I do not know what to do next."

"I have often felt the same," said Albern. "Well, we

have a long walk back to Lan Shui. We can discuss it on the way."

Sun nodded. "That sounds agreeable."

They walked on in silence for a while, Sun mulling things over in her mind. She thought of the maps she had studied of this part of the kingdom. There were some things she had always wanted to see in Dorsea. She thought of its history, and of the ancient and great figures of Underrealm's beginnings, many of them her long-distant kin.

"What if we went to Bertram?" she said.

Albern looked at her, his brows raised. "Bertram?"

"I have often wanted to see it," said Sun. "My family was going to travel there, though not for some time yet. It was one of the few places along our route that I looked forward to. Renna the Sunmane made her home there, before she built Dorsea's capital of Danfon."

"So she did," said Albern. "Bertram would be a fine place to visit. In fact, there is a man there who owes me some money, and I would be happy to give you a fair share of it, if you will have it."

Sun frowned. "A fair share?"

He tilted his head. "As a partner."

"But what is the money for?"

"Ah." He smiled. "For services I rendered to him, which I shall tell you about once we reach Bertram. But I promise it is a benign surprise, far more innocent than our business tonight. I would split it with you, with your portion being in recognition of your accompaniment, and of your skill with a blade. I am afraid you are a bit of a sellsword now, Sun—at least as long as you stick the road."

Sun smiled. "A sellsword. I think I might like that."

He swept his arm out as if in invitation, and then he continued on west. Sun followed him into the moonslight, full of wonder at what her future might yet hold. Wonder, but no longer any fear.

KEEP READING

Your next book of Underrealm is *Hell Skin*.

What is the Shades' next step in their war? How will Albern and Mag ever find Kaita now? And what power was promised to Kaita?

Find out in *Hell Skin,* the next book in the Tales of the Wanderer. Get it here:

Underrealm.net/TOW3

AUTHOR'S NOTE

This book was not meant to be timely. To paraphrase the bard, it had timeliness thrust upon it.

Albern is a trans man—referred to in Underrealm as "ander." If you've read this novel, you likely heard about Underrealm in the first place because it is meant to be a diverse and inclusive fantasy universe. When I started working on this story (the very earliest roots of which are over a year and a half old), Albern was "only" supposed to be another form of representation. We had no trans main character in an Underrealm book series. As with all our representation, this aspect of Albern's identity wouldn't be the main focus of the story, but it would of course be a significant part of him.

Things have changed since then. Trans people in the real world have come under attack in new and horrifying ways, and it has been especially explicit in America.

The attacks are baseless, horrific, and without reason. There is no purpose to them other than to inflict pain on a community that has already had more than its fair share of pain. There is no reason for a society to hate its own citizens who have done nothing wrong, but who instead have been at the forefront of every significant push for social justice for decades.

Underrealm was designed to be a world that could demonstrate the needlessness and uselessness of bigotry and hate. Now more than ever, I hope that idea is a comfort to those who need it.

I also hope you will join me in contributing to PFlag, an organization that has been incredibly helpful to one of my friends when he needed them most. You can see their work and donate at PFlag.org.

Garrett Robinson,
November 2018

THE BOOKS OF UNDERREALM

THE NIGHTBLADE EPIC

NIGHTBLADE

MYSTIC

DARKFIRE

SHADEBORN

WEREMAGE

YERRIN

THE ACADEMY JOURNALS

THE ALCHEMIST'S TOUCH

THE MINDMAGE'S WRATH

THE FIREMAGE'S VENGEANCE

THE TALES OF THE WANDERER

BLOOD LUST

STONE HEART

HELL SKIN

THE BOOKS OF UNDERREALM

CHRONOLOGICAL ORDER

NIGHTBLADE

MYSTIC

DARKFIRE

SHADEBORN

BLOOD LUST

THE ALCHEMIST'S TOUCH

WEREMAGE

THE MINDMAGE'S WRATH

STONE HEART

THE FIREMAGE'S VENGEANCE

HELL SKIN

YERRIN

THE CHRONICLES OF UNDERREALM

TAVERN CROSSINGS

THE NIGHT OF TWO KINGS

A NIGHT ON THE SEAT

THE MAN AND THE SATYR

THE BEAST WITHIN

CHASING MOONSLIGHT

BLOOD ON THE SNOW

THE HAMMER OF THE KING

THE TIDES OF WAR

THE LEGEND OF CABRUS

THE SUNMANE PASS

ABOUT THE AUTHOR

Garrett Robinson was born and raised in Los Angeles. The son of an author/painter father and a violinist/singer mother, no one was surprised when he grew up to be an artist.

After blooding himself in the independent film industry, he self-published his first book in 2012 and swiftly followed it with a stream of others, publishing more than two million words by 2014. Within months he topped numerous Amazon bestseller lists. Now he spends his time writing books and directing films.

A passionate fantasy author, his most popular books are the novels of Underrealm, including The Nightblade Epic, The Academy Journals, and The Tales of the Wanderer series.

However, he has delved into many other genres. Some works are for adult audiences only, such as *Non Zombie* and *Hit Girls,* but he has also published popular books for younger readers, including The Realm Keepers series and *The Ninjabread Man*, co-authored with Z.C. Bolger.

Garrett lives in Oregon with his wife Meghan, his children Dawn, Luke, and Desmond, and his dog Chewbacca.

Garrett can be found on:

BLOG: garrettbrobinson.com/blog
EMAIL: garrett@garrettbrobinson.com
TWITTER: twitter.com/garrettauthor
FACEBOOK: facebook.com/garrettbrobinson

EPILOGUE

Oh, by the by—you should know something of what Rogan was doing during this time.

Not long after Kaita fled from Kahaunga, he was sitting in a chamber in Dorsea's northeastern reaches. A cup of mulled wine was in his hand, but he drank from it slowly, twirling it in his hands and staring into its depths.

A voice spoke from the shadows. "My son."

Rogan shot to his feet, his eyes shining.

"Father?"

"Kaita has failed."

Rogan's hands clenched to fists at his sides. "She . . . how do you—"

"It is enough that I know."

"Father, tell me that she is not—"

"She lives."

Rogan sank back into his chair in relief, casting a hand over his eyes. "Thank the sky." But then he lifted his head, and there was fear in his eyes. "Do not blame her for this, Father. It was with my counsel that she set upon her road. If she could not succeed in Tokana, no one could have. Do not punish her."

"She did her best. She could not have done any more than she did. But now she is searching for you. You made her a vow."

"As you commanded." Rogan shook his head, staring at his own boots. "I was reluctant."

"Kaita cannot be allowed to find you. Not right away. Not until the time is right. But when you reunite with her at last, you must give her what was promised."

Slowly, Rogan stood from his chair. He went to the table in the center of the chamber. Upon it had been laid a map of the nine kingdoms. Small figures in blue stood upon the map, marking every place where the Shades had an agent or a fighting force. There were many. Far more than we would have guessed, in those days.

"You said you would not punish her," he said quietly.

"It is not punishment."

"I have seen it, Father," whispered Rogan. "If Kaita gets her wish, it will only lead to her death."

"You can see farther than any other, my son. Any other except me. Trust me when I say that this is no punishment." Rogan felt a hand on his shoulder, comforting him. "But yes. I am afraid that if we are to achieve our aims, you are right. Kaita will have to die."

www.ingramcontent.com/pod-product-compliance
Lightning Source LLC
Chambersburg PA
CBHW030809310726
48980CB00006B/437/J

* 9 7 8 1 9 4 1 0 7 6 5 6 9 *